Pride and Prejudice and Zombies
by Jane Austen and Seth Grahame-Smith

"Jane Austen isn't for everyone. Neither are zombies. But combine the two and the only question is, why didn't anyone think of this before? The judicious addition of flesh-eating undead to this otherwise faithful reworking is just what Austen's gem needed."—*Wired*

Sense and Sensibility and Sea Monsters
by Jane Austen and Ben H. Winters

"Quirk commissioned Ben H. Winters to punch up Jane Austen's *Sense and Sensibility* with man-eating beasts from the briny deep. And once again, to the consternation of purists everywhere, the result is sheer delight."—*Onion A. V. Club*

"It's a monsterpiece."—*Real Simple*

"The effect is strangely entertaining, like a Weird Al version of an opera aria, and Eugene Smith's amusing illustrations add an extra touch of bizarre hilarity."—*Library Journal*

"A very funny idea, and there's a pleasure in watching someone be so silly with the kind of book generally treated as sacrosanct."—*Philadelphia Inquirer*

"Bring on the kraken lit, man!"—*io9.com*

"Now that's my kind of love story! Bloody, gory, awkward, and odd—kind of like it is in real life."—*TheFrisky.com*

ANDROID
KARENINA

by Leo Tolstoy & Ben H. Winters

Illustrations by Eugene Smith

TRANSLATED BY CONSTANCE GARNETT &
THE II/ENGLISHRENDERER/94

QUIRK BOOKS
PHILADELPHIA

Library of Congress Cataloging in Publication Number: 2010924948

ISBN: 978-1-59474-460-0

Printed in Canada

Typeset in Bembo

Designed by Doogie Horner

Cover illustration by Lars Leetaru

Cover art research courtesy the Bridgeman Art Library International Ltd.

Interior illustrations by Eugene Smith

Production management by John J. McGurk

Distributed in North America by Chronicle Books

680 Second Street

San Francisco, CA 94107

10 9 8 7 6 5 4 3 2 1

Quirk Books

215 Church Street

Philadelphia, PA 19106

www.quirkclassics.com

www.irreference.com

LIST OF ILLUSTRATIONS

*Amidst all the skaters who hovered electromagnetically atop
the tracks, Kitty was as easy to find as a rose among nettles*   *page 41*

*She shrouded the light in her eyes, but it shone against her will;
the android, walking behind, glowed a regal indigo*   *page 74*

*"It's time, it's time," he said, with a meaningful smile; his
telescoping oculus zoomed in as he entered their bedroom*   *page 123*

*The quick-moving death machines fanned out, aiming their
bomb-hurlers and echo-cannons at one another*   *page 179*

*The robots swarmed around him—the Pitbots, the Glowing
Scrubblers, the Extractors; Levin counted forty-two altogether*   *page 202*

*"My God!" Vronsky shouted, at last noticing: "Anna! You
are floating!"*   *page 241*

*"No!" he shrieked, and Anna felt her body slammed into the ceiling,
pressure squeezing upon her throat*   *page 266*

*"A girl cannot be wed without the soothful presence of her Class III,"
the prince had pleaded*   *page 318*

*Anna emerged in perambulating togs, her pale and lovely hand
holding the handle of her dainty ladies'-size oxygen tank*   *page 328*

Nikolai Dmitrich issued his last gurgling scream before his head lolled backward at a terrible angle   page 361

Twitching, snarling, their massive reptilian heads bubbling with eyeballs, the aliens poured into the opera house   page 396

Vronsky chewed on the ends of his moustache as he barked orders at his mechanical charges   page 427

Knowing the direction this conversation would take, Android Karenina opened her arms and patted her lap for Lupo   page 450

"I will punish him, and I will escape from this hateful machine that I have become"   page 521

Quietly, invisibly, they would keep humanity's flame burning until the Golden Hope could finally fly free   page 539

A NOTE ON NAMES

Russian names consist of three parts: the given name, the patronymic (derived from the father's first name), and the family name. Often, individuals also go by a nickname. Hence the first character introduced is Stepan Arkadyich Oblonsky—Stepan is his given name, Arkadyich the patronymic, and Oblonsky the family name. But the man is often called "Stiva," his nickname.

Class I and II robots also use a three-part nomenclature: a Roman numeral for class type, a function-designation, and an indication of model. Hence the I/Samovar/1(8) is a Class I device, designed to steep and serve tea, model number 1(8).

Class III robots are universally known by the nickname bestowed by their master or mistress.

MAJOR CHARACTERS IN ANDROID KARENINA

Stepan Arkadyich Oblonsky (Stiva), a Moscow gentleman
and **Small Stiva,** Stiva's Class III

Darya Alexandrovna Oblonskaya (Dolly), Oblonsky's wife
and **Dolichka,** Dolly's Class III

Anna Arkadyevna Karenina, Oblonsky's sister
and **Android Karenina,** Anna's Class III

Alexei Alexandrovich Karenin, Anna's husband

Sergey Alexeich Karenin (Seryozha), the Karenins' young son

Konstantin Dmitrich Levin, Oblonsky's old friend
and **Socrates,** Levin's Class III

Nikolai Dmitrich Levin, Levin's brother
and **Karnak,** Nikolai's Class III

Ekaterina Alexandrovna Shcherbatskaya (Kitty), Dolly's sister
and **Tatiana,** Kitty's Class III

Prince Alexander Dmitrievich Shcherbatsky,
Kitty and Dolly's father

The Princess Shcherbatskaya, Kitty and Dolly's mother
and **La Scherbatskaya,** the Princess's Class III

Count Alexei Kirillovich Vronsky, a war hero
and **Lupo,** Vronsky's Class III

Countess Vronsky, Vronsky's mother
and **Tunisia,** the Countess's Class III

Elizaveta Fyodorovna Tverskaya (Betsy), Vronsky's cousin and a friend of Anna

and **Darling Girl**, Betsy's Class III

Marya Nikolaevna, Nikolai Levin's companion

Madame Stahl, a society woman and prominent xenotheologist

Varenka, a poor girl attached to Madame Stahl

Yashvin, Count Vronsky's friend and fellow officer

Vassenka Veslovsky, a gentleman of society

VENGEANCE IS MINE;

I SHALL REPAY.

PART ONE: A CRACK IN THE SKY

CHAPTER 1

FUNCTIONING ROBOTS are all alike; every malfunctioning robot malfunctions in its own way.

Everything was in confusion in the Oblonskys' house. The wife had discovered that the husband was carrying on an intrigue with the French girl who had been a *mécanicienne* in their family, charged with the maintenance of the household's Class I and II robots. Stunned and horrified by such a discovery, the wife had announced to her husband that she could not go on living in the same house with him. This position of affairs had now lasted three days, and not only the husband and wife themselves, but all the robots in the household were terribly affected by it. The Class IIIs were keenly aware of their respective masters' discomfort, and the Class IIs sensed in their rudimentary fashion that there was no logic in their being agglomerated together, and that any stray decoms, junkering in a shed at the Vladivostok R.P.F., had more in common with one another than they, the servomechanisms in the household of the Oblonskys.

The wife did not leave her own room; the husband had not been at home for three days. The II/Governess/D145, its instruction circuits pitifully mistuned, for three days taught the Oblonsky children in Armenian instead of French. The usually reliable II/Footman/C(c)43 loudly announced nonexistent visitors at all hours of the day and night. The children ran wild all over the house. A II/Coachman/47-T drove a sledge directly through the heavy wood of the front doors, destroying a I/Hourprotector/14 that had been a prized possession of Oblonsky's father.

Three days after the quarrel, Prince Stepan Arkadyich Oblonsky—Stiva, as he was called in the fashionable world—woke at eight o'clock in the morning, not in his wife's bedroom, but within the oxygen-tempered Class I comfort unit in his study. He woke as usual to the clangorous *thumpthumpthump* of booted robot feet crushing through the snow, as a regiment of 77s tromped in lockstep along the avenues outside.

Our tireless protectors, he thought pleasantly, and uttered a blessing over the Ministry as he turned over his stout, well-cared-for person, as though to sink into a long sleep again. He vigorously embraced the pillow on the other side and buried his face in it; but all at once he jumped up, banging his rotund forehead against the glass ceiling of the I/Comfort/6, and opened his eyes.

He suddenly remembered that he was not sleeping in his wife's room, but in his study, and why: the smile vanished from his face, he knitted his brows.

Small Stiva, Stepan Arkadyich's Class III companion robot, clomped happily into the room on his short piston-actuated legs, carrying his master's boots and a telegram. Stiva, as yet unprepared to undertake the day's obligations, bid his Class III come a bit closer, and then swiftly pressed three buttons below the rectangular screen centered in Small Stiva's midsection. He sat back glumly in the I/Comfort/6, while every detail of his quarrel with his wife was displayed on Small Stiva's monitor, illuminating the hopelessness of Stiva's position and, worst of all, his own fault.

"Yes, she won't forgive me, and she can't forgive me," Stepan Arkadyich moaned when the Memory ended. Small Stiva made a consoling chirp and piped, *"Now, master: She might forgive you."*

Stiva waved off the words of consolation. "The most awful thing about it is that it's all my fault—all my fault, though I'm not to blame. That's the point of the whole situation."

"Quite right," Small Stiva agreed.

"Oh, oh, oh!" Stiva moaned in despair, while Small Stiva motored closer, angled his small, squattish frame 35 degrees forward at the midsection, and rubbed his domed head in a catlike gesture against his master's belly. Stepan Arkadyich then re-cued the Memory on the monitor and stared desolately at the most unpleasant part: the first minute when, on coming, happy and good-humored, from the theater, with a huge pear in his hand for his wife, he had found his wife in her bedroom viewing the unlucky communiqué that revealed everything.

She, his Dolly, forever fussing and worrying over household details, supervising the *mécaniciennes*, limited in her ideas, had been sitting perfectly still while the incriminating communiqué played on the monitor of her Class III, Dolichka, and looking at him with an expression of horror, despair, and indignation. Dolichka, despite the rounded simplicity of her forms, appeared equally distraught, and her perfectly circular peach-colored eyes glowed fiercely from her ovoid silver faceplate.

"What's this?" Dolly asked, gesturing wildly toward the images displayed upon Dolichka's midsection.

Stepan Arkadyich, as is so often the case, was not so much annoyed at the fact itself as at the way in which he had met his wife's words. What happened to him at that instant happens to people when they are unexpectedly caught in something very disgraceful. He did not succeed in adapting his face to the position in which he was placed toward his wife by the discovery of his fault. Instead of being hurt, denying, defending himself, begging forgiveness, instead of remaining indifferent even— anything would have been better than what he did do—his face utterly involuntarily (reflex spinal action, reflected Stepan Arkadyich, who from his work at the Ministry understood the simple science of motor response)—utterly involuntarily assumed its habitual, good-humored, and therefore idiotic smile. Still worse, Small Stiva emitted a nervous, high-pitched series of chirps, clearly indicating a guilty thought-string.

Dolly shuddered as though at physical pain, broke out with her characteristic heat into a flood of cruel words, and rushed out of the room, Dolichka springing pneumatically along behind her. Since then, Dolly had refused to see her husband.

"But what's to be done? What's to be done?" he said to Small Stiva in despair, but the little Class III had no answer.

CHAPTER 2

S TEPAN ARKADYICH was a truthful man in his relations with himself. He wasn't the type to tell small, self-consoling lies to his Class III, and Small Stiva was programmed to console, but not to offer or confirm dishonest impressions. So Stiva was incapable of pretending that he repented of his conduct, either to himself or to his Class III. He could not at this date repent of the fact that he, a handsome, susceptible man of thirty-four, was not in love with his wife, the mother of five living and two dead children, and only a year younger than himself. All he repented of was that he had not succeeded better in hiding it from his wife. But he felt all the difficulty of his position and was sorry for his wife, his children, and himself. Possibly he might have managed to conceal his sins better from his wife if he had anticipated that the knowledge of them would have had such an effect on her. He had vaguely conceived that his wife must long ago have suspected him of being unfaithful to her, and shut her eyes to the fact. He had even supposed that she, a worn-out woman no longer young or good-looking, and in no way remarkable or interesting, merely a good mother, ought from a sense of fairness to take an indulgent view. It had turned out quite the other way.

He idly activated the Galena Box, praying the gentle fluttering of the Class I device's thinly hammered groznium panels would have their usual salutary effect on his disposition.

"Oh, it's awful!" said Stepan Arkadyich to Small Stiva, who echoed him, chirping *"Awful awful awful"* from his Vox-Em, but neither could think of anything to be done. "And how well things were going up till now!"

"How well you got on," noted the Class III, falling into his familiar role as comforter and confidant.

"She was contented and happy in her children!"

"You never interfered with her in anything!"

"I let her manage the children and the Is and IIs just as she liked. It's true it's bad *her* having been a *mécanicienne* in our own house."

"Yes, bad. Very very very very bad!"

"There's something common, vulgar, in flirting with one's *mécanicienne*, in getting the grease-oil on one's cuffs, as it is said. Oh—but what a *mécanicienne*!" Responding unhesitatingly to his master's implied request, Small Stiva cued his monitor with a flattering Memory of Mlle Roland: her roguish black eyes; her smile; her figure slyly making itself known within her silver jumpsuit.

Stiva sighed, and Small Stiva sighed with him, and in unison they murmured, "But what is to be done?"

Small Stiva had a relatively advanced empathetic and communicative function, compared for instance to Dolly's Class III, Dolichka, whose Vox-Em could barely produce sentences—but on the other hand, she had more advanced use of her end-effectors. Small Stiva's stubby midtorso appendages were several clicks short of full phalangeal function. His short legs worked adequately on their pistons, but Stiva's Class III was for all intents and purposes a very clever little torso and head. In moments of pique or jovial teasing, Stiva called him his little bustling samovar.

Drawing a deep breath of air into his broad, bare chest, Stepan Arkadyich walked to the window with his usual confident step, turning out his feet that carried his full frame so easily. He pulled up the blind and signaled Small Stiva to bring him his clothes and boots and activate the II/Sartorial/943. The Class II automaton motored to life, a pair of long, flat "arms" unfolding and extending forward from the sides of its hatbox-sized body as it wheeled over to Stiva on its thick treads. As Stiva settled into his comfortable armchair and presented his face and neck, one of the Class II's end-effectors grew thick with shaving cream, and from the other flicked forth a gleaming silver straight razor.

As the II/Sartorial/943 began carefully lathering Stepan Arkadyich's cheeks and jowls, Small Stiva emitted a series of three sharp pings: A communiqué was arriving. Stiva gestured for his little beloved-companion to play it, and soon his face brightened.

"My sister Anna Arkadyevna will be here tomorrow," he said, checking for a minute the efficient end-effector of the II/Sartorial/943 cutting a pink path through his long, curly whiskers.

As the communiqué from Anna Arkadyevna concluded, Small Stiva's whole frontal display lit up brightly, and his gleaming dome of a head spun rapidly around atop his little body. He, like his master, realized the significance of this arrival—that is, that Anna Arkadyevna, the sister Stiva was so fond of, might bring about a reconciliation between husband and wife.

"Alone, or with her husband?" the Class III inquired.

As he opened his mouth to answer, the II/Sartorial/943 let out a shriek as loud and piercing as a boiling kettle and sank the razor end-effector deeply into Stiva's top lip, causing him to jerk backward and yelp.

"Ah! Ah!" he shouted in genuine pain, hot blood streaming from the wound into his mouth and down his neck. The Class II screeched again, deafeningly, its razor-tipped end-effector drawn back for a second slash. Stepan Arkadyich raised his hands feebly before his face, trying to protect his eyes, and to wave away the noxious cloud of sweet perfume the II/Sartorial/943 was spraying from the Third Bay at the base of its midsection. The Class II swept its blood-smeared end-effector directly at Stepan Arkadyich's plump neck, nicking his Adam's apple and missing the carotid artery by a matter of inches.

Stepan Arkadyich hollered wildly over the din of the Class II's feverish beeping. "The thing is maltuned! It's become maleficent! Small Stiva!"

But Small Stiva, programmed in keeping with the Iron Laws to defend his master even past the point of his own destruction, was already in action. The loyal Class III bent forward at a 45-degree angle and launched himself like a little cannonball directly into the black metal frame of the malfunctioning robot. The II/Sartorial/943 was knocked off its treads and thrown across the room, where it smashed against the glass top of the comfort unit.

"Bravo, little samovar," said Stepan Arkadyich through his wadded handkerchief, which he had stuffed up against his lip in a half-successful effort to staunch the crimson flow from his face.

The Class II's horrid beeping had not yet ceased, and the malfunctioning of the sartorial unit was more dire than Stepan Arkadyich had realized. It righted itself and shot back across the floor with demonic energy, whirling gyroscopically as it came, firing hot, thick globs of shaving cream toward Stepan Arkadyich's eyes, its straight-razored end-effector swinging in wild, deadly circles. Stepan Arkadyich cowered back into the corner, his arms flung up helplessly before him.

Small Stiva, faster and more complex in his functioning than the smartest of Class IIs, which this simple household sartorial certainly was not, easily intercepted the smaller machine. Holding it at arm's length with one midtorso effector, Small Stiva flung himself open at the torso, revealing the intensely hot groznium furnace that burned within him. Then, suddenly, he let go of the II/Sartorial/943 and let the thing fling itself forward—the errant Class II flew into the torso furnace, and Small Stiva clanged the door shut behind it.

"My Lord. I have never seen such a severe maltuning in a Class II, to so wantonly contravene the Iron Laws," mused Stepan Arkadyich, dabbing more blood from his gashed lip with his shirttail. "I am lucky, as ever, that you were here, *mon petit ami.*"

Small Stiva whistled proudly and stoked his groznium core for one hot instant—and from within him came the hiss and pop of the II/Sartorial/943's polymers disintegrating. The casings and trim would be destroyed, but the machine's thousands of groznium parts, indestructible and reusable, would, by a remarkable process, be "internalized" into Small Stiva's own biomechanical infrastructure.

Stepan Arkadyich struggled to his feet and was casting about for a fresh shirt when Dolichka whirred officiously into the room.

On her monitor was displayed a simple message: "Darya Alexandrovna is going away." After Stiva had read it glumly and nodded, Dolichka pivoted on her thick metal legs and whirred out. Stepan Arkadyich was silent a minute. Then a good-humored and rather pitiful smile showed itself on his handsome face.

"Eh, Small Stiva?" he said, shaking his head.

The android turned his head all the way around, flashed a cheerful red from within his frontal display, and piped, *"Worry not, master. For you, all things will turn out right."*

With a midbody effector he was holding up Stepan Arkadyich's fresh shirt like a horse's collar, and blowing off some invisible speck with a burst of air from his Third Bay, he slipped it over the body of his master.

CHAPTER 3

STEPAN ARKADYICH, IN SPITE OF his unhappiness and his natural irritation at the sacrifice of a particularly good household Class II, walked with a slight swing of each leg into the dining-room, where coffee was already waiting for him, piping hot from the I/Samovar/1(8).

Sipping his coffee, he activated Small Stiva's monitor to display the first of several business-related communiqués he had to review. One was very unpleasant, from a merchant who was buying a small but valuable patch of groznium-rich soil on his wife's property. To sell this property was absolutely essential; but at present, until he was reconciled with his wife, the subject could not be discussed. The most unpleasant thing of all was that his pecuniary interest should in this way enter into the question of his reconciliation with his wife. And the idea that he might be led on by his interests, that he might seek a reconciliation with his wife on account of the sale of the land—that idea hurt him.

When he had finished viewing his communiqués, Stepan Arkadyich dismissed Small Stiva, enjoyed a sip of coffee, and allowed the morning news feed to wash over him.

Stepan Arkadyich took a liberal feed, not an extreme one, but one advocating the views held by the majority. With the liberal party and his liberal feed, Stepan Arkadyich held that marriage is an institution quite out of date, and that it needs reconstruction; that religion is only a curb to keep in check the barbarous classes of the people; that the progress of technology was too slow, especially in the realm of Class III vocalization and action/reaction; and that there could be no mercy shown the terrorists and assassins of UnConSciya—even though it was that very technological progress those terrorists claimed to be fighting for.

Having finished the feed, a second cup of coffee and a roll and butter, Stiva got up, shaking the crumbs of the roll off his waistcoat; and, squaring his broad chest, he smiled joyously: not because there was anything particularly agreeable in his mind—the joyous smile was evoked by a good digestion, and by the gentle oscillations of the Galena Box.

Just then Small Stiva bustled back into the room and chirruped out a message. *"The carriage is ready,"* he said, *"and there's someone to see you with a petition."*

"Been here long?" asked Stepan Arkadyich.

"Half an hour."

"How many times have I told you to tell me at once?"

"One must let you drink your coffee in peace," answered Small Stiva in that affectionately tinny tone with which it was impossible to be angry. For the hundredth time, Stepan Arkadyich promised himself to have the Class III's relevant circuits adjusted, to tend him more toward formal attendance to duties, and away from pleasant appeasement of perceived wishes—but he knew he never would do so.

"Well, show the person up at once," said Oblonsky, frowning with vexation.

After dealing with the petitioner, Stepan Arkadyich took his hat and stopped to recollect whether he had forgotten anything. It appeared that he had forgotten nothing except what he wanted to forget—his wife.

"Ah, yes!" He bowed his head, and his handsome face assumed a harassed expression. "To go, or not to go!" he said to Small Stiva, who made a gesture charmingly imitative of a human shrug. An inner voice told Stiva he must not go, that nothing could come of it but falsity; that to amend, to set right their relations was impossible, because it was impossible to make her attractive again and able to inspire love, or to make him an old man, not susceptible to love. Except deceit and lying, nothing could come of it now; and deceit and lying were opposed to his nature.

"It must be some time, though: it can't go on like this," he said to Small Stiva, who said, *"No no can't go on no."* Thus encouraged, Stiva squared his chest, took out a cigarette, took two whiffs at it and flung it into a Class I mother-of-pearl ashtray, which instantly and automatically filled with a half inch of water, extinguishing the smoldering butt. With rapid steps he walked through the drawing room, and opened the other door into his wife's bedroom.

CHAPTER 4

DARYA ALEXANDROVNA, in a dressing jacket, with her now scanty, once luxuriant and beautiful, hair fastened up with hairpins on the nape of her neck, was standing before an open bureau among a litter of all sorts of things scattered all over the room. Hearing her husband's steps, she stopped, looking toward the door; Dolichka, by angling her linear eyebrows into a sharp V, gave her features a severe and contemptuous expression. Dolly and her companion android alike felt afraid of Stepan Arkadyich, and afraid of the coming interview. They were just attempting to do what they had attempted to do ten times already in these last three days—to sort out the children's things so as to take them to her mother's—but again Darya Alexandrovna could not bring herself to do this. She said to Dolichka, as each time before, "Things cannot go on like this! I must take some step to punish him!" and as always Dolichka confirmed her in her opinions, supporting her in all things, exactly as it was the sole purpose of her existence to do.

"I shall leave him!" Dolly pronounced, and Dolickha in her metallic soprano echoed her: *"Yes! Leave!"* But Dolly knew in her heart of hearts what Dolichka, in the mechanical limitations of her imagination, could not understand: to leave him was impossible. It was impossible because Darya Alexandrovna could not get out of the habit of regarding him as her husband and loving him. Besides this, she realized that if even here in her own house she could hardly manage to look after her five children properly, along with their several dozen Class IIs and countless Class Is, they would be still worse off where she was going with them all.

Seeing her husband, followed closely by the obnoxious oblong form of Small Stiva, she dropped her hands into the drawer of the bureau as though looking for something. But her face, to which she tried to give a severe and resolute expression, betrayed bewilderment and suffering.

"Dolly!" Stepan Arkadyich said in a subdued and timid voice, while Small Stiva bent at midline in a supplicating position toward Dolichka. In a rapid glance Dolly scanned her husband's figure, and that of his robot. Man and machine both radiated health and freshness. "Yes, he is happy and content!" she whispered to Dolichka, and the bitter confirmation came from the Class III's Vox-Em, *"Happy. Content."*

"While I . . . ," Dolly continued, but her mouth stiffened, the muscles of the cheek contracted on the right side of her pale, nervous face.

"What do you want?" Dolly said to her husband in a rapid, deep, unnatural voice.

"Dolly!" he repeated, with a quiver in his voice. "Anna and Android Karenina are coming today."

"Well, what is that to me? I can't see them!" she cried.

"But you must, really, Dolly . . . "

"Go away, go away, go away!" she shrieked, not looking at him, as though this shriek were called up by physical pain.

The Galena Box, its simple external sensors attuned to those vocal tonalities indicative of emotional distress, reactuated, pulsing more rapidly.

Stepan Arkadyich could be calm when he thought of his wife, and could immerse himself in the news feed and drink the coffee that the II/Samovar/1(8) provided; but when he saw her tortured, suffering face, heard the tone of her voice, submissive to fate and full of despair, there was a catch in his breath and a lump in his throat, and his eyes began to shine with tears.

"My God! What have I done? Dolly! For God's sake! . . . You know . . . " He could not go on; there was a sob in his throat. "Might we . . . " he began, gesturing meaningfully at their two androids. Dolly gave an agitated nod, and both of the Class IIIs were sent into Surcease, with head units slightly forward and sensory circuits deactivated, to allow their masters their absolute privacy.

"Dolly, what can I say . . . ?" He paused, trying to arrange his thoughts appropriately, and there was no machine buzz in the room, not a single milli-Maxwell of hum. In this uncanny silence, Stiva blundered onward. "One thing: forgive . . . Remember, cannot nine years of my life atone for an instant—"

She dropped her eyes and listened, expecting what he would say, yet silently beseeching him in some way or other to make her believe differently.

"—an instant of passion?" he said, and would have gone on, but at that word, as at a pang of physical pain, her lips stiffened again, and again the muscles of her right cheek worked. The razor wound on Stiva's upper lip sent a pulse of fresh pain radiating through the nerves of his face.

"Go away, go out of the room!" she shrieked still more shrilly. "And don't talk to me of your passion and your loathsomeness."

She tried to go out, but tottered, and clung to the back of a chair to support herself. His face quivered in a fresh wave of agony, and his eyes swam with tears.

"Dolly!" he said, sobbing now. "For mercy's sake, think of the children! I am to blame, and punish me, make me expiate my fault. Anything I can do, I am ready to do anything! I am to blame, no words can express how much I am to blame! But, Dolly, forgive me!"

She sat down. He listened to her hard, heavy breathing, and he was unutterably sorry for her. She tried several times to begin to speak, but could not. He waited.

"Tell me, after what . . . has happened, can we live together?" Dolly answered finally, glancing at the stiff, silent form of Dolichka, missing the comfort of her animated presence. "Is that possible? Tell me, eh, is it possible?" she repeated, raising her voice, "after my husband, the father of my children, enters into a love affair with a common household *mécanicienne*?"

"But what could I do? What could I do?" he kept saying in a pitiful voice, not knowing what he was saying, as his head sank lower and lower.

"You are loathsome to me, repulsive!" she shrieked, getting more and more heated. "Your tears mean nothing! You have never loved me; you have neither heart nor honorable feeling! You are hateful to me, disgusting, a stranger—yes, a complete stranger!" With pain and wrath she uttered the word so terrible to herself—*stranger*.

He looked at her, and the fury expressed in her face alarmed and amazed him. He did not understand how his pity for her exasperated her. She saw in him sympathy for her, but not love. *No, she hates me. She will not forgive me,* he thought.

"Dolly! Wait! One word more," he said.

"Dolichka!" Dolly cried, turning her back to him and agitatedly flicking the red switch beneath her Class III's chin; the angular machine-woman's circuits sprang to life, and together the two of them fled the room.

"If you come near me, I will call in the neighbors, the children! Every Class II in the house will know you are a scoundrel! I am going away at once, and you may live here with your jumpsuited mistress!"

And she went out, slamming the door.

CHAPTER 5

STEPAN ARKADYICH WORKED in the Moscow Tower, as a Deputy Vice President for Class I Manufacture & Distribution, Branch: Toys & Misc. It was an honorable and lucrative position, but one which required very little of him. The substantive decisions were made and relayed to him from elsewhere in his department, or from the St. Petersburg Tower, where the Higher Branches of the Ministry had their headquarters. He had received his post through his sister Anna's husband, Alexei Alexandrovich Karenin, who held an extremely important position in the Higher Branches, the details of which were unclear and uninteresting to Stiva. But if Karenin had not gotten his brother-in-law this post, then through a hundred other personages—brothers, sisters, cousins, uncles, and aunts—Stiva Oblonsky would have received this post, or some other similar one, together with the salary of six thousand absolutely needful for him, as his affairs, in spite of his wife's considerable property, were in an embarrassed condition.

Half of Moscow and Petersburg were friends and relations of Stepan Arkadyich. He was born in the midst of those who had been and are the powerful ones of this world: men in government, roboticists, engineers, landowners, and above all those with positions in the Ministry. Consequently the distributors of earthly blessings in the shape of places, rents, and precious groznium were all his friends.

Stepan Arkadyich was not merely liked by all who knew him for his good humor, but for his bright disposition, unquestionable honesty, and adorable little walking armoire of a Class III. In Stepan Arkadyich—in his handsome, radiant figure, his sparkling eyes, black hair and eyebrows, and the white and red of his face—there was something that produced a physical effect of kindliness and good humor on the people who met him. "Aha! Stiva and Small Stiva! Here they are!" was almost always said with a smile of delight on meeting the affable pair.

The principal qualities in Stepan Arkadyich that had gained him this universal respect consisted, in the first place, of his extreme indulgence for others, founded on a consciousness of his own shortcomings; secondly, of his perfect liberalism—not the liberalism he read of in the papers, but the liberalism that was in his blood, in virtue of which he treated all men and their machines perfectly equally and exactly the same, whatever their fortune or calling might be; and thirdly—the most important point—his complete indifference to the business in which he was engaged, in consequence of which he was never carried away, and never made mistakes.

Stepan Arkadyich arrived at his place of work and looked adoringly up at the massive onion-shaped bulb that rotated slowly atop the Tower, forever scanning Moscow's streets. "The Tower, she keeps her loving eye upon us," went the saying, and indeed there was something decidedly ocular about the single round opening on one side of the giant rotating bulb, keeping its eternal, and eternally loving, watch over the city and her people.

Waiting for Stiva at the top of the stairs was the welcome sight of his old friend, Konstantin Dmitrich Levin.

"Why, it's actually you, Levin, at last!" Stiva said with a friendly mocking smile, taking in Levin and his Class III as he bounded up the stairs toward them, Small Stiva clumsily following one step at a time. "Welcome to the Ministry!" As he uttered the words, both men crossed themselves and glanced upward, as if to heaven—the instinctual gesture of reverence for the most cherished of Russian institutions.

"How is it you have deigned to look me up in this den?" said Stepan Arkadyich, and not content with shaking hands, he kissed his friend. "Have you been here long?"

"I have just come, and very much wanted to see you," said Levin, looking shyly and at the same time angrily and uneasily around. Stiva could now see Levin's Class III, an oddly unpleasant-looking, tall, copper-plated humanoid called Socrates, hovering by his side. Ringing Socrates' chin was an array of useful items—a knife, a corkscrew, a spring, a small shovel, and so on—which jangled on his neck like a thick beard of springs and cogs, and which he tugged as he also looked uneasily around, mimicking his master's discomfited manner.

"Well, let's go into my room," said Stepan Arkadyich, who knew his friend's sensitive and irritable shyness, and, taking his arm, he drew him along, the trigger-latch that caused the door to his inner office to open with an audible pneumatic gasp.

Levin was almost of the same age as Oblonsky, and had been the friend and companion of his early youth. They were fond of one another in spite of the difference of their characters and tastes, as friends are fond of one another who have been together in early youth. Their bond had been cemented when both boys were merely sixteen, unshaven lads not yet possessed of their Class IIIs. An UnConSciya trap called a godmouth had suddenly yawned open in a Moscow open-air vegetable market a few yards from where they were standing. Levin tackled Oblonsky, who had been obliviously eating a peach, and dragged him to safety before the other boy even realized that the terrible, glowing vortex had appeared. The near miss left a lasting impression on both boys, and guaranteed a lifelong brotherly friendship.

In spite of this bond, each of them, as is often the way with men who have selected careers of different kinds, despised the other's career— though in discussion he would even justify it. It seemed to each of them that the life he led himself was the only real life, and the life led by his friend was a mere apparition, no more tangible than a communiqué relayed in the monitor of a Class III. Oblonsky could not restrain a slight mocking smile at the sight of Levin. How often he had seen him come up to Moscow from the country where he was doing something, but what precisely Stepan Arkadyich could never quite make out, and indeed he took no interest in the matter. Levin arrived in Moscow always excited and in a hurry, rather ill at ease and irritated by his own want of ease, and for the most part with a perfectly new, unexpected view of things. Stepan Arkadyich laughed at this, and liked it. In the same way Levin in his heart despised the town mode of life of his friend, and his official duties, which he laughed at, and regarded as trifling. But the difference was that Oblonsky, as he was doing the same as everyone did, laughed complacently and good-humoredly, while Levin laughed without complacency and sometimes angrily.

"We have long been expecting you," said Stepan Arkadyich, going into his room and letting Levin's hand go as though to show that here all danger was over. "I am very, very glad to see you," he went on. "That is, to see *both* of you."

Socrates bowed awkwardly. Stepan Arkadyich marveled, as
he always did on greeting his friend's Class III, at how different the
machine was from his genial, pleasant little Small Stiva. But as they said,
everyone gets the Class III that he deserves; such was the miracle of
the technology that had created the beloved-companions. Companion
robots were built-to-suit, their qualities created to match the needs
of the recipient; some were glib and some grave; some reassuring and
some critical; every one played the role in the life of the master that the
master needed it to play.

"I have to sizzle a whole container of outmoded Ones," Stiva said
to his old friend. "Shall we take turns?"

"Ah, no," said Levin, with his characteristic unsmiling awkwardness.
"No, thank you."

Oblonsky smiled and flicked a red switch on his desk, which caused
a copper panel to slide open. From this hidden chamber he produced
a sleek, handsome Ministry-issued Class I called a sizzler, a one-trigger
shooting device for neatly destroying small robots. Then from a box
beside his desk he took out the first of the Class Is slated for sizzling.
They were simple I/Mouse/9s, household favorites for keeping one's
kitchen or backyard free of roaches and other pests. These were perfectly
functional—indeed, as Oblonsky held it aloft by the tail, the I/Mouse/9
squeaked and looked around the room with its little glass eyes—but
they were no longer desired for distribution, since the I/Mouse/10s had
become available.

"Well, how are you?" asked Stiva, and zapped the Class I in its little
lifelike face with the sizzler. The thing arced its back and dropped from
his hand onto the desk. "When did you come? How is your groznium
mine?" Levin was silent.

As it writhed on the desk, the mouselike automaton let out a loud,
pained squeal. Stiva wrinkled his nose and shot Levin a helpless, apologetic smile.

"Makes conversation difficult, but it is in their circuits—they can't help it."

"They don't feel pain?" asked Levin.

Stiva selected a second I/Mouse/9 and zapped it in the face. "What? Oh, yes. Certainly they do." Levin said nothing, only shot a disapproving glance to Socrates, who flashed his dark-yellow eyebank and tugged at his cluster of springs.

"What brings you to our fair Babylon this time?" Stiva inquired with a wink, as he felt around in the box, finally snatching up another squirming I/Mouse/9.

"I have nothing very particular. Only a few words to say, and a question I want to ask you."

"Well, say the few words, then, at once!"

Levin paused, unsure how to proceed, and turned to his companion android. Socrates regarded him sternly. *"Just say it,"* urged the Class III tinnily sotto voce.

"I cannot simply say it."

"Can and must."

"Do not badger me, Socrates."

Stiva regarded this conversation with a sardonic expression, and looked knowingly at his own Class III, Small Stiva, who whirred with amusement.

"Well, it's this," said Levin to Stiva finally, "but it's of no importance, though."

"Oh?" Stiva tossed the next I/Mouse/9 up into the air and sizzled it with a twirling trick shot.

Levin's face all at once took an expression of anger from the effort he was making to surmount his shyness. Socrates angled his head forward with a significant gesture, bidding his master summon the nerve to say his piece.

"What are the Shcherbatskys doing? Everything as it used to be?" Levin said finally.

Stepan Arkadyich had long known that Levin was in love with his sister-in-law Kitty. His eyes sparkled merrily as he plucked up two I/ Mouse/9s at once and sizzled them both with a single shot by allowing the electric burst to flow through the "brain" of the first into the "brain" of the second.

He smiled slowly, teasingly, extending Levin's discomfort. "I can't answer in a few words, because . . . Excuse me a minute. . . . "

A small II/Secretary/44 with respectful familiarity and modest consciousness flitted through the door on hummingbird-like wings, its end-effector clutching some papers for Oblonsky.

"*Sir? Sir?*" it said, *sir* being the one word this Class II was programmed to employ, and flapped the papers. "*Si—*" Stepan Arkadyich, distracted by his enjoyment of the conversation with Levin, zapped the thing in the face.

"Drat!" Stiva said in frustration, as the II/Secretary/44 sputtered. For a moment Oblonsky thought the machine might be recovered, but the sizzler was a powerful device. The Class II's faceplate was already melting, bits of exterior plating dripping like tears along its flesh-tinted skull, while it made crazy circles around the room, banging against the desk and the walls. "Small Stiva?" Oblonsky said with resignation. The dutiful Class III opened his torso and, for the second time that day, destroyed a fellow robot inside of himself.

During this incident Levin had completely recovered from his embarrassment. He was standing with his elbows on the back of a chair, and on his face was a look of ironical attention.

"I don't understand it, I don't understand it," he said.

"What don't you understand?" said Oblonsky, trying to maintain his sardonic smile, though the small cloud of blue-black smoke emerging from Small Stiva's Third Bay darkened the room along with his mood. Stepan Arkadyich was a relatively prestigious personage, but two destroyed machines in one day was pushing the limits of what would go unnoticed. The last thing he needed, to compound the difficulty of a household in disarray, was the curious attention of the

Higher Branches.

"I don't understand what you are doing," Levin continued, shrugging his shoulders and gesturing at the sizzler, still smoking in Stiva's hand. "How can you do all this seriously?"

"Why not?"

"Why, because there's nothing in it."

"You think so, but we're overwhelmed with work."

"On paper. But, there, you've a gift for it," added Levin.

"That's to say, you think there's a lack of something in me?"

"Perhaps so," said Levin. "But all the same, I admire your grandeur, and am proud that I've a friend in such a great person. You've not answered my question, though," he went on, with a desperate effort looking Oblonsky straight in the face.

"Oh, that's all very well. You wait a bit, and you'll come to this yourself. It's very nice for you to have over six thousand acres of groznium-saturated soil in the Karazinsky district, and such muscles, and the freshness of a girl of twelve; still you'll be one of us one day. Yes, as to your question, there is no change, but it's a pity you've been away so long."

"Oh, why so?" Levin queried, panic-stricken.

"Oh, nothing," responded Oblonsky. "We'll talk it over. But what's brought you up to town?"

"Oh, we'll talk about that, too, later on," said Levin, reddening again up to his ears.

"All right. I see," said Stepan Arkadyich. "I should ask you to come to us, you know, but my wife's not quite the thing. But I tell you what: if you want to see them, they're sure now to be at the skate-maze from four to five. Kitty skates. You drive along there, and I'll come and fetch you, and we'll go and dine somewhere together."

"Capital. So good-bye till then."

CHAPTER 6

WHEN OBLONSKY HAD ASKED Levin what had brought him to town, Levin blushed, and was furious with himself for blushing, because he could not answer, "I have come to make your sister-in-law an offer," though that was precisely what he had come for.

As he reflected on this lack of will, he and Socrates sat down across from one another at a small café along the banks of the Moskva. Together they had wandered some miles from the Tower, but could still see its tall spire in the distance, slowly rotating, scanning, keeping watch, ensuring the safety of the city and her people.

"Our tireless protectors," Levin said absently, and then activated Socrates' monitor. Sipping his tea, he viewed the Memories he had already viewed so many times, over and over in the carriage, all the way from his country estate.

The families of the Levins and the Shcherbatskys were old, noble Moscow families, and had always been on intimate and friendly terms. This intimacy had grown still closer during Levin's student days. He had trained in mine management with the young Prince Shcherbatsky, the brother of Kitty and Dolly, and had entered Moscow Groznium Institute at the same time with him. In those days Levin used often to be in the Shcherbatskys' house, and he was in love with the Shcherbatsky household. Strange as it may appear, it was with the household, the family, that Konstantin Levin was in love, especially with the feminine half of the household. Why it was the three young ladies had one day to speak French, and the next English; why it was that at certain hours they played by turns on the piano, the sounds of which were audible in their brother's room above, where the students used to work; why they were visited by those professors of French literature, of music, of drawing, of dancing; it was the first time he had heard French spoken in a household.

A ragged, high-pitched scream interrupted Levin's enjoyment of these reveries. He looked up from his Memories, and saw the source of the screaming: a dusty-faced woman in a tattered apron stood on the stoop of her home, yelling the words, "No, it cannot be!" in a high-pitched, desperate voice. An equally disheveled-looking man, evidently her husband, was being hoisted and his arms pinned behind his body by the strong metallic arms of a 77. More 77s stood on either side of the doorway, their onion-bulb-shaped heads revolving slowly, visual sensors glowing from within, constantly taking in and analyzing the surroundings. One of them, with his thick pipe-like arms, was restraining the woman; meanwhile, a tall, handsome Caretaker, his gold uniform glittering in the midday sun, directed the 77s with sharp commands to secure the block and search the house.

"Ah! They have captured a Janus," said Levin admiringly.

"This close to the market, it is likely a black marketeer," suggested Socrates, *"or a groznium hoarder."*

"Yes, or even an agent of UnConSciya," Levin agreed, becoming excited despite himself at this close-up look at the function of the state apparatus. He marveled at the brisk efficiency of the Caretaker and his cadre of 77s as they went about the business of interrogating the Janus. It had been some months since his last visit to Moscow, and in the countryside one rarely got to see the assured work of the majestic bulb-headed 77s in action.

At last Levin tore himself away and turned back to Socrates' monitor, and his precious Memories. He watched how the three young Shcherbatsky sisters drove along the Tversky Boulevard, dressed in their satin cloaks: Dolly in a long one, Natalia in a half-long one, and Kitty in one so short that her shapely legs in tightly drawn red stockings were visible to all beholders; how they had to walk about the Tversky Boulevard escorted by their parents, their parents' stately Class IIIs, and a II/Gendarme/439 with a copper-plated smoker, drawn and engaged—all this and much more that was done in their mysterious world he did not understand, but he was sure that everything that was done there was very good, and he was in love precisely with the mystery of the proceedings.

When he looked up from this pleasing Memory stream, Levin saw that a crowd had grown at either end of the cordoned block. The Caretaker had dispatched a 77 to keep the onlookers from becoming too curious, while the massive 77 holding the Janus lifted him high into the air, clutching the man's arms with his fat, gloved end-effectors, and shook him roughly back and forth. Now Levin heard the tromp of metal boots close at hand, and saw that 77s were fanning through the crowd at the café. Levin, accurately judged a nobleman by the presence of his Class III robot, was left alone, even as the 77s began briskly running their physiometers over the other diners.

He and Socrates watched as the Caretaker loudly demanded answers of his prisoner, answers which evidently did not come quickly enough: the 77 restraining the Janus snaked a gold-tipped cord from a compartment in his upper torso and attached it roughly to the man's left temple. A blast of voltage traveled from the 77's core into the man's forehead, and the Janus gibbered and shook, his body rattling from the pain.

The Janus's wife, still standing in the doorway, shrieked and fainted dead away on her stoop.

"*Swift justice,*" said Socrates, but at this bit of violence Levin grimaced and turned away. Noting his master's pained expression, Socrates echoed back what he himself had said a moment ago: "*Probably he is an agent of UnConSciya. Almost certainly, now that I have had a chance to reflect.*" But Socrates had not run an analysis on the question, could not really know, and Levin said nothing. This time it was Socrates who re-engaged his own monitor, drawing his master back into the soothing consolations of the past.

In his student days Levin had all but been in love with the eldest daughter of the Shcherbatsky family, Dolly, but she was soon married to Oblonsky. Then he began being in love with the second. He felt, as it were, that he had to be in love with one of the sisters, only he could not quite make out which. But Natalia, too, had hardly made her appearance in the world when she was married to the mathementalics engineer Lvov. Kitty was still a child when Levin left the university. Young Shcherbatsky began in the mines, was crushed in a cave-in, and Levin's relations with the Shcherbatskys, in spite of his friendship with Oblonsky, became less intimate. But when early in the winter of this year Levin came to Moscow, after a year in the country, and saw the Shcherbatskys, he realized which of the three sisters he was indeed destined to love.

But Levin was in love, and so it seemed to him that Kitty was so perfect in every respect that she was a creature far above everything terrestrial; and that he was a creature so low and so earthly that it could not even be conceived that other people and she herself could regard him as worthy of her. Levin's conviction that it could not be was founded on the idea that in the eyes of her family he was a disadvantageous and worthless match for the charming Kitty, and that Kitty herself could not love him.

In her family's eyes he had no ordinary, definite career and position in society; yes, he had his patch of rough land in the country, but like all pit-operators he was ultimately a functionary, proudly mining his soil on behalf of the Ministry, which owned all the Russian groznium beds; while his contemporaries by this time, when he was thirty-two, were already one a colonel, and another a robotics professor, another director of a bank, or Vice President of a Division, like Oblonsky. But he (he knew very well how he must appear to others) was a country gentleman, occupied only in extraction and excavation and smelting; in other words, a fellow of no ability, who had not turned out well, and who was doing just what, according to the ideas of the world, is done by people fit for nothing else.

The mysterious, enchanting Kitty herself could not love such an ugly person as he conceived himself to be, and, above all, such an ordinary, in no way striking person. He had heard that women often did care for ugly and ordinary men, but he did not believe it, for he judged by himself, and he could not himself have loved any but beautiful, mysterious, and exceptional women.

After spending two months in Moscow in a state of enchantment, seeing Kitty almost every day in society, into which he went so as to meet her, his circuits (to employ the crass expression) went haywire: he abruptly decided that it could not be, and went back to the country. But after several months . . .

"No! No, please—"

This was the voice of the Janus's wife.

"We confess. We have done it. My husband and I. We released the koschei at St. Catherine Square . . . Thursday last. It was us! Please—"

"This, madame, we were already aware," said the Caretaker in command of the troop of state robots, casually brushing a speck of dirt from his gleaming golden uniform. Meanwhile a second cord had writhed forward from a second compartment in the 77's bulky torso, and attached itself to the other side of the man's temples. Again electricity flowed from within the 77, along the deadly conduits of the cords, and into the Janus's skull. His body lifted off the ground, his feet rattled like empty cans, and then he went slack.

As Levin and Socrates looked on, the gold-uniformed Caretaker shouted an order at the 77, and the old man was lifted by the massive man-machine like a sack of potatoes, and tossed bodily into the river, while the crowd of peasants cheered lustily.

"Master?" came the cautious inquiry from Socrates' Vox-Em, when all was concluded and the troop of 77s had disappeared.

"Never fear, old friend. My stomach is strong enough to bear witness to the cost of safety for Mother Russia. Still . . . rather an ill omen for my undertaking in the city."

Levin sighed as he rose from the café table, and bid Socrates to rise with him. He could not leave without completing his quest. After spending two months alone in the country, he was convinced that his feeling for Kitty was not one of those passions of which he had had experience in his early youth; that this feeling gave him not an instant's rest; that he could not live without deciding the question, would she or would she not be married to him, and that his despair had arisen only from his own imaginings, that he had no sort of proof that he would be rejected. And he had now come to Moscow with a firm determination to make an offer, and get married if he were accepted. Or . . . he could not conceive what would become of him if he were rejected.

The body of the Janus bobbed past them, floated down the river, and away.

CHAPTER 7

A T FOUR O'CLOCK, conscious of his heart hammering like a maltuned Class I sleep-waker, Levin stepped out of a hired sledge at the skating park, and turned along the path to the frozen mounds and the skate-maze, knowing that he would certainly find her there, as he had seen the Shcherbatskys' carriage at the entrance.

It was a bright, frosty day. Rows of carriages, sledges, drivers, and policemen—not 77s, just workaday Moscow II/Policeman/12s in their cheerful bronze weather-coating—were in the approach. Crowds of well-dressed people, with hats bright in the sun, swarmed about the entrance and along the well-swept little paths between the little houses adorned with carving in the Russian style. The old, curly birches of the gardens, all their twigs laden with snow, looked as though freshly decked in sacred vestments.

Levin walked along the path toward the skate-maze, while angular Socrates, programmed to dampen his master's anxiety when it grew too frenzied, droned in his ear:

"You mustn't be excited. You must be calm. Be quiet, be quiet, be quiet!"

But the more Levin tried to heed this warning, and keep himself composed, the more breathless he found himself. An acquaintance met him and called him by his name, but Levin did not even recognize him. He went toward the elaborate interlacing paths of magnetized track that made up the skate-maze, heard the familiar electric purr of skates gliding above its surface and the sounds of merry voices. He walked on a few steps, and the skating ground lay open before his eyes, and at once, amidst all the skaters, he knew her.

He knew she was there by the rapture and the terror that seized on his heart. She was talking to a woman at the opposite end of the ground, both ladies hovering just above track level, their skates set on neutral as they conversed. There was apparently nothing striking either in Kitty's dress or in her attitude. But for Levin she was as easy to find in that crowd as a rose among nettles. Everything was made bright by her. She was the smile that shed light on all around her. In that moment, it was to Levin like *she* was the Eye in the Tower, keeping loving watch over all Moscow.

"Be quiet-be calm-be quiet-calm-quiet-calm . . . ," Socrates repeated over and over in his ear.

"Is it possible I can go over there on the tracks, go up to her?" he murmured. The place where she stood seemed to him a holy shrine, unapproachable, as if encircled by a moat of radiant liquid groznium, and there was one moment when he was almost retreating, so overwhelmed was he with terror. With Socrates' help, he made an effort to master himself: People of all sorts were moving about her! He too was permitted to come there to skate! He walked down, for a long while avoiding looking at her as at the sun, but seeing her, as one does the

AMIDST ALL THE SKATERS WHO HOVERED ELECTROMAGNETICALLY ATOP
THE TRACKS, KITTY WAS AS EASY TO FIND AS A ROSE AMONG NETTLES

sun, without looking.

On that day of the week and at that time of day people of one set, all acquainted with one another, used to meet on the skate-maze. In skates with razor-thin, magnetized blades, revelers navigated the miles of inter-weaving tracks, the positive charge of the maze surface gently repelling the positive charge of the skates, so everyone glided along, elevated precisely one quarter inch above the track. There were crack skaters there, showing off their skill: happily they whooshed forward, weaving their way across the metal maze, greeting each other gaily, leaping up with bold tricks, skating forward and (when the track vectors were reversed by the II/Skatemaster/490) skating backward.

There were, too, learners clinging to chairs with timid, awkward movements, and elderly noblewomen skating slowly, leaning for support on their Class IIIs. All seemed to Levin an elect band of blissful beings because they were here, near her. All the skaters, it seemed, with perfect self-possession, skated toward her, skated by her, even spoke to her, and were happy, quite apart from her, enjoying the capital ice and the fine weather.

She was in a corner, and turning out her slender feet in their high boots with obvious timidity, she skated toward him.

"*Be calm! Be calm becalmbecalmbecalm . . . ,*" urged Socrates.

As she approached, a young boy skating down a track some distance away pitched head over heels, tumbling abruptly off the track and onto the frozen ground. This kind of accident was most unusual, even for the most unsteady skaters, given the self-correcting mechanisms built into the magnetic-repulsion skate technology. Konstantin Dmitrich had no time or inclination to ponder this event, had he even noticed it; his eyes, along with his heart, were focused only and entirely upon the slim pleasing figure of Kitty Shcherbatskaya.

"Have you been here long?" she said, giving him her hand and nodding pleasantly to Socrates.

"I? I've not long . . . yesterday . . . I mean today . . . I arrived," answered Levin, in his emotion not at once understanding her question. Directly behind where they were talking, a stout middle-aged man flew off the track and onto the ground, just as the boy had, landing with an audible *thump*. "I was meaning to come and see you," Levin continued, and then, recollecting with what intention he was trying to see her, he was promptly overcome with confusion and blushed.

Before he could recover his composure, suddenly, without warning, Kitty's body jerked violently backward and flew down the track like a rag doll hurled by a willful child. In the space of an instant, she was a dozen yards away, her body accelerating at an alarming rate from where Levin and Socrates stood, astounded. Worse, she was flying toward another skater, a mustachioed Moscow dandy, who was mysteriously shooting forward as rapidly as Kitty was speeding backward.

"Socrates!" shouted Levin desperately. "They shall collide!" and the Class III launched himself forward, his long springy legs telescoping open to become still longer as he leapt forward toward the impending collision. The bearded yellow machine-man, his massive bristle of springs and cogs bobbling, caught Kitty about the waist, pulling her off the track just before the mustachioed man would have caromed into her.

All over the maze, similar scenes of havoc unfolded. Some skaters flew backward down the track, others forward, while still others were stuck in place, gyrating violently in their skates. No one, it seemed, was any longer in control of his own feet; the electromagnetic whims of the skates, or of the track, or of both together, had taken control. As Levin watched, an old matron, whom he had seen moments earlier, plodding steadily forward on the track reserved for slower skaters, rocketed forward at a dizzying speed until she was hurled entirely off the course, over the side of a hill and down a snow-crusted embankment.

After satisfying himself that Kitty was out of danger, Levin ran about the perimeter of the skate-maze, saving those he could with a series of flying tackles that intercepted the terrified skaters and flung them off the grid. Socrates sprinted off in the opposite direction and did his part as well, plucking from his beard a powerful handheld destabilizer and using it to short-circuit the magnetic force in patches along the track, disrupting its power long enough to let skaters jump to freedom.

"UnConSciya," said Levin gravely to his Class III when they reconvened at the entrance to the park, where Kitty Shcherbatskaya sat beneath a snow-dusted aspen tree, shaken but unhurt.

"Who but they?" Socrates agreed bitterly. None but the rogue scientists in the so-called Union of Concerned Scientists had the technological ability or the anarchic spirit to launch such a terrible attack. Frustrated by the slow pace of scientific progress, even in the face of all that had been accomplished since the discovery of groznium, the futurists who had quit the government service and established UnConSciya were hellbent on bringing down the Ministry at all costs.

Today, mercifully, the chaos was short-lived; already, Levin heard the klaxon bell of the Tower ringing out as troops of 77s marched in. The wounded wailed, here and there a broken body lay in the snow, and those who had emerged unscathed were upset and terrified, exactly as the terrorists of UnConSciya wanted them to be.

In the aftermath, Levin and Kitty stood panting next to each other, recovering their breath. He wrapped her in his coat, and then, summoning his courage, Levin signaled Socrates into Surcease and grabbed at an excuse to say something, anything that might lead him back to that declaration which even now, after such chaos all around, threatened to burst from his lungs with more violence than any UnConSciya attack could ever muster.

"I didn't know you could skate, and skate so well," he said to Kitty.

"Your praise is worth having. The tradition is kept up here that you yourself are the best of skaters," she said. For a moment, then, both were silent, lowering their eyes respectfully as a corpse, wrapped in rough burlap, was loaded onto a carriage.

After a discreet pause, Levin replied simply: "Yes, I once used to skate with passion; I wanted to reach perfection."

"You do everything with confidence, I think," she said.

"I have confidence in myself when you are near me," he said, but was at once panic-stricken at what he had said, and blushed. And indeed, no sooner had he uttered these words, when all at once, like the sun going behind a cloud, her face lost all its friendliness, and Levin detected the familiar change in her expression that denoted the working of thought; a crease showed on her smooth brow.

"Is there anything troubling you? Which is to say, besides . . . " He indicated with a meaningful gesture the sad scene lying on the skate-maze before them. "Though I've no right to ask such a question," he added hurriedly.

"No, I have nothing to trouble me, beyond this latest diabolical assault on our beloved Moscow," she responded coldly. Levin cursed internally; there was no discounting that this horrid event had cast a pall over his intentions, and he could feel Kitty shying away from him. When she looked back at him, her face was no longer stern; her eyes looked at him with the same sincerity and friendliness, but Levin saw that in her friendliness there was a certain note of deliberate composure. And he felt depressed, even as she questioned him about his life.

"Surely you must be dull in the country in the winter, aren't you?" she said.

"No, I'm not dull, I am very busy," he said, feeling that she was holding him in check by her composed tone, which he would not have the force to break through. Around them, the injured and dead had been removed, and, as was the common practice, the skate-maze would be reopened as quickly as possible; it only remained for the 77s to conclude their safety-scan of the park. The machine-men, supervised by a gold-uniformed Caretaker, moved swiftly on that mission, overturning benches and lifting up sections of track, their sensors glowing purposefully.

"Are you going to stay in town long?" Kitty questioned him.

"I don't know," he answered, not thinking of what he was saying. The thought that if he were restrained by her tone of quiet friendliness he would end by going back again without deciding anything came into his mind, and he resolved to make a struggle against it.

"How is it you don't know?"

"I don't know. It depends upon you," he said, and was immediately horror-stricken at his own words. At that same moment, a tinkling little bell began to ring, signaling that the skate-maze was revivified: the track had been cleaned and polished by the II/Skatemaster/490, and was ready for use. Whether it was that she had heard his words, or that she did not want to hear them, Kitty made a sort of stumble, twice struck out, and hurriedly skated away from Levin.

Levin brought Socrates back from Surcease and immediately began muttering bitter curses to him.

"My God, what have I done! Merciful God! Help me, guide me."

"Yes," echoed the Class III, somewhat less than helpfully. *"God help you."*

CHAPTER 8

"THEY SHOULD BE rounded up," said Stepan Arkadyich, reaching for another oyster from the large pile that sat on the table between he and Konstantin Dmitrich. "Every last one of them should be rounded up and slaughtered in the streets, like the vile beasts they are."

Such was the gist of the evening news feed, and such therefore was the firm opinion espoused by Stepan Arkadyich over dinner. Levin, though he had witnessed the violence firsthand, offered a more tempered and analytical response. "You do not think, old friend, that we have had enough bloodshed in our struggle with UnConSciya? You do not think an offer of amnesty, to discuss and perhaps address their grievances, might be the wiser path?"

"Yes, yes! A truce for the moderate elements, certainly, certainly!" Stepan Arkadyich agreed genially. "But these violent lunatics? With their koschei and their godmouths and their emotion bombs? Let them be rounded up and subjected to the harshest possible punishment, in the most public of ways."

The conversation continued in this vein for another five or ten minutes before trailing away. Oblonsky held no real opinions on the subject, beyond what he had received from the evening's feed, and Levin was too distracted by the undertaking that had brought him to Moscow to let his mind be consumed, as often it could be, by political questions.

"You don't care much for oysters, do you?" said Stepan Arkadyich finally, emptying his wine glass. "Or you're worried about something. Eh?"

He wanted Levin to be in good spirits. But it was not that Levin was not in good spirits; he was ill at ease. With what he had in his soul, he felt sore and uncomfortable in the restaurant, in the midst of private rooms where men were dining with ladies, in all this fuss and bustle; the surroundings of bronzes, looking glasses, gas, and II/Server/888s—all of it was offensive to him.

He glanced anxiously toward Socrates, looking to have his own emotions explained to him. *"You are afraid,"* the beloved-companion pronounced in a simple and quiet voice. *"Afraid of sullying what your soul is brimful of."*

"Oh, I say, are you going tonight to our people, the Shcherbatskys', I mean?" said Stiva suddenly, alighting unerringly on the very topic causing Levin's consternation. His eyes sparkled significantly as he pushed away the empty rough shells, and drew the cheese plate toward him with a snappy little wrist-borne force projector.

"Yes, I shall certainly go," replied Levin slowly and with emotion,

"Oh, what a lucky fellow you are!" broke in Stepan Arkadyich, looking into Levin's eyes.

"Why?"

"I know a gallant steed by tokens sure,
And by his eyes I know a youth in love,"

declaimed Stepan Arkadyich. "Everything is before you!"

"Why, is it over for you already? "

"No; not over exactly, but the future is yours! You are the master of present and future alike, as surely as if you were a part of the Phoenix Project."

Oblonsky laughed heartily at his own jest, reaching for a third oyster. For all the technological strides that had been made in Russia in the Age of Groznium, the Phoenix Project—through which, it had been hoped, a machine could be built, using the unique properties of the Miracle Metal, that could tear a hole in the fabric of space-time—was one that had been long since abandoned. Indeed, it was the abandonment of that project, among several others of similar ambition, which had outraged the cell of government scientists who ultimately would form the dreaded UnConSciya. By now the very idea of time travel was so ridiculous as to be a source of ready amusement for Stiva and his fashionable set.

"Hi! Take away!" he called to their II/Server/888, and then turned back to his friend. "Well, why have you come to Moscow, then?"

"You guess?" responded Levin, his eyes like deep wells of light fixed upon Stepan Arkadyich.

"I guess, but I can't be the first to talk about it. You can see by that whether I guess right or wrong," said Stiva, gazing at Levin with a subtle smile.

"Well, and what have you to say to me?" said Levin in a quivering voice, feeling that all the muscles of his face were quivering too. "How do you look at the question?"

Stepan Arkadyich slowly emptied his glass of Chablis, never taking his eyes off Levin. He tossed a scrap of beef to Small Stiva, who opened a

fist-sized hole in his faceplate and vacuumed it up with a hoselike extension that suddenly snapped forward. The loyal little servomechanism did
not need the food, of course, but both master and Class III found delight
in the ritual.

"I?" said Stepan Arkadyich. "There's nothing I desire so much as
that—nothing! It would be the best thing that could be."

"But you're not making a mistake? You know what we're speaking of?" said Levin, piercing him with his eyes. "You think it's possible?"
Socrates bent forward at a precisely calibrated, inquiring angle.

"I think it's possible. Why not possible?"

"No! Do you really think it's possible? No, tell me all you think!"
Socrates bent forward another six degrees, his deepening incline reflect-
ing Levin's urgency. "Oh, but if . . . if refusal's in store for me! . . . Indeed
I feel sure . . . "

"Why should you think that?" said Stepan Arkadyich, smiling at
his excitement.

"It seems so to me sometimes. That will be awful for me, and for
her too."

"Oh, well, anyway there's nothing awful in it for a girl. Every girl's
proud of an offer."

"Yes, every girl, but not she."

Stepan Arkadyich smiled. He so well knew that feeling of Levin's,
that for him all the girls in the world were divided into two classes: one
class—all the girls in the world except her, and those girls with all sorts
of human weaknesses, and very ordinary girls: the other class—she alone,
having no weaknesses of any sort and higher than all humanity.

"Stay, take some sauce," he said, holding back Levin's hand as it
pushed away the sauce.

Levin obediently helped himself to sauce, but would not let Stepan
Arkadyich go on with his dinner.

"No, stop a minute, stop a minute," he said. "You must understand
that it's a question of life and death for me. I have never spoken to anyone

of this. And there's no one I could speak of it to, except you. You know we're utterly unlike each other, different tastes and views and everything; but I know you're fond of me and understand me, and that's why I like you awfully. But for God's sake, be quite straightforward with me."

Socrates bent forward further and a sharp luteous light began to flash from within his eyebank.

"I tell you what I think," said Stepan Arkadyich, smiling. "But I'll say more: my wife is a wonderful woman. . . . " He sighed, remembering his position with his wife, and, after a moment's silence, resumed. "She has a gift of foreseeing things. She sees right through people, as if she had a physiometer in her face; but that's not all; she knows what will come to pass, especially in the way of marriages!"

Both of them laughed lightly, though Levin's laughter was more out of nervousness than anything like genuine amusement. His true state was reflected by what was happening in Socrates' eyebank, where lights were blinking rapidly, in alternating shades of yellow, topaz, and orange.

"She foretold, for instance, that Princess Shahovskaya would marry Brenteln. No one would believe it, but it came to pass. And she's on your side."

"How do you mean?"

"It's not only that she likes you—she says that Kitty is certain to be married to you."

Levin's face suddenly lighted up with a smile, a smile not far from tears of emotion.

"She says that!" cried Levin. "I always said she was exquisite, your wife. There, that's enough, enough said about it," he said, getting up from his seat. Socrates got up just after him, one step behind his master, the deep-set lamps of his eyebank now a flickering blur of red and orange, orange and yellow, yellow and red.

"Do sit down," cried Stiva to both of them, as Small Stiva twittered with alarm at the other robot's wild display of lights.

But Levin could not sit down. He walked with his firm tread twice up and down the little cage of a room, blinked his eyelids so that his tears might not fall, and only then sat down to the table.

"You must understand," he said, "it's not love."

"Not merely *love,"* Socrates echoed in a high-pitched burble.

"I've been in love, but it's not that. It's not my feeling, but a sort of force outside me has taken possession of me."

"A force, a force, a powerful force!"

"I went away, you see, because I made up my mind that it could never be, you understand, as a happiness that does not come on earth; but I've struggled with myself, I see there's no living without it. And it must be settled."

"It must, it must, it must be settled now!" blared Socrates.

"What did you go away for?" inquired Oblonsky, but Levin charged on: "Ah, the thoughts that come crowding on one! The questions one must ask oneself!" Socrates now was pacing at furious speed around the dining table, beeping and whirring and whistling in a paroxysm of agitation. "You can't imagine what you've done for me by what you said. I'm so happy that I've become positively hateful; I've forgotten everything. I heard today that my brother Nikolai . . . you know, he's here . . . he's ill. . . . I had even forgotten him. But what's awful . . . Here, you've been married, you know the feeling. . . . " Socrates was now turning, twisting rapidly in place, his eyebank a wild xanthic blur, but Levin hardly noticed. "It's awful that we—old—with a past . . . not of love, but of sins . . . are brought all at once so near to a creature pure and innocent; it's loathsome—"

"Loathsome! Loathsome!"

"And that's why one can't help feeling oneself unworthy."

"Unworthy! Unworthy! Unworthy!" Socrates bleated, and then there was a loud grinding noise and a small hiss of steam, as Socrates overheated, and went to unintentional Surcease.

CHAPTER 9

LEVIN CURSED, REVIVIFIED HIS beloved-companion, and emptied his glass. The two old friends sat in silence for a time, waiting for Socrates' circuits to realign. Tea cups clinked elsewhere in the restaurant; a I/Samovar/1(8) burbled in the kitchen; a Class I *lumière* flickered to life automatically just as the gathering twilight demanded it; off in the distance on the streets outside was the tromp of 77s, the sharp hoot of their Caretaker.

"There's one other thing I ought to tell you," said Stepan Arkadyich while they waited. "Do you know Vronsky?"

"No, I don't. Why do you ask?"

"Give us another bottle," Stepan Arkadyich directed the II/Server/888 who was filling up their glasses, motoring round them just when he was not wanted. "And then turn off your sensors, will you?" Not needing to watch to make sure the white-jacketed Class II complied, since the Iron Laws demanded obedience to a human's every order, Stepan Arkadyich freely turned back to Levin to share his secret.

"Why you ought to know Vronsky is that he's one of your rivals."

"Who's Vronsky?" said Levin, and his face was suddenly transformed from the look of childlike ecstasy which Oblonsky had just been admiring to an angry and unpleasant expression.

"Vronsky is one of the sons of Count Kirill Ivanovitch Vronsky, and one of the finest specimens of the gilded youth of Petersburg. I made his acquaintance in Tver when I was there on official business, and he came there for the levy of recruits. Fearfully rich, handsome, great connections, a hero of the Border Wars, and authorized to carry a hot-whip and a pair of smokers on his belt. And with all that a very nice, good-natured fellow. But he's more than simply a good-natured fellow, as I've found out here—he's a cultivated man, too, and very intelligent; he's a man who'll make his mark."

Levin scowled and was dumb.

"Well, he turned up here soon after you'd gone, and as I can see, he's over head and ears in love with Kitty, and you know that her mother ... "

"Excuse me, but I know nothing," said Levin, frowning gloomily. And immediately he recollected his ill brother Nikolay and how hateful he was to have been able to forget him.

"You wait a bit, wait a bit," said Stepan Arkadyich, smiling and touching his hand. "I've told you what I know, and I repeat that in this delicate and tender matter, as far as one can conjecture, I believe the chances are in your favor."

Levin dropped back in his chair; his face was pale.

"But I would advise you to settle the thing as soon as may be," pursued Oblonsky, filling up his glass.

"No, thanks, I can't drink any more," said Levin, pushing away his glass. "I shall be drunk. . . . Come, tell me how are you getting on?" he went on, obviously anxious to change the conversation. He glanced with frustration at Socrates, willing the robot to swiftly revivify, but his beloved-companion's faceplate remained blank and black.

"One word more: in any case I advise you to settle the question soon. Tonight I don't advise you to speak," said Stepan Arkadyich. "Go round tomorrow morning, make an offer in due form, and God bless you. . . . "

At once Levin's whole soul was full of remorse that he had begun this conversation with Stepan Arkadyich. A feeling such as his was profaned by talk of the rivalry of some Petersburg officer, of the suppositions and the counsels of Stepan Arkadyich. He immediately moved to change the subject.

"Oh, do you still think of coming to me for the Hunt-and-be-Hunted? Come next spring, do," said Levin.

"I'll come Hunt some day," he said. "But women, my boy, they're the pivot everything turns upon. Things are in a bad way with me, very bad. And it's all through women. Tell me frankly now," he pursued, lighting the cigar that Small Stiva proffered, and keeping one hand on his glass, "give me your advice."

"Why, what is it?"

"I'll tell you. Suppose you're married, you love your wife, but you're fascinated by another woman. . . . "

"Excuse me, but I'm absolutely unable to comprehend how . . . just as I can't comprehend how I could now, after my dinner, go straight to a baker's shop and steal a roll."

Stepan Arkadyich's eyes sparkled more than usual. Suddenly both felt that though they were friends, though they had been dining and drinking together, which should have drawn them closer, each was thinking only of his own affairs, and they had nothing to do with one another. Oblonsky had more than once experienced this extreme sense of aloofness, instead of intimacy, coming on after dinner, and he knew what to do in such cases.

"Bill!" he called, and waited impatiently, patting the table with his hands, before remembering he had demanded the II/Server/888 turn off its sensors.

CHAPTER 10

THE YOUNG PRINCESS Kitty Shcherbatskaya was eighteen. It was the first winter that she had been out in the world, and shortly she would at last receive her very own beloved-companion robot. Kitty's success in society had been greater than that of either of her elder sisters, and greater even than her mother had anticipated. To say nothing of the young men who danced at the Moscow floats being almost all in love with Kitty, two serious suitors had already this first winter made their appearance: Levin, and immediately after his departure, that dashing, smoker-wielding hero of the Border Wars, Count Vronsky.

Levin's appearance at the beginning of the winter, his frequent visits, and evident love for Kitty had led to the first serious conversations between Kitty's parents as to her future, and to disputes between them. The prince was on Levin's side; he said he wished for nothing better for Kitty. The princess for her part, going round the question in the manner peculiar to women, maintained that Kitty was too young, that Levin had done nothing to prove that he had serious intentions, that Kitty felt no great attraction to him, and other side issues; but she did not state the principal point, which was that she looked for a better match for her daughter, and that Levin was not to her liking, and she did not understand him. A groznium miner with a pit-burnt face and alloy dust on his hands? When Levin had abruptly departed, the princess was delighted, and said to her husband triumphantly: "You see, I was right. Let him return to his smoldering hole in the ground!"

When Vronsky appeared on the scene, she was still more delighted, confirmed in her opinion that Kitty was to make not simply a good, but a brilliant match. Vronsky satisfied all the mother's desires. Very wealthy, clever, of aristocratic family, a known sharpshooter with a smoker, on the highroad to a brilliant career at court, and a fascinating man. Nothing better could be wished for.

Vronsky openly flirted with Kitty at the floats, hovered and flipped at her side, and came continually to the house; consequently there could be no doubt of the seriousness of his intentions. But, in spite of that, the mother had spent the whole of that winter in a state of terrible anxiety and agitation; her Class III, a matronly machine with a French inflection called La Shcherbatskaya, had spent many an evening fanning her mistress and offering calming jets of scented air from her Third Bay.

Now she was afraid that Vronsky might confine himself to simply flirting with Kitty. She saw that her daughter was in love with him, but tried to comfort herself with the thought that he was an honorable man, and would not do this. But at the same time she knew how easy it is, with the freedom of manners of today, to turn a girl's head, and how lightly men generally regard such a crime.

Today, with Levin's reappearance, a fresh source of anxiety arose. "I am afraid for my daughter," she said to La Shcherbatskaya, who stood beside her, folding laundry.

"Afraid? Oh dear, madame!"

"At one time I think she had a feeling for Levin."

"Oh yes, oh yes, a feeling. A certain feeling!"

"Perhaps from some extreme sense of honor she will refuse Vronsky!"

"Refuse him! No, no, madame. Oh dear oh dear oh dear!"

"Or that Levin's arrival might generally complicate and delay the affair so near being concluded."

At that moment the daughter entered the room to greet her mother, and the Class III politely put herself into Surcease.

"Has he been here long?" the princess asked about Levin, after Kitty related to her the dramatic events at the skate-maze, including the heroics exhibited by Konstantin Dmitrich and his Class III.

"He came today, Mamma."

"There's one thing I want to say . . . ," began the princess, and from her serious and alert face, Kitty guessed what it would be.

"Mamma," she said, flushing hotly and turning quickly to her. "Please, please don't say anything about that. I know, I know all about it."

She wished for what her mother wished for, but the motives of her mother's wishes wounded her.

"I only want to say that to raise hopes . . . "

"Mamma, darling, for goodness' sake, don't talk about it. It's so horrible to talk about it."

"I won't," said her mother, seeing the tears in her daughter's eyes, "but one thing, my love: You promised me you would have no secrets from me. You won't?"

"Never, Mamma, none," answered Kitty, flushing a little, and looking her mother straight in the face, "but there's no use in my telling you anything, and I . . . I . . . if I wanted to, I don't know what to say or how . . . I don't know. . . . "

No, she could not tell an untruth with those eyes, thought the mother, smiling at her agitation and happiness. The princess smiled that what was taking place just now in her soul seemed to the poor child so immense and so important.

CHAPTER 11

AFTER DINNER, AND TILL the beginning of the evening, Kitty was feeling a sensation akin to the sensation of a young man before a battle. Her heart throbbed violently, and her thoughts would not rest on anything.

She turned on the Galena Box, trying to calm her nerves. She felt that this evening, when they would both meet for the first time, would be a turning point in her life. And she was continually picturing them to herself, at one moment each separately, and then both together. She wished she had already received her Class III, so she could review her past experiences more efficiently, by cuing them in the monitor of her own beloved-companion; instead she was forced to remember in the way of children, with her mind. Still she dwelt with pleasure, with tenderness, on the memories of her relations with Levin. The memories of childhood and of Levin's friendship with her dead brother gave a special poetic charm to her relations with him. His love for her, of which she felt certain, was flattering and delightful to her; and it was pleasant for her to think of Levin. In her memories of Vronsky there always entered a certain element of awkwardness, though he was in the highest degree well-bred and at ease, as though there were some false note—not in Vronsky, he was very simple and nice, but in herself, while with Levin she felt perfectly simple and clear. But, on the other hand, when she thought of the future with Vronsky, there arose before her a perspective of brilliant happiness; with Levin the future seemed misty.

She turned up the Galena Box and carried it with her when she went upstairs to dress. Looking into the looking-glass, she noticed with joy that it was one of her good days, and that she was in complete possession of all her forces—she needed this so for what lay before her: she was conscious of external composure and free grace in her movements.

At half past seven she had only just gone down into the drawing room, when the II/Footman/C(c)43 announced, in its grandiloquent way, *"Konstantin Dmitrich Levin."* The princess was still in her room, and the prince had not come in. *So it is to be,* thought Kitty, and all the blood seemed to rush to her heart. She was horrified at her paleness, as she glanced into the looking-glass. At that moment she knew beyond doubt that he had come early on purpose to find her alone and to make her an offer. And only then for the first time the whole thing presented itself in a new, different aspect; only then she realized that the question did not affect her only—with whom she would be happy, and whom she loved—but that she would have that moment to wound a man whom she liked. And to wound him cruelly. She wished she could render herself invisible . . . though of course invisibility was impossible, and indeed experimentation into it was strictly forbidden.

Konstantin Dmitrich, dear fellow, loved her, was in love with her. But there was no help for it, so it must be, so it would have to be.

"My God! Shall I myself really have to say it to him? Can I tell him I don't love him? That will be a lie. What am I to say to him? That I love someone else? No, that's impossible. I'm going away, I'm going away."

She had reached the door when she heard his step. "What have I to be afraid of? I have done nothing wrong. What is to be, will be! I'll tell the truth. And with him one can't be ill at ease. Here he is," she said to herself, seeing his powerful, shy figure, and directly behind him that of his gangling Class III, both of them with their shining eyes fixed on her. She looked straight into his face, as though imploring him to spare her, and gave her hand.

"It's not time yet; I think we're too early," he said glancing round the empty drawing room. When he saw that his expectations were realized, that there was nothing to prevent him from speaking, his face became gloomy. Socrates continued to stare directly at her, as if his sensors bore into her very soul—as always, she found Levin's tall, strange-looking companion droid powerfully unsettling.

"Oh, no," said Kitty, and sat down at the table.

"But this was just what I wanted, to find you alone," he began, not sitting down, and not looking at her, so as not to lose courage.

"Mamma will be down directly. She was very much tired. . . . Yesterday . . . "

She talked on, not knowing what her lips were uttering, and not taking her supplicating and caressing eyes off him. She wished she had brought the Galena Box down from her bedroom, and could feel its machine-lent courage already draining away.

He glanced at her, and then more pointedly at Socrates, who dutifully sent himself into Surcease.

"I told you I did not know whether I should be here long," Levin began, "that it depended on you. . . . "

She dropped her head lower and lower, not knowing herself what answer she should make to what was coming.

"That it depended on you," he repeated. "I meant to say . . . I meant to say . . . I came for this . . . to be my wife!" he brought out, not knowing what he was saying. Levin felt that the most terrible thing was said; he stopped short and looked at her.

Kitty was breathing heavily, not looking at him. She was feeling ecstasy. Her soul was flooded with happiness. She had never anticipated that the utterance of love would produce such a powerful effect on her.

But it lasted only an instant. She remembered Vronsky. She lifted her clear, truthful eyes, and seeing his desperate face, she answered hastily:

"That cannot be . . . forgive me."

A moment ago, and how close she had been to him, of what importance in his life! And how aloof and remote from him she had become now!

"It was bound to be so," he said, not looking at her. He flicked Socrates back on, and man and machine bowed together, preparing to retreat.

CHAPTER 12

BUT AT THAT VERY MOMENT the princess came in. There was a look of horror on her face when she saw them alone, and their disturbed faces. Levin bowed to her, and said nothing. Kitty did not speak nor lift her eyes. *Thank God, she has refused him,* thought the mother, and her face lighted up with the habitual smile with which she greeted her guests on Thursdays. She sat down and began questioning Levin about his life operating the groznium mine. He sat down again, waiting for other visitors to arrive, so he might retreat unnoticed.

Five minutes later there came in a friend of Kitty's, married the preceding winter, Countess Nordston.

She was a thin, sallow, sickly, and nervous woman, with brilliant black eyes, and a short, green, cheap-looking Class III called Courtesana. Countess Nordston was fond of Kitty, and her affection for her showed itself, as the affection of married women for girls always does, in the desire to make a match for Kitty after her own ideal of married happiness; she wanted her to marry Vronsky. Levin she had often met at the Shcherbatskys' early in the winter, and she had always disliked him.

"Well, Kitty," she began. "Were you badly hurt in the attack upon the skate-maze?"

And she began talking to Kitty. Awkward as it was for Levin to withdraw now, it would still have been easier for him to perpetrate this awkwardness than to remain all the evening and see Kitty, who glanced at him now and then and avoided his eyes.

But as he was preparing to leave, he saw the officer who came in behind the countess.

"That must be Vronsky," murmured Levin to Socrates, who nodded glumly. To be sure of it, Levin glanced at Kitty. She had already had time to look at Vronsky, and looked round at Levin. And simply from the look in her eyes, which grew unconsciously brighter, Levin knew that she loved that man, knew it as surely as if she had told him so in words. But what sort of a man was he? Now, whether for good or for ill, Levin could not choose but remain; he must find out what the man was like whom she loved.

Levin studied Vronsky. There are people who, on meeting a successful rival, no matter in what, are at once disposed to turn their backs on everything good in him, and to see only what is bad. There are people, on the other hand, who desire above all to find in that lucky rival the qualities by which he has outstripped them, and seek with a throbbing ache at heart only what is good. Levin belonged to the second class. But he had no difficulty in finding what was good and attractive in Vronsky. It was apparent at the first glance. Vronsky was a squarely built, dark man, not very tall, with a good-humored, handsome, and exceedingly calm and resolute face. His belt line was marked by two large smoker holsters; the electric crackle of a hot-whip laced around his upper thigh, a coiled cord of restrained power, waiting only for the flick of the master's thumb to snap to life, whereupon it would pour upward into the air, crackling with deadly potential. Vronsky's Class III, like all those awarded to border officers, was a simulative animal, in this case, one built in the shape of a powerful, silver-trimmed black wolf. Everything about Count Vronsky's face and figure, from his short-cropped black hair and freshly shaven chin down to his loosely fitting, brand-new uniform, was simple and at the same time elegant. Making way for the lady who had come in, Vronsky went up to the princess and then to Kitty.

As he approached her, his beautiful eyes shone with a specially tender light, and with a faint, happy, and modestly triumphant smile (so it seemed to Levin), bowing carefully and respectfully over her, he held out his small broad hand to her.

Greeting and saying a few words to everyone, he sat down without once glancing at Levin, who had never taken his eyes off him.

"Let me introduce you," said the princess, indicating Levin. "Konstantin Dmitrich Levin, Count Alexei Kirillovich Vronsky."

Vronsky got up and, looking cordially at Levin, shook hands with him.

"I believe I was to have dined with you this winter," he said, smiling his simple and open smile, "but you had unexpectedly left for the country."

"Konstantin Dmitrich despises and hates the town and us townspeople," said Countess Nordston.

Levin hoped again to make a graceful exit from the Shcherbatskys' drawing room, and he rose and nodded meaningfully to Socrates, who gathered up his master's coat from the II/Footman/74 of the household. In the next moment, however, they were trapped by Countess Nordston's sudden announcement of a most tedious exercise.

The countess, much to Levin's annoyance, had long been a fervent believer in a race of extraterrestrial beings called the Honored Guests; members of this faith had created over several decades an elaborate xenotheology, which held at its core that the Honored Guests were for now merely a watchful benevolent presence, but one day they would arrive to bless the human race with their munificence.

"They will come for us," intoned Countess Nordston, invoking the central creed of the faith. "In three ways they will come for us." Tonight, the countess declared, due to the sudden and furious electrical storm raging outside, was an excellent evening to provoke a brief and healing contact with one of these benevolent light-beings, through an elaborate ceremony.

"Before we begin," Countess Nordston continued. "I must know if the psychic energy of our shared space is primed for the arrival of the Honored Guests." Courtesana then rotated her head unit three times, and beeped accusingly at Levin and Socrates. "Konstantin Dmitrich, do you believe in it?" Countess Nordston asked Levin.

"Why do you ask me? You know what I shall say."

"But I want to hear your opinion."

"My opinion," answered Levin, "is only that this alien-communing simply proves that educated society—so called—is no higher than the peasants. They believe in the evil eye, and in witchcraft and omens, while we stand in drawing rooms making circles with our hands raised, chanting obscurely, every time a lightning storm happens to raise the level of electricity in the air."

"Oh, then you don't believe in it?"

"I can't believe in it, Countess."

"But if I've seen them myself?"

"The peasant women, too, tell us they have seen goblins."

"Then you think I tell a lie?"

"Oh, no, Masha, Konstantin Dmitrich said he could not believe in it," said Kitty, blushing for Levin. Levin saw this, and, still more exasperated, would have answered, but Vronsky with his bright, frank smile rushed to the support of the conversation, which was threatening to become disagreeable.

"You do not admit the conceivability at all?" he queried. "But why not? We admit the existence of groznium, a wondrous alloy unimagined before the time of Tsar Ivan. Why should there not be some new beings, still unknown to us, which . . . "

"When *groznium* was discovered," Levin countered hotly, "it was found, after careful experimentation over many years, to hold all those useful qualities originally claimed of it by its champions. Far from being the stuff of parlor games and hopeful acolytes, it has revolutionized every sphere of Russian life!"

Vronsky listened attentively to Levin, as he always did listen, obviously interested in his words.

"Yes, but the xenotheologists such as the Countess only say we don't know at present what these beings *are*, only that such beings do exist," he argued mildly, "And these are the conditions in which they might appear to us."

As if to reinforce Vronsky's point, the sky just then began to rumble with thunder, and a bolt of lightning leapt forth from the clouds outside the Shcherbatskys' big front window.

"Let the scientific men find out what these aliens might be," Vronsky continued. "No, I don't see why there should not be a new race somewhere in the universe, if we found a new *metal* . . . "

"Why, because with groznium," Levin interrupted again, "all the promises of its potential have been *proven*! It has allowed for every positive change in our society! Every easeful thing, every moment of leisure we enjoy thanks to the helpful machines that do such work for us—all this we owe to groznium: the Grav, the transports, the robots—!" He gestured with energy at the ring of quiet and attentive Class IIIs, who stood in a respectful semicircle at the outskirts of the room.

But the conversation had ended, and the ceremony, so nonsensical to Levin, began. It took more than an hour of chanting and elaborate prayers before the ceremony was concluded—abruptly, and to Levin's secret pleasure—when Countess Nordston threw open the parlor window to urge the Honored Guests to be swift in blessing us with their presence, but all that entered the Shcherbatskys' magnificent front room was rain.

CHAPTER 13

VRONSKY SAT UP that night, viewing Memories in the monitor of his Class III, which was located in a smooth, furless patch of the animal's exterior, where the "soft underbelly" of a real *Canis lupus* would be found.

Alexei Kirillovich had never had a real home life. His mother had been in her youth a brilliant society woman, who had had during her married life, and still more afterward, many love affairs notorious in the whole fashionable world. His father he scarcely remembered, and he had been educated in the Regimental Underschool, where he was assigned and instructed in his special military issue Class III, soon growing to cherish the ersatz hunting wolf with its thick collar of bristling metal "fur" and menacing voice-box growl.

Leaving the school very young as a brilliant officer, after a distinguished six-month tour along the border, Vronsky had at once gotten into the circle of wealthy Petersburg army men. Although he did go more or less into Petersburg society, his love affairs had always hitherto been outside it. In Moscow he had for the first time felt, after his luxurious and coarse life at Petersburg, all the charm of intimacy with a sweet and innocent girl of his own rank, who cared for him. It never even entered his head that there could be any harm in his relations with Kitty. At the floats he danced principally with her. He was a constant visitor at their house. He talked to her as people commonly do talk in society—all sorts of nonsense, but nonsense to which he could not help attaching a special meaning in her case. Although he said nothing to her that he could not have said before everybody, he felt that she was becoming more and more dependent upon him, and the more he felt this, the better he liked it, and the more tender was his feeling for her. He did not know that his mode of behavior in relation to Kitty had a definite character, that of courting young girls with no intention of ever marrying, and that such courting is one of the evil actions common among brilliant young men such as he was. It seemed to him that he was the first who had discovered this pleasure, and he was enjoying his discovery.

If he could have put himself at the point of view of the family and have heard that Kitty would be unhappy if he did not marry her, he would have been greatly astonished, and would not have believed it. He could not believe that what gave such great and delicate pleasure to him, and above all to her, could be wrong. Still less could he have believed that he ought to marry.

Marriage had never presented itself to him as a possibility. He not only disliked family life, but the very idea of starting a family was, in accordance with the general views in the bachelor world in which he lived, as alien and ridiculous as the so-called Honored Guests so fervently awaited by Countess Nordstron and her set.

Lupo finished the Memory and, before cuing the next one, chased a I/Mouse/9 across the floor. The beasts had recently become decommed, and Vronsky had begged a box of them from his friend Stepan Arkadyich, in the Ministry, as a source of amusement and exercise for Lupo. The fierce animal machine, having caught the unfortunate little Class I in his jaws and efficiently cracked its groznium spine, rolled again onto his back to reveal his monitor and the next Memory.

Vronsky felt on coming away from the Shcherbatskys' that the secret spiritual bond which existed between him and Kitty had grown so much stronger that evening that some step must be taken. But what step could and ought to be taken, he could not imagine.

"What is so exquisite," he mused to Lupo, "is that not a word has been said by me or by her, but we understand each other so well in this unseen language of looks and tones, that this evening more clearly than ever she told me she loves me. And how secretly, simply, and most of all, how trustfully! I feel myself better, purer, like I have exited Earth's atmosphere, and am moon-bound. I feel that I have a heart, and that there is a great deal of good in me. Those sweet, loving eyes! When she said: 'Indeed I do ... '"

He trailed off, whereupon Lupo tilted his head and barked inquiringly.

"Well, what then? Oh, nothing. It's good for me, and good for her." And he began wondering where to finish the evening.

He passed in review the places he might go to. "The Blasting Club? A game of Flickerfly, champagne with Ignatov? No, I'm not going. Château des Fleurs; there I shall find Oblonsky, songs, the cancan. No, I'm sick of it. That's why I like the Shcherbatskys', because I'm growing . .. *better*." Instead of going out, he ordered supper, and then undressed, and as soon as his head touched the pillow and he felt the reassuring weight of Lupo's warm, gently thrumming metal snout curled against his chest, he fell into a sound sleep.

CHAPTER 14

NEXT DAY AT ELEVEN o'clock in the morning Vronsky drove to the station of the Petersburg-Moscow Grav to meet his mother, and the first person he came across on the great flight of steps was Oblonsky, who was expecting his sister by the same train.

"Ah! Your Excellency!" cried Oblonsky. "Whom are you meeting?"

"My mother," Vronsky responded, smiling, as everyone did who met Oblonsky and his funny little Class III. "She is to be here from Petersburg today." Vronsky shook hands with Stiva, patted Small Stiva amiably on his hemispheric head-dome, and together they all ascended,

Lupo prowling along at the rear, nose down, examining the steps with his keen scent sensors as they went.

"I was looking out for you till two o'clock last night. Where did you go after the Shcherbatskys'?"

"Home," answered Vronsky. "I must own I felt so content yesterday after the Shcherbatskys' that I didn't care to go anywhere."

> *"I know a gallant steed by tokens sure,*
> *And by his eyes I know a youth in love,"*

declaimed Stepan Arkadyich, just as he had done before to Levin.

Vronsky smiled with a look that seemed to say that he did not deny it, but he promptly changed the subject.

"Look there: Our tireless protectors are out in force today. I hope there are not koschei along the lines. Mother so hates to be discomfited."

Even as he spoke, the distinct heavy thud of the 77s in their metal boots echoed through the station. Dozens of the elite bots, bulbed heads performing their endless all-seeing rotations, roamed through all corners of the vast terminus, magnifying sensors clipped to their end-effectors, searching for the monstrous little bugs known and feared as koschei

"And whom are you meeting?" Vronsky asked of Oblonsky.

"I? I've come to meet a pretty woman," said Oblonsky, and maintained a sly, elusive expression, even as he raised his arms in the air to allow a 77 swiftly to scan his entire body. Even members of the nobility, when traveling by rail, had to submit to this relative indignity, and Oblonsky took it, like most all inconveniences, with ease and good humor.

"A pretty woman?" Vronsky replied meanwhile. "You don't say so!"

"*Honi soit qui mal y pense!* My sister Anna."

"Ah! That's Madame Karenina," said Vronsky. The 77 leveled his physiometer at Count Vronsky, who, with an officious scowl, whistled to the accompanying Caretaker and directed the man's attention to a small pin he wore on his lapel, identifying him as an officer of the Border Regiments.

"If you need assistance, I am here," he with quiet arrogance to the gold-uniformed soldier, who, mollified, gestured curtly to the 77 and departed.

"You know my sister Anna, no doubt?" Stepan Arkadyich was saying as together they approached the platform.

"I think I do. Or perhaps not . . . I really am not sure," Vronsky answered heedlessly, with a vague recollection of something stiff and tedious evoked by the name Karenina.

"But Alexei Alexandrovich, my celebrated brother-in-law, you surely must know. All the world knows him. He is in the Higher Branches."

"Ah, yes," said Vronsky. "And . . . he is, enhanced, yes?"

Oblonsky nodded with mock gravity. "Oh, that he most certainly is."

"I know him by reputation and by sight," Vronsky continued. "I know that he's clever, learned, religious somewhat. . . . But you know that's not . . . *not in my line*," said Vronsky in English.

"Yes, he's a very remarkable man; rather a conservative, but a splendid man," observed Stepan Arkadyich, "a splendid man."

A chorus of shrill beeps erupted from the center of the station, as a dozen of the bioscanners rang out as one. The 77s and their Caretaker converged around a fat peasant with a battered rucksack, who stood wide-eyed and trembling as one of the massive machine-men snaked a winding, pincer-tipped cord from a slot on his lower-mid-torso and plucked a tiny koschei from the pocket of his vest.

"They've got one," said Vronsky with evident enjoyment. He and Oblonsky watched as the 77 held the wriggling, roach-like koschei aloft. The fat peasant recoiled in horror from the twitching little bug-machine, its armor-plated back lined with quivering antennae, that had been playing stowaway in his shirtfront, while the fearsome 77 held the tiny thing carefully by the tip of its tail, carried it to a rubbish bin, and flicked it inside. While Vronsky and Oblonsky watched approvingly, a second 77 tossed a miniature I-bomb in after it, and slammed down the lid.

With one motion, everyone in the station covered their ears, and Small Stiva and Lupo dampened their auditory sensors. A moment later came the deafening explosion, followed by silence, as the station filled with heavy, acrid smoke. A child burst into tears and was comforted by the heavy mechanical arms of a II/Governess/646.

"Good show." Oblonsky clapped, waving appreciatively at the 77s. "That will teach UnConSciya to trifle with the power of the Ministry. Nothing sneaks past us."

Vronsky shook his head and sighed. "Yes, yes. Though the Grav will be delayed, and Mother will be agitated."

"Of course," Stepan Arkadyich agreed. "This is the price we pay for happiness," he added, parroting one of the popular slogans which together comprised his political opinions.

"By the way, did you make the acquaintance of my friend Levin?" asked Stepan Arkadyich of Count Vronsky, as the station's normal hum of activity resumed and they waited at the platform's edge for the Grav to arrive.

"Yes; but he left rather early."

"He's a capital fellow," pursued Oblonsky. "Isn't he?"

"I don't know why it is," responded Vronsky, "in all Moscow people—present company of course excepted," he put in jestingly, "there's something uncompromising. They are all on the defensive, lose their tempers, as though they all want to make one feel something. . . . "

"Yes, that's true, it is so," said Stepan Arkadyich, laughing good-humoredly.

"*Are* the tracks cleared? Will the Grav soon be in?" Vronsky asked a II/StationAgent/L26, when the last of the 77s had marched away.

"*Grav has signaled,*" answered the Class II, a green light glowing affirmatively in the dead center of his faceplate.

The approach of the magnificent Moscow–St. Petersburg High-Speed Antigravitational Massive Transport, was more and more evident by the preparatory bustle in the station, the rush of II/Porter/7e62s, the movement of II/Policeman/R47s, and people meeting the train. Through the frosty vapor could be seen II/GravWorker/X99s in their impregnable groznium outer-sheaths and soft, felt-lined roller wheels crossing the magnetized rails of the curving line.

"No," said Stepan Arkadyich, who felt a great inclination to tell Vronsky of Levin's intentions in regard to Kitty. "No, you've not got a true impression of Levin. He's a very nervous man, and is sometimes out of humor, it's true, and his Class III is an odd duck indeed, but then he is often very nice. He has such a true, honest nature, and a heart of gold. But yesterday there were special reasons," pursued Stepan Arkadyich, with a meaningful smile, totally oblivious of the genuine sympathy he had felt the day before for his friend, and feeling the same sympathy now, only for Vronsky. "Yes, there were reasons why he could not help being either particularly happy or particularly unhappy."

Vronsky stood still and asked directly: "How so? Do you mean he made your *belle-soeur* an offer yesterday?"

This moment of exchanged confidences was interrupted by Lupo, who sat back on his haunches, flattened his ears against his head, and howled. Vronsky looked down at his beloved-companion inquiringly, but in the next moment the rest heard what Lupo had sensed: The gentle pulse of the Grav *shooshing* forward could be both heard and felt reverberating along the magnet bed.

"Maybe," said Stepan Arkadyich. "I fancied something of the sort yesterday. Yes, if he went away early, and was out of humor too, it must mean it . . . He's been so long in love, and I'm very sorry for him."

"So that's it! I should imagine, though, she might reckon on a better match," said Vronsky, "though I don't know him, of course," he added. "Yes, that is a hateful position! That's why most fellows prefer to have to do with II/Klara/X14s. If you don't succeed with them it only proves that you've not enough cash, but in this case one's dignity's at stake. But here's the Grav."

Now the platform was quivering, and with visible lines of electric force quivering above the magnet bed, the great hovering massive transport eased magnificently forward into the station, the stern figure of the II/Engineer/L42 covered with frost. Behind the tender, setting the platform more and more slowly swaying, came the luggage van with a dog whining in it. At last the passenger carriages whooshed in, de-oscillating for a full three minutes after the circuits were switched off and the Grav came to a standstill.

A II/GravGuard/FF9 appeared, emitted a high whistle from a slanting slot in his groznium torso, and after him one by one the impatient passengers began to get down: an officer of the Border Regiments, holding himself erect in his silver uniform, and looking severely about him; a nimble little merchant with a Class II suitcase tucked under his arm, smiling gaily; a whistling peasant with a sack over his shoulder.

Vronsky, standing beside Oblonsky, watched the carriages and the passengers, totally oblivious of his mother. What he had just heard about Kitty excited and delighted him. Unconsciously he swelled his chest, and his eyes flashed. He stooped to run his hand through Lupo's bristling metallic fur. He drew himself erect and stood with his hand on the handle of the hot-whip that curled along his thigh. He felt himself a conqueror.

"Countess Vronskaya is in that compartment," said the Border Officer, going up to Vronsky.

The officer's words roused him, and forced him to think of his mother and his approaching meeting with her.

CHAPTER 15

VRONSKY FOLLOWED HIS FELLOW officer to the carriage, and at the door of the compartment he stopped short to make room for a lady getting out, followed by a tall, elegant Class III.

As the woman and her beloved-companion stepped from the carriage, Lupo, uncharacteristically, narrowed his eyes to slits and growled in the back of his throat. Alexei Kirillovich, horrified at the implied insult, gestured sharply to his Class III for silence and then stood back from the door of the compartment to allow the woman and her android to pass. But for a long moment they simply stood in this tableau at the door of the carriage: Vronsky with his head bowed, Lupo back on his haunches, the stranger and her striking robot standing regally in the doorway.

With the insight of a man of the world, it was clear to Vronsky that this woman belonged to the best society. When at last the tableau broke, and she and her Class III exited, and Vronsky was finally getting into the carriage, he felt he must glance at her once more; not because she was very beautiful, not on account of the elegance and modest grace which were apparent in her whole figure, but because in the expression of her charming face, as she passed close by him, there was something peculiarly caressing and soft. As he looked round, she too turned her head. Her shining gray eyes, which looked dark from the thick lashes, rested with friendly attention on his face, as though she were recognizing him, and then promptly turned away to the passing crowd, as though seeking someone. In that brief look Vronsky had time to notice the suppressed eagerness that played over her face, and flitted between the brilliant eyes and the faint smile that curved her red lips. It was as though her nature

SHE SHROUDED THE LIGHT IN HER EYES, BUT IT SHONE AGAINST HER
WILL; THE ANDROID, WALKING BEHIND, GLOWED A REGAL INDIGO

were so brimming over with something that, against her will, it showed itself now in the flash of her eyes, and now in her smile. Deliberately she shrouded the light in her eyes, but it shone against her will in the faintly perceptible smile. The android, walking a half step behind the woman, glowed a deep and regal indigo, allowing no expression, only accenting all that was remarkable about her mistress as she traveled at her side.

Vronsky stepped into the carriage. His mother, a dried-up old lady with black eyes and ringlets, screwed up her eyes, scanning her son, and smiled slightly with her thin lips. Getting up from the seat and handing her robot a bag, she gave her little wrinkled hand to her son to kiss, and lifting his head from her hand, kissed him on the cheek.

"You got my communiqué? Quite well? Thank God."

"You had a good journey?" said her son, sitting down beside her, and involuntarily listening to a woman's voice outside the door. He knew it was the voice of the lady he had met at the door.

In the next moment, the mysterious woman and her robot appeared again in the door of the Grav. "Could you see if Stepan Arkadyich Oblonsky is here, and send him to me?" she said politely to a II/Porter/7e62, who scuttled off obligingly. Vronsky understood now that this was Madame Karenina, and this her Class III, Android Karenina.

"Your brother is here," he said, standing up. "Excuse me, I did not know you, and, indeed, our acquaintance was so slight," said Vronsky, bowing, "that no doubt you do not remember me."

"Oh, no," she said, "I should have known you because your mother and I have been talking, I think, of nothing but you all the way." As she spoke she let the eagerness that would insist on coming out show itself in her smile. "And still no sign of my brother."

"Do call him, Alexei," said the old countess. Vronsky stepped out onto the platform, and shouted, "Oblonsky! Here!" Lupo let out a corresponding howl, long and low.

Madame Karenina, meanwhile, did not wait for her brother, but catching sight of him she stepped out with her light, resolute step. And as soon as her brother had reached her, with a gesture that struck Vronsky by its decision and its grace, she flung her left arm around his neck, drew him rapidly to her, and kissed him warmly. Vronsky gazed, never taking his eyes from her, and smiled; he could not have said why. But recollecting that his mother was waiting for him, he went back again into the carriage.

"She's very sweet, isn't she?" said the countess of Madame Karenina. "Her husband put her with me, and I was delighted to have her." Madame Karenina entered the carriage again to say good-bye to the countess.

"Well, Countess, you have met your son, and I my brother," she said. "And all my gossip is exhausted. I should have nothing more to tell you."

"Oh, no," said the countess, taking her hand. "I could go all around the world with you and never be dull. You are one of those delightful women in whose company it's sweet to be silent as well as to talk. Now please don't fret over your son; you can't expect never to be parted."

Madame Karenina stood quite still, holding herself very erect, and her eyes were smiling. Vronsky noted with interest how his mother's beloved-companion, a wiry gray machine-woman called Tunisia, looked distractedly about the carriage during this exchange, while Android Karenina's careful and attentive posture mimicked that of her mistress precisely.

"Anna Arkadyevna," the countess was saying to him in explanation, "has a little boy eight years old, I believe, and she has never been parted from him before, and she keeps fretting over leaving him."

"Yes, the Countess and I have been talking all the time, I of my son and she of hers," said Madame Karenina, and again a smile lighted up her face, a caressing smile intended for him.

"I am afraid that you must have been dreadfully bored," he said, promptly catching the ball of coquetry she had flung him. He thrust one leg forward in an offhandedly dashing pose, displaying the hot-whip that flickered in its transparent sheath along the outer curve of his leg. But apparently she did not care to pursue the conversation in that strain, and she turned to the old countess.

"Thank you so much. The time has passed so quickly. Good-bye, Countess."

"Good-bye, my love," answered the countess. "Let me kiss your pretty face. I speak plainly, at my age, and I tell you simply that I've lost my heart to you."

Clichéd as the phrase was, Madame Karenina obviously believed it and was delighted by it. She flushed, bent down slightly, and put her cheek to the countess's lips, drew herself up again, and with the same smile fluttering between her lips and her eyes, she gave her hand to Vronsky. He pressed the little hand she gave him, and was delighted, as though at something special, by the energetic squeeze with which she freely and vigorously shook his hand.

Just as she did, a great *BOOM* echoed through the Grav station. All present silenced their conversation and paused in their activity—even the industrious II/Porter/7e62s stopped short on their stubby legs and wheeled in small circles, aural sensors pulsing. This *BOOM*, despite its tremendous power, came from no evident source; it was as if a crack had opened in the sky, through which had come the sound of God pounding his fist upon a table. And though others would later deny it, even scoff at the notion, many present later swore that the sky, at the moment of the blast, flickered an uncanny shade of blackish purple.

Vronsky hastened to calm his mother, patting her hand and saying soothingly, "Koschei, Madame. The 77s captured one and detonated it in the station. Likely this was another." Vronsky was aware, of course, that this was a well-meaning but preposterous falsehood: the *BOOM* had sounded nothing like that of the koschei being junkered in the rubbish bin—indeed it sounded like no explosion he had heard in his life, and he had heard many.

Anna Karenina, meanwhile, stared uneasily up at the sky, feeling the reverberations of the *BOOM* to the pit of her stomach. Only when Android Karenina placed a gentle, reassuring hand at the small of her back could Anna shake off the unpleasant sensation. She then exited with the rapid step which bore her rather fully developed figure with such strange lightness.

"Very charming," said the countess.

That was just what her son was thinking. Vronsky's eyes followed her till her graceful figure was out of sight, and then the smile remained on his face. Vronsky saw out of the window how this remarkable woman went up to her brother, put her arm in his, and began telling him something eagerly, obviously something that had nothing to do with him, Vronsky, and at that he felt annoyed.

"Well, Mamma, are you perfectly well?" he said, and gave his mother his arm. But just as they were getting out of the carriage, a small fleet of Class II/StationMaster/44s buzzed officiously past, their alarm lights flashing an urgent red. Obviously something unusual had happened. The crowd who had left the Grav were running back again.

A cold feeling crept over Vronsky, as he caught a whiff of some terrible burning rising off the tracks.

"What? . . . What? . . . Where? . . . Burned? . . . Crushed! . . . " was heard among the crowd. Stepan Arkadyich, with his sister on his arm, turned back. They too looked scared, and stopped at the carriage door to avoid the crowd. Vronsky interposed himself between Madame Karenina and the platform edge, instinctively desiring to block from her vision whatever gruesome scene lay on the magnet bed below.

It was a battered corpse, evidently first fallen on the magnet bed then crushed by the rushing force of the oncoming Grav. The rumor making its way rapidly through the agitated crowd said the dead man had been a stowaway, riding the Grav without a ticket, when he was discovered by a troop of 77s. The heavy-booted machine-men had brought the anonymous rider to their Caretaker, who had demanded his name and occupation. The stowaway had refused to answer and the gold-uni-formed Caretaker had dutifully declared him a Janus, a hateful enemy of Mother Russia, and ordered him thrown in front of an arriving Grav.

But Vronsky, who knew that such stories were often mere concoc-tions to shield the public from some unpalatable truth, retained an agi-tated feeling about this accident. He averted his eyes from the wrapped, smoldering corpse as the 77s with their strong pipe-like arms tossed it unceremoniously into the back of a carriage.

Before Vronsky and Oblonsky came back, the ladies had heard the tale from other onlookers. Oblonsky was evidently upset. He frowned and seemed ready to cry.

"Ah, how awful! Ah, Anna, if you had seen it! Ah, how awful!" he said.

Madame Karenina walked with her brother, Small Stiva and Android Karenina walking a few paces behind. Anna was lost in thought: twice in the last half hour, a disturbing feeling had passed through her, a penumbra of creeping dread radiating from some unknown origin. This feeling had first occurred when the station rattled with that reverberat-ing *BOOM* and again when she glanced at the platform edge—and seen, despite Count Vronsky's efforts to block her view, the hooded corpse lifted without ceremony from the magnet bed.

Madame Karenina seated herself in his carriage, and Stepan Arkadyich saw with surprise that her lips were quivering, and she was with difficulty restraining her tears.

"What is it, Anna?" he asked, when they had driven a few hun-dred yards.

"This death, it touches me somehow," she said. "I cannot understand it."

"What nonsense!" said Stepan Arkadyich, his genial nature reas-serting itself against the mess and unpleasantness of death. "Our 77s have discovered a traitor, and acted swiftly and appropriately! Bravo, and praise God for our tireless protectors! You've come, that's the chief thing. You can't conceive how I'm resting my hopes on you."

"Have you known Vronsky long?" she asked, trying to match her brother's easy calm. She glanced at Android Karenina, who bathed her in reassuring silence and a gentle lavender glow. Unusual for a Class III robot, Android Karenina never spoke, only buttressed by her constant reassuring presence Anna's natural feeling of dignity and reserve.

"Yes," Stiva answered cheerily. "You know we're hoping he will marry Kitty."

"Yes?" said Anna softly. "Come now, let us talk of you," she added, tossing her head as though she would physically shake off something superfluous oppressing her. "Let us talk of your affairs. I got your letter, and here I am."

"Yes, all my hopes are in you," said Stepan Arkadyich.

"Well, tell me all about it."

CHAPTER 16

THOUGH SHE HAD SENT word the day before to her husband that it was nothing to her whether his sister came or not, Darya Alexandrovna Oblonskaya had made everything ready for her arrival, and was expecting her sister-in-law with emotion.

Dolly was crushed by her sorrow, utterly swallowed up by it. Still she did not forget that Anna, her sister-in-law, was the wife of an official in the Higher Branches of the Ministry, and was a Petersburg *grande dame*. And, thanks to this circumstance, she did not carry out her threat to her husband—that is to say, she remembered that her sister-in-law was coming, along with her elegant and imposing Class III. "And, after all, Anna is in no way to blame," Dolly said to Dolichka, who nodded vigorously and agreed.

"Oh no, not at all to blame! The dear."

"I know nothing of her except the very best, and I have seen nothing but kindness and affection from her toward myself."

"Only kindness, true kindness indeed."

And it was true that as far as she could recall her impressions of Petersburg at the Karenins', she did not like their household itself; Karenin was a strange and distant man, as were most men she had ever known from the Higher Branches, and there was something artificial in the whole framework of their family life. "But why should I not receive her? If only she doesn't take it into her head to console me!" said Dolly to Dolichka, who clucked *"Oh dear"* and *"I should think not,"* while the two of them together folded laundry.

"All consolation and counsel and Christian forgiveness, all that I have thought over a thousand times, and it's all no use."

"No use, no use at all!"

Dolly did not want to talk of her sorrow, but with that sorrow in her heart she could not talk of outside matters. She knew that in one way or another she would tell Anna everything, and she was alternately glad at the thought of speaking freely, and angry at the necessity of speaking of her humiliation with her, his sister, and of hearing her ready-made phrases of good advice and comfort. She had been on the lookout for her, glancing at her watch every minute, and, as so often happens, let slip just that minute when her visitor arrived, so that she did not hear the three happy tinkles of the I/Doorchime/6.

She got up and embraced her sister-in-law.

"What, here already!" she said as she kissed her. Dolichka gave a low bow to Android Karenina, who offered a reserved nod in return.

"Dolly, how glad I am to see you!" Anna began.

"I am glad, too," said Dolly, faintly smiling, and trying by the expression of Anna's face to find out whether she knew. *Most likely she knows,* she thought, noticing the sympathy in Anna's face. "Well, come along, I'll take you to your room," she went on, trying to defer as long as possible the moment of confidences.

Anna greeted the children, and handed her kerchief and her hat to Android Karenina. She tossed her head and shook out her mass of black curls.

"You are radiant with health and happiness!" said Dolly, almost with envy.

"I? . . . Yes," said Anna. They sat down to coffee in the drawing room, and Anna meaningfully sent Android Karenina into Surcease.

"Dolly," Anna said, pushing the coffee tray away, "he has told me."

Dolly flicked off her own Class III, but she looked coldly at Anna. She was waiting now for phrases of conventional sympathy, but Anna said nothing of the sort.

"Dolly, dear," she said, "I don't want to speak for him to you, nor to try to comfort you; that's impossible. But, darling, I'm simply sorry, sorry from my heart for you!"

Under the thick lashes of her shining eyes tears suddenly glittered. She moved nearer to her sister-in-law and took her hand in her own vigorous little hand. Dolly did not shrink away, but her face did not lose its blank expression. She said:

"To comfort me is impossible. Everything's lost after what has happened, everything's over!"

And as soon as she had said this, her face suddenly softened. Anna lifted the wasted, thin hand of Dolly, kissed it, and said:

"But, Dolly, what's to be done, what's to be done? How is it best to act in this awful position—that's what you must think of."

"All's over, and there's nothing more," said Dolly. "And the worst of all is, you see, that I can't cast him off: there are the children, I am tied. And I can't live with him! It's a torture to me to see him."

"Dolly, darling, he has spoken to me, but I want to hear it from you: tell me about it."

Dolly looked at her inquiringly.

Sympathy and love unfeigned were visible on Anna's face.

"Very well," she said all at once. "But I will tell you it from the beginning. You know how I was married. With the education Mamma gave us, I knew nothing. I know they say men tell their wives of their former lives, but Stiva"—she corrected herself—"Stepan Arkadyich told me nothing. You'll hardly believe it, but till now I imagined that I was the only woman he had known. So I lived, for eight years.

"You must understand that I was so far from suspecting infidelity, I regarded it as impossible, and then—try to imagine it—with such ideas, for all to be revealed, played back in a communiqué, suddenly all the horror, all the loathsomeness. . . . You must try and understand me. To be fully convinced of one's happiness, and all at once . . . " continued Dolly, holding back her sobs, "a mistress, my *mécanicienne*, with grease on her jumpsuit, and metal shavings beneath her nails! No, it's too awful!" She hastily pulled out her handkerchief and hid her face in it. "I can understand being carried away by feeling," she went on after a brief silence, "but deliberately, slyly deceiving me . . . and with whom? . . . To go on being my husband together with her . . . it's awful! You can't understand. . . . "

"Oh, yes, I understand! I understand! Dolly, dearest, I do understand," said Anna, pressing her hand.

"And do you imagine he realizes all the awfulness of my position?" Dolly resumed. "Not the slightest! He's happy and contented."

"Oh, no!" Anna interposed quickly. "He's to be pitied, he's weighed down by remorse. . . . "

"Is he capable of remorse?" Dolly interrupted, gazing intently into her sister-in-law's face.

"Yes. I know him. I could not look at him without feeling sorry for him. We both know him. He's good-hearted, but he's proud, and now he's so humiliated. What touched me most . . . " (and here Anna guessed what would touch Dolly most) "he's tortured by two things: that he's ashamed for the children's sake, and that, loving you—yes, yes, loving you beyond everything on earth," she hurriedly interrupted Dolly, who would have answered—"he has hurt you, pierced you to the heart. 'No, no, she cannot forgive me,' he keeps saying."

Dolly looked dreamily away beyond her sister-in-law as she listened to her words, and then responded angrily.

"She's young, you see, she's pretty, she's technically proficient. Do you know, Anna, my youth and my beauty are gone, taken by whom? By him and his children."

Again her eyes glowed with hatred.

"And after that he will tell me . . . . What! Can I believe him? Never! No, everything is over, everything that once made my comfort, the reward of my work, and my sufferings . . . . What's so awful is that all at once my heart's turned, and instead of love and tenderness, I have nothing but hatred for him; yes, hatred. I could kill him."

Dolly grew calmer, and for two minutes both were silent.

"What's to be done? Think for me, Anna, help me. I have thought over everything, and I see nothing."

Anna could think of nothing, but her heart responded instantly to each word, to each change of expression of her sister-in-law.

"One thing I would say," began Anna. "I am his sister, I know his character, that faculty of forgetting everything, everything." She waved her hand before her forehead, as if a person's circuits could be unspooled in the same way as those of a Class III. "That faculty for being completely carried away, but for completely repenting too. He cannot believe it, he cannot comprehend now how he can have acted as he did."

"No, he understands, he understood!" Dolly broke in. "But I . . . you are forgetting me . . . does it make it easier for me?"

Anna cut her short, kissing her hand once more.

"I know more of the world than you do," she said. "I know how men like Stiva look at it. They project a sort of electric barrier that can't be crossed between them and their families. I don't understand it, but it is so."

"Yes, but he has kissed her . . . "

"Dolly, hush, darling. I saw Stiva when he was in love with you. I remember the time when he came to me and cried, talking of you, and all the wild oscillations of his heart for you, and I know that the longer he has lived with you the loftier you have been in his eyes. You know we have sometimes laughed at him for putting in at every word: 'Dolly's a marvelous woman.' You have always been a divinity for him, and you are that still, and this has not been an infidelity of the heart. . . . "

"But if it is repeated?"

"It cannot be, as I understand it. . . . "

"Yes, but could you forgive it?"

"I don't know, I can't judge. . . . Yes, I can," said Anna, thinking a moment; and grasping the position in her thought and weighing it in her inner balance, she added: "Yes, I can, I can, I can. Yes, I could forgive it. I could not be the same, no; but I could forgive it, and forgive it as though it had never been, never been at all . . . "

"Oh, of course," Dolly interposed quickly, as though saying what she had more than once thought, "else it would not be forgiveness. If one forgives, it must be completely, completely. Come, let us go; I'll take you to your room," she said, getting up to flick Dolichka back to life, while Anna did the same with Android Karenina. As the Class IIIs reanimated, their respective mistresses embraced.

"My dear, how glad I am you came," Dolly said, and then offered a polite bow to Android Karenina, who tilted her head with kindness in place of a smile. "That *both* of you came. It has made things better, ever so much better."

CHAPTER 17

THE WHOLE OF THAT DAY ANNA and Android Karenina spent at the Oblonskys', and received no one, though some of Anna's acquaintances had already heard of their arrival, and came to call. Anna spent the whole morning with Dolly and the children. She merely sent a brief note to her brother to tell him that he must not fail to dine at home. "Come, God is merciful," she wrote.

Oblonsky did dine at home: the conversation was general, and his wife, speaking to him, addressed him as "Stiva," as she had not done before. In the relations of the husband and wife the same estrangement still remained, but there was no talk now of separation, and Stepan Arkadyich saw the possibility of explanation and reconciliation. Small Stiva, while attending as usual to his master, once dared to flash the red eye-shapes of his frontal display flirtatiously at Dolichka, who turned away but did not swat him.

Immediately after dinner Kitty came in. She knew Anna Arkadyevna, but only very slightly, and she came now to her sister's with some trepidation at the prospect of meeting this fashionable Petersburg lady, whom everyone spoke so highly of. But she made a favorable impression on Anna Arkadyevna—she saw that at once. Anna was unmistakably admiring her loveliness and her youth, and before Kitty knew where she was she found herself not merely under Anna's sway, but in love with her, as young girls do fall in love with older and married women. Anna was not like a fashionable lady, nor like the mother of a boy of eight years old. In the elasticity of her movements, the freshness and the unflagging eagerness which persisted in her face and broke out in her smile and her glance, she would rather have passed for a girl of twenty, had it not been for a serious and at times mournful look in her eyes, which struck and attracted Kitty. Her Class III, Android Karenina, too, seemed even in her perfect silence to be marked by a soulful depth of emotions—inaccessible, complex, and poetic—unlike any companion robot Kitty had ever seen.

After dinner, when Dolly went away to her own room, Anna rose quickly and went up to her brother, who was just lighting a cigar, having flicked open Small Stiva's torso to use his groznium core for a light.

"Stiva," she said to him, winking gaily, crossing him and glancing toward the door, "go, and God help you."

He chucked the cigar into Small Stiva's core, where it was consumed, winked back at his sister, and departed through the doorway.

"And when is your next float?" Anna asked Kitty.

"Next week, and a splendid float it shall be! Finally I am considered a woman, old enough to receive my very own Class III at last."

"My congratulations," murmured Anna Karenina, trying to remember the days of her own life, so many years ago, before her android had been brought to her—it seemed she could hardly recall a time when she hadn't had the comforting presence of her beloved-companion at her heel.

"Yes," Kitty added brightly. "I feel it will be one of those floats where one always enjoys oneself."

"For me there are no floats now where one enjoys oneself," said Anna, and Kitty detected in her eyes that mysterious world which was not open to her. "For me there are some less dull and tiresome."

"How can *you* be dull at a float?"

"Why should *I* not be dull at a float?" inquired Anna.

"Because you always look nicer than anyone."

Anna had the faculty of blushing. She blushed a little, and said: "In the first place it's never so; and secondly, if it were, what difference would it make to me?"

"Are you coming to this float?" Kitty asked. "I shall be so glad if you go. I should so like to see you dancing."

"Anyway, if I do go, I shall comfort myself with the thought that it's a pleasure to you."

"I imagine your android at the ball glowing with a lilac hue," Kitty said, daring a quick glance at Android Karenina, who had her faceplate turned toward the window, gazing it seemed at the Eye in the Tower, in its slow, eternal revolution.

"And why lilac precisely?" asked Anna, smiling. Class IIIs were often programmed, at public events, to glow from "bow to stern" in fanciful colors, to lend an extra *je ne sais quoi* to their mistresses' appearance. "I know why you press me to come to the float. You expect perhaps to leave this float with your companion robot and a *human* companion as well! And you want everyone to be there to take part in it."

"How do you know? Yes."

"Oh! What a happy time you are at," pursued Anna. "I remember, that feeling as if gravity has been oh-so-slightly suspended, not just at the float, but everywhere you go! That mist which covers everything in that blissful time when childhood is just ending, and out of that vast circle, happy and gay, there is a path growing narrower and narrower, and it is delightful and alarming to enter the ballroom, bright and splendid as it is. . . . Who has not been through it?"

Kitty smiled without speaking. *But how did she go through it? How I should like to know all her love story!* thought Kitty, recalling the foreboding, unromantic appearance of Alexei Alexandrovich, her husband.

"I know something. Stiva told me, and I congratulate you. I liked him so much," Anna continued. "I met Vronsky at the Grav station."

"Oh, was he there?" asked Kitty, blushing. "What was it Stiva told you?"

"Stiva gossiped about it all. I traveled yesterday with Vronsky's mother," she went on, "and his mother talked without a pause of him; he's her favorite. I know mothers are partial, but . . . "

"What did his mother tell you?"

"Oh, a great deal! And I know that he's her favorite; still one can see how chivalrous he is. . . . Well, for instance, she told me that he has served in the Border Wars, and is now with a regiment hunting UnConSciya operatives. He has destroyed many koschei, saving many lives. He's a hero, in fact," said Anna.

But she did not tell Kitty about her encounter with Vronsky at the Grav station, nor how Vronsky had gallantly interposed himself before her line of sight, to protect her from seeing the person dead upon the magnet bed. She was about to, when she glanced at Android Karenina, who bent her head forward by several degrees toward her lap, and for some reason made Anna feel it was disagreeable to her to think of it. She felt that there was something that had to do with her in it, and something that ought not to have been.

CHAPTER 18

STIVA AND DOLLY soon emerged, their Class IIIs scuttling noisily behind them like happy children, and both Kitty and Anna could tell that a reconciliation had taken place. The whole evening Dolly was, as always, a little mocking in her tone to her husband, while Stepan Arkadyich was happy and cheerful, but not so as to seem as though, having been forgiven, he had forgotten his offense.

At half past nine o'clock a particularly joyful and pleasant family conversation over the tea table at the Oblonskys' was broken up by an apparently simple incident. But this simple incident for some reason struck everyone as strange. Anna had gone upstairs with her light, resolute step to retrieve a favorite polishing cloth from her valise, so that she might give Android Karenina's monitor a sheen before displaying Memories of her Sergey. The stairs up to her room came out on the landing of the great warm main staircase.

Just as she was leaving the drawing room, the I/Doorchime/6's tinkling greeting was heard in the hall.

"Who can that be?" said Dolly.

"It's early for me to be fetched, and for anyone else it's late," observed Kitty.

"Sure to be someone from the Ministry for me," put in Stepan Arkadyich. When Anna was passing the top of the staircase, a Class II was buzzing up to announce the visitor, while the visitor himself was standing under a lamp. Anna glancing down at once recognized Vronsky, for the crackle of the hot-whip and the twin bulges of the smokers were unmistakable. A strange feeling of pleasure and at the same time dread of something stirred in her heart; as she looked at Count Vronsky, she remembered with a kind of violence in her head the tremendous *BOOM* that had rent the sky at the Grav station, when last they had met.

Vronsky was standing still, not taking off his gleaming silver outer-coat, pulling something out of his pocket. At the instant when she was just facing the stairs, he raised his eyes, caught sight of her, and in the expression of his face there passed a shade of embarrassment and dismay. With a slight inclination of her head she passed, hearing behind her Stepan Arkadyich's loud voice calling him to come up, and the quiet, soft, and composed voice of Vronsky refusing.

By the time Anna rejoined the group, he was already gone, and Stepan Arkadyich was telling them that he had called to inquire about the dinner they were giving the next day for a celebrated engineer who had just arrived. "And nothing would induce him to come up. What a queer fellow he is!" added Stepan Arkadyich.

Kitty blushed. She thought that she was the only person who knew why he had come, and why he would not come up. *He has been at home,* she thought, *and didn't find me, and thought I should be here, but he did not come up because he thought it late, and Anna's here.*

All then turned their attention to Android Karenina's monitor, where Anna's Memories of handsome young Sergey were sequentially displayed.

CHAPTER 19

THE FLOAT WAS ONLY JUST beginning as Kitty and her mother walked up the great staircase, flooded with light, and lined with flowers and II/Footmen/74s in red linings. Bracing them-selves against the banister, they bent at the leg and waited with keen anticipation at the top step until the special chime was sounded, signaling the first blasts of jet-powered air from the hidden matrix of pipes in the floor and walls. At the same moment, the notes of the waltz began, and mother and daughter leaped from the top step and caught the air, dancing in airborne three-quarters time about the room.

A beardless youth, one of those society youths whom the old Prince Shcherbatsky called "young bucks," in an exceedingly open waistcoat, straightening his white tie as he went, waved to them as he bounced awkwardly past on a puff of air, then did a clumsy midair course reversal to ask Kitty for a quadrille. As the first quadrille had already been given to Vronsky, she had to promise this youth the second. He bowed and sailed past on the next surge of air, stroking his mustache, admiring rosy Kitty.

Although her dress, her coiffure, and all the preparations for the float had cost Kitty great trouble and consideration, at this moment she flew into the floatroom in her elaborate tulle dress over a pink slip as easily and simply as though all the rosettes and lace, all the minute details of her attire, had not cost her or her family a moment's attention, as though she had been born in that tulle and lace, bobbing and bouncing gracefully above the floor, with her hair done up high on her head, and a rose and two leaves on the top of it.

It was one of Kitty's best days. Her dress was not uncomfortable anywhere; her lace bertha did not droop anywhere; her rosettes were neither crushed nor torn off; her pink slippers with high, hollowed-out heels did not pinch, but gladdened her feet; and the thick rolls of fair chignon kept up on her head as if they were her own hair. All three buttons buttoned up without tearing on the long glove that covered her hand without concealing its lines. The black velvet of her locket nestled with special softness round her neck. That velvet was delicious; at home, looking at her neck in the looking glass, Kitty had felt that that velvet was speaking. She had asked her father if her Class III could have a skin of soft velvet, and she wanted to be dressed to match when it arrived.

About all the rest there might be a doubt, but the velvet was delicious. Kitty smiled now too, at the float, when she glanced at it in the glass. Her bare shoulders and arms gave Kitty a sense of chill marble, a feeling she particularly liked. Her eyes sparkled, and her rosy lips could not keep from smiling from the consciousness of her own attractiveness.

She had scarcely jumped from the stairs into the interlocking airstreams and reached the throng of ladies, all tulle, ribbons, lace, and flowers, all of the feminine trim gently oscillating in the carefully controlled winds, when she was asked for the next waltz, and asked by the best partner, the first star in the hierarchy of the ballroom, a renowned director of dances, a married man, handsome and well-built, Yegorushka Korsunsky. Without even asking her if she cared to dance, Korsunsky put out his arm to encircle her slender waist, bent deeply at the waist, and at the sound of the next air-chime launched them up together. They ascended rapidly on three subsequent puffs, Kitty's dress billowing beneath her, leaving below them the throngs of ladies and elegant gentlemen angling for partners.

Three regiments of 77s stood guard at the edges of the room, their dense metal frames resolutely, reassuringly earthbound, their heads tirelessly rotating, even as the supernatant revelry proceeded all around, beside, and above them. Their Caretaker in gold uniform and epaulets kept his vigilant, protective gaze upon the crowd.

"How nice you've come in good time," Korsunsky said to Kitty, as they dropped a foot and then shot giddily back up on the three-beat. "Such a bad habit to be late." Bending her left hand, she laid it on his shoulder, and her little feet in their pink slippers followed his as he led them through a tricky maneuver, moving over and up, over and up, catching each new burst of air at just the right moment, waltzing diagonally toward the ceiling.

"It's a rest to waltz with you," he said to her, as they glided through the waltz. "It's exquisite—such lightness, precision." He said to her the same thing he said to almost all his partners whom he knew well.

She smiled at his praise, and continued to look down at the room below them. She was not like a girl at her first float, for whom the tops of all the heads melt into one vision of fairyland. And she was not a girl who had gone the stale round of floats till every pate was familiar and tiresome. But she was in the middle stage between these two; she was excited, and at the same time she had sufficient self-possession to be able to observe.

Kitty turned her attention to her fellow dancers, as the music slowed from triple time to a common four-four and the air slowed with it, transforming from the swift, giddy *puff-puff-puff* of waltzfloating to a controlled series of magisterial gusts. Doing a slow pirouette in the air was the beauty Lidi, Korsunsky's wife; swanning past, nearly horizontal, was the lady of the house; dancing upside down, catching the air with his rear end and kicking his legs in a comical bicycling motion, was old Krivin, always to be found where the best people were. Down below, in the seating area, Kitty caught sight of Stiva, and beside him the exquisite figure and head of Anna, with Android Karenina beside her, glowing not lilac, but purest black.

And *he* was here too, silver uniform gleaming in the candlelight, his hot-whip crackling wickedly where it encircled his upper thigh. Kitty had not seen him since the evening she refused Levin. With her long-sighted eyes, she knew him at once, and was even aware that he was looking at her.

"Where shall I alight you?" said Korsunsky, a little out of breath, as the air song came to the end and the airstreams began to weaken in force, bringing the dancers closer to the floor with each subsequent gust.

"Madame Karenina's here, I think . . . take me to her."

"Wherever you command."

And Korsunsky began waltzing their measured way, downward and diagonally, straight toward the group in the left corner, continually saying, "*Pardon, Mesdames, pardon, pardon, Mesdames,*" and steering his course through the sea of lace, tulle, and ribbon.

"This is one of my most faithful supporters," said Korsunsky, bowing to Anna Arkadyevna, whom he had not yet seen, and exchanging polite nods with Android Karenina. "Anna Arkadyevna, a waltz?" he said, bending down to her.

"I don't dance when it's possible not to dance," she said.

"But tonight it's impossible," answered Korsunsky.

At that instant Vronsky came up.

"Well, since it's impossible tonight, let us start," she said, not noticing Vronsky's bow, and she hastily put her hand on Korsunsky's shoulder as the air-chime sounded for the next waltz, the steady huffing of the hidden pipes began anew, and he launched them into the air.

"What is she vexed with him about?" thought Kitty, discerning that Anna had intentionally not responded to Vronsky's bow. Vronsky went up to Kitty reminding her of the first quadrille, and expressing his regret that he had not seen her all this time. Kitty gazed in admiration at Anna waltzing, and listened to him. She expected him to ask her for a waltz, but he did not, and she glanced wonderingly at him. Kitty looked into his face, which was so close to her own, and long afterward—for several years after—that look, full of love, to which he made no response, cut her to the heart with an agony of shame.

He flushed slightly, and hurriedly asked her to waltz, but they had only just ascended to the first tier when a whistle blew, the music stopped, the air jets cut off abruptly, and everybody tumbled toward the ground.

Kitty cried out as she fell, but the floor of the ballroom was of course lined with plush mats of eiderdown, and so the greatest risk was not physical injury but embarrassment, which in fact was the result. As the erstwhile floaters, some laughing, some calling out in confusion and discompose, struggled to their feet, Kitty blushed to find herself entangled with Count Vronsky, who calmly pulled them both upright.

Korsunsky, who had landed on top of Anna Karenina, assumed the drop was triggered accidentally, and was among those taking the incident with good-natured merriment, until, in the next moment, he and Anna were encircled by four 77s. The Caretaker who controlled them—and who had ordered the drop—was striding manfully toward them, dragging behind him a fat, bright orange Class III who was twittering confusedly.

"Your Excellency," began this Caretaker, who wore a thin black mustache and a smirk of self-satisfaction. "Can you confirm the provenance of this machine?"

"Why, indeed," replied Korsunsky readily, pulling away from Anna and to the side of his beloved-companion. "This is my Class III, Portcullis. Is there some sort of difficulty?"

Kitty watched Korsunsky's eyes darting rapidly from his robot to the suspicious and hawk-like gaze of the Caretaker to the strong, pincer-like end-effectors of the 77s.

"Pardon, your Excellency. I did not inquire as to the machine's name or master. I asked if you can vouch for its origins."

The Caretaker's tone was unmistakably hardening. Looking away from Korsunsky, Kitty's gaze fell on Anna, who had not set Android Karenina to glow in lilac, as Kitty had so urgently wished, but instead to gently silhouette her, with the subtlest overtones of velvet, brilliantly complementing Anna's throat and shoulders, which looked as though carved in old ivory, and her rounded arms, with tiny, slender wrists. On Anna's head, among her black hair—her own, with no false additions—was a little wreath of pansies, and a bouquet of the same in the black ribbon of her sash among white lace. Her coiffure was not striking. All that was noticeable were the little willful tendrils of her curly hair that would always break free about her neck and temples. Round her well-cut, strong neck was a thread of pearls.

Kitty had been seeing Anna every day; she adored her, and had pictured her invariably haloed in lilac. But now seeing her silhouetted in black, Kitty felt that she had not fully seen her charm. She saw her now as someone quite new and surprising to her. Now she understood that Anna could not have been in lilac, and that her charm was just that she always stood out against her attire, that her companion light could never be noticeable on her. It was only that, the light, and all that was seen was she—simple, natural, elegant, and at the same time gay and eager.

"The difficulty is simply this, sir," the Caretaker continued in a smooth, almost supplicating tone. "This Class III device has been implanted with a recorder/transmitter by enemies of the state, and sadly must be destroyed."

An audible gasp came from the assembled crowd, followed by a ripple of disapproval and excitement. Korsunsky could only throw up his hands with confusion. "What? This cannot be! I am not with UnConSciya!"

"No one has suggested so," the Caretaker responded, his lips tightening and turning up almost imperceptibly. "No one, that is, until yourself, at this moment. But this machine, your excellency, has been corrupted, and must be destroyed."

"Wait! No—no," cried Korsunsky, as the massive 77s, their heads performing their slow, watchful revolutions, surrounded his small orange Class III, which clucked and whirred frightfully. "Portcullis!"

Count Vronsky separated from Kitty's side and strode across the floor, raising his hands before him in a calming manner. The Caretaker, noting Count Vronsky's air of presumed authority and glinting silver regimental uniform, stepped slightly backward and gestured to the 77s to allow him entry into the tight circle of enforcer robots around the terrified Korsunsky and his Class III.

"Alexei Kirillovich," said Korsunsky imploringly to Vronsky, sensing his chance to make an appeal. "This is an old and dearly beloved family android. It belonged to my grandfather and to his grandfather before him. It fought beside him in Kazakhstan."

"In Kyrgyzstan."

"Don't correct me, Portcullis, not now of all times!"

"Sorry, sorry."

"Hmmm," Count Vronsky mused, displaying for all at the party his mien of wise and dutiful authority. "If it is an UnConSciya device, sir, then the thing must be destroyed, its history as a member of your household notwithstanding." Korsunsky choked out a sob even as he nodded mutely, and all those present looked away, terrified for him, and ashamed as well by such unmanful behavior. "And yet," Vronsky continued sympathetically, "it would be irresponsible to deprive you of a beloved-companion without reason."

"Respectfully, sir," the Caretaker interjected, glancing with agitation at the red and emotional face of Korsunsky, "there is of course no safe way to check the thing; as you must know, automatons when corrupted with such devices are often rigged with trigger bombs as well."

Vronsky, clearly put off with the Caretaker's effrontery in presuming to know what he in his position knew or did not know, stood for a moment in thought, his thumb idly tracing a circle on the hilt of his hot-whip. From where she stood at the periphery of the incident, Kitty Shcherbatskaya saw with pained clarity how Vronsky cast a quick, distracted glance toward Anna Arkadyevna, to be sure, despite the gravity of the situation, that he had *her* attention.

At last he gave a small wave of his hand, and bent before the twittering orange Class III. Not waiting for permission from the Caretaker, he carefully, with evident expertise, dismantled Portcullis's exterior safeguards and cracked open the torso of the servomechanism.

A long, tense moment then passed, during which Korsunsky wrung his hands, and whined helplessly from where he stood between the powerful forms of two 77s.

"Yes," Vronsky said finally, straightening up and roughly wiping metal grease off his hands onto his sharply pressed silver trousers. "This is a Janus machine."

"No! No, it cannot be . . . " Korsunsky shook violently, tears streaming down his face. The Caretaker, wasting no more time, motioned to the 77s, and the cords began to snake out of their torsos, searching automatically for the necessary points along the Class III's wide orange torso—Portcullis now quivered wildly, emitting terrified squawks and beeps.

"No," said Vronsky to the 77s. "Allow me."

"Vronsky!" said Korsunsky. "Vronsky, please . . . " The air sizzled with fire. In the space of an instant, he had drawn both of his twin smokers and fired off the necessary ordnance at the droid's face, and Portcullis was junkered.

"Ah, God," cried Korsunsky, kneeling at the mechanized feet of his companion robot, which never again would give him comfort and consolation through life's trials. "Merciful God."

The crowd, while sympathizing with Korsunsky's grief, still clapped enthusiastically, for the threat was eliminated, the mechanism of the state had overcome the peril, and—most importantly from the perspective of the young romantic people in search of polite amusement and not spy-bots and laser fire—the float could proceed. The music began again, the air-chime sounded and the windblasts resumed, and the waltz continued. Vronsky holstered his smokers, and he and Kitty waltzed several times through the air. After the first waltz Kitty went to her mother, and she had hardly time to say a few words to Countess Nordston when Vronsky came up again for the first quadrille. During the quadrille—as the air-patterns busily evolved, blowing faster and slower, harder and weaker, in keeping with the complexity of the music—nothing of any significance was said: only once the conversation touched her to the quick, when he asked her about Levin, whether he was here, and added that he liked him so much. But Kitty did not expect much from the quadrille. She looked forward with a thrill at her heart to the mazurka. She fancied that in the mazurka everything must be decided. The fact that he did not during the quadrille ask her for the mazurka did not trouble her. She felt sure she would dance the mazurka with him as she had done at former floats, and refused five young men, saying she was engaged for the mazurka. The whole float up to the last quadrille was for Kitty an enchanted vision of delightful colors, sounds, and motions. She only sat down when she felt too tired and begged for a rest. But as she was dancing the last quadrille with one of the tiresome young men whom she could not refuse, she chanced to be vis-á-vis with Vronsky and Anna.

She had not been near Anna again since the destruction of Korsunsky's Class III, and now again she saw her suddenly quite new and surprising. She saw in her the signs of that excitement of success she knew so well in herself; she saw that she was intoxicated with the delighted admiration she was exciting. She knew that feeling and knew its signs, and saw them in Anna—saw the quivering, flashing light in her eyes, and the smile of happiness and excitement unconsciously play-ing on her lips, and the deliberate grace, precision, and lightness of her movements.

It's not the admiration of the crowd that has intoxicated her, Kitty thought, *but the adoration of one. And that one? Can it be he?* Every time he spoke to Anna the joyous light flashed into her eyes, and the smile of happiness curved her red lips. She seemed to make an effort to control herself, to try not to show these signs of delight, but they came out on her face of themselves. *But what of him?* Kitty looked at him and was filled with ter-ror. What was pictured so clearly to Kitty in the mirror of Anna's face, she saw in him as well. What had become of his always self-possessed, reso-lute manner, and the carelessly serene expression of his face? Now every time he turned to her, he bent his head, as though he would have fallen at her feet, and in his eyes there was nothing but humble submission and dread. *I would not offend you*, his eyes seemed every time to be saying, *but I want to save myself, and I don't know how.* On his face was a look such as Kitty had never seen before.

"Kitty, what is it?" said Countess Nordston, setting down gracefully on the carpet beside her. "I don't understand it."

Kitty's lower lip began to quiver; she got up quickly.

"Kitty, the chime has sounded. You're not dancing the mazurka?"

"No, no," said Kitty in a voice shaking with tears.

Countess Nordston found Korsunsky, with whom she was to dance the mazurka; he was sunk in a corner, insensible to the world around him, sobbing quietly and cradling the melted wreck of his beloved-companion's head in his lap. The countess shook him vigorously and told him to get a hold of himself and go ask Kitty.

Kitty danced in the first couple, and luckily for her she had not to talk, because Korsunsky was all the time weeping for his dear Portcullis, and how "there must have been some mistake, there *must* have been." Vronsky and Anna floated almost opposite her. She saw them with her long-sighted eyes, and saw them, too, close by, when they met in the figures, dipping and swooping, spinning and leaping over each other on those trickily swift triple-time mazurka air-blasts. The more she saw of them, the more convinced she was that her unhappiness was complete. She saw that they felt themselves alone in that crowded room. And on Vronsky's face, always so firm and independent, she saw that look that had struck her, of bewilderment and humble submissiveness, like the expression of an intelligent dog when it has done wrong.

Anna smiled, and her smile was reflected by him. She grew thoughtful, and he became serious. Some supernatural force drew Kitty's eyes to Anna's face. She was fascinating against the deep black midnight shadows cast by Android Karenina; fascinating were her round arms with their bracelets, fascinating was her firm neck with its thread of pearls, fascinating the straying curls of her loose hair, gaily swaying in the airstreams, fascinating the graceful, light movements of her little feet and hands, fascinating was that lovely face in its eagerness, but there was something terrible and cruel in her fascination.

Kitty admired her more than ever, and more and more acute was her suffering. Kitty felt overwhelmed, and her face showed it. When Vronsky saw her, sailing by in the mazurka, he did not at once recognize her, she was so changed.

"Delightful float!" he said to her, for the sake of saying something.

"Yes," she answered.

The float concluded with the presentation of Kitty's Class III, a

tall, graceful android constructed with the lithe form and pink coloring of a ballet dancer, just as Kitty in her childish fancy had long
desired. The companion robot was named Tatiana, and the beauty of
her face and figure were applauded by the crowd. But Kitty could
barely muster an appreciative smile, and shortly thereafter she hurriedly left the dance, her new Class III fluttering along behind her,
her tutu flapping as they fled.

CHAPTER 20

Y ES, THERE IS SOMETHING in me hateful, repulsive," said
Levin bitterly to Socrates, who nodded his yellow metal head
slowly, reluctantly. Together they came away from the Shcherbatskys'
and walked in the direction of his brother Nikolai's lodgings. "And I don't
get on with other people. Pride, they say. No, I have no pride. If I had any
pride, I should not have put myself in such a position." And he pictured to
himself Vronsky, happy, good-natured, clever, that handsome wolf of a Class
III bounding along at his feet, so self-possessed, and felt sure he had never
been placed in the awful position in which he had been that evening.

"Yes, she was bound to choose him."

"*It had to be,*" agreed Socrates sadly. "*You cannot complain of anyone
or anything.*"

"I am myself to blame. What right had I to imagine she would care
to join her life to mine?"

"*Who are you? What are you?*"

"A nobody, not wanted by anyone, nor of use to anybody."

Man and machine sighed heavily in melancholy unison.

To prepare Levin for what was to be a difficult visit to his brother,
Socrates initiated his monitor and displayed for his master a sequence of

Nikolai Memories: Nikolai tottering drunkenly, sneering, with his torn coat and his disdain for the world and all the people in it.

"Isn't he right that everything in the world is base and loathsome?"

"No," said Socrates, who felt at such times a programmatic responsibility to balance his master's gloomy emotional state with a more sober analysis. *"No, it cannot be."*

"And are we fair in our judgment of brother Nikolai? Of course, from the point of some, tipsy and wearing his torn cloak, accompanied by that battered, old, oil-stained Class III, he's a despicable person. But I know him differently. I know his soul, and know that we are like him. And I, instead of going to seek him out, went out to dinner, and came here." Levin sighed again, had Socrates call Nikolai's address up from his internal archives, and called a sledge. All the long way to his brother's, Levin continued to view all the vivid Memories familiar to him of his brother Nikolai's life.

He watched how his brother, while at the university, and for a year afterward, had, in spite of the jeers of his companions, lived like a monk, strictly observing all religious rites, services, and fasts, and avoiding every sort of pleasure, especially women. And afterward, how he had all at once broken out: he had associated with the most horrible people, and rushed into the most senseless debauchery—including, it had been whispered, relationships of an intimate nature with robots, relationships that were forbidden in even the most liberal construction of the Ministry's laws, and of God's.

It was all horribly disgusting, yet to Levin it appeared not at all in the same disgusting light as it inevitably would to those who did not know Nikolai, did not know all his story, did not know his heart.

Levin felt that, in spite of all the ugliness of his life, his brother Nikolai, in his soul, in the very depths of his soul, was no more in the wrong than the people who despised him. He was not to blame for having been born with his unbridled temperament and his somehow limited intelligence. But he had always wanted to be good. And now, or so he had written, he had fallen ill—terribly ill, if Levin could judge by his brother's latest letter, though the precise nature of his illness remained unclear.

I will tell him everything, without reserve, and I will make him speak without reserve, too, and I'll show him that I love him, and so understand him, Levin resolved to himself, as, toward eleven o'clock, he reached the hotel of which he had the address.

"The top . . . twelve and thirteen," the II/Porter7e62 answered automatically to Levin's inquiries.

The door of No. 12 was half open, and there came out into the streak of light thick fumes of cheap, poor tobacco, and the sound of a woman's voice, unknown to Levin. But he knew at once that his brother was there; he heard his cough.

"Whom do you want?" said the voice of Nikolai Levin, angrily.

"It's I," answered Konstantin Levin, coming forward into the light.

"Who's *I*?" Nikolai's voice said again, still more angrily. He could be heard getting up hurriedly, stumbling against something, and Levin saw, facing him in the doorway, the big, scared eyes, and the huge, thin, stooping figure of his brother, so familiar, and yet astonishing in its weirdness and sickliness. Karnak hunched in the shadows of the corner, a battered and dented old can of an android, with black-orange streaks of rust and acid staining his copper-colored sides.

Nikolai was even thinner than three years before, when Konstantin Levin had seen him last. He was wearing a short coat, and his hands and big bones seemed huger than ever. His hair had grown thinner, the same straight mustache hid his lips, the same eyes gazed strangely and naively at his visitor.

"Ah, Kostya!" he exclaimed suddenly, recognizing his brother, and his eyes lit up with joy. Karnak raised his creaky head and groaned tiredly. But the next second Nikolai's face took on a quite different expression: wild, suffering, and cruel.

"I wrote to you that I don't know you and don't want to know you. What is it you want?"

He was not at all the same as Konstantin had been fancying him. The worst and most tiresome part of his character, what made all relations with him so difficult, had been forgotten by Konstantin Levin when he thought of him, and now, when he saw his face, and especially that nervous twitching of his head, he remembered it all. Karnak let out a strange, metallic belch, and from within him some set of bedeviled gears ground together with an unbearable screech.

"I didn't want to see you for anything," he answered timidly. "I've simply come to see you."

His brother's timidity obviously softened Nikolai. His lips twitched. For the first time, Levin noticed a small, gray pustule pulsing just above his brother's left eyelid.

"Come to see me. Oh, so that's it?" Nikolai spat angrily.

"Thaaaaat's itttt?" croaked Karnak. Socrates took a step away from the other Class III, as if afraid his rust and gear-degeneracy could be infectious.

"Well, come in. Sit down," Nikolai continued. "Like some supper? Masha, bring supper for three, and fresh humectant for the machineman. Yes, we have it! No, stop a minute. Do you know who this is?" he said, addressing his brother.

"This woman," he said, pointing to her, "is the partner of my life, Marya Nikolaevna. I took her out of a bad house," and Levin knew what was meant by this, and blushed for it. "But I love her and respect her, and anyone who wants to know me," he added, raising his voice and knitting his brows, "I beg to love her and respect her. She's just the same as my wife, just the same. So now you know whom you've to do with. And if you think you're lowering yourself, well, here's the floor, there's the door."

And again his eyes traveled inquiringly over all of them. Karnak's big, rusty head lolled in its neck socket.

"Why I should be lowering myself, I don't understand."

"Then, Masha, bring supper: three portions, the humectant, the spirits and wine. . . . No, wait a minute. . . . No, it doesn't matter. Go along."

As they ate, Nikolai coughed and spat big clumps of mucous onto the floor, and Levin noticed a second gray pustule, slightly larger than the first, throbbing on his brother's cheek. It was difficult to eat.

"Yes, of course," said Konstantin Levin, as his brother rambled about some new idea he had, a theory about forming a new membership association for Class IIIs. He tried not to look at the patch of red that had come out on his brother's projecting cheekbones.

"Why such an association? What use is it?"

"Why? Because robots have been made slaves, just as the peasants once were in the time of the Tsars! We feel we can treat them as objects, because we have created them, but we created them to possess consciousness, and to have free will—"

"Free will as bounded by the Iron Laws," Levin reminded his brother.

"Yes, yes, the Iron Laws. But free will they nevertheless possess, free will of a *kind*. And just as God made man to pursue his own ends as he saw fit, surely we must allow magnificent automatons like these to try and get out of their slavery," said Nikolai, exasperated by the objection. He gestured to Karnak, as if his own Class III's magnificence were evidence enough—and at that moment one of Karnak's arms fell off with a weak, tinny *clank*.

Levin sighed, looking meanwhile about the cheerless and dirty room. This sigh seemed to exasperate Nikolai still more.

It became increasingly difficult for Nikolai even to speak, as he was consumed by a series of shuddering coughs. Finally he stepped out onto the landing to expectorate mightily over the side; he found enjoyment, he announced wickedly, evacuating his sputum onto passing sledges—he considered it the one small pleasure that life had still afforded him.

Left alone with Marya Nikolaevna, Levin turned to her.

"Have you been long with my brother?" he said to her.

"Yes, more than a year." She lowered her voice, turning away from Karnak's sensors, although it seemed to Levin that they were pitifully befogged and incapable of registering much. "Nikolai Dmitrich's health has become very poor. Nikolai Dmitrich drinks a great deal," she said.

"That is . . . how does he drink?"

"Drinks vodka, and it's bad for him."

"And a great deal?" whispered Levin.

"Yes," she said, looking timidly toward the doorway, where Nikolai Levin had reappeared. Soon he resumed his tired oration, turning to a bizarre warning that: "If we do not allow robots to control their own destiny, they will control ours." But his speech had begun to falter, and he passed abruptly from one subject to another. Konstantin, with the help of Masha, persuaded him not to go out anywhere, and got him to bed hopelessly drunk.

Masha promised to write to Konstantin in case of need, and he departed. As he and Socrates descended the creaky stairs, Levin considered his suspicion that there was something wrong with his brother far beyond the effects of drink, and wondered what exactly it could be.

CHAPTER 21

IN THE MORNING Konstantin Levin left Moscow, and toward evening he reached home. On his journey on the Grav he talked to his neighbors about politics and the new gravways, and, just as in Moscow, he was overcome by a sense of confusion of ideas, dissatisfaction with himself, shame of something or other. But when he got out at his own station, when he saw the cyclopian II/Coachman/47-T, its sturdy torso perfectly perpendicular at the controls; when, in the dim light reflected by the station fires, he saw his own sledge, his own four-treaded Puller at

its head, trimmed with rings and tassels; when the Coachman mechanically relayed the village news, he began to see what had happened to him
in quite a different light. He felt himself, and did not want to be anyone
else. All he wanted now was to be better than before.

Then, riding on the coach from the Grav station, came the heat: the
radiating warmth of the pit, his pit, which he began to feel on his skin
several versts before his massive groznium mine came into view. At last,
there it was, a vast and craggy crater blasted out of the countryside. The
pit was half a verst long and twice again as wide, its rough rock walls
sloping down into a rutted rock-lined bottom, which was dotted with a
thousand small smelting fires, which rung twenty-four hours a day with
the clang of pickaxes and shovels.

Konstantin Levin climbed from the sledge, waved robustly to a
gang of Pitbots with their battered but firm charcoal bodies and wide
treads, donned his goggles, and stood at the outer radius of the pit. As
he stared down into the vast crater, watching his dozens of diligent
Pitbots at work, diligent and industrious as honeybees, scurrying to and
fro, churning up the Earth with their axes, he felt that little by little the
confusion was clearing up, and the shame and self-dissatisfaction were
passing away.

He took a last breath of the sulfurous air and walked with Socrates
to the house from the side of the pit. As they walked, Levin expressed to
his Class III his new resolutions.

"In the first place, from this day I will give up hoping for any extraordinary happiness," he said. "Such as marriage might have given me."

"One, no happiness for you," Socrates parroted faithfully, his master's
use of the set phrase "in the first place" having activated his recording/
retaining function-set.

"Consequently I will not so disdain what I really have."

"Subset of one: no happiness equals no disdain."

"Secondly, I will never again let myself give way to low passion, the
memory of which tortured me so while I was making up my mind to

make an offer."

"*Two: absence of low passion.*"

Then Levin remembered his brother Nikolai, and made one further resolution. "I will never allow myself to forget him, Socrates."

"*Three: Nikolai preservation dedication.*"

"I will follow him up, and not lose sight of him. I will be ready to help if his illness should continue to worsen."

The snow of the little quadrangle before the house was lit up by a light in the bedroom window of his old *mécanicienne*, Agafea Mihalovna. She was not yet asleep.

"You're soon back again, sir," said Agafea Mihalovna as Levin and Socrates entered.

"I got tired of it, Agafea Mihalovna. With friends, one is well; but at home, one is better," he answered, and, together with his beloved-companion, went into his study.

CHAPTER 22

COME, IT'S ALL OVER, and thank God!" was the first thought that came to Anna Arkadyevna, when at the Moscow Grav Station she bid good-bye to her brother, who stood blocking the entrance to the carriage till the third bell was heard. She sat down on her lounge beside Android Karenina, and looked about her in the twilight of the sleeping carriage.

On the morning after the float, Anna Arkadyevna had sent her husband a telegram that she was leaving Moscow the same day.

"No, I must go, I must go." She had explained to her sister-in-law the change in her plans in a tone that suggested that she had to remember so many things that there was no enumerating them: "No, it had really better be today!"

Stepan Arkadyich came to see his sister off at seven o'clock. Kitty had not come, sending a note that she had a headache.

"Thank God!" Anna murmured to her beloved-companion as they settled in the carriage. "Tomorrow I shall see Seryozha and Alexei Alexandrovich, and my life will go on in the old way, all nice and as usual."

Still in the same anxious frame of mind, as she had been all that day, Anna took pleasure in arranging herself for the journey with great care. With her long, deft fingers Android Karenina opened a discreet mid-body compartment, took out a cushion, and laid it on Anna's knees. Anna smiled and stroked Android Karenina's gentle hands in thanks: she had long felt, and felt all the more so at such moments, that she and her darling android enjoyed a bond that was, somehow, stronger than that between other humans and their beloved-companions—even though Android Karenina never breathed a word, indeed lacked even the capacity to elocute, Anna knew in her own heart that there was no one else on Earth, human or robot, who understood or loved her so well.

They were seated across from a kindly elderly lady, but, intending to enjoy a novel, rather than to engage her fellow passengers in conversation, Anna leaned back in her seat and engaged a chitator, putting Android Karenina into partial Surcease. At first her attention was too distracted to follow the story. She could not help listening to the magical, propulsive noises of the Grav as it shot forward on the magnet bed; then the snow beating on the left window and sticking to the pane, and the sight of the muffled II/Gravman/160 rolling by, covered with snow on one side, and the conversations about the terrible snowstorm raging outside distracted her attention.

At last, Anna began to understand the story. Anna Arkadyevna listened and understood, but it was distasteful to follow the reflection of other people's lives. She had too great a desire to live herself. If she heard that the heroine of the story had fallen ill with malaria, she longed to move with noiseless steps about a sick room; if the chitator had a pirate ship laying siege to a houseboat, she longed to be the one active in its defense. But there was no chance of doing anything, and she forced herself to relax and let the chitator wash over her.

The heroine of the story was already almost reaching her English happiness, a handsome husband and a lakeside estate, and Anna was feeling a desire to go with them to the estate, when she suddenly felt that *he* ought to feel ashamed, and that she was ashamed of the same thing. But what had he to be ashamed of? *What have I to be ashamed of?* she asked herself in injured surprise. She switched off the chitator, sank against the back of the chair, and glanced at Android Karenina to help her understand, but her faceplate in Surcease was perfectly smooth and unreflective, revealing nothing.

There *was* nothing! She went over all her Moscow recollections. All were good, pleasant. She remembered the ball, remembered Vronsky and the crackle of his hot-whip and his face of slavish adoration, remembered all her conduct with him: there was nothing shameful. And for all that, at the same point in her memories, the feeling of shame was intensified, as though some inner voice, just at the point when she thought of Vronsky, were saying to her, "Warm, very warm, hot."

"Well, what is it?" she demanded of Android Karenina, though she knew the Class III could hardly respond while in Surcease. "What does it mean? Am I afraid to look it straight in the face? Why, what is it? Can it be that between me and this officer boy there exists, or can exist, any other relations than such as are common with every acquaintance?"

But, as is the way with many people who have difficult questions, but not the will to hear them answered, she asked her questions of a Surceased robot, who of course offered no response.

Anna laughed contemptuously at her own foolishness, and reactivated the chitator; but now she was definitely unable to follow what she heard.

Unthinkingly, she lifted Android Karenina's smooth hand and laid its cool surface onto her cheek, and almost laughed aloud at the feeling of delight that all at once without cause came over her. She felt as though her nerves were strings being strained tighter and tighter on some sort of screwing peg. She felt her eyes opening wider and wider, her fingers and toes twitching nervously, something within oppressing her breathing, while all shapes and sounds seemed in the uncertain half-light to strike her with unaccustomed vividness.

In this strange and disjointed sense of hyperawareness, it took her eyes a long moment to fully register what she then saw across from her: a koschei, bronzish, pencil-thin and centipedal, crawling on dozens of tiny, hideous feet across the wrinkled neck of the dozing elderly lady seated across from her.

The skittering steps of the miniature bug-robot were hardly heavy enough to wake the sleeping woman, and Anna thanked God at least for that small mercy. Surely the very sight of the skittering koschei—for that must be what this was, one of the hideous little insect-like death-machines used by UnConSciya to terrify the Russian populace—would cause the old woman to panic, and panic would seal her doom. Anna, murmuring a prayer for courage, scrunched forward in her seat, raising one hand, her fore- and middle fingers primed for plucking . . . slowly, carefully, she raised her hand, never taking her eyes off the automaton crawling in and out of the wrinkled folds of the ancient woman's neck flesh.

She was about to grasp the glowing, creeping thing, not yet considering what she would do with it once it was in her grasp, when three things happened in rapid succession.

A flat, jellyfish-like blob of undulating silver flew over Anna's head from behind her and landed with a thick, disgusting splat across the old woman's face, causing her to wake and begin thrashing in her seat; Anna herself also began screaming, loud enough to wake the devil; and the koschei she had been grasping for escaped her clutches, leapt off the old woman and onto Anna's forearm, and escaped up the sleeve of her dress.

The sensation of the koschei twitching rapidly forward inside her dress was viscerally horrifying, the countless tiny feet dancing about on her flesh—but worse by far was her knowledge of what was surely the koschei's intention, programmed like an animal instinct: to find her breast-bone, to pierce her flesh, to plunge its heat-sucking electrode antennae into the chambers of her heart. Anna clawed at her chest with one hand, and with the other she desperately flicked Android Karenina's red switch, praying with every breath that she would not be long in emerging from Surcease.

There was nothing to be done for the elderly woman, even if she could: the jellyfish koschei was still clenched over the old woman's face and was oozing out in all directions, covering the woman's body like a wriggling sheath, sucking the heat from her body.

While Anna slapped at her flesh, trying to squash the centipede koschei inside her dress, she became aware that all over the Grav car, other koschei were attacking other passengers. A slavering robotic beast in the shape of a gigantic cockroach, with coal-black wings and teeth like needles, buzzed down the aisle and landed on the eyes of a digni-fied Petersburg gentleman. Anna saw the roach thing sink its pulsing antennae into a dozen places in the unfortunate man's face, before her attention was seized by a most welcome distraction: Android Karenina, animated and in action, her smart, thin fingers inside Anna's bodice, catching up the wriggling koschei, crushing it neatly between thumb and forefinger.

Android Karenina then scooped up her mistress around the waist and hustled them both to the end of the carriage, where they escaped down the running board and toward the platform, for the Grav had made an emergency stop at a rural station. As they stepped from the carriage, the driving snow and the wind rushed to meet them. Android Karenina greeted the cold burst of air silently, but to Anna, the wind seemed as though lying in wait for her; with gleeful whistle it tried to snatch her up and bear her off, but she clung to the cold doorpost, and holding her skirt got down onto the platform and under the shelter of the carriages. The wind had been powerful on the steps, but on the platform, under the lee of the carriages, there was a lull. With a giddy, life-embracing thrill of having survived, she drew deep breaths of the frozen, snowy air, and standing near the carriage looked about the platform and the lighted station.

The carriages, posts, people, everything that was to be seen was covered with snow on one side, and was getting more and more thickly covered. For a moment there would come a lull in the storm, but then it would swoop down again.

Meanwhile, inside the carriage from whence they had escaped, a troop of 77s charged in, heads spinning rapidly, spitting pincer-tipped cords from their midsections to catch up koschei, sending rapid-fire bursts of bolts around the carriage, pinning the little beasts against chair backs and doorposts. Anna saw several more of the dog-sized cockroach koschei, along with at least one blackly gleaming spider-bot and a small cadre of flying wasp koschei, which buzzed and swooped through the carriage like demonically possessed birds, stinging passengers in their necks and ears.

Android Karenina gently turned her mistress's eyes from such horrors, and for a long time they stood quietly in the freezing dark of the station. But then it sounded like the tenor of the battle was changing, and Anna risked another glance through the window; what she saw heartened her, for it seemed that koschei were being dispatched rapidly now, one after the other, their hideous clacketing metal feet stilled, their fangs loosened from the necks and arms of the passengers.

Anna realized after a moment that the changing tide of the fight appeared to be the doing of one man—not a 77 at all, but a regimental soldier in a crisp silver uniform, who moved briskly but unpanicked up and down the length of the carriage, slashing and shooting and calling out orders with a loud, authoritative voice. And even before Anna heard the rumbling growl of a mechanical wolf, before she could see the sizzle and crackle of a hot-whip in action, before she could see his face, she knew that it was *he*.

The battle won, the koschei thrown together into a portable sizzle unit and destroyed, Vronsky emerged from the carriage, put his hand to the peak of his cap, bowed to her, and asked if she had been hurt? Could he be of any service to her? She gazed rather a long while at him without answering, and, in spite of the shadow in which he was standing, she saw, or fancied she saw, both the expression of his face and his eyes. It was again that expression of reverential ecstasy which had so worked upon her the day before. More than once she had told herself during the past few days, and again only a few moments before, that Vronsky was for her only one of the hundreds of young men, forever exactly the same, that are met everywhere, that she would never allow herself to bestow a thought upon him. But now at the first instant of meeting him, she was seized by a feeling of joyful pride. She had no need to ask why he was here. She knew as certainly as if he had told her that he was here to be where she was.

"It is lucky you were on this train, it seems, Count Vronsky," she said. "But what are you coming for?" she then added, barely masking the irrepressible delight and eagerness that shone in her eyes.

"What am I coming for?" he repeated, looking straight into her eyes. "You know that I have come to be where you are," he said. "I can't help it."

At that moment the wind, surmounting all obstacles, sent the snow flying from the carriage roofs, and clanked some sheet of iron it had torn off, while the mechanisms of the Grav's engine eased back to life. All the awfulness of the storm, all the terror of the koschei, seemed to her almost splendid now. He had said what her soul longed to hear, though she feared it with her reason. She made no answer, and in her face he saw conflict.

"Forgive me, if you dislike what I said," he said humbly.

He had spoken courteously, deferentially, yet so firmly, so stubbornly, that for a long while she could make no answer. Android

Karenina, for all this long silence, looked off with studied disinterest into the distance, while Lupo, less instinctively decorous, sniffed with curiosity at the hem of her skirts.

"It's wrong, what you say, and I beg you, if you're a good man, to forget what you've said, as I shall forget it," she said at last.

"Not one word, not one gesture of yours shall I, could I, ever forget. . . . "

"Enough, enough!" she cried, trying assiduously to give a stern expression to her face, into which he was gazing greedily. And clutching at the cold doorpost, she clambered up the steps and got rapidly into the corridor of the carriage. Settled again in the carriage, fumigated and revivified already by the Grav's assiduous crew of IIs, she cued in Android Karenina's monitor a Memory of what had just occurred. As she watched, she realized instinctively that the momentary conversation had brought them fearfully closer; and she was panic-stricken and blissful at it. The overstrained condition which had tormented her before did not only come back, but was intensified, and reached such a pitch that she was afraid every minute that something would snap within her from the excessive tension. She did not sleep all night. But in that nervous tension, and in the visions that filled her imagination, there was nothing disagreeable or gloomy: on the contrary, there was something blissful, glowing, and exhilarating. Even the painful recollection of the multitudinous cold steel feet of the koschei, tickling their way up toward her breastbone, could not dampen this powerful rush of feeling.

Toward morning Anna sank into a doze, sitting in her place, and when she woke it was daylight and the Grav was gliding into the Petersburg station. At once thoughts of home, of husband and of son, and the details of that day and the following came upon her.

* * *

At Petersburg, as soon as the Grav stopped and she got out, the first person that attracted Anna's attention was her husband. "Oh, mercy! That face!" she murmured to Android Karenina. Covering the right side of Alexei Alexandrovich's face as always, nearly entirely hiding it, was a mask of steely silver, descending from brow to chin, with only enough metal cut away to allow his nose and mouth their full functioning. While Alexei's left eyebrow could and did twitch sardonically, and while his left cheek could and did rise in wry humor, the corresponding parts on the opposite side were hidden behind an unreadable sheen of metallic cold, laced with dark veins of pure groznium—not tempered or alloyed by the Ministry's metallurgists, but the raw, scarlet-black ore itself. Where his right eye once had sat was a large aperture, a cyborgicist's reinvention of a human eye socket, from which emerged a telescoping oculus. It was with this rotating orbital that Alexei Alexandrovich was now scanning the crowd, looking for his wife.

Catching sight of her, he came to meet her, his lips sliding into their habitual, sarcastic smile, and his left human eye looking straight at her, while its mechanized companion eye mechanically scanned the station. An unpleasant sensation gripped at her heart when she met his obstinate and weary glance, as though she had expected to see him different. She was especially struck by the feeling of dissatisfaction with herself that she experienced on meeting him. That feeling was an intimate, familiar feeling, like a consciousness of hypocrisy, which she experienced in her relations with her husband. But hitherto she had not taken note of the feeling; now she was clearly and painfully aware of it.

"Yes, as you see, your tender spouse, as devoted as the first year after marriage, burned with impatience to see you," he said in his deliberate, high-pitched voice, and in that tone which he almost always took with her, a tone of jeering at anyone who should say in earnest what he said. He took his wife's valise from Android Karenina, offering her Class III no greeting, and naturally receiving none in return.

"Is Seryozha quite well?" Anna asked.

"This is all the reward," said he, "for my ardor? He's quite well. . . . "

CHAPTER 23

A FTER THE MAYHEM with the koschei, Vronsky had not even tried to sleep all that night. Rather, as Lupo lay curled in Surcease at his feet, he sat in his Grav carriage, looking straight before him or examining the people who got in and out. If he had indeed on previous occasions struck and impressed people who did not know him by his air of unhesitating composure, he seemed now more haughty and self-possessed than ever. He looked at people as if they were things. A nervous young man, a clerk in a law court, sitting opposite him, hated him for that look. The young man asked him for a light, and entered into conversation with him, and even pushed against him, to make him feel that he was not a thing, but a person. But Vronsky gazed at him exactly as he would a Class I device, and the young man made a wry face, feeling that he was losing his self-possession under the oppression of this refusal to recognize him as a person.

Vronsky saw nothing and no one. Occasionally, he passed his eye over the revivified carriage to ensure no more of the vicious skittering koschei were aboard, even while he was certain in his heart that none remained: not when he, Alexei Kirillovich, with all his battlefield acuity and self-assurance, had junkered the lot.

He felt himself a king, not because he believed that he had made an impression on Anna—he did not yet believe that—but because the impression she had made on him gave him happiness and pride. His hot-whip crackled pleasantly along his thigh, an old fellow soldier whose very presence reminded him of past successes.

What would come of it all he did not know, he did not even think.

He felt that all his forces, hitherto dissipated, wasted, were centered on one thing, and bent with fearful energy on one blissful goal. And he was happy at it. He knew only that he had told her the truth, that he had come where she was, that all the happiness of his life, the only meaning in life for him, now lay in seeing and hearing her. When he had climbed out on the platform and seen her, in the adrenalin-charged moments after the koschei were destroyed, involuntarily his first word had told her just what he thought. And he was glad he had told her it, that she knew it now and was thinking of it. He did not sleep all night. When he was back in the carriage, he kept unceasingly going over every position in which he had seen her, every word she had uttered, and before his fancy, making his heart faint with emotion, floated pictures of a possible future.

When he got out of the train at Petersburg, he felt after his sleepless night as keen and fresh as after a cold bath. He paused near his compartment, waiting for her to get out. "Once more," he said quietly to Lupo, who growled happily, "once more I shall see her walk, her face, her striking beloved-companion; she will say something, turn her head, glance, smile, maybe." But before he caught sight of her, he saw her husband, whom the stationmaster was deferentially escorting through the crowd. "Ah, yes! The husband." Only now for the first time did Vronsky realize clearly the fact that there was a person attached to her, a husband. He knew that she had a husband, but had hardly believed in his existence, and only now fully believed in him, with his head and shoulders, his cold, mechanical faceplate, his legs clad in black trousers; especially when he saw this husband calmly take her arm with a sense of property.

Seeing Alexei Alexandrovich with his severely self-confident figure, in his round hat, with his rather prominent spine, he believed in him, and was aware of a disagreeable sensation, such as a man might feel tortured by thirst, who, on reaching a spring, should find a dog, a sheep, or a pig who has drunk of it and muddied the water. Alexei Alexandrovich's outsize automated eye, now slowly scanning Anna from within its prominent metal socket, particularly annoyed Vronsky. He could recognize in no one but himself an indubitable right to love her. But she was still the same, and the sight of her affected him the same way, physically reviving him, stirring him, and filling his soul with rapture.

He saw the first meeting between the husband and wife, and noted with a lover's insight the signs of slight reserve with which she spoke to her husband. Lupo, at his feet, bristled and arched his back. "Yes, Lupo, I notice it too," Vronsky said in a low voice to the beast. "She does not love him and cannot love him."

He strode toward the pair, and at the moment before approaching them, he noticed too with joy that Anna Arkadyevna was conscious of his being near, and looked round, and seeing him, turned again to her husband.

"The koschei certainly provided us with a restless evening," Vronsky greeted her. "Are you feeling well this morning?" he asked, bowing to her and her husband together, and leaving it up to Alexei Alexandrovich to accept the bow on his own account, and to recognize it or not, as he might see fit.

"Thank you, yes," she answered.

Lupo's narrow canine eyes looked into the single robotic oculus of Alexei Alexandrovich, and the theriomorphic Class III let out a loud, gear-grinding bark. Vronsky silenced him with one raised finger.

Anna's face looked weary, and there was not that play of eagerness in it peeping out in her smile and her eyes; but for a single instant, as she glanced at Vronsky, there was a flash of something in her eyes, and although the flash died away at once, he was happy for that moment. She glanced at her husband to find out whether he knew Vronsky. Alexei Alexandrovich looked over Vronsky's silver uniform with displeasure, vaguely recalling who this was. Vronsky's composure and self-confidence here struck, like a scythe against a stone, upon the cold imperturbability of Alexei Alexandrovich.

"Count Vronsky," said Anna.

"Ah! We are acquainted, I believe," said Alexei Alexandrovich indifferently, giving his hand. To Anna he said, "You set off with the mother and you return with the son," articulating each syllable, as though each were a separate favor he was bestowing.

Lupo barked a second time, sharp and clear, raising his back and baring his teeth at Alexei Alexandrovich, who regarded the beast with weary irritation before addressing his wife in a jesting tone: "Well, were a great many tears shed in Moscow at parting?"

By addressing his wife like this he gave Vronsky to understand that he wished to be left alone, and, turning slightly toward him, he touched his hat; but Vronsky turned to Anna Arkadyevna.

"I hope I may have the honor of calling on you," he said.

Lupo, his circuits for some reason keenly activated, now emitted from his Vox-Em a piercing, willful *aroof.* Before Vronsky could chastise the dog-robot, Alexei Alexandrovich cocked his head and stared straight at the Class III with his dark metallic eye for a long moment. Lupo yelped feebly, shuddered, and fell to the ground like a broken Class I plaything. Alexei Alexandrovich then glanced with his biological eye at Vronsky, who was staring with open-mouthed shock at his beloved-companion.

"On Mondays we're at home," Alexei Alexandrovich said blandly. Vronsky crouched on the spotless floor of the Grav station cradling Lupo's great, bristly head in his lap. Lupo stirred feebly, issuing hollow little whimpers and moans.

"How fortunate," Alexei Alexandrovich said to his wife in the same jesting tone, dismissing Vronsky altogether, "that I should just have half an hour to meet you, so that I can prove my devotion."

"You lay too much stress on your devotion for me to value it much," she responded in the same jesting tone, involuntarily glancing backward at the stricken Vronsky. "But what has it to do with me?" she murmured to Android Karenina. She began asking her husband how Seryozha had got on without her.

"Oh, capitally! The II/Governess says he has been very good.

And ... I must disappoint you ... but he has not missed you as your husband has. Well, I must go to my committee. I shall not be alone at dinner again," Alexei Alexandrovich went on, no longer in a sarcastic tone. "You wouldn't believe how I've missed ..." And with a long pressure of her hand and a meaningful smile, he put her in her carriage.

Vronsky remained on the silver floor of the Petersburg Grav station, watching with relief as signs of full functioning returned one by one to his Class III. He shook his head, contemplating the beauty of Anna Karenina, the austere elegance of Android Karenina—and wondering, of her strange, metal-faced husband: *What in God's name is he?*

CHAPTER 24

THE FIRST PERSON to meet Anna at home was her son. He dashed down the stairs to her, in spite of his II/Governess/D147's call, and with desperate joy shrieked: "Mother! Mother!" Running up to her, he hung on her neck.

"I *told* you it was mother!" he shouted to the II/Governess/D147, who issued scolding clucks at this rudeness. "I knew!"

But the son, like the husband, aroused in Anna a feeling akin to disappointment. She had imagined him better than he was in reality. She had to let herself drop down to the reality to enjoy him as he really was. But even as he was, he was charming, with his fair curls, his blue eyes, and his plump, graceful little legs in tightly pulled-up stockings. Anna experienced almost physical pleasure in the sensation of his nearness and his caresses, and moral soothing when she met his simple, confiding, and loving glance and heard his naive questions.

Anna took out the Class Is that Dolly's children had sent him, and told her son what sort of little girl his cousin was in Moscow, how she could read, and even taught the other children.

"Why, am I not so nice as she?" asked Seryozha.

"To me you're nicer than anyone in the world."

"I know that," said Seryozha, smiling.

Various friends visited with Anna, glad to have her back, while Alexei Alexandrovich spent the day at the Ministry, busy with some momentous project that he himself had initiated and was directing. Anna, finally left alone, spent the time till dinner in helping with her son's dinner (he dined apart from his parents) and in putting her things in order, and in reading and answering the notes and letters that had accumulated on her table.

The feeling of causeless shame, which she had felt on the journey, and her excitement, too, had completely vanished. In the habitual conditions of her life she felt again resolute and irreproachable; in her physical body she felt only the occasional phantasmal tingling just above her breastbone, where the koschei had danced with its dozens of disgusting feet across her chest.

She shuddered at the memory, and then recalled with wonder her curiously joyful state of mind after the nightmare of the attack. *What was it? Nothing. Vronsky said something silly, which was easy to put a stop to, and I answered as I ought to have done. To speak of it to my husband would be unnecessary and out of the question. To speak of it would be to attach importance to what has no importance.* She remembered how she had told her husband of what was almost a declaration made to her at Petersburg by a young man, one of her husband's subordinates in the Ministry, and how Alexei Alexandrovich had answered that every woman living in the world was exposed to such incidents, but that he had the fullest confidence in her tact, and could never lower her and himself by jealousy. Neither ever mentioned the incident again, and the man had, anyway, later been revealed as a Janus, and given appropriate punishment in Petersburg Square.

"So then there's no reason to speak of it? And indeed, thank God, there's nothing to speak of," she said to Android Karenina, who nodded

"IT'S TIME, IT'S TIME," HE SAID, WITH A MEANINGFUL SMILE; HIS
TELESCOPING OCULUS ZOOMED IN AS HE ENTERED THEIR BEDROOM

her quiet agreement.

Alexei Alexandrovich came back from his meeting at four o'clock, but as often happened, he had not time to come in to her. Later they dined together, and after dinner Anna sat down at the hearth to write a letter to Dolly, and waited for her husband. Precisely at twelve o'clock, when Anna was still sitting at her writing table, she heard the sound of measured steps in slippers, and Alexei Alexandrovich, freshly washed and combed, his faceplate glinting in the hearth light, came in to her.

"He's a good man, truthful, good-hearted, and remarkable in his own line," Anna whispered to Android Karenina, as her husband approached. "And really, the visible half of his face is handsome in its way."

"It's time, it's time," he said, with a meaningful smile; his right eye zoomed slowly toward her, its lens opening visibly, before he went into their bedroom.

"And what right had he to look at him like that?" Anna said to her android, recalling Vronsky's glance at Alexei Alexandrovich. Undressing, she went into the bedroom, and sent Android Karenina, as was appropriate, into Surcease; but her face had none of the eagerness that, during her stay in Moscow, had fairly flashed from her eyes and her smile; on the contrary, now the fire seemed quenched in her, hidden somewhere far away.

PART TWO: VOYAGE OF THE SHCHERBATSKYS

CHAPTER 1

A T THE END OF THE WINTER, in the Shcherbatskys' house, a consultation was being held, which was to pronounce on the state of Kitty's health and the measures to be taken to restore her failing strength. It was hoped by her family that she was suffering from nothing worse than a broken heart. But she had been severely ill, and as spring came on she grew worse. A celebrated physician was called in, and, with his valise crammed full of the latest physiolographical instruments, accompanied by an industrious hospital-green Class II with an impressive effector array, he examined the patient.

For more than an hour the doctor ran his Class I physiometers along every inch of Kitty Shcherbatskaya's naked flesh, carefully working the thread-thin vital-estimators into her windpipe and the chambers of her ears, listening with his echolocater pressed against the sides of her skull. Throughout this invasive and degrading process, Princess Shcherbatskaya, the patient's mother, hovered anxiously at the edges of the room, as did Tatiana, the lithe, balletic Class III who had, as yet, been little used and hardly noticed by her ailing mistress.

"Well, doctor, decide our fate," said the princess. "Tell me everything."

"Yes, yes, tell! What hope is there? Is there hope?" said La Scherbatskaya, the princess's Class III, wringing her hands beside her mistress.

"Princess. Allow me to examine the results of the various physiolographs and then I will have the honor of laying my opinion before you."

"So we had better leave you?"

"As you please."

When the doctor was left alone, he flicked on his II/Prognosis/M4, and fed into it all the data he had collected. After thirty long seconds, during which the wise little machine ran its efficient tabulation of the various symptoms that had been discovered, the Class II reported that there was possibly a commencement of tuberculosis trouble . . . that there were indications: malnutrition, nervous excitability, and so on.

The celebrated physician looked impatiently at the Class II. "Yes, but in the presence of tuberculosis indications, what is to be done to maintain nutrition?"

The Class II mulled over this follow-up, a faint steam indicative of second-tier information-processing escaping from its Third Bay, while the doctor glanced at his gold-plated watch and waited, thinking about the opera. Meanwhile in the drawing room the family whispered anxiously, surrounding Kitty where she lay prostrate on the sofa, blushing and anticipating her fate. Her Class III, Tatiana, performed nervous *jetés* from one corner of the room to the other.

At last the physician received the final results from the Class II and entered the drawing room. When the doctor came in, Kitty flushed crimson and her eyes filled with tears. All her illness and treatment struck her as a thing so stupid, ludicrous even! Doctoring her seemed to her as absurd as putting together the pieces of a broken vase. Her heart was broken. Why would they try to cure her with pills and powders and vitasonic recalibrations? But she could not grieve her mother, especially as her mother considered herself to blame.

"May I trouble you to sit down, princess?" the celebrated doctor said to her.

He sat down with a smile, facing her, felt her pulse, and again began asking her tiresome questions. Suddenly sensing an opportunity to be of use to her mistress, Tatiana pirouetted over and took first position directly between the doctor and Kitty.

"Excuse me, doctor," she said, her sweet, still-developing soprano Vox-Em tone showing surprising strength. *"But there is really no object in this. For this is the third time you've asked her the same things!"* Kitty looked up with wide-eyed gratitude at this intercession, experiencing for the first time that mysterious feeling of true, deep kinship between a human and her beloved-companion; and then, arm in arm, Kitty Shcherbatskaya and her pink-hued android left the room.

The celebrated doctor did not take offense.

"What a charming Class III," he said to the princess. "However, I had finished . . . "

And the doctor began scientifically explaining to the princess, repeating word for word the phrases he had heard only a few minutes earlier from the II/Prognosis/M4. At the question whether they should "go abroad," the doctor plunged into deep meditation, as though resolving a weighty problem. He glanced furtively at the Class II, saw it indicate *yes* with a barely perceptible 2.5-degree head unit rotation, and thusly pronounced his decision: they *were* to "go abroad," but to put no faith in foreign quacks, and to apply to him in any need.

It seemed as though some piece of good fortune had come to pass after the doctor had gone. The mother was much more cheerful when she went back to her daughter, and Kitty pretended to be more cheerful. She even spent a half hour walking the grounds of the estate with Tatiana, which made the rose-accented Class III immeasurably joyful.

"Really, I'm quite well, Mamma. But if you want to go abroad, let's go!" she said, and trying to appear interested in the proposed tour, she began talking of the preparations for the journey.

So it was that several weeks later the Shcherbatskys marked the coming of Lent by giving up their terrestrial moorings. They traveled first by Puller carriage and then by Grav to Russia's grand departure port, the town of Pushkin, where stood the pride of the century: the Ballistic Cross-Orbital Cannon.

Thus were the Scherbatskys blasted into space.

CHAPTER 2

THE HIGHEST PETERSBURG SOCIETY is essentially one: in it everyone knows everyone else, everyone visits everyone else. But this great set has its subdivisions. Anna Arkadyevna Karenina had friends and close ties in various circles of this highest society. One circle was her husband's government official set, consisting of his colleagues and subordinates in the Higher Branches of the Ministry of Robotics and State Administration. Anna found it difficult now to recall the feeling of almost awe-stricken reverence that she had at first entertained for these persons, who were together responsible for the management and advancement of groznium-derived technologies, and therefore for the welfare of all Mother Russia. Now she knew all of them as people know one another in a country town; she knew their habits and weaknesses, and where the shoe pinched each one of them. She knew their relations with one another and with the head authorities, knew who was for whom, and how each one maintained his position, and where they agreed and disagreed.

The second circle with which Anna had ties was preeminently the fashionable world—the world of floating balls, of dinners, of sumptuous dresses. Her connection with this circle was kept up through Princess Betsy Tverskaya, her cousin's wife, who had an income of a hundred and twenty thousand rubles, and who had taken a great fancy to Anna since she came of age and received her Class III, showed her much attention, and drew her into her set, which followed all the latest trends.

Anna had at first avoided as far as she could Princess Tverskaya's world, because it necessitated an expenditure beyond her means, and besides in her heart she preferred the first circle. But since her visit to Moscow she had done quite the contrary. She avoided her serious-minded friends in that circle around the Ministry, and went out into the fashionable world. There she saw Vronsky, and experienced an agitating joy at those meetings. She met Vronsky especially often at Betsy's, for Betsy was a Vronsky by birth and his cousin. Vronsky was everywhere where he had any chance of meeting Anna and speaking to her, when he could, of his love. She gave him no encouragement, but every time she met him there surged up in her heart that same feeling of quickened life that had come upon her that day in the Grav, when he saw her for the first time. She was conscious herself that her delight sparkled in her eyes and curved her lips into a smile, and she could not quench the expression of this delight.

At first Anna sincerely believed, and earnestly expressed to Android Karenina, that she was displeased with him for daring to pursue her. But soon after her return from Moscow, on arriving at a soiree where she had expected to meet him, and not finding him there, she realized distinctly from the rush of disappointment that she had been deceiving herself, and that this pursuit was not merely not distasteful to her, but that it made the whole interest of her life.

Their next meeting occurred soon after, at another soiree, this one at the home of Princess Betsy.

As the princess's guests arrived at the wide entrance one by one, the stout II/Porter/7e62 noiselessly opened the immense door, letting the visitors pass by into the house. Almost at the same instant the hostess, with freshly arranged coiffure and freshened face, walked in at one door and her guests at the other door of the drawing room, a large room with dark walls, downy rugs, and a brightly lighted table, gleaming with the light of *lumiéres*, white cloth, a II/Samovar/1(16) in fashionable platinum, and transparent china tea things.

Some guests were amused, and others discomfited, to find in attendance at the gathering a Class III named Marionetta, who had no owner—she was a decom, an android whose owner had died without heir, or else been denounced as a Janus and exiled. Betsy thought it endlessly amusing to have such pitiful creatures at her *petites fêtes*, where she would treat the humanless robots as if they were her own sad little bear cubs to be baited. Typically decoms were junkered within days of their obsolescence, but Betsy obtained them, it was rumored, through some secret connection in the Ministry—though surely *not* within the Higher Branches, as no one from that elite cadre would dare enact such brazen pilferage.

Princess Betsy sat down at the table and took off her gloves, handing them with a flourish to Marionetta, who folded them neatly before stowing them carefully in a drawer, pathetically grateful for the small assignment. The party began, and chairs were set with the aid of II/Footman/74s, moving almost imperceptibly about the room; the party settled itself, divided into two groups: one round the samovar near the hostess, the other at the opposite end of the drawing room, round the handsome wife of an ambassador, in black velvet, with sharply defined black eyebrows and a Class III with nearly identical, equally imposing facial features. In both groups conversation wavered, as it always does, for the first few minutes, broken up by meetings, greetings, offers of tea, and, as it were, feeling about for something to rest upon.

Marionetta meanwhile flickered her feeble eyebank at everyone, offering small gestures of usefulness, lighting cigars and distributing drinks. Betsy's beloved-companion, Darling Girl, laughed mercilessly at her fellow robot, her own eyebank flashing scarlet.

Round the samovar and the hostess the conversation vacillated in just the same way between three inevitable topics: the latest piece of public news, the theater, and scandal. It finally came to rest on the last topic, that is, ill-natured gossip.

"Anna Karenina is quite changed since her stay in Moscow. There's something strange about her," said Betsy, having noted that Anna had not yet arrived. "Though not as strange, one cannot help observing, as her husband's face!" Darling Girl emitted a sly, appreciative giggle.

"The great change is that she brought back with her the shadow of Alexei Vronsky," said the ambassador's wife.

"Well, what of it? There's a fable of Grimm's about a man without a shadow, a man who's lost his shadow. And that's his punishment for something. I never could understand how it was a punishment. But a woman must dislike being without a shadow."

"Yes, but women with a shadow usually come to a bad end," said Anna's friend.

"Bad luck to your tongue!" said Princess Myakaya suddenly. "Madame Karenina's a splendid woman. I don't know much of her husband, but I like her very much."

"There is something extremely odd about her husband," said the ambassador's wife, lowering her voice to a confidential tone. "You know, he possesses no Class III robot."

"Well, many members of the Higher Branches have begun to eschew them."

"And you do not find that strange?"

"Princess Betsy! Is that a decom?" said a strong voice from the doorway.

"Ah, here you are at last!" Betsy said, turning with a smile to Vronsky, as he came in, removing his coat to reveal his powerful legs, accentuated by the outline of the whip along his thigh. "And in answer to your question, yes, Marionetta here is indeed a decommissioned Class III—and I have a plan for her that I think shall offer considerable amusement."

CHAPTER 3

B ETSY INTENDED TO PLACE the unfortunate Marionetta in the center of a pastime called the One-or-the-Other Game, which was designed to measure a robot's relative fidelity to the Iron Laws. That is, it would test the relative strength of their obedience to one law ("robots shall obey humans") weighed against another ("robots shall not allow themselves to be damaged").

"A game?" vocalized Marionetta with pitiful eagerness. *"How delightful!"*

Just then steps were heard at the door, and Princess Betsy, knowing it was Madame Karenina, glanced at Vronsky. He was looking toward the door, and his face wore a strange new expression. Joyfully, intently, and at the same time timidly, he gazed at the approaching figure, and slowly he rose to his feet. Anna walked into the drawing room. Holding herself extremely erect, as always, looking straight before her, and moving with her swift, resolute, and light step, Android Karenina a pace or two behind her and casting her in a fetching crimson, she crossed the short space to her hostess, shook hands with her, smiled, and with the same smile looked around at Vronsky. Vronsky bowed low and pushed a chair up for her.

Marionetta stood with an old-fashioned mask of black crepe drawn down over her eyebank, a sickly smile of anticipation plastered across her faceplate. But for the moment, however, the eyes of all humans present were focused upon Alexei Kirillovich and Anna Karenina.

Anna acknowledged him only by a slight nod, flushed a little, and frowned. But immediately, while rapidly greeting her acquaintants, and shaking the hands proffered to her, she addressed Princess Betsy:

"I have been at Countess Lidia's, and meant to have come here earlier, but I stayed on."

"I think you shall be glad you tore yourself away, when we begin our little game," Princess Betsy responded with a wicked smile.

"I do so love games!" said Marionetta, from behind her mask.

Betsy raised her eyebrows at the crowd with wry amusement and began the first of the tests, which she herself, as hostess, would administer. A chalice, containing superheated humectant, the powerful lubricant used to treat groznium gears, was brought to Betsy on a gleaming tray by one of the II/Footman/74s. Betsy gripped the tray carefully and then ordered Marionetta to plunge her hand downward, into the chalice.

The robot did so, but then, actuated by the delicate lacing of sense receivers in her end-effector, jerked back.

"Leave your hand in place, Marionetta," commanded Betsy calmly. "Be still."

A expression of evident pain washed over the visible portion of Marionetta's face, and for a long moment it seemed uncertain whether she would obey the Iron Law demanding her self-preservation, or the one which required obedience to Betsy's command.

But as the struggle in her face lessened and then disappeared, replaced by a stoic mien, attention turned away and the gossip continued, passing to the case of a love-match that Princess Myakaska had heard of, and of which she disapproved. "I was in love in my young days with a deacon," she was saying. "I don't know that it did me any good."

"No, I imagine, joking apart, that to know love, one must make mistakes and then correct them," said Princess Betsy from where she stood. "Stay there, Marionetta," she barked to the decom, who had, sensing the loss of attention, begun to draw her hand up from its torment. "Stay where you are."

"Yes, yes, of course," the decom responded with difficulty. *"Stay stay I shall stay."*

"Correct them, even after marriage?" said the ambassador's wife to Princess Myakaska playfully.

"'It's never too late to mend.'"

"Just so," Betsy agreed. "One must make mistakes and correct them. What do you think about it?" She turned to Anna, who was listening in silence to the conversation, though her eyes were fixed on Marionetta— apparently alone among the partygoers, Anna felt an intense pang of conscience relating to such ill use of any machine, whether it retained its human master or not.

"I think," said Anna, playing absently with the glove she had taken off, "I think . . . of so many men, so many minds, certainly so many hearts, so many kinds of love."

Vronsky was gazing at Anna, and with a fainting heart waiting for what she would say. He sighed as after a danger escaped when she uttered these words.

Princess Betsy, satisfied with the answer she had drawn from Anna Arkadyevna, permitted Marionetta to remove her hand from the chalice, which the decom did with a gasp of relief. Betsy turned to the crowd: "The law of obedience wins this round," she announced, to general applause and laughter. Anna suddenly turned to Vronsky.

"Oh, I have had a letter from Moscow. They write me that Kitty Shcherbatskaya's very ill. She may be sent into orbit."

"Really?" said Vronsky, knitting his brows.

Anna looked sternly at him.

"That doesn't interest you?"

"On the contrary, it does, very much. What was it exactly they told you, if I may know?" he questioned.

"And now, Round Two," announced Princess Betsy.

"Please," protested Anna Arkadyevna. "You have proved the machine's fidelity to the Iron Laws. Let there be no more of this game."

"More games? Is the game to continue?" said Marionetta with piti- ful earnestness, and at that moment Betsy, ignoring Anna's objection,

signaled to the old ambassador's wife, who activated a Class I device called a bolt-shot, part of a child's game not unlike darts. As dozens of tiny electric bursts exploded along the length of her torso, Marionetta jumped backward, but Betsy ordered her to stay still. Her struggle to do so was obvious, and as a second round of blazing bolts struck her, she turned and began, as if against her will, to leave the room.

Betsy shouted "*Stay*! Stay in place!" Others of the party joined in—"Stay!" "Stay, robot!" "Remain where you are!"—and Marionetta did so.

"What?" Vronsky repeated to Anna, who was only half-listening, watching the progress of the "game" with horrified fascination. "What is it they write to you?

"I often think men have no understanding of what's not honorable though they're always talking of it," Anna replied sharply.

"I don't quite understand the meaning of your words," Vronsky said. The bolt-shot jammed, the ambassador's wife shrugged, and the fusillade ceased; Anna, assuming that the cruel sport was over, turned her full attention to Alexei Kirillovich. "I have been wanting to tell you," she said to him, "You behaved wrongly, very wrongly."

"Do you suppose I don't know that I've acted wrongly?" he replied. "But who was the cause of my doing so?"

"What do you say that to me for?" she said, glancing severely at him.

"You know what I say these things for," Vronsky answered boldly and joyfully, meeting her glance and not dropping his eyes.

"That only shows you have no heart," said Anna to Vronsky, but her eyes said that she knew he had a heart, and that was why she was afraid of him.

"Ah! There we are!" said the ambassador's wife, and a new fusillade sung out from the device, its full force this time striking Marionetta's leg; the robot cried out in alarm at the fresh round of pain.

"What you spoke of just now was a mistake, and not love."

"Remember that I have forbidden you to utter that word, that hateful word," said Anna with a shudder, overcome both by the conversation and the wash of empathy she was experiencing meanwhile for this poor decom; she reached out for Android Karenina's hand to steady herself. "I have long meant to tell you this! I've come on purpose this evening, knowing I should meet you. I have come to tell you that this must end. I have never blushed before anyone, and you force me to feel to blame for something."

He looked at her and was struck by a new spiritual beauty in her face. "I . . . ," he began, but Anna interrupted: "I can't abide this any longer!" And, dropping Android Karenina's hand, she herself jumped in front of the reverberating bolt-shots, protecting Marionetta's body with her own, and hollering into the robot's face: "*Move, Move*! Move, Marionetta! You may move!"

The robot danced away, the ambassador's wife stopped shooting, and the room was suddenly terribly silent and still, as everyone grasped what had happened; the game was over, and Anna was hurt. She clutched at her leg, rolled onto her back and grimaced in pain.

"I didn't . . . it was not my intention . . ." stammered Princess Betsy, while Count Vronsky rushed to Anna Arkadyevna's side, crouched over her, quickly and expertly cutting off her boot with his crackle dagger and examining the electrical burn. At the same time, Android Karenina crouched over Marionetta, running her hands along the body of the other robot, enacting a dozen small solderings, activating the other bot's self-repair mechanisms. The rest of the partygoers milled about, discussing in low voices the singular event they had witnessed—a human interceding, even placing herself in danger, to save a robot!

While Vronsky tended to Anna's wound he whispered desperately in her ear, "What do you wish of me?"

"I want you to go to Moscow and ask for Kitty's forgiveness," she said.

"You don't wish that?" he said.

He saw she was saying what she forced herself to say, not what she wanted to say.

"If you love me, as you say," she whispered, "do so that I may be at peace."

His face grew radiant.

"Don't you know that you're all my life to me? But I know no peace, and I can't give it to you. All myself—and love . . . yes. I can't think of you and myself apart. You and I are one to me. And I see no chance before us of peace for me or for you. I see a chance of despair, of wretchedness . . . or I see a chance of bliss, what bliss! . . . Can it be there's no chance of it?" he murmured with his lips; but she heard.

She strained every effort of her mind to say what ought to be said. But instead of that she let her eyes rest on him, full of love, and made no answer.

It's come! he thought in ecstasy. *When I was beginning to despair, and it seemed there would be no end—it's come! She loves me! She owns it!*

"Then do this for me: never say such things to me, and let us be friends," she said in words; but her eyes spoke quite differently.

"Friends we shall never be, you know that yourself. Whether we shall be the happiest or the most wretched of people—that's in your hands."

She would have said something, but he interrupted her.

"I ask one thing only: I ask for the right to hope, to suffer as I do," he said as he tied off his handkerchief and smoothed down the hem of her dress over the tidy makeshift bandage. "But if even that cannot be, command me to disappear, and I shall disappear. You shall not see me if my presence is distasteful to you."

"I don't want to drive you away."

"Only don't change anything, leave everything as it is," he said in a shaky voice. "Here's your husband."

At that instant Alexei Alexandrovich did in fact walk into the room with his calm, awkward gait, his robotic right eye turning slowly in his head, scanning everyone in all corners of the room. Lupo, who had been curled up in the corner, waiting loyally for his master to conclude his conversation, slunk hurriedly away.

Glancing at his wife and Vronsky, Alexei Alexandrovich went up to the lady of the house, and sitting down for a cup of tea, began talking in his deliberate, always audible voice, in his habitual tone of banter, laced with menace.

"Your Rambouillet is in full conclave," he said, looking round at all the party, "the graces and the muses."

But Princess Betsy could not endure that tone of his—"sneering," as she called it, using the English word, and like a skillful hostess she at once brought him into a serious conversation on the subject of universal conscription. Alexei Alexandrovich was immediately interested in the subject, and began seriously defending the Ministry's latest decree against Princess Betsy, who had attacked it.

Vronsky and Anna still sat at the little table.

"This is indecorous," whispered one lady, with an expressive glance at Madame Karenina, Vronsky, and her husband.

"What did I tell you?" said Anna's friend.

Not only those ladies, but almost everyone in the room, even Princess Myakaya and Betsy herself, looked several times in the direction of these two, withdrawn from the general circle, as though that were a disturbing fact. Alexei Alexandrovich was the only person who did not once look in that direction, having entered into an interesting discussion elsewhere in the room.

Noticing the disagreeable impression that was being made on everyone, Princess Betsy slipped someone else into her place to listen to Alexei Alexandrovich, and went up to Anna.

"I'm always amazed at the clearness and precision of your husband's language," she said.

"Oh, yes!" said Anna. She crossed over to the big table and took part in the general conversation.

Alexei Alexandrovich, after staying half an hour, went up to his wife and suggested that they should go home together. But she answered, not looking at him, that she was staying for supper. Alexei Alexandrovich made his bows and withdrew.

After supper, Madame Karenina at last excused herself, and found her streamlined II/Coachman/47-T outside, chilled with the cold. A II/Footman/C(c)43 stood opening the carriage door. The II/Porter/7e62 stood holding open the great door of the house. Android Karenina, with her dexterous metal fingers, was unfastening the lace of her mistress's sleeve caught in the hook of her fur cloak, and averting her faceplate while, with bent head, Anna listened to the words Vronsky murmured as he escorted her down.

"You've said nothing, of course, and I ask nothing," he was saying, "but you know that friendship's not what I want: that there's only one happiness in life for me, that word that you dislike so . . . yes, love! . . . "

"Love," Anna repeated slowly, feeling the painful burn on her calf. "Love." (Later, as she fell asleep that night, Anna thought she remembered hearing Android Karenina say it too— *"love"*—though of course this was impossible: her dear beloved-companion had no capacity to speak, no Vox-Em at all.)

"I don't like the word," she said to Vronsky. "I don't like it that it means too much to me, far more than you can understand," and she glanced into his face. *"Au revoir!"*

She gave him her hand, and with her rapid, springy step she passed by the II/Porter/7e62 and vanished into the carriage.

Her glance, the touch of her hand, set him aflame. He kissed the palm of his hand where she had touched it. Lupo reared back and bayed his artificial bay, almost but not quite real, up toward the light of the full moon, as if in greeting to the people who lived there.

CHAPTER 4

I T WAS NOT TRUE, as the wagging tongues at Princess Betsy's would have it, that the members of the Higher Branches, those who had ascended to the highest ranks of service in the Ministry, had eschewed Class III companion robots. In fact their experiments, experiments hidden from most of the world, had been quietly advancing the art of robotic engineering, so much so that a new generation of Class IIIs had been born, as yet unknown to the public.

Alexei Alexandrovich's Class III, for example, was his Face. That cold sheath of metal that covered the right front portion of his skull, which people (including his wife) assumed existed for purely cosmetic reasons, was in fact a servomechanism of the most advanced technological achievement, with which he communed directly, using not his voice but the synapses of his brain. It was a Thinking Machine, quite literally, for Alexei Alexandrovich did not rely upon his Class III to pour him tea or carry his suitcases, but rather to help him reason out those problems that confronted him in his work—that is to say, the most crucial questions of Russian life.

Lately, though, Alexei Alexandrovich's Face had been evolving to better serve its master, exactly as all Class IIIs were designed to do; its counsel had begun to extend, for example, past professional considerations into personal issues as well. So, though Alexei Alexandrovich had seen nothing striking or improper in the fact that his wife was sitting with Vronsky at a table apart, in eager conversation with him about something, his Face disagreed, and suggested to him in the carriage on the way home that there was something in the relationship that was striking and improper, and for that reason it seemed to him too to be improper. He made up his mind that he must speak of it to his wife.

On reaching home Alexei Alexandrovich went to his study, as he usually did, seated himself in his low chair, activated a chitator relating to tank-tread construction at the place where he had paused it, and listened till one o'clock, just as he usually did. At his usual time he got up and made his toilet for the night. Anna Arkadyevna had not yet come in. With a book under his arm he went upstairs. But this evening, instead of his usual thoughts and meditations upon official details, his thoughts were absorbed by his wife and something disagreeable connected with her. Contrary to his usual habit, he did not get into bed, but fell to walking up and down the rooms with his hands clasped behind his back. He could not go to bed, feeling that it was absolutely needful for him first to think thoroughly over the position that had just arisen.

When Alexei Alexandrovich had made up his mind that he must talk to his wife about it, it had seemed a very easy and simple matter. But now, when he began to think over the question that had just presented itself, it seemed to him very complicated and difficult.

I am not jealous, of course, he thought.

OH?

This was the Face. Its voice appeared in Alexei Alexandrovich's mind, as clear and strong as if he were in conversation with another man, though no one could hear it but he.

No. Jealousy according to my notions is an insult to one's wife, and one ought to have confidence in one's wife.

AND YOU HAVE NO SUCH LACK OF CONFIDENCE. The Face's tone was decidedly neutral, implying no opinion.

"Yes," Alexei Alexandrovich replied aloud. "For though my conviction that jealousy is a shameful feeling and that one ought to feel confidence has not broken down—I feel that I was standing face to face—"

AS IT WERE.

"Yes, very clever, face to face, as it were, with something illogical and irrational, and I do not know what is to be done."

INDEED. FOR YOU STAND FACE TO FACE WITH LIFE, WITH THE POSSIBILITY OF YOUR WIFE'S LOVING SOMEONE OTHER THAN YOU, AND THIS FEELS IRRATIONAL AND INCOMPREHENSIBLE.

Alexei Alexandrovich silently contemplated this position, and the Face remained silent as well. All his life he had lived and worked in official spheres having to do with the reflection of life. And every time he had stumbled against life itself he had shrunk away from it. Now he experienced a feeling akin to that of a man who, while calmly crossing a precipice by a bridge, should suddenly discover that the bridge is broken, and that there is a chasm below. That chasm was life itself, the bridge that artificial life in which Alexei Alexandrovich had lived. His focus had been on his work, on the innovations in technology and weaponry, in physi-olography and transportation—those innovations so crucial to his beloved country's continued advancement, to protect her from her enemies.

Now, for the first time, the question presented itself to him of the possibility of his wife's loving someone else, and he was horrified at it.

He did not undress, but walked up and down with his regular tread over the resounding parquet of the dining room, where one *lumière* shone bright, over the carpet of the dark drawing room, in which the light was reflected on the big new portrait of himself hanging over the sofa, and across her boudoir, where two *lumières* glowed, lighting up the portraits of her parents and woman friends, and the pretty knickknacks of her table, that he knew so well. He walked across her boudoir to the bed-room door, and turned back again. At each turn in his walk, especially at the parquet of the lighted dining room, he halted and announced to his Face, "Yes, this I must decide and put a stop to; I must express my view of it and my decision."

BUT EXPRESS WHAT? WHAT DECISION? the Face asked innocently, and Alexei Alexandrovich had no ready reply.

"But after all," Alexei added, "what has occurred? Nothing!"

NOTHING?

He hesitated. "Yes. *Nothing*. She was talking a long while with him. But what of that? Surely women in society can talk to whom they please. And then, jealousy means lowering both myself and her."

For some reason Alexei remembered at this moment Sarkovich, the underling from his department who had made impertinent overtures to Anna. Alexei had not been jealous, for then, as now, he had considered the emotion beneath him. He next recalled, with a twinge of unease, how he had later found the man out to be a Janus. Or, rather, the Face—having performed unbidden the relevant set of analyses—had discovered that the man was a spy for UnConSciya, Alexei Alexandrovich had announced the finding, and Sarkovich had been appropriately punished.

For some reason this led Alexei Alexandrovich's restless mind to a more recent recollection—the encounter at the Grav station with Vronsky and his incessantly barking Class III. He had been thinking how much he wished the animal would be quiet, had even been saying to himself: *Quiet. Quiet!* And then, echoing through the chambers of his mind came the Face repeating the same word: **QUIET!**

And the next moment the irritating canine Class III had been lying on the floor of the Grav station, quivering and stricken.

Now, shaking these reflections away, postponing their analysis for another time, he entered the dining room of his house and said aloud, "Yes, I must decide and put a stop to it, and express my view of it. . . . "

DECIDE HOW? HOW MUST WE DECIDE?

But Alexei's thoughts, like his body, went round a complete circle, without coming upon anything new. He noticed this, rubbed his forehead, and sat down in Anna's boudoir.

And the worst of it all, he thought, *is that just now, at the very moment when my great work is approaching completion*—he was thinking of the long-term project for Class III improvement, a project of which the Face represented but the first phase—*when I stand in need of all my mental peace and all my energies, just now this stupid worry should fall foul of me. But what's to be done? I'm not one of those men who submit to uneasiness and worry without having the force of character to face them.*

HERE IS WHAT YOU MUST DO, pronounced the Face in a calming, even fatherly tone. **YOU MUST THINK IT OVER, COME TO A DECISION, AND PUT IT OUT OF YOUR MIND.**

There was the sound of a carriage driving up to the front door. Alexei Alexandrovich halted in the middle of the room.

CHAPTER 5

ANNA CAME IN with hanging head, with Android Karenina at her heels, glowing an easy nighttime red-orange glow. On seeing her husband, Anna raised her head and smiled, as though she had just woken up.

"You're not in bed? What a wonder!" she said, letting fall her hood, and without stopping, she went on into the dressing room. "It's late, Alexei Alexandrovich," she said, when she had gone through the doorway.

"Anna, it's necessary for me to have a talk with you."

"With me?" she said, wonderingly. She came out from behind the door of the dressing room, and looked at him. His one human eye blinked back, while the mechanical iris of the other dilated with a barely audible whir, adjusting automatically to the room's semidarkness. "Why, what is it? What about?" she asked, sitting down. "Well, let's talk, if it's so necessary. But it would be better to get to sleep."

Anna said what came to her lips, and marveled, hearing herself, at her own capacity for lying. How simple and natural were her words, and how likely that she was simply sleepy! She felt herself clad in an impenetrable force field of falsehood.

"Anna, I must warn you," he began, and flicked Android

Karenina—*her* Class III—into Surcease, exercising a crude patriarchal prerogative that caused Anna's eyes to widen with startlement. The warm glow that Android Karenina had been shedding snapped off, plunging the room into a preternatural gloom.

"Warn me?" Anna said, when she had recovered from the start of surprise. "Of what?"

She looked at him so simply, so brightly, that anyone who did not know her as her husband knew her could not have noticed anything unnatural, in either the sound or the sense of her words. Moving bit by minute bit, his steely oculus scanned every inch of her flesh, gathering in an instant a universe of physiognomic datum points: the subtle flinch of her retinas, her skin's agitated flush. He saw that the inmost recesses of her soul, which had always hitherto lain open before him, were closed against him. More than that, he heard from her tone that she was not even perturbed at that, but, as it were, said straight out to him: *Yes, it's shut up, and so it must be, and will be in the future.* Now he experienced a feeling such as a man might have, returning home and finding his own house locked up.

BUT PERHAPS THE KEY MAY YET BE FOUND, suggested the ever-thinking Face of Alexei Alexandrovich.

"I want to warn you . . ." he said in a low voice, and then found himself embarrassed, unable to continue.

"Yes?"

Alexei Alexandrovich continued, lamely, "To, to warn you of the likelihood of more UnConSciya violence, in the form of koschei. A woman was set upon by a leech-like machine-beast, and had her spinal column pierced and drained of its fluid, as she shopped in the open-air fruit and vegetable market Thursday last."

"Very well," replied Anna Karenina, and smiled with evident relief, as if daring him to continue, to announce the true cause of his vexation.

HAVE STRENGTH, FRIEND ALEXEI. HAVE STRENGTH.

"I want to warn you, too, that through thoughtlessness and lack of caution you may cause yourself to be talked about in society. Your too-an-imated conversation this evening with Count Vronsky—" he enunciated the name firmly and with deliberate emphasis—"attracted attention."

He talked and looked at her laughing eyes, which frightened him now with their impenetrable look.

HAVE STRENGTH.

"You're always like that," Anna answered, as though completely misapprehending him, and, of all he had said, only taking in the last phrase. "One time you don't like my being dull, and another time you don't like my being lively. I wasn't dull. Does that offend you?"

Alexei Alexandrovich shivered, and out of old habit raised a hand before his chin and tapped a neat fingernail against the cold, hard metal of his right cheek.

"Oh, please, don't do that, I so dislike it," she said. "But what is this all about? What do you want of me?"

Alexei Alexandrovich struggled to speak. Indeed, what did he want of her? The answer came from his Class III: **INSTEAD OF DOING WHAT YOU HAD INTENDED—THAT IS TO SAY, WARNING YOUR WIFE AGAINST A MISTAKE IN THE EYES OF THE WORLD—YOU HAVE UNCONSCIOUSLY BECOME AGITATED OVER WHAT WAS THE AFFAIR OF HER CONSCIENCE.**

Yes. Why, that is it precisely.

YOU STRUGGLE AGAINST THE BARRIER YOU FANCY BETWEEN YOU.

Alexei drew strength from the calm counsel of his Face, and he continued. "This is what I meant to say to you, and I beg you to listen to it. I consider jealousy, as you know, a humiliating and degrading feeling, and I shall never allow myself to be influenced by it; but there are certain rules of decorum that cannot be disregarded with impunity. This evening it was not *I* who observed it, but judging by the impression made on the company, everyone observed that your conduct and deportment were not altogether what could be desired."

"I positively don't understand," said Anna, shrugging her shoulders, believing that it was other people who had upset him, the fact that they had noticed it. "You're not well, Alexei Alexandrovich," she said, and she got up, and would have gone toward the door, but for a strange, thick power that suddenly welled up in the atmosphere around her, like invisible fingers of fog, holding her body in place. She gasped, and looked to Alexei Alexandrovich.

He for his part saw that his wife had stopped by the door, and was gladdened, and felt she had done so because she was now willing to listen to reason. For in the previous moment he had been silently willing her to do so: he had been thinking, *Stop, Anna, do stop, try and understand what I ask of you.* He did not understand that this will had been translated, somehow, into physical reality—that it was the force of his desire holding her in place.

When she looked at her husband, Anna saw that the natural portion of his face had a most relaxed, calm expression, and was even smiling; while the metal half was alive with movement, glowing with a weird grey-green light. The thin lines of groznium that laced his faceplate were pulsing furiously, as if they were rushing veins, alive with the movement of blood. Anna forced herself to remain calm, and idly began taking out her hairpins, as if no queer thickening of the air around her were holding her in place where she stood.

"Well, I'm listening to what's to come," she said, calmly and ironically, "and indeed I listen with interest, for I should like to understand what's the matter."

She spoke, and marveled at the confident, calm, and natural tone in which she was speaking, and the choice of the words she used.

"To enter into all the details of your feelings I have no right, and besides, I regard that as useless and even harmful," began Alexei Alexandrovich. As he continued, she slowly, slowly felt the pressure around her release like a fist unclenching, and that she could again move normally. "Ferreting in one's soul, one often ferrets out something that might have lain there unnoticed. Your feelings are an affair of your own conscience; but I am in duty bound to you, to myself, and to God, to point out to you your duties. Our life has been joined, not by man, but by God, blessed in the eyes of Mother Russia, and sanctified by the Ministry. That union can only be severed by a crime, and a crime of that nature brings its own chastisement."

"I don't understand a word. And, oh dear! How sleepy I am, unluckily," she said, rapidly passing her hand through her hair, feeling for the remaining hairpins.

"Anna, for God's sake, don't speak like that," he said gently. "Perhaps I am mistaken, but believe me, what I say, I say as much for myself as for you. I am your husband, and I love you."

For an instant the mocking gleam in her eyes died away, but the word "love" threw her into revolt again. She thought: *Love? Can he love? If he hadn't heard there was such a thing as love, he would never have used the word. He doesn't even know what love is.* She looked longingly at the still-Surceased Android Karenina, wishing for the warm comfort of her activated eyebank.

"Alexei Alexandrovich, really I don't understand," she said. "Define what it is you find . . . "

"Pardon, let me say all I have to say." The pulsating movement along the thin lines of the Face had stopped now, Anna noted fleetingly, and again the thing upon her husband's skull was a simple cold mask of silver. "I love you. But I am not speaking of myself; the most important persons in this matter are our son and yourself. It may very well be, I repeat, that my words seem to you utterly unnecessary and out of place; it may be that they are called forth by my mistaken impression. In that case, I beg you to forgive me. But if you are conscious yourself of even the smallest foundation for them, then I beg you to think a little, and if your heart prompts you, to speak out to me. . . . "

"I have nothing to say. And besides," she said hurriedly, with difficulty repressing a smile, "it's really time to be in bed."

Alexei Alexandrovich sighed, and, without saying more, went into the bedroom.

* * *

From that time a new life began for Alexei Alexandrovich and for his wife. Nothing special happened. Anna went out into society, as she had always done, was particularly often at Princess Betsy's, and met Vronsky everywhere. Alexei Alexandrovich saw this, but could do nothing. Prompted by occasional reminders that appeared in his mind, issued in the dispassionate voice of the Face, he made continual efforts to draw her into open discussion, all of which she confronted with a barrier that he could not penetrate, made up of a sort of amused perplexity.

Outwardly everything was the same, but their inner relations were completely changed. Alexei Alexandrovich, a man of great power in the Higher Branches of the Ministry, great power in the world of politics, felt himself helpless in this. Like a decommissioned Class II, awaiting its destruction, he submissively awaited the blow that he felt was lifted over him. Every time he began to think about it, he felt that he must try once more, that by kindness, tenderness, and persuasion there was still hope of saving her, of bringing her back to herself, and every day he made ready to talk to her. But every time he began talking to her, he felt that the spirit of evil and deceit, which had taken possession of her, had possession of him too, and he talked to her in a tone quite unlike that in which he had meant to talk. Involuntarily he talked to her in his habitual tone of jeering at anyone who should say what he was saying. And in that tone it was impossible to say what needed to be said to her.

CHAPTER 6

THAT WHICH FOR VRONSKY had been, for almost a whole year, the one absorbing desire of his life, replacing all his old desires; that which for Anna had been an impossible, terrible, and for that reason even more entrancing dream of bliss; that desire had been fulfilled. They were alone, entirely alone; their respective Class IIIs were not present. By unspoken agreement, they had left them behind as each traveled to the place of assignation, for robots were barred from viewing this most human of phenomena.

Vronsky stood before her, pale, his lower jaw quivering, and besought her to be calm, not knowing how or why.

"Anna! Anna!" he said with a choking voice, "Anna, for pity's sake . . . !"

But the louder he spoke, the lower she dropped her once proud and gay, now shame-stricken head, and she bowed down and sank from the sofa where she was sitting, down on the floor, at his feet; she would have fallen on the carpet if he had not held her.

"My God! Forgive me!" she said, sobbing, pressing his hands to her bosom.

She felt so sinful, so guilty, that nothing was left for her but to humiliate herself and beg forgiveness; and as now there was no one in her life but him, to him she addressed her prayer for forgiveness. Looking at him, she had a physical sense of her humiliation, and she could say nothing more. He felt what a murderer must feel when he sees the body he has robbed of life. That body, robbed by him of life, was their love, the first stage of their love. There was something awful and revolting in the memory of what had been bought at this fearful price of shame. Shame at their spiritual nakedness crushed her and infected him. But in spite of all the murderer's horror before the body of his victim, he must hack it to pieces, hide the body, must use what he has gained by his murder.

And with fury, as it were with passion, the murderer falls on the body, and drags it and hacks at it; so he covered her face and shoulders with kisses. She held his hand, and did not stir.

"Yes, these kisses—that is what has been bought by this shame. Yes, and one hand, which will always be mine—the hand of my accomplice." She lifted up that hand and kissed it. He sank on his knees and tried to see her face; but she hid it, and said nothing. At last, as though making an effort over herself, she got up and pushed him away. Her face was still as beautiful, but it was only the more pitiful for that.

"All is over," she said. "I have nothing but you. Remember that."

"I can never forget what is my whole life. For one instant of this happiness . . . "

"Happiness!" she said with horror. She felt that at that moment she could not put into words the sense of shame, of rapture, and of horror at stepping into a new life, and she did not want to speak of it, to vulgarize this feeling with inappropriate words. "For pity's sake, not a word, not a—"

As if to underscore her determination for him to be silent, Anna stopped speaking midway through her sentence. Indeed, Vronsky realized, it was not only her lovely mouth but her entire body: Anna had stopped moving, her body locked in place, eyes half-open, limbs stilled, frozen like a statue upon the bed.

"Anna?" he cried out. "Anna! What is the matter?"

It is he, Vronsky thought immediately, meaning the husband—*her bizarre and cruel husband has discovered us, and somehow poisoned her . . .* but this was something stranger and more powerful than any poison: for as Vronsky watched, Anna's body, still frozen like it was carved from marble, rose slowly several inches off the bed and oscillated wildly in the air.

"Anna!"

He reached toward her with a shaking hand, unsure of how to proceed, ashamed to admit to himself that he was afraid even to touch her—when, as suddenly as this extraordinary episode had begun, it ended. Anna's body stopped quivering, fell back softly onto the mattress, and reanimated; indeed, Anna returned to their conversation exactly where she had stopped.

"—a word more," she concluded, while Vronsky stared back at her, trying to comprehend what he had witnessed.

"Anna," he finally began. "Anna, I . . . "

But it was too late. With a look of chill despair, incomprehensible to him, she parted from him.

*   *   *

In dreams, when she had no control over her thoughts, her position presented itself to her in all its hideous nakedness. One dream haunted her almost every night. She dreamed that both were her husbands at once, that both were lavishing caresses on her. Alexei Alexandrovich was weeping, kissing her hands, and saying, "How happy we are now!" And Alexei Vronsky was there too, and he *too* was her husband. And Lupo was also there, prowling in circles, sniffing the tangled bedsheets; and Alexei's metal Face was there, glinting in the light of the *lumiéres*; and then Anna, glancing down, saw that while she embraced Vronsky, her own human head had been fused somehow onto Android Karenina's gleaming robot body.

This dream weighed on her like a nightmare, and she awoke from it in terror.

CHAPTER 7

I N THE EARLY DAYS after his return from Moscow, whenever Levin shuddered and grew red, remembering the disgrace of his rejection, he said to himself: *This was just how I used to shudder and blush, thinking myself utterly lost, when I was plucked in physics and did not get my remove; and how I thought myself utterly ruined after I built that first surface mine and it collapsed. And yet, now that years have passed, I recall it and wonder that it could distress me so much. It will be the same thing too with this trouble. Time will go by and I shall not mind about this either.*

But three months had passed and he had not left off minding about it; and it was as painful for him to think of it as it had been those first days. He could not be at peace because after dreaming so long of family life, and feeling himself so ripe for it, he was still not married, and was further than ever from marriage.

Meanwhile spring came on, beautiful and kindly, without the delays and treacheries of spring—one of those rare springs in which plants, beasts, and man rejoice alike. This lovely spring roused Levin still more, and strengthened him in his resolution of renouncing all his past and building up his lonely life firmly and independently.

One day, as he rode up to the house in this happy frame of mind, Levin heard the bell ring at the side of the principal entrance of the house.

"Yes, that's someone from the station," he said to Socrates. "Just the time to be here from the Moscow Grav. . . . Who could it be? What if it's brother Nikolai? He did say: 'Maybe I'll go to the waters, or maybe I'll come down to you.'"

He felt dismayed and vexed for the first minute, that his brother Nikolai's presence should come to disturb his happy mood of spring. But he felt ashamed of the feeling, and at once he opened, as it were, the arms of his soul, and with a softened feeling of joy and expectation, now he hoped with all his heart that it was his brother. He pricked up his horse, and riding out from behind the acacias he saw a hired three-horse sledge from the Grav station, and a gentleman in a fur coat.

"Ah," cried Levin joyfully, flinging up both his hands. "Here's a delightful visitor! Ah, how glad I am to see you!" he shouted, recognizing Stepan Arkadyich, with Small Stiva balanced like a fat, happy child between his legs.

"Now you shall find out for certain whether she's married, or when she's going to be married," Socrates muttered to him with a cautious tone, anxious to protect his master's feelings. But on that delicious spring day Levin felt that the thought of Kitty did not hurt him at all.

"Well, you didn't expect me, eh?" said Stepan Arkadyich, getting out of the sledge, splashed with mud on the bridge of his nose, on his cheek, and on his eyebrows, but radiant with health and good spirits. "I've come to see you in the first place," he said, embracing and kissing him, while Socrates plucked an air-blasting end-effector to clean the mud from Small Stiva's frontal display. "To participate in the Hunt-and-be-Hunted second, and to sell that little patch of soil at Ergushovo third."

Stepan Arkadyich told him many interesting pieces of news, but not one word in reference to Kitty and the Shcherbatskys; he merely gave him greetings from his wife. Levin was grateful to him for his delicacy and was very glad of his visitor. As always happened with him during his solitude, a mass of ideas and feelings had been accumulating within him, which he could not communicate to those about him. And now he poured out upon Stepan Arkadyich his poetic joy in the spring, and his failures and plans for the seasonal extraction. Stepan Arkadyich, always charming, understanding everything at the slightest reference, was particularly charming on this visit, and Levin noticed in him a special tenderness, as it were, and a new tone of respect that flattered him.

They determined that they would Hunt-and-be-Hunted the very next day, and Levin ordered the Huntbears to be warmed and baited overnight.

CHAPTER 8

THE PLACE FIXED ON for the Hunt-and-be-Hunted was not far above a stream in a little aspen copse. On reaching the copse, Levin led Oblonsky to a corner of a mossy, swampy glade, already quite free from snow. He went back himself to a double birch tree on the other side, and leaning his gun on the fork of a dead lower branch, he took off his full overcoat, fastened his belt again, and worked his arms to see if they were free.

The sun was setting behind a thick forest, and in the glow of sunset the birch trees, dotted about in the aspen copse, stood out clearly with their hanging twigs, and their buds swollen almost to bursting. Levin sighed with contentment, for the Hunt-and-be-Hunted was to him the ideal way to spend a day: shooting at grackles and geese with one's old-fashioned cartridge rifle, while simultaneously trying to escape the claws of the heat-seeking, man-chasing mechanical monsters called Huntbears.

How, Levin had long wondered, had hunting ever held the slightest enchantment before the introduction of the Huntbears?

From the thickest parts of the copse, where the snow still remained, came the faint sound of narrow, winding threads of water running away. Tiny birds twittered, and now and then fluttered from tree to tree. They heard the rustle of last year's leaves, stirred by the thawing of the earth and the growth of the grass. Small Stiva optimized his aural and optical sensors, rotating his head unit nervously around and around; he loathed the Hunt-and-be-Hunted, and envied Socrates, who had been left at the estate doing bookkeeping.

"Imagine! One can hear and see the grass growing!" Levin said, noticing a wet, slate-colored aspen leaf moving beside a blade of young grass. Oblonsky laughed gaily at this observation, and then Small Stiva beeped shrilly six times, the birds fled in one urgent fluttering cloud, and the Huntbear thundered into the copse. The huge mechanized bear, over eight feet high, crashed toward them with great, lumbering steps, opening its gaping mouth to display two rows of oversize teeth. Levin, even as he leveled his rifle at the thing, admired the simple but effective craftsmanship; the Bear looked not so much like a real bear as like a child's rendering of a bear, with massively exaggerated paws and fangs.

Oblonsky, rattled, fired first but wildly, and most of his cartridge rounds ended up in the surrounding trees, or tinged harmlessly off the Huntbear's thick groznium legs. While the Huntbear advanced another crashing step toward them, Small Stiva skittered off into the cover of the undergrowth.

Levin, calmly taking aim at the thrashing beast, noticed for the first time that the Huntbear was accompanied by a cub—a nice naturalistic touch. He would try to remember to thank his groundskeeper for providing an especially delightful day's Hunt-and-be-Hunted.

Levin shot once and missed. The Huntbear swatted Oblonsky with the back of its paw, hard enough to knock him down but not to kill; Oblonsky cried out in genuine terror—like most first-time Hunt-and-be-Hunters, he forgot in the heat of the action that Huntbears were programmed with the Iron Laws and so could never do real harm to humans.

Levin shot again and scored a clean hit in the belly of the beast— the ursine robot monster reared back in simulated pain. At that moment, a hawk flew high over a forest far away with a slow sweep of its wings, and another flew with exactly the same motion in the same direction and vanished. The Huntbear paused in its rampage, its sensors distracted by the graceful black swoop of the hawk, and Levin took his opportunity:

he fired his rifle exactly four times, with deadly precision—bang, bang, bang, bang—alternating, one shot to bring down a hawk, one shot in the right eye of the Bear, one for the other hawk, one for the other eye.

Birds twittered more and more loudly and busily in the neighboring thicket. An owl hooted not far off. The Bear, its brain circuits shattered by Levin's shots, clattered to the ground like a fallen tree. Oblonsky hesitantly rose to his feet, laughing with easy good humor at his momentary panic, just as Small Stiva emerged from the bush clutching both dead hawks with the pincer of a single end-effector.

* * *

The Hunt-and-be-Hunted was capital. Stepan Arkadyich shot two more birds and Levin two, of which one was not found. It began to get dark. Venus, bright and silvery, shone with her soft light low in the west behind the birch trees, and Levin gazed happily at the planet with a loving look, wondering why the sight, which he had seen so many times before, should inspire in him such a sense of pleasure and calm.

The snipe had ceased flying; but Levin resolved to stay a little longer, till Venus, which he saw below a branch of birch, should be above it. Then Venus had risen above the branch, yet still he waited.

"Isn't it time to go home?" said Stepan Arkadyich.

It was quite still now in the copse, and not a bird was stirring.

"Let's stay a little while," answered Levin.

"As you like."

They were standing now about fifteen paces from one another.

"Stiva!" said Levin unexpectedly. "How is it you don't tell me whether your sister-in-law's married yet, or when she's going to be?"

Levin felt so resolute and serene that no answer, he fancied, could affect him. But he had never dreamed of what Stepan Arkadyich replied.

"She's never thought of being married, and isn't thinking of it; but she's very ill, and the doctors have sent her into orbit around Venus."

Venus. Levin stared up again at the distant body, and felt its tug upon his heart.

"They're positively afraid she may not live."

"What!" cried Levin. "Very ill? What is wrong with her? How has she . . . ?"

Before he could inquire further into her condition, at that very instant both suddenly heard a shrill whistle which, as it were, smote on their ears; it was Small Stiva, bleating out the alarm again. Both suddenly seized their guns and two flashes gleamed as they pumped a combined seventeen rounds into the tiny groznium body of the Huntbear cub.

They stood together over the smoldering heap of the fallen Huntbear, flushed with pleasure at the unexpected victory, each humorously blaming the other for having forgotten about the cub.

"Splendid! Together!" cried Levin. *Oh, yes, what was it that was unpleasant?* he wondered. *Yes, Kitty's ill. . . . Well, it can't be helped; I'm very sorry*, he thought.

*   *   *

They tromped back to Levin's estate, and did not see that, as soon as they turned their backs, a head like that of a worm, only closer in size to a dog's head, emerged from the rough forest ground as if from a tunnel; and they did not see this worm head open a grotesque, gaping mouth and suck up the shattered groznium skeleton of the Huntbear cub, before disappearing again beneath the earth's surface.

CHAPTER 9

LTHOUGH ALL VRONSKY'S INNER LIFE was absorbed in
his passion, his external life unalterably and inevitably followed
along the old accustomed lines of his social and regimental ties and interests. The interests of his regiment, the Circling Hawks of the Borderland,
took an important place in Vronsky's life, both because he was fond of
the regiment, and because his regiment was fond of him. They were not
only fond of Vronsky in his regiment, they respected him too, and
were proud of him; proud that this man, with his immense wealth, his
brilliant education and abilities, and the path open before him to every
kind of success, distinction, and ambition, had disregarded all that, and
of all the interests of life had the interests of his Border regiment and his
comrades nearest to his heart. Vronsky was aware of his comrades' view
of him, and in addition to his liking for the life, he felt bound to keep
up that reputation.

It need not be said that he did not speak of his love to any of his
comrades, nor did he betray his secret even in the wildest drinking bouts
(though indeed he was never so drunk as to lose all control of himself). And he shut up any of his thoughtless comrades who attempted
to allude to his connection. But in spite of that, his love was known to
all the town; everyone guessed with more or less confidence at his relations with Madame Karenina. The majority of the younger men envied
him for just what was the most irksome factor in his love—the exalted
position of Karenin, and the consequent publicity of their connection in
society. Only a few of the younger members, men who harbored half-
secret jealousies of Vronsky's rank and ambition, whispered that such an

assignation—to the wife of a man in the secretive world of the Higher Branches—might carry dangers beyond that attending to a commonplace adulterous intrigue.

Besides the service and society, Vronsky had another great interest—the annual gladiatorial contest, known as the Cull, by which advancement in the regiment was determined. He was passionately fond of these contests, had done particularly well in the last, and looked forward with savage glee to the next, which was now rapidly approaching.

The contest took place in a great arena, witnessed by vast crowds of spectators. Every member of the regiment donned their own customized, death-dealing, armor-plated suit known as an Exterior, and entered into mass free-for-all combat, man against man against man, until the weaker ones were destroyed. Those that emerged victorious—as Vronsky, so far, always had—earned not only glory but advancement in rank.

That year's intra-regimental Exterior battle had been arranged for the officers and was rapidly approaching. In spite of his love affair, he was looking forward to the match with intense, though reserved, excitement.

These two passions did not interfere with one another. On the contrary, he needed occupation and distraction quite apart from his love, so as to recruit and rest himself from the violent emotions that agitated him.

CHAPTER 10

A KIND OF METAL SHED known as "the silo" had been put up close to the battle arena, and there Vronsky's Exterior was to have been taken the previous day. He had not yet seen her there. During the last few days he had not ridden her out for practice himself, and so now he positively did not know in what condition his Exterior had arrived yesterday and was in today.

Vronsky was justifiably proud of his Exterior, Frou-Frou, which he had built and modified to his tastes, in consultation with a brilliant English engineer whom he retained as *mécanicien* at great cost. Frou-Frou's every movement was controlled by Vronsky, encased inside her, his body attached to her delicate sensory system by dozens of wires.

"Well, how's Frou-Frou?" Vronsky asked the engineer in English.

"All right, sir," the Englishman's voice responded somewhere in the inside of his throat. "Come along, then," said the Englishman, frowning and speaking with his mouth shut, and with swinging elbows he went on in front with his disjointed gait.

They went into the little yard in front of the shed. A target boy, trembling a bit in the head-to-toe padded suit he wore, followed them. As they walked through the silo Vronsky knew five other Exteriors stood in their separate stalls, and he knew that Matryoshka, the Exterior belonging to his chief rival, Mahutin, had been brought there, and must be standing among them.

Even more than his own Exterior, Vronsky longed to see Matryoshka, whom he had never seen. But he knew that by the etiquette of the Cull it was not merely impossible for him to see another of the exoskeletons, but improper even to ask questions about it. Just as he was passing along the passage, the boy opened the door into the second stable on the left, and Vronsky caught a glimpse of exactly that fighting machine he was most curious about: Matryoshka was a curiously innocent-looking Exterior, with an immense and rounded bottom, a smaller but equally rounded upper portion, and the crude, clownishly painted face of a bearded old peasant man. He lingered, surprised that Mahutin's Exterior should be so pleasant, even silly looking; then, with the feeling of a man turning away from another man's open letter, he turned round and went into Frou-Frou's stall.

Frou-Frou was an Exterior of medium size, constructed to roughly humanoid shape from a dozen enormous, curved, and overlapping metal plates. He had paid dearly to acquire the masses of groznium alloy required to plate her entire body, and such was the cleverness of her jointures that no enemy ordnance Vronsky had yet encountered could pierce her. As to offensive capability, Frou-Frou was equipped with a trio of rotating heavy-fires set in cones at chest level, plus a grill across the "face" of the machine, from which, when Vronsky wished it, could launch cannonball-sized bursts of globular electricity, directed at the opponent of his choosing.

About all Frou-Frou's figure, and especially her head, there was a certain expression of energy, of overwhelming offensive capability, and yet of softness. Some Exteriors seem only like deadly furniture, large weapons with a hole to climb inside; but Frou-Frou was one of those Exteriors—less than a Class III but more than a simple Class II—which seem not to speak only because they were built without a mouth hole. To Vronsky, at any rate, it seemed that she understood all he felt at that moment as he looked at her.

As soon as Vronsky was attached to the dozen pulse-point electrodes allowing him to communicate with Frou-Frou's control relays, she shifted the massive armor plates at the joints, rotated her eyes in their cavernous ocular cavities, and pointed her three heavy-fires in three different directions.

"There, you see how fidgety she is," said the Englishman.

"There, darling! There!" said Vronsky, speaking soothingly to the suit. "Quiet, darling, quiet!" he said, patting her again over her rear section, which glinted in the dim light of the shed. "Let's give her a go."

In another moment the engineer had opened her metal torso, and Vronsky had climbed inside, attaching the dozen wires to the corresponding input points along Frou-Frou's contact board. Vronsky felt that his heart was throbbing, and that he, too, like the suit, longed to move, to open fire; it was a feeling both dreadful and delicious. As the machine warmed up, and Vronsky felt the familiar delectable tingle of his limbs seeming to merge with the synthetic reflexes of the suit, the target boy made a run for it, but was corralled by Lupo, who growled warningly to hold him at bay until Vronsky was ready to test-fire.

"Please, your Excellency," said the target boy. "Perhaps—"

The Englishman rolled his eyes and walloped him on the back of the head. "It's only a half-power round."

Vronsky, as comfortable in Frou-Frou's familiar confines as a child in the womb, directed his Exterior to shoot, and shoot she did, loosing a jolt of pure electric force from behind the face grill directly at the target boy. Though it was indeed only a half-power jolt, when Vronsky climbed out of the suit and he and the Englishmen stepped from the shed into the sunlight, they left the target boy behind them, his body shivering as he slowly recovered on the rock-hard floor of the silo.

"Well, I rely on you, then," Vronsky said to the Englishman. "Half past six on the ground."

"All right," said the Englishman. "Ah, where are you going, my lord?" he asked suddenly, using the title which he had scarcely ever used before.

Vronsky in amazement raised his head, and stared, as he knew how to stare, not into the Englishman's eyes, but at his forehead, astounded at the impertinence of his question. But realizing that in asking this the Englishman had been looking at him not as an employer, but as a combatant, he answered:

"I've got to pay a visit; I shall be home within an hour." He blushed, a thing which rarely happened to him.

The Englishman looked gravely at him; and, as though he, too, knew where Vronsky was going, he added: "The important thing's to keep quiet before a contest. Don't get out of temper or upset about anything. And watch the roads. The rumor is circulating that UnConSciya has mined the roads around the arena with emotion bombs." Vronsky scowled. Emotion bombs were a nasty business: detonators triggered by mood-based physiological surges in passersby, such as their perspiration chemistry.

"All right," answered Vronsky, and departed, still wearing the set of miniaturized sense-plates attached to his body, with which he would later resume his connection with Frou-Frou—and through which, via vibratory telegraphy, the engineer could monitor his physiological condition until then.

Before he had driven many paces away, the dark clouds that had been threatening rain all day broke, and there was a heavy downpour.

CHAPTER 11

THE RAIN DID NOT last long, and by the time Vronsky arrived at the Karenins' the sun had peeped out again, the roofs of the summer villas and the old lime trees in the gardens on both sides of the principal streets sparkled with wet brilliance, and from the twigs came a pleasant drip and from the roofs rushing streams of water. He thought no more of the shower spoiling the match ground, but was rejoicing now that—thanks to the rain—he would be sure to find her at home and alone, as he knew that Alexei Alexandrovich had not moved from Petersburg.

Hoping to find her alone, Vronsky alighted, as he always did, to avoid attracting attention, before crossing the bridge, and walked to the house. He did not go up the steps to the street door, but went into the court.

"Has your master come?" he asked a *mécanicien*, who was irritatedly tinkering with a maltuned II/Topiary/42-9.

"No, sir. The mistress is at home. But will you please go to the front door; there are II/Footmen/74s there," the *mécanicien* answered. "They'll open the door."

"No, I'll go in from the garden."

And feeling satisfied that she was alone, and wanting to take her by surprise, since he had not promised to be there today, and she would certainly not expect him to come before the match, he walked, with one hand on the handle of his hot-whip, and stepping cautiously over the sandy path bordered with flowers to the terrace that looked out upon the garden. Vronsky forgot now all that he had thought on the way of the hardships and difficulties of their position. He thought of nothing but that he would see her directly, not in imagination, but living, all of her, as she was in reality.

Anna Karenina was sitting on the terrace waiting for the return of her son, who had gone out for his walk and been caught in the rain. She had sent a II/Porter/7e62 and a II/Maid/467 out to scan for him. Dressed in a white gown, deeply embroidered, she was sitting in a corner of the terrace watering some flowers with a Class I water-spritzer, which sensed the precise amount of mist to properly water each individual leaf and stem, and therefore did not hear him. In his Cull undersuit, with the dozen electrodes still attached to various vital points along his body, Vronsky was aware that he must look strange and vulnerable. Bowing her curly black head, she pressed her forehead against a cool watering pot that stood on the parapet, and both her lovely hands, with the rings he knew so well, clasped the pot. The beauty of her whole figure, her head, her neck, her hands, struck Vronsky every time as something new and unexpected. He stood still, gazing at her in ecstasy. His heart palpitated rapidly; at the same moment, away in the battleground silo, the English engineer, monitoring Vronsky's telemetry readings on a Class I physi-olographer, grimaced at the way his pulse was escalating.

But, just as he was about to make a step to come nearer to her, Anna was aware of his presence, pushed away the watering pot, and turned her flushed face toward him.

"What's the matter? You are ill?" he said to her in French, going up to her. He would have run to her, but remembering that there might be spectators, he looked round toward the balcony door, and reddened a little, as he always reddened, feeling that he had to be afraid and be on his guard.

"No, I'm quite well," she said, getting up and pressing his out-stretched hand tightly. "I did not expect . . . thee. What in God's name are you wearing?"

"Mercy! What cold hands!" he said, and quickly he explained the undersuit and the need for his vital signs to be monitored in the hours preceding the Cull.

"You startled me," she said. "I'm alone, and expecting Seryozha. He's out for a walk; they'll come in from this side."

But, in spite of her efforts to be calm, her lips were quivering.

"Forgive me for coming, but I couldn't pass the day without seeing you," he went on, speaking in French, as he always did to avoid using the stiff Russian plural form, so impossibly frigid between them, and the dangerously intimate singular.

"Forgive you? I'm so glad!"

"But you're ill or worried," he went on, not letting go her hands and bending over her. "What were you thinking of?"

"Always the same thing," she said, with a smile, and back in the stable the engineer muttered a curse in English, watching the various needles of his box shoot up into the red.

Anna had spoken the truth. If ever at any moment she had been asked what she was thinking of, she could have answered truly: of the same thing, of her happiness and her unhappiness. She was thinking, just when he came upon her, of this: Why was it that to others it was all easy, while to her it was such torture? Today this thought gained special poignancy from certain other considerations. She asked him about the impending death matches. He answered her questions, and, seeing that she was agitated, trying to calm her, he began telling her in the simplest tone the details of his preparations for the races.

Tell him or not tell him? she thought, looking into his quiet, affectionate eyes. *He is so happy, so absorbed in his upcoming Cull that he won't understand as he ought, he won't understand all the gravity of this fact to us.*

"But you haven't told me what you were thinking of when I came in," he said, interrupting his narrative. "Please tell me!"

She did not answer, and, bowing her head a little, she looked inquiringly at him from under her brows, her eyes shining under their long lashes. Her hand shook as it played with a leaf she had picked. He saw it, and his face expressed that utter subjection, that slavish devotion, which had done so much to win her; the needles on the Englishman's Class I registered the calming effect of adoration on his bloodstream.

"I see something has happened. Do you suppose I can be at peace, knowing you have a trouble I am not sharing? Tell me, for God's sake," he repeated imploringly.

Abruptly Anna rose and walked to Android Karenina, whom Vronsky had not even noticed, sitting perfectly still on the opposite side of the fountain.

"Yes," Anna sighed to her Class III. "I shan't be able to forgive him if he does not realize all the gravity of it. Better not tell; why put him to the test?"

"For God's sake!" he repeated, circling the fountain and taking her hand.

"Shall I tell you?"

"Yes, yes, yes . . . "

But Anna could not bring herself to speak, and it was Android Karenina who revealed to him the truth, without saying a word: holding her two end-effectors interlaced in front of her midsection, she slowly brought them outward and upward, miming the appearance of a growing stomach, heavy with child.

As Android Karenina enacted this dumb show, the leaf in Anna's hand shook more violently, but she did not take her eyes off Vronsky, watching how he would take it. He turned white, would have said something, but stopped; he dropped her hand, and his head sank on his breast. His reaction might have been still more dramatic, had not the Englishman, noting the sudden spiking wildness on his monitor, keyed the right combination of buttons to moderate his heartbeat.

"Yes, he realizes all the gravity of it," Anna said to Android Karenina.

But Anna was mistaken in thinking he felt the weight of the fact in the same way as she, a woman, felt it. What Vronsky felt was that the turning-point he had been longing for had come now; that it was impossible to go on concealing things from her husband, and it was inevitable in one way or another that they should soon put an end to their unnatural position. But, besides that, her emotion physically affected him in the same way. He looked at her with a look of submissive tenderness, kissed her hand, got up, and, in silence, paced up and down the terrace.

"Yes," he said, going up to her resolutely. "Neither you nor I have looked on our relations as a passing amusement, and now our fate is sealed. It is absolutely necessary to put an end"—he looked round as he spoke—"to the deception in which we are living."

"Put an end? How put an end, Alexei?" she said softly.

She was calmer now, and Android Karenina was glowing with an intense but not unpleasant violet, lending a romantic backlight to her mistress's tender expression.

"Leave your husband and make our life one."

"It is one as it is," she answered, scarcely audibly.

"Yes, but altogether, altogether."

"But how, Alexei, tell me how?" she said in melancholy mockery at the hopelessness of her own position. "Is there any way out of such a position? Am I not the wife of my husband?"

"There is a way out of every position. We must take our line," he said. "Anything's better than the position in which you're living. Of course, I see how you torture yourself over everything—the world and your son and your husband."

"Oh, not over my husband," she said, with a quiet smile. "I don't know him, I don't think of him. He doesn't exist."

"You're not speaking sincerely. I know you. You worry about him too."

"Oh, he doesn't even know," she said, and suddenly a hot flush came over her face; her cheeks, her brow, her neck crimsoned, and tears of shame came into her eyes. "But we won't talk of him."

CHAPTER 12

VRONSKY HAD SEVERAL TIMES ALREADY, though not so resolutely as now, tried to bring her to consider their position, and every time he had been confronted by the same superficiality and triviality with which she met his appeal now. It was as though there were something in this that she could not or would not face, as though the moment she began to speak of this, she, the real Anna, retreated some-how into herself, and another strange and unaccountable woman came out, whom he did not love, and whom he feared, and who was in oppo-sition to him. But today he was resolved to have it out.

"Whether he knows or not," said Vronsky, in his usual quiet and resolute tone, "that's nothing to do with us. We cannot . . . you cannot stay like this, especially now."

"What's to be done, according to you?" she asked with the same frivolous irony. She who had so feared he would take her condition too lightly was now vexed with him for deducing from it the necessity of taking some step.

"Tell him everything, and leave him."

"Very well, let us suppose I do that," she said. "Do you know what the result of that would be? I can tell you it all beforehand," and a wicked light gleamed in her eyes, which had been so soft a minute before. "'Eh, you love another man, and have entered into criminal intrigues with him?'" (Mimicking her husband's singular appearance, she covered one side of her face with the flat of her hand). "'I warned you of the results in the religious, the civil, and the domestic relation. You have not listened to me. Now I cannot let you disgrace my name'"—*and my son*, she had meant to say, but about her son she could not jest—"'disgrace my name, and'—and more in the same style," she added. "In general terms, he'll say in his official manner, and with all distinctness and precision, that he cannot let me go, but will take all measures in his power to prevent scandal. And he will calmly and punctually act in accordance with his words. That's what will happen. He's not a man, but a machine, and a spiteful machine when he's angry," she added, recalling Alexei Alexandrovich as she spoke, with all the peculiarities of his figure and manner of speaking and bifurcated apperance, and reckoning against him every defect she could find in him, softening nothing for the great wrong she herself was doing him.

It was then she sensed that Vronsky was not listening, and saw that his eyes were fixed on some spot behind her head.

"The swirling . . . ," he said in a low voice, as if hypnotized, and Anna felt irritated by his lack of attention.

"What?"

"The fountain . . . the swirling. . . . " he repeated, and then with sudden force shouted, "Jump!"

Anna, shocked into action by this sudden urgency, leapt forward from where she sat on the wall of the fountain, landing in a disordered heap at Vronsky's feet; he scrambled forward to grasp as her forearms and pulled as hard as he could. Directly behind her, hovering like a storm cloud over the fountain's swirling waters, was what could only be described as a terrible, undulating *nothingness*: a grey-black hole in the fabric of the atmosphere, wavering in the air above the fountain, and pulling, pulling Anna Karenina in toward itself.

Vronsky gripped her with all his strength, bracing his feet against the wall of the fountain, resisting with all his strength the violent force, ten times stronger than gravity, that was drawing Anna in. Android Karenina joined the struggle, lacing her fingers around Anna's waist and digging in the base of her heels at the base of the fountain wall.

"What . . . what is . . . ," Anna began, and Vronsky answered immediately: "A godmouth!" Anna's skirts billowed up behind her, rustled by the phantasmagoric wind bellowing from the portal. "UnConSciya creates them . . . somehow . . . *oof* . . . "

His fingers slipping a little, Vronsky cursed. "Hold on, Anna. Only hold on, a bit longer . . . it will not last long."

"Let me go," said Anna weakly.

"What?"

"What good is living," she said, louder now, "if our life is to be under *my husband's* control? Let me go!" She directed this last command to Android Karenina, who by virtue of the Iron Laws could not disobey; she turned her faceplate apologetically to Vronsky and released her grasp.

"But, Anna," said Vronsky, renewing his grip and putting steel into his voice, "we simply must, anyway, tell him, and then be guided by the line he takes."

"And what, run away?"

"And why *not* run away?" he shouted desperately. "I don't see how we can keep on like this. And not for my sake—I see that you suffer!"

A fierce wind blew from the terrible depths of the demonic spiral; one of Anna's shoes slipped from her feet and was sucked into the vortex. Vronsky redoubled his efforts to pull her free, nearly dislodging Anna's arm from the socket. He stared over her shoulder at the space-hole still hovering in the air behind her, glowing like the malevolent eye of a hungry beast. One of Anna's hands came loose from his, and she made no effort to let him grab it again. Her body was virtually slack, and he felt she had given up, in her body and her mind, and was ready to be consumed.

"Anna," he pleaded, "do not quit!"

"Yes," she muttered, almost talking to herself. "Run away, become your mistress, and complete the ruin of . . . "

And she would have said "my son," but she could not utter those words—whether because she could not bear to, or because the force on her body was squeezing the very air from her lungs, Vronsky could not say.

Anna thought of her son, pictured his innocent body hovering before the unfathomable grey void behind her, imagined him caught in such a trap. It came to her that *she* had set a trap for him, by falling in love; she thought of his future attitude toward his mother, who had abandoned his father, and she felt such terror at what she had done that she could not face it. She cried out and writhed, and Vronsky lost his grip. The god-mouth widened, like a snake mouth opening to accommodate a rabbit or possum.

It was then that Android Karenina broke the Iron Law of obedience.

Dismissing the earlier command to let go, she grabbed Anna by the waist, and with furious mechanical strength pulled her to safety. Together, mistress and robot landed with a thud on the stones of the fountain, and Anna watched with shaded eyes as the queer dimensional portal *whooshed* shut and disappeared.

For a long moment, Anna stared into the pale purple gleam of Android Karenina's faceplate—and then mouthed the words *thank you*. Android Karenina, as ever, said nothing, only straightened up and motored respectfully away, as Vronsky rushed to his lover's side and placed her head lovingly in his lap.

"I beg you, I entreat you," Anna said, turning her head away from Vronsky's eyes. "Never speak to me of that!"

"To the contrary!" Vronsky began. "I shall not rest until I discover what cell, what madman, would dare to launch such an attack on you—and why—"

"No," said Anna, shaking her head with impatience. "Never speak to me of my becoming your mistress. Of my ruin, and that of . . . "

"But, Anna . . . "

"Never. Leave it to me. I know all the baseness, all the horror of my position; but it's not so easy to arrange as you think. And leave it to me, and do what I say. Never speak to me of it. Do you promise me? . . . No, no, promise!"

"I promise everything, but I can't be at peace, especially after what you have told me. I can't be at peace, when you can't be at peace . . . "

"I?" she repeated. "Yes, I am worried sometimes; but that will pass, if you will never talk about this. When you talk about it—it's only then it worries me."

"I don't understand—" he said.

"I know," she interrupted him, "how hard it is for your truthful nature to lie, and I grieve for you. I often think that you have ruined your whole life for me."

"I was just thinking the very same thing," he said. "How could you sacrifice everything for my sake? I can't forgive myself that you're unhappy!"

"I unhappy?" she said, coming closer to him, and looking at him with an ecstatic smile of love. "I am like a hungry man who has been given food. He may be cold, and dressed in rags, and ashamed, but he is not unhappy. I unhappy? No, this is my unhappiness. . . . "

She could hear the sound of her son's voice coming toward them, and glancing swiftly round the terrace, she got up impulsively. Her eyes glowed with the fire he knew so well; with a rapid movement she raised her lovely hands, covered with rings, took his head, looked a long moment into his face, and, raising her face with smiling, parted lips, swiftly kissed his mouth while Android Karenina kept her gaze discretely averted, then pushed him away. She would have gone, but he held her back.

"When?" he murmured in a whisper, gazing in ecstasy at her.

"Tonight, at one o'clock," she whispered, and, with a heavy sigh, she walked with her light, swift step to meet her son.

Vronsky, looking at his watch, went away hurriedly, plagued by questions about the encounter: Why would UnConSciya plant such a trap here? Was it meant for Anna . . . or for him?

And was it UnConSciya at all?

CHAPTER 13

WHEN VRONSKY LOOKED at his watch, he was so greatly agitated and lost in his thoughts that he saw the figures on the watch's face, but could not take in what time it was. He came out onto the highroad and walked, picking his way carefully through the mud, to his carriage, detaching and reattaching the electrodes to his chest and forehead as he went. He was so completely absorbed in his confusion about the godmouth that he did not even think what o'clock it was. But the excitement of the approaching Cull gained upon Vronsky as he drove further and further into the atmosphere of the arena, overtaking carriages driving up from the summer villas or out of Petersburg.

He arrived to find Frou-Frou standing in the silo, torso door hanging open, at the ready. They were just going to lead her out.

"I'm not too late?"

"It's all right! It's all right!" said the Englishman, looking nervously at his I/Physiolographer/99. "For Heaven's sakes, don't upset yourself!"

Vronsky once more took in, in one glance, the exquisite lines of his Exterior, which was oscillating all over, quivering with excitement up and down its sleek lines. He surveyed the rows of pavilion seating, quickly scanning the crowd before climbing inside his death-suit to begin combat.

"Oh, there's Karenin!" said an acquaintance from his regiment. "He's looking for his wife, and she's in the middle of the pavilion. Didn't you see her?"

"No," answered Vronsky, and without even glancing round toward
the pavilion where his friend was pointing out Madame Karenina, he
went up to his Exterior.

In a moment, the cry was heard: *"Entrez!"*

Vronsky climbed inside Frou-Frou's groznium torso door and with
a series of deft movements attached himself to her contact board. He
then slipped his forefinger and index fingers under the palm-sized steering disc, which was his secondary means of control, and pressed its small
central button firmly, once, with his thumb. Instantly the war-machine
reared back, tilted her head upward, and fired a massive jolt of electricity
into the sky. Vronsky smiled: *She is ready.*

Outside the beast, the Englishman puckered up his lips, leaned
against the torso door, and shouted in:

"Good luck, your Excellency." And then, in English, added his traditional final word of support: "Survive."

Vronsky peered into the long-tube, a periscope-like exterior sen-
sor, to gain a last look at his rivals. Once the match began, they would in
the grand tradition of the Cull no longer be his beloved fellow Border
Officers, but targets. One Exterior, belonging to a drinking companion
of his, Oposhenko, was in the shape of a massive arachnid, with glittering golden "eyes" that Vronsky knew could exert a powerful magnetic
force, to draw enemies into the Exterior's "web." A second battle-suit
was a modified sledge, with engines attached to the back, allowing it to
function as a kind of battering ram, simple but effective. Galtsin, a friend
of Vronsky's and one of his more formidable rivals, had an Exterior
patriotically fashioned in the shape of a massive sickle, such as that used
in the time of the Tsars by traditional peasants in their fields; she could
roll with deadly speed along the periphery of the conflict, and then dart
in to slice through heavy armor plating with her sharpened edge.

A little light hussar was boldly taking the field in a modified
Exterior, which one did not wear at all; in tight riding breeches he shot

by astride a missile, which he had harnessed and sat upon like a cat on the saddle, in imitation of English jockeys. How this hussar could hope to kill his opponents and yet survive himself, it was impossible for Vronsky to conceive. Prince Kuzovlev rode out inside a monolithic block of black groznium, which Vronsky knew to be well-armored but utterly useless in offensive capability. Vronsky and all his comrades knew Kuzovlev and his peculiarity of "weak nerves" and terrible vanity. They knew that he was afraid of everything, and therefore had entered the field in this upright coffin of an Exterior, prepared to *survive* a Cull, but never to *win* one.

The combatants were ambling and motoring forward past a dammed-up stream on their way to the starting point. Several of the riders were in front and several behind, when suddenly Vronsky heard the sound of a loud, primitive engine in the mud behind him, and he was overtaken by Mahutin inside his fat-bellied, curiously adorable Exterior, Matryoshka, with the fat, rounded bottom, tapered top, and jaunty, painted peasant's face. Vronsky grimaced and looked angrily at him; there was something curious about that Exterior, and Vronsky regarded him now as his most formidable rival.

Frou-Frou, feeding off Vronsky's anticipation like a horse lapping at a clearwater stream, engaged her powerful rear legs in an excited dash to the starting point, thrusting Vronsky back against the rear wall of the cockpit.

"This is going to be a worthy match," he thought.

CHAPTER 14

THERE WERE SEVENTEEN Border Officers in all competing in the Cull. The arena was a large three-mile ring in the form of an ellipse in front of the pavilion. On this course nine obstacles had been arranged: the stream, a big and solid barrier five feet high, just before the pavilion, a dry ditch, a ditch full of water, a precipitous slope, an Irish barricade (one of the most difficult obstacles, consisting of a mound fenced with brushwood); then two more ditches filled with water, and one dry one; and the end of the race was just facing the pavilion.

Every eye, every opera glass, was turned on the gleaming, brightly colored group of exoskeletons at the moment they were in line to start.

At last the umpire shouted, "Away!" and the omnidirectional destruction began

"They're off! They're starting!" was heard on all sides after the hush of expectation.

And little groups and solitary figures among the public began running from place to place to get a better view. In the very first minute the group of quick-moving death machines fanned out across the course, taking positions around and under the barrier, the ditch, and the Irish barricade, aiming their sparkers and bomb-hurlers and echo-cannons at one another, blasting vividly away. To the spectators it seemed as though they had all started simultaneously, the field erupting in one bright blossom of furious movement and electrical fire, but to the gladiators there were seconds of difference that had great value to them.

First to fall was Vronsky's drinking companion, Oposhenko, in his spider-like exterior, who foolishly directed his powerful magnet at the worst possible foe: the confident hussar astride the missile, who flew directly at him and into one of the arachnid Exterior's gleaming "eyes." Both Exteriors exploded violently, and the eight spider legs were sent flying helter-skelter around the course. A huge shambling golem of an Exterior stopped shambling abruptly and tipped over, caught just below the neck plate by the sharpened tip of one of these spider legs. The golem suit owner, Pyotrovich, tumbled out onto the course, cursing and clutching at his legs.

Frou-Frou, excited and over-nervous by all of the activity, spun around in the first moments, unloading her heavy-fires at will, but

Vronsky soon gained control, expertly maneuvering his fingers beneath the palm disc. Sweating inside the cockpit, teeth gritted, he stared intently through the long-tube, scanning the field till he found whom he wanted: timid Kuzovlev in his monolithic obsidian crate of an Exterior.

"Low-hanging fruit," Vronsky murmured, loosing a sharp discharge of electricity from Frou-Frou's front grill directly at the midline of Kuzovlev's ugly black battleship. But the electric blast ricocheted off the front of the monolith, and Vronsky scowled with disappointment— *how has he plated the thing?*—before laughing with astonishment at his good luck: the fiery charge, sailing through the sky like a blazing croquet ball, caught Mahutin's Matryoshka instead. The blast slammed directly into the gaudy peasant-man face of the exosuit, and Vronsky was pleased that this happy accident had taken out his main rival.

In celebration, Frou-Frou drew up her legs and back and leapt like a cat, and, clearing the wreckage of Mahutin's downed Exterior, alit beyond her.

O the darling! thought Vronsky.

"Bravo!" cried a voice from the stands.

At the same instant, under Vronsky's eyes, right before him flashed the palings of the barrier. As he directed Frou-Frou in her efforts to navigate it, Vronsky glanced backward through the long-tube and cursed what he saw: his chief rival was not, in fact, dispatched. As Vronsky watched in horror, Matryoshka's smoldering upper portion, decorated with the face of a peasant man, molted like a layer of skin—revealing a *second*, fresh Exterior beneath, this one painted with the gaudy colors of a peasant *woman*.

"Drat!" Vronsky shouted. "Nested!"

He turned back to the barrier and regretted at once that he had allowed himself to be distracted: his position had shifted and he knew that something awful had happened. He could not yet make out what had happened, when the sledge-shaped Exterior rocketed by close to him, and the new, matronly Matryoshka gamboled by in pursuit. Frou-

THE QUICK-MOVING DEATH MACHINES FANNED OUT, AIMING THEIR
BOMB-HURLERS AND ECHO-CANNONS AT ONE ANOTHER

Frou was attempting to clear the barrier, but her massive back leg had smashed into it, and she went spiraling end over end, banging Vronsky violently against the interior walls of the tiny cockpit. They lay then on the muddy course just past the barrier, an open target, and Vronsky knew what would come next—his clumsy movement in clearing the barrier had doomed her.

Desperately he willed Frou-Frou back onto her feet, but it was too late—he looked into the long-tube and saw that his vulnerable state had not gone unnoticed by his rival. By this time Galtsin's sickle-suit had destroyed Matryoshka's matriarch-tier, but of course now Vronsky was not surprised to see a still smaller war-suit had emerged from within. The last thing to register upon his eyes before impact was the happy, painted peasant-boy face of Matryoshka's third metal shell flying through the air directly at him and his poor disabled Frou-Frou.

Somehow, in the crazed, fiery moments after the collision, Vronsky kicked open the door of the cockpit and rolled onto the match ground.

"A–a–a!" groaned Vronsky, clutching at his head, tearing his helmet from it, tiny fires still burning on various spots of his body. "Ah! What have I done!" he cried. "The battle lost! And my fault! Shameful, unpardonable! And the poor darling, ruined machine! Ah! What have I done!"

A crowd of men, a doctor and his assistant, the officers of his regiment, ran up to him as he exited the arena. To his misery he felt that he was whole and barely burnt, but the poor machine had been wounded past repair, and it was decided to junker it. Vronsky could not answer questions, could not speak to anyone. He turned, and leaving his helmet in a charred mess by the pond, walked away from the match course, not knowing where he was going. He felt utterly wretched. For the first time in his life he knew the bitterest sort of misfortune, misfortune beyond remedy, and caused by his own fault.

Half an hour later Vronsky had regained his self-possession. But the memory of that Cull remained for long in his heart, the cruelest and bitterest memory of his life.

CHAPTER 15

WHEN ALEXEI ALEXANDROVICH reached the death-match arena Anna was already sitting in the stands beside Betsy, in that area where all the highest society had gathered. She caught sight of her husband in the distance. Two men, her husband and her lover, were the two centers of her existence, and even unaided by Android Karenina's vibratory sensors she was aware of their nearness. She was aware of her husband approaching a long way off, and she could not help following him in the surging crowd in the midst of which he was moving. She watched his progress toward the pavilion, saw him now responding condescendingly to an ingratiating bow, now exchanging friendly and nonchalant greetings with his equals, now assiduously trying to catch the eye of some great one of this world, and tapping his metal cheek with an elegant forefinger. All these ways of his she knew, and all were hateful to her. *Nothing but ambition, nothing but the desire to get on, that's all there is in his soul,* she thought. *As for these lofty ideals, love of culture, religion, they are only so many tools for getting on.*

From his glances toward the ladies' pavilion she saw that his mechanical oculus was scanning the stands for her, but she purposely avoided noticing him.

"Alexei Alexandrovich!" Princess Betsy called to him. "I'm sure you don't see your wife: here she is."

He smiled his chilly smile, and his metal face glinted almost beautifully in the bright sun.

"There's so much splendor here that one's eyes are dazzled," he said, and then added, humorlessly, "or rather, one's *eye*." He smiled to

his wife as a man should smile on meeting his wife after only just parting from her, and greeted the princess and other acquaintances. There
was an interval between the races, and so nothing hindered conversation. An adjutant-general expressed his disapproval of the death matches,
and Alexei Alexandrovich, carrying when he spoke the authority of the
Higher Branches, defended them at length, explaining grandiloquently
why the contests had been deemed necessary by those in a position to
understand their importance.

Anna heard his high, measured tones, not losing one word, and
every word struck her as false and stabbed her ears with pain.

When the Cull was beginning and the dazzle of heavy fire lit up
the course, she bent forward and gazed with fixed eyes at Vronsky as he
went up to his Exterior and climbed inside it, and at the same time she
heard that loathsome, never-ceasing voice of her husband. She was in
an agony of terror for Vronsky, but a still greater agony was the never-
ceasing, as it seemed to her, stream of her husband's shrill voice with its
familiar intonations.

"I'm a wicked woman, a lost woman," she said in a grave whisper
to Android Karenina. "But I don't like lying, I can't endure falsehood,
while as for *him*—" her eyes flickering quickly toward her husband—"it's
the breath of his life, falsehood. He knows all about it, he sees it all; what
does he care if he can talk so calmly? If he were to kill me, if he were
to kill Vronsky, I might respect him. No, all he wants is falsehood and
propriety." Android Karenina offered no reply, other than to decorously
suggest, with a small motion of one hand, that her mistress would do well
to lower her voice.

Anna did not understand that Alexei Alexandrovich's peculiar
loquacity that day, so exasperating to her, was merely the expression of
his inward distress and uneasiness. As a child who has been hurt skips
about, putting all his muscles into movement to drown the pain, so in
that same way Alexei Alexandrovich needed mental exercise to drown
the thoughts of his wife that, in her presence and in Vronsky's, and with

the continual iteration of his name, would force themselves on his attention. And it was as natural for him to talk well and cleverly as it is natural for a child to skip about.

"Princess, bets!" sounded Stepan Arkadyich's voice from below, addressing Betsy. "Who's your favorite?"

"Anna and I are for Kuzovlev," replied Betsy. "That thing looks well-nigh impenetrable!"

"I'm for Vronsky. A Class One on it? Winner's choice?"

"Done!"

"But it is a pretty sight, isn't it?"

Alexei Alexandrovich paused in what he was saying while there was talking about him, but he began again directly.

"I admit that manly sports do not . . . ," he was continuing.

But at that moment the racers started, and all conversation ceased. Alexei Alexandrovich too was silent, and everyone stood up and turned toward the stream. Alexei Alexandrovich took no interest in the Cull, and so he did not watch the combatants, but fell listlessly to scanning the spectators with his weary eyes. His mechanized eye bore into Anna.

Her face was white and set. She was obviously seeing nothing but one Exterior, thinking of no one but the man inside it. Her hand had convulsively clutched her fan, and she held her breath. Alexei Alexandrovich looked at her and hastily turned away, scrutinizing other faces.

"But here's this lady too, and others very much moved as well; it's very natural," Alexei Alexandrovich thought for the benefit of the Face, but the Face did not answer—did it chuckle? was it possible he heard a droll, low chuckle reverberating in the chambers of his mind?—and he gazed as if absently through his I/Binocular/8 and tried to remain calm. He tried not to look at her, but unconsciously his gaze was drawn to her. His oculus scanned her again, trying not to read what was so plainly written on her face, and against his own will, with horror read on it what he did not want to know.

The first massive collisions—when the arachnid Exterior was exploded by the hussar's missile and sent its razor-sharp leg into the neck of the shambling golem suit—these agitated everyone, but Alexei Alexandrovich saw distinctly on Anna's pale, triumphant face that the man she was watching had not fallen. A shudder of horror passed over the whole public, but Alexei Alexandrovich saw that Anna did not even notice it, and had some difficulty in realizing what everyone was talking of. But more and more often, and with greater persistence, he watched her. Anna, wholly engrossed as she was with the Cull, became aware of her husband's cold eyes fixed upon her from one side.

She glanced round for an instant, looked inquiringly at him, and with a slight frown turned away again.

"Ah, I don't care!" he thought he saw her say to her android, and she did not once glance at him again.

CHAPTER 16

THE CULL WAS UNUSUALLY, even disturbingly, successful in its purpose of identifying the weak officers and the strong: mere minutes into the bout, more than half of the seventeen officers competing had already been downed, and half of that number clearly had not survived.

Everyone was loudly expressing their unease at all the death and violence, and everyone was feeling horrified; so that when Frou-Frou was dispatched by Matryoshka, and Vronsky rolled out of it on fire, there was nothing very out of the way in it. But afterward a change came over Anna's face which really was beyond decorum. She utterly lost her head. She began fluttering like a caged bird, at one moment got up and moved away, at the next turned to Betsy.

"Let us go, let us go!" she said.

But Betsy did not hear her. She was bending down, talking to a general who had come up to her.

Alexei Alexandrovich went up to Anna and courteously offered her his arm.

"Let us go, if you like," he said in French, but Anna did not notice her husband.

Without answering her husband, Anna lifted her opera glass and gazed toward the place where Vronsky's machine had blown up; but it was so far off, and there was such a crowd of people about it, that she could make out nothing. She laid down the opera glass, and would have moved away, but at that moment an officer galloped up and made some announcement. Anna craned forward, listening.

"Stiva! Stiva!" she cried to her brother.

But her brother did not hear her.

"Small Stiva!" she cried, but the fat little robot did not hear her, either.

"Once more I offer you my arm if you want to be going," said Alexei Alexandrovich, reaching toward her hand.

She drew back from him with aversion, and without looking into that face which so unsettled her.

"No, no, let me be, I'll stay."

She saw now that from the place of Vronsky's accident an officer was running across the course toward the pavilion. Betsy waved her handkerchief to him. The officer brought the news that the rider was not killed, but the machine was to be junkered.

On hearing this Anna sat down hurriedly, and hid her face in her I/Fan/9. Alexei Alexandrovich saw that she was weeping, and could not control her tears, nor even the sobs that were shaking her bosom. Alexei Alexandrovich stood so as to screen her, giving her time to recover herself.

"For the third time I offer you my arm," he said to her. Anna gazed at him and did not know what to say. Princess Betsy came to her rescue.

"No, Alexei Alexandrovich; I brought Anna and I promised to take her home," put in Betsy.

"Excuse me, princess," he said, smiling courteously but looking her very firmly in the face, "but I see that Anna's not very well, and I wish her to come home with me."

Anna looked about her in a frightened way, got up submissively, and laid her hand on her husband's arm.

"I'll send to him and find out, and let her know," Betsy whispered to Android Karenina, who received this input obediently and motored after her distressed mistress.

As they left the pavilion, Alexei Alexandrovich, as always, talked to those he met, and Anna had, as always, to talk and answer; but she was utterly beside herself, and moved hanging on her husband's arm as though in a dream.

Is he killed or not? Is it true? Will he come or not? Shall I see him today? she was thinking.

She took her seat in her husband's carriage in silence, and in silence drove out of the crowd of carriages. In spite of all he had seen, Alexei Alexandrovich still did not allow himself to consider his wife's real condition. He merely saw the outward symptoms. He saw that she was behaving unbecomingly, and it was his *duty* to tell her so. He opened his mouth to tell her she had behaved unbecomingly, but he could not help saying something utterly different.

"What an inclination we all have, though, for these cruel spectacles," he said. "I observe . . ."

"Eh? I don't understand," said Anna contemptuously.

BE A MAN. SHOW YOUR METTLE, pronounced the Face, suddenly resonating inside Alexei Alexandrovich's mind. Never before had he heard the Face speak so loudly, and the vehemence and power of the voice scattered his thoughts and sent a vivid shiver down his spine.

"I am obliged to tell you," Alexei Alexandrovich began again, and then hesitated.

I AM METAL AND YOU ARE ME.

SHOW *METAL*.

Anna shuddered to see a strange ripple pass over the metal portion of her husband's face, like a cluster of shadowy spiders rushing from forehead to chin and then disappearing. "So now we are to have it out," she murmured quietly to Android Karenina.

"I am obliged to tell you that your behavior has been unbecoming today," her husband said to her in French.

YES . . . TELL HER . . . TELL HER. . . .

"In what way has my behavior been unbecoming?" she said aloud, turning her head swiftly and looking at him straight in the face, not with the bright expression that seemed to be covering something, but with a look of determination, under which she concealed with difficulty the dismay she was feeling. Android Karenina glowed a deep, soothing purple and lay her fingers on Anna's shoulder, trying to exert what calming influence she could.

"What did you consider unbecoming?" Anna repeated.

"The despair you were unable to conceal at the accident of one of the riders."

THERE. THERE, ALEXEI. TELL HER. CHASTISE HER.

CONTROL HER.

Alexei, agitated by this continuing imprecation inside of him, waited for his wife to answer, but she was silent, looking straight before her.

"I have already begged you so to conduct yourself in society that even malicious tongues can find nothing to say against you. There was a time when I spoke of your inward attitude, but I am not speaking of that now."

GO ON, GO ON, GO ON. MAKE HER UNDERSTAND. YOU WILL NOT BE MADE A FOOL OF.

"Now I speak only of your external attitude. You have behaved improperly, and I would wish it not to occur again."

OR THERE WILL BE CONSEQUENCES. *CONSEQUENCES!*

Anna did not hear half of what he was saying; she felt panic-stricken before him, before the harsh sound of his voice and the uncanny expression on his face. She was thinking whether it was true that Vronsky was not killed. Was it of him they were speaking when they said the combatant was unhurt, but the machine had been broken past repair? She merely smiled with a pretense of irony when he finished, and made no reply, because she had not heard what he said. Alexei Alexandrovich had begun to speak boldly, but as he realized plainly what he was speaking of, the dismay she was feeling infected him too. He saw the smile, and a strange misapprehension came over him.

She is smiling at my suspicions, he thought, and the Face eagerly threw fuel on the fire of his anger. **SMILING! LAUGHING! HOW DARE SHE? TO HER IT IS ALL A COMEDY, AND YOU ARE CHIEF AMONG THE CLOWNS.**

But Alexei could not yet feel so hateful toward her as his Class III implored. At that moment, when the revelation of everything was hanging over him, there was nothing he expected so much as that she would answer mockingly as before that his suspicions were absurd and utterly groundless. So terrible to him was what he knew that now he was ready to believe anything. But the expression of her face, scared and gloomy, did not now promise even deception.

"Possibly I was mistaken," he said. "If so, I beg your pardon."

"No, you were not mistaken," she said deliberately, looking desperately into his eyes, one mechanical, one real, both radiating sadness and anger. Android Karenina tightened her grip on Anna's shoulder, trying to warn her back from the brink of this confession, but it was too late—Anna placed her hand upon that of her Class III, for strength, and pressed on.

"You were not mistaken. I was, and I could not help being in despair. I hear you, but I am thinking of him. I love him, I am his mistress; I can't bear you; I'm afraid of you, and I hate you. . . . You can do what you like to me."

Alexei reeled back, shocked, and in the next instant the carriage rocked violently, as if it, too, was stricken by Anna's confession, and flew up into the air.

As Vronsky had been warned by his engineer, the roads leading in and out of the arena were mined with emotion bombs, among the most ingenious of UnConSciya's cruel arsenal of terroristic weaponry. In Alexei Alexandrovich and his wife, they had, at this moment, an ideal target. Alexei's heart pounded with wild emotion in response to Anna's outburst, while Anna felt flushed and half-mad over what she had announced, and the biological effects of these passionate feelings were together enough—far more than enough—to trigger the physiochemical-sensing bombs that pitted the roadway.

The carriage was flung high into the air, then landed on its side and spun along the roadway until it smashed into the carriage in front of them, which carried the junkered bodies of Exteriors destroyed in the Cull. The shock and terror of that carriage's passenger, a Ministry engineer, triggered a second blast; the junkered Exteriors flew up and were soon coming down again, a rain of deadly metal shrapnel pelting the tipped-over carriage of Anna and Karenin.

All of this Anna hardly noticed; dropping back into the corner of the upset carriage, she was sobbing, her face hidden in her hands; she did not notice, either, that with each wave of despair, a fresh explosion went off along the roadway, causing more dirt and gravel and bits of fractured metal to explode into the air. Android Karenina spread her arms widely, valiantly laying her metal body over that of her mistress.

Alexei Alexandrovich did not stir, and kept looking straight before him. But the telescopic eye embedded in the left side of his face slowly extended outward, and then upward, and as it did, the burning chunks of metal hurtling down toward the carriage halted in midair and hovered there. Anna raised her head from the crook of her arm and watched confusedly as, responding to minute movements from her husband's mechanical eye—or so it seemed—the burning hunks of shrapnel crumpled harmlessly, one after the other, in the air above them.

A few minutes later the carriage was once more righted and along its way, its passengers still perfectly silent.

*   *   *

On reaching the house Alexei Alexandrovich turned his head to her, still with the same expression. He only cleared his throat decorously, and responded to her earlier declaration as if nothing had happened. "Very well! But I expect a strict observance of the external forms of propriety till such time—" his voice shook "—as I may take measures to secure my honor and communicate them to you."

He got out first and helped her to get out. In range of the Class IIs and their senors, he pressed her hand, took his seat in the carriage, and drove back to Petersburg. Immediately afterward a II/Footman/c43 came from Princess Betsy with a communiqué.

"I sent to Alexei to find out how he is, and he writes me he is quite well and unhurt, but in despair."

So he will be here, she thought. *What a good thing I told him all!*

Then for a fleeting moment she recalled the hail of shrapnel, and the cold efficiency with which her husband had defused it. She looked in the direction of Petersburg, where Alexei Alexandrovich had gone off to his office at the Ministry, and thought: *What in God's name is he?*

CHAPTER 17

ON THE MAJESTIC SPACE VESSEL orbiting the planet Venus, to which the Shcherbatskys had betaken themselves, as in all places indeed where people are gathered together, the usual process of the crystallization of society went on, assigning to each member of that society a definite and unalterable place. Though this vessel was the property of the Russian Ministry of Robotics and State Administration (and operated by the sub-Ministry of Extraterrestrial Trade & Travel), berths were sold to all peoples of the world. And just as the particle of water in frost definitely and unalterably takes the special form of the crystal of snow, so each new person who arrived aboard was at once placed in his special place. The Shcherbatskys, from their name and from the friends they made, were immediately crystallized into a definite place marked out for them.

It was characteristic of Kitty that she always imagined everything in people in the most favorable light possible, especially so in those she did not know. Kitty wandered the long, illuminated halls of the grand old vessel, as it slowly rotated in the ancient blackness of space, arm in arm with her now-beloved Class III, Tatiana, observing and delighting in her fellow passengers. This massive satellite they now inhabited was an Orbiting Purification Retreat, on which the air was carefully recirculated to cleanse it of impurities, in order to maintain maximum recuperative qualities.

Of these people the one who attracted her most was a Russian girl who had blasted off in the company of an invalid Russian lady, Madame Stahl, as everyone called her. Madame Stahl belonged to the highest society, but she was so ill that she could not walk, and was borne about the passageways of the vessel not by a Class III, but dragged in a Class I wheelbarrow piloted by the girl, whom Madame Stahl called Varenka.

The two girls, Kitty and Varenka, met several times a day, and every time they met, Kitty's eyes said: "Who are you? What are you? Are you really the exquisite creature I imagine you to be? But for goodness' sake don't suppose," her eyes added, "that I would force my acquaintance on you, I simply admire you and like you."

"I like you too, and you're very, very sweet. And I should like you better still, if I had time," answered the eyes of the unknown girl. Kitty saw indeed that she was always busy, either dragging Madame Stahl around on the Class I sledge or resting her arms from a long day of doing so.

Soon after the arrival of the Shcherbatskys there appeared on the morning transport two persons who attracted universal and unfavorable attention. These were a tall man with a stooping figure and huge hands, with black, simple, and yet terrible eyes, and a squat, sputtering Class III; and a pockmarked, kind-looking woman, very badly and tastelessly dressed. Recognizing these persons as Russians, Kitty had already in her imagination begun constructing a delightful and touching romance about them. But her mother, having ascertained from the visitors' list that this was Nikolai Levin and Marya Nikolaevna, explained to Kitty what a bad man this Levin was, and all her fancies about these two people vanished. Not so much from what the princess told her, as from the fact that it was Konstantin's brother, this pair suddenly seemed to Kitty intensely unpleasant. This Levin, with his continual twitching of his head, and a cluster of suppurating sores above and around his eyes, aroused in her now an irrepressible feeling of disgust. It seemed to her that his big, terrible eyes, and their dreadful outline of pustules, expressed a feeling of hatred and contempt, and she tried to avoid meeting him.

But Kitty soon found an excuse to make the acquaintance of Varenka, and of Madame Stahl too, and these friendships comforted her in her mental distress. She found this comfort through a completely new world being opened to her by means of this acquaintance, a world having nothing in common with her past, an exalted, noble world, from the height of which she could contemplate her past calmly. It was revealed to her that besides the instinctive life to which Kitty had given herself up hitherto, there was a spiritual life. This life was disclosed in religion, but a religion having nothing in common with that one which Kitty had known from childhood, and which found expression in litanies and all-night services at the Widow's Home, where one might meet one's friends, and in learning by heart Slavonic texts with the priest. Madame Stahl's religion was xenotheologism, the lofty, mysterious faith that Kitty had experienced only slightly, through her friend Countess Nordston:

the religion that worshipped mysterious light-beings called the Honored Guests; they who, Madame Stahl explained rapturously, would "come for us in three ways" in days to come, traveling from the farthest reaches of the interplanetary ether to redeem all humankind.

Countess Nordston's version of this faith, Kitty now understood, had reflected only a limited understanding. When it was presented to her in its full, luminescent complexity by Madame Stahl, xenotheologism brought to Kitty a whole series of noble thoughts and feelings. And Kitty found all this out not from words. Madame Stahl talked to Kitty as to a charming child whom one looks on with pleasure, as on the memory of one's youth, and only once she said in passing that in all human sorrows nothing gives comfort but love and faith, and that in the knowledge of the Honored Guests' compassion for us no sorrow is trifling—and immediately talked of other things. But in every gesture of Madame Stahl, in every word, in every heavenly—as Kitty called it—look, and above all in the whole story of her life, which she heard from Varenka, Kitty recognized that "something important," of which, till then, she had known nothing.

At first the princess noticed nothing but that Kitty was much under the influence of her *engouement*, as she called it, for Madame Stahl, and still more for Varenka. She saw that Kitty did not merely imitate Varenka in her conduct, but unconsciously imitated her in her manner of walking, of talking, of blinking her eyes. But later on the princess noticed that, apart from this adoration, some kind of serious spiritual change was taking place in her daughter. In the evenings, the four of them—Varenka, Madame Stahl, Kitty, and Tatiana—would gather at the huge bay windows of the grand old orbiter, staring off at the clusters of stars, waiting patiently with uplifted hands and hearts for the arrival of the Honored Guests.

Yet, elevated as Madame Stahl's character was, touching as was her story, and exalted and moving as was her speech, Kitty could not help detecting in her some traits that perplexed her. She noticed that when questioned about her family, Madame Stahl had smiled contemptuously, which was not in accord with Honored meekness. She wore the same contemptuous expression when speaking to Tatiana, and made Kitty understand, never outrightly, but by vague suggestions, that the Honored Guests were disapproving of human reliance upon robots.

For Kitty, who had come to rely deeply, in the way of young girls, on her beloved-companion, this doubt poisoned the charm of her new life.

CHAPTER 18

BEFORE THE END of their recuperative stay aboard the purification satellite, Prince Shcherbatsky, who had sojourned nearby on a Venusian colony orbiter to visit some Russian friends—to get a breath of Russian air, as he said—came back to his wife and daughter.

The prince returned thinner, with the skin hanging in loose bags on his cheeks, marked here and there by mild red burns from occasional exposure to the closer-than-usual sun, but in the most cheerful frame of mind. His good humor was even greater when he saw Kitty completely recovered. The news of Kitty's friendship with Madame Stahl and Varenka, and the reports the princess gave him of some kind of change she had noticed in Kitty, troubled the prince and aroused his habitual feeling of jealousy of everything that drew his daughter away from him, and a dread that his daughter might have gone out of the reach of his influence into regions inaccessible to him. But these unpleasant matters were all drowned in the sea of kindliness and good humor that was always within him.

The evening after his arrival the prince, in his long overcoat, with his Russian wrinkles and baggy cheeks propped up by a starched collar, set off with his daughter down the long, brightly lit passageways of the orbiter. She had invited him to join her this night, in the company of

Madame Stahl and Varenka, to take part in the joy she had discovered in
the xenotheological ritual of invitation to the Honored Guests.

"Present me to your new friends," he said to his daughter, squeezing her hand with his elbow as they arrived at the darkened arcade, with
the wide windows looking out at the universe of stars, where Madame
Stahl held the nightly ceremony. "Only it's melancholy, very melancholy
here. Who's that?"

It was Varenka herself. She was walking rapidly toward them carrying an elegant red bag.

"Here is Papa," Kitty said to her.

Varenka made—simply and naturally as she did everything—a
movement between a bow and a curtsey, and immediately began talking
to the prince, without shyness, naturally, as she talked to everyone.

"Of course I know you; I know you very well," the prince said
to her with a smile, in which Kitty detected with joy that her father
liked her friend. Kitty saw that her father had meant to make fun of
Varenka, but that he could not do it because he liked her.

"I look forward, too, to meeting the famous Madame Stahl," he
went on, "if she deigns to recognize me."

"Why, did you know her, Papa?" Kitty asked apprehensively, catching the gleam of irony that kindled in the prince's eyes at the mention
of Madame Stahl.

"I used to know her husband, and her too a little, before she became
a stargazer."

"What do you mean by stargazer, Papa?" asked Kitty, dismayed by
the teasing tone with which he had pronounced the word.

"I don't quite know myself. I only know that she thanks these
magical light-beings for everything, for every misfortune, and thanks
them too that her husband died. And that's rather droll, as they didn't
get on together."

"Oh, here she is now," said Kitty, as Varenka returned, now tugging laboriously on the Class I wheelbarrow in which lay, propped on

pillows, something in gray and blue and lying under a sunshade—a sunshade, though they were quite well protected from outer space. This was Madame Stahl.

The prince went up to her, and Kitty detected that disconcerting gleam of irony in his eyes. He went up to Madame Stahl and addressed her with extreme courtesy and affability in that excellent French that so few speak nowadays.

"I don't know if you remember me, but I must recall myself to thank you for your kindness to my daughter," he said, taking off his hat and not putting it on again.

"Prince Alexander Shcherbatsky," said Madame Stahl, lifting upon him her heavenly eyes, in which Kitty discerned a look of annoyance. "Delighted! I have taken a great fancy to your daughter."

"You are still in weak health?"

"Yes, I'm used to it," said Madame Stahl.

"You are scarcely changed at all," the prince said to her. "It's ten or eleven years since I had the honor of seeing you."

"Yes, our Guests send the darkness and the strength to bear it. Often one wonders what is the goal of this life? . . . The other side!" she said angrily to Varenka, who had rearranged the rug over her feet not to her satisfaction.

"To do good, probably," said the prince with a twinkle in his eye.

"That is not for us to judge," said Madame Stahl, perceiving the shade of expression on the prince's face.

"I meant to warn you, Madame," said the prince, his tone losing its genial teasing quality and growing serious, "there is talk on Venus of a changing attitude among the Ministry, regarding the practice of xenotheology. To me and other tired old cynics like me, it is merely amusing, but I feel I should warn you, the Ministry seems to be finding it less amusing of late."

"What do you mean?" she said, her eyes growing wary.

"What once was a silly fad is lately considered to be a form of

Janusism."

Kitty and Varenka gasped, and Tatiana in shock clapped a pink-clad metal hand before her mouth. Madame Stahl offered no reply to the prince. Instead she turned a cold eye to Kitty, apologized that she was not feeling well and there would be no ceremony tonight. Then she snapped her fingers, and Varenka dragged her from the room.

Kitty turned to her father and objected hotly to this treatment of her new mentor.

"Do not be cross with me, dear," replied the Prince. "I only warn her as a caution, though I cannot pretend I did not take some pleasure in spoiling her fun."

"Oh, Papa! How can you be so mocking? Varenka worships her."

"Of course she does. And I suppose she has told you how the relations between Class IIIs and humans are against the good principles of xenotheologism? You might ask her, or her poor Varenka, how it can be thought more moral to treat fellow human beings as if *they* were the robots—or, to use the ancient word, servants."

"But she does so much good! Ask anyone! Everyone knows her!"

"Perhaps so," said the prince, squeezing her hand with his elbow, "but it's better when one does good so that you may ask everyone and no one knows."

Kitty did not answer, not because she had nothing to say, but because she did not care to reveal her secret thoughts even to her father. But, strange to say, although she had so made up her mind not to be influenced by her father's views, not to let him into her inmost sanctuary, she felt that the heavenly image of Madame Stahl, which she had carried for a whole month in her heart, had vanished, never to return, just as the fantastic figure made up of some clothes thrown down at random vanishes when one sees that it is only some garment lying there. All that was left was a woman with short legs, who worried patient Varenka for not arranging her rug to her liking. And by no effort of the imagination could Kitty bring back the former Madame Stahl.

And nor was it necessary to do so, as four days later, the rumors the prince had heard on the Venusian colony were proved true in the most shocking way. Madame Stahl was arrested by the shipboard troop of 77s, denounced as a heretic and a traitor to Mother Russia; but the rumor on the orbiter was that the Ministry, having discovered that there may actually *be* aliens in the far reaches of the universe, ruled that those fervently awaiting their arrival were not religious fanatics, but conspirators with a potential enemy.

Kitty was devastated that this person she had come to love, even to worship, in such a short time, could turn out to be a Janus. With Varenka holding onto one trembling arm and Tatiana onto the other, she went to watch the sentence carried out; Madame Stahl struggled as she was lifted from her wheelbarrow and dragged all the way down the long hallway that led to the portal. She struggled as she was stripped of her clothing and bound head and feet. She struggled and wept as she was shoved into the exit dock, and the airlock was shut behind her. She pounded on the interior door as the exterior door was opened from within by remote telegraphy, and she screamed, wordlessly, as her body was launched into the cold vastness of the void. At last, as Kitty watched, weeping, from the bay window of the orbiter, Madame Stahl stopped screaming, stopped crying, and her body became entirely still, floating rapidly away into echoing black eternity.

After that solemn event, all the world in which she had been living was transformed for Kitty. She did not give up everything she had learned, but she became aware that she had deceived herself in supposing she could be what she wanted to be. Her eyes were, it seemed, opened; she felt all the difficulty of maintaining herself without hypocrisy and self-conceit on the pinnacle that she had wished to mount. Moreover, she became aware of all the dreariness of the world of sorrow, of sick and dying people, in which she had been living. The efforts she had made to like it seemed to her intolerable, and she felt a longing to get back quickly into the fresh air, to Russia, to Ergushovo, where, as she knew from letters, her sister Dolly had already gone with her children.

But her affection for Varenka did not wane. As she said good-bye, Kitty begged her to come to them in Russia.

"I'll come when you get married," said Varenka.

"I shall never marry."

"Well, then, I shall never come."

"Well, then, I shall be married simply for that. Mind now, remember your promise," said Kitty.

The doctor's prediction was fulfilled. Kitty returned home to Russia cured. She was not so gay and thoughtless as before, but she was serene. Her Moscow troubles had become a memory to her.

PART THREE: WHAT LIES WITHIN

CHAPTER 1

ONCE, IN A PREVIOUS YEAR, Levin had gone to look in on the work in the groznium mine, and being made very angry by the deteriorated condition of the chief II/Excavator/8, and the lazy *mécanicien* who had not reported it, he had sought recourse in what would become his favorite means for regaining his temper: he retrieved an antique pickaxe (such as peasants had once wielded) from the cellar of his home, donned a helmet and everlit, was lowered by the great pneumatic dumbwaiter to the floor of the mine pit, chose a tunnel extension, entered the inky blackness, and began to dig.

He liked the work so much that he had several times tried his hand at mining since. This year, ever since the early spring, he had cherished a plan for digging for a whole day together with the nimble Pitbots, light-shedding Glowing Scrubblers, and big and inexhaustible II/Extractor/4s who served in his groznium mine.

"I must have physical exercise, or my temper will certainly be ruined," he announced one spring day to loyal Socrates, who was bent at the Herculean task of tabulating the receipts and filling out the Ministry paperwork relating to that season's excavation and extraction. "I fancy the spring extraction is in full swing. Tomorrow I shall start mining."

Socrates lifted his head, and looked with interest at his master.

"Mine like a Pitbot? All day long?"

"Yes, it's very pleasant," said Levin.

"*Splendid exercise, except you'll hardly be able to stand it,*" replied Socrates, without a shade of irony.

"No, I don't think so. It's so delightful, and at the same time such hard work, that one has no time to think about it."

The next morning, Konstantin Levin got up earlier than usual, but he was detained reviewing communiqués from the Ministry's Department of Groznium Management, and by the time he arrived pitside and donned his goggles, air canister, lead-lined suit, and thick-soled boots, the miners were already at the declension point.

He stared down from the outer rim of the crater, surveying his beloved gash in the earth. Lying in rich deposits in this crater and the soil below it were vast quantities of groznium, the Miracle Metal, the blood of Russian life. But before it could be transformed into devices of every shape and class, it had to be pried out by the mechanical axes of the Pitbots and the shovels of the imperturbable Extractors; pried from where it lay buried in thick chunks along tunnel walls; from where it sat in thick clusters along cragged rock walls, each rough nugget of groznium more valuable than any diamond.

Gripping the edge of the dumbwaiter as it descended, Levin gazed at the cluster of tunnel entrances on the far wall of the pit: in and out of the tunnel entrances flowed his dear rough-hewn Class IIs like ants, clutching their buckets and axes in their sturdy end-effectors. He waited impatiently, his soul crying out to begin work, as the dumbwaiter clicked slowly downward, inch by inch, before at last depositing him on the floor of the pit.

From the declension point, he hastily picked his way down the sloping crater wall into the heart of the pit, and the main tunnel entrance. The robots swarmed around him—the industrious surface-machines; the Pitbots gunmetal gray where they weren't yet caked in ore; the Glowing Scrubblers shedding their famous dirty-red subterranean glow; and the heavy, tank-like Extractors, rumbling like sentient carriages, their shovel-like face attachments primed to bore into the soil. Levin counted forty-

THE ROBOTS SWARMED AROUND HIM—THE PITBOTS, THE GLOWING
SCRUBBLERS, THE EXTRACTORS; LEVIN COUNTED FORTY-TWO ALTOGETHER

two robots altogether.

Just as Levin joined the line of robots they broke off into a dozen or more small groups and branched off the pit floor into the small side-tunnels where the good clusters of extractable ore could be found. He fell in with a small buzzing band as they moved slowly into an uneven, freshly dug tunnel, sloping steadily downward away from the honey-comb of tunnel entrances and into the pit's sulfurous heart. Levin recog-nized some of his own robots, many of whom his old father had given names to, when he was lord of the mine: here was old Yermil, a dented Pitbot with a very long, white frontplate, bending forward to swing his axe; there was a newer model, Vaska, thrusting at the pit wall with a wide sweep. Here, too, was Tit, a thin little android whose thin fingertips were built for crevice-cleaning. Tit was in front of all, and swung away at the tunnel wall without bending, as though playing with the axe.

Levin, carrying his old-fashioned axe and shining his headlamp for-ward in the dim gloom of the cavern, went to meet Tit, who burbled respectfully at the master. Tit produced a newer pickaxe from his torso, more appropriate to the task at hand, and gave it to him.

"Like a razor, sir," intoned Tit. *"Like a razor, cuts of itself."*

Levin took the axe, and clacked it three times against the wall of the tunnel before pronouncing himself ready to begin. The robots all stared at him till a tall, old Glowing Scrubbler bent its red-glowing frame respectfully at Levin's side.

"Look'ee now, master," tweedled the Scrubbler apologetically in the curious argot of the hypogeal Class IIs. *"Look'ee, look'ee, look'ee. Once join-ing the line there's no going back!"*

"I shall not be turning back," Levin said, taking his stand behind Tit, and waiting for the time to begin. Tit made room, and Levin started swinging his axe. The wall here was thick with chunks of groznium, so large you could see big pieces glinting at you, as if winking, begging to be driven free. But Levin knew that it was harder than it seemed, that the alloy did not simply crumble forth, that it took strength and the precise angling of one's axe to drive it forth. The group's II/Extractor/4, nick-named Old Georgy, scuttled forward, its treads working laboriously over the rutted, rock-strewn path, its brush-and-magnet effectors collecting the precious dust left behind by the extraction of the bigger rocks. The Pitbots buzzed efficiently in the Extractor's wake, axing out or vacuum-ing up chunks of groznium that Old Georgy missed with its broader efforts.

Levin, who had not done any mining for a long while, and was disconcerted by the robots' curious lenses locked upon him, dug badly for the first moments, though he swung his axe vigorously. Behind him he heard soft mechanical chirrups:

"Not set right. . . . "

"Handle's too high. . . . "

"He has to stoop to it. . . . "

"He's going to hit a hot one. . . . "

"Never mind, he'll get on all right," countered Tit sharply, and Levin felt a burst of fellow feeling with the lithe Pitbot, a feeling which some-what unsettled him, considering the machine was but a Class II.

With each step forward, the tunnel grew smaller and dimmer, and Levin followed Tit, trying to do the best he could. They moved a hundred paces. Tit kept moving on, without stopping, not showing the slightest weariness, but Levin was already beginning to be afraid he would not be able to keep it up: he was so tired.

He felt as he swung his axe that he was at the very end of his strength, and was making up his mind to ask Tit to stop. But at that very moment Tit stopped of his own accord, and bending at the midsection, rubbed his axe, and began whetting it on the whetstone embedded in his fore-arm. Levin straightened himself, and drawing a deep breath looked round. Behind him came another Pitbot, who stopped at once without waiting to get to Levin, and began whetting his own axe. Tit sharpened his tool and Levin's, and they went on. The next time it was just the same. Tit moved on with sweep after sweep of his axe, not stopping nor showing signs of weariness. Levin followed him, trying not to get left behind, and he found it harder and harder: the moment came when he felt he had no strength left, but at that very moment Tit stopped and whetted the axes.

He marveled at the sensitivity of this Class II, at the evolutionary design of it; Tit's circuits were designed to adjust to the needs of the other worker robots in his line, to maintain each other as they worked together in the Scrubbler-lit gloom. Since today Levin worked among them, Tit now treated him automatically as a member of the cadre, making allowances for his slow pace and (compared to the robots) limited strength.

So they completed the first tunnel. And this first branch seemed particularly hard work to Levin; when the tunnel ended abruptly, the mechanical crew reversed its course, retracing their steps to the declension point, and headed down a second tunnel to continue their work. What delighted Levin particularly was that he now knew he would be able to hold out.

He thought of nothing, wished for nothing, but not to be left behind by the robots, and to do his work as well as possible. He heard nothing but the clang of metal on rock and the constant dull buzz emitted by Old Georgy. He saw before him Tit's upright figure swinging away, the thick chunks of alloy falling free with each swing.

How odd, thought Levin, *to think that in centuries past this land was intact, unscarred by tunnels and mines, covered instead by fields of gently swaying wheat.* Before groznium was discovered, in the ancient days of the Tsar, before there were robots or even the idea of robots, all this was cropland, and where now was heard the clang of the axe and the whir of the Extractor was heard the whisper of the scythe, the tromp of peasant boots on grass, the endless mowing of rows. And all that work, that grueling and backbreaking labor, performed not by tireless machines, but by human beings. This work that he did today as a sort of lark, to rid his irritable soul of excess energy, had in those days been the daily toil of the Russian people in their thousands and millions.

Levin found it hard to imagine . . . and yet he could not help but consider what price his people had paid for the glorious transformation of the Age of Groznium. *The robots have assumed the burden of our labors, but have taken from us, too, the benefits of that labor: the clarifying moral force of discipline, the redemptive pain of long exertion.*

Such were the thoughts working through Konstantin Dmitrich's mind, as the man himself worked through the tunnels of his mine. Long tunnels and short tunnels, with easy walls and with poor walls. As the hours ticked by in the inky darkness, Levin lost all sense of time and could not have told whether it was late or early now. A change began to come over his work, which gave him immense satisfaction. In the midst of his toil there were moments during which he forgot what he was doing, and it all came easy to him, and at those same moments his wall was almost as smooth and well-plucked as the robots'.

Even as they descended further and further below the surface of the earth, and the heat grew and grew until it felt he was standing in a very oven, the mining did not seem such hard work to him. The perspiration with which he was drenched cooled him, while the fulvous lucency of the Glowing Scrubbler seemed to give a vigor and dogged energy to his labor; more and more often now came those moments of unconsciousness, when it was possible not to think of what one was doing. The pick-axe dug of itself. These were happy moments. Still more delightful were the moments when they reached a cool underground stream, and old Tit rinsed his blade in the murky water, ladled out a little in a tin dipper, and offered Levin a drink.

"*Humans experience thirst, correct?*" he said. "*For water?*"

And truly Levin had never drunk any liquor so good as this cold, black water with purplish, glowing pinpricks of groznium floating in it, and a taste of rust from the tin dipper. And immediately after this came the delicious, slow saunter, with his hand on the axe, during which he could wipe away the streaming sweat, breathe deeply from his oxygen canister, and look about at the long string of automated miners tromping along in their dark underground universe.

The longer Levin mined and the deeper below the surface his labor took him, the oftener he felt the moments of unconsciousness in which it seemed not his hands that swung the axe, but the axe swinging of itself, a body full of life and consciousness of its own; and as though by magic, without thinking of it, the work turned out regular and well-finished of itself. These were the most blissful moments. He suspected that some portion of this blissful sensation was the result of oxygen deprivation, and pulled deeply on his canister.

Emerging from the tunnel at last, Levin blinked back at the startling brightness of daylight. He looked at the crater floor and hardly recognized the place, everything was so changed. While he was immersed in the mine, the surface-machines had transformed the crater floor into a bustling assembly line, where buckets full of mined ore were first weighed by efficient little Class I scales, then bundled by the busy boxing end-effectors of II/Packagers/97s, then run up on hundred-yard-long conveyer belts from the tunnel entrance to the dumbwaiters. The crater floor was like a busy and happy factory floor, with surface machines and Pitbots buzzing and beeping gaily to one another and navigating their way around Surceased Extractors and busy Packagers, while the conveyer track carried the freshly plucked groznium off to the smeltworks.

The work done was exceptionally much for forty-two machines. But Levin felt a longing to get as much mining done that day as possible, and he was vexed with the sun sinking so quickly in the sky. He felt no weariness; all he wanted was to pick a fresh tunnel, grab his axe once more, and get as much done as possible.

But the day's work was to come to a sudden end, for from deep within the pit came a series of concussive booms. Likely a maltuned Pitbot had struck a "hot one," a tiny pocket of heavily concentrated groznium mixed with nitrates, and the impact had caused an explosion. In the next instant robots came pouring out, red lights flashing on their head units, klaxons blaring, scuttling out of danger as quickly as possible in compliance with the Iron Law of self-preservation.

Levin joined the hastening crowd, sprinting full bore for the crater-side; he clambered fist over foot up the side of the crater wall, caught amidst a crush of robots ascending beside him on sturdy metal feet. Halfway up the face of the crater Levin risked a glance behind him and saw a great cloud of dust billowing out from within the tunnels; he saw the opposite wall of the crater fracture and avalanche, as the earth convulsed with the power of the mine explosion; he saw Old Georgy, come automatically out of Surcease but too slow on his fat treads to escape the massive tumble of rock, buried in boulders and rubble.

Levin turned away in sadness and continued his own escape. It was hard work finishing his climb up the steep side of the crater. But this did not trouble old Tit, who was next to Levin. Brandishing his axe just as ever, and moving his feet in their big, plaited casings with firm, little steps, he climbed slowly up the steep place, and though a bolt rattled on his frontplate, and his whole frame trembled with effort, he continued to find little chunks of loose groznium, and to scoop them up as they went—this was his programming. This was the purpose of his existence.

Levin walked after him and did the same; he often thought he would fall, as he climbed with an axe up the steep side of a crater where it would have been hard work to clamber without anything. But he climbed up and did what he had to do. He felt as though some external force were moving him.

CHAPTER 2

LEVIN GOT ON HIS TWO-TREAD and, parting regretfully from the Pitbots, rode homeward.

He found Socrates pacing anxiously, looking through a newly

delivered stack of mail. Levin rushed into the room with his wet and matted hair sticking to his forehead, and his back and chest grimed and moist. Despite his physical state, he was merry.

"We excavated four tunnels!" he announced buoyantly to his beloved-companion, who regarded him with a warily flickering eye-bank. "And some maltuned Pitbot struck a hot one, and an explosion shook the mines, and the crater floor was buried in rock! And how have you been getting on?"

"Dirt! Grime! Filth! What do you look like?" said Socrates scoldingly, for the first moment looking round with some dissatisfaction. *"And the door, shut the door!"* he cried. *"You must have let in a dozen at least."*

Socrates could not endure flies, for he had an inexplicable fear that one would fly into his joints and lay eggs, disabling him.

"Not one, on my honor," Levin replied with a hearty laugh. "But if I have, I'll catch them. You wouldn't believe what a pleasure it is! How have you spent the day?"

Five minutes later the two old friends met in the dining room. Although it seemed to Levin that he was not hungry, when he began to eat, the dinner struck him as extraordinarily good.

A small red bulb alongside Socrates' monitor lit up. *"A communiqué has arrived for you,"* the Class III said. The communiqué was from Oblonsky, and Socrates cued it for Levin to view:

"Dolly is at Ergushovo," said the little hologrammatic vision of Oblonsky, "And everything seems to be going wrong there. Her I/Butterchurn/19 has exploded, the well is not running clear, and a II/MilkExtractor/47 had a disastrous accident. Poor Dolly, never mind the cow! Do ride over and see her, please; help her with advice; you know all about it. She will be so glad to see you. She's quite alone, poor thing. My mother-in-law and all of them are still in orbit."

"That's capital! I will certainly ride over to her," said Levin. "Or we'll go together. Darya Alexandrovna is such a splendid woman, isn't she? They're not far from here! Twenty-five miles."

"*Thirty,*" Socrates corrected, with a wry smile, for he knew what was already in his master's mind: To meet with Dolly and find out news of Kitty Shcherbatskaya.

CHAPTER 3

ON THE SUNDAY of St. Peter's week Dolly drove to mass for all her children to take the sacrament. Driving home from church, with all her children round her, their heads still wet from their bath, and a kerchief tied over her own head, Dolly was getting near the house, when the II/Coachman/199's antennae began to quiver, and his Vox-Em rumbled, "*Gentleman coming . . . gentleman coming . . . the master of Provokovskoe . . .* "

Dolly peeped out in front, and was delighted when she recognized in the gray hat and gray coat the familiar figure of Levin walking to meet them. She bade the children sit up straight and prepare to greet Konstantin Dmitrich Levin, and Grisha grumbled as he put away the I/Flashpop/4 with which he was irritating his sister. Dolly was glad to see Levin at any time, but at this moment she was specially glad he should see her in all her glory. No one was better able to appreciate her grandeur than Levin.

Seeing her, he found himself face to face with one of the pictures of his daydream of family life.

"You're like a hen with your chickens, Darya Alexandrovna."

"Ah, how glad I am to see you!" she said, holding out her hand to him.

"Glad to see me, but you didn't let me know. I got a communiqué from Stiva that you were here."

"From Stiva?" Dolly asked with surprise.

"Yes. He said that you are here, and that he thinks you might allow me to be of use to you," said Levin. He was embarrassed through a sense that Darya Alexandrovna would be annoyed by receiving from an outsider help that should by rights have come from her own husband.

Dolly certainly did not like this little way of Stepan Arkadyich's of foisting his domestic duties on others. But she was at once aware that Levin was aware of this. It was for just this fineness of perception, for this delicacy, that she liked Levin.

And his usefulness to her was immediately proved apparent, when in the next instant the carriage in which Dolly and her children were riding rose ten feet up into the air, as if borne aloft on the crest of a geyser. Levin and Socrates stared upward to where the vehicle was balanced on the frontal section of a hideous wormlike beast, like an earthworm swelled to an unnatural size. As Levin and Socrates tried to conceive of the provenance of such a creature, the carriage fell with a bone-rattling bang from the heights to which the thing had borne it. The children, unhurt but wildly terrified, screamed and huddled in their mother's skirts, while the creature turned its frontal portion toward Levin; he saw now its toothless chasm of a mouth, the dark indentations in lieu of eyes, the entire absence of a nose. But most of all that mouth—a gray and puckering maw, smacking wetly, a physical incarnation of the idea of appetite. The upper portion of the long body writhed balefully, with the lower half still hidden from view, only in part emerged from the earth.

A sound accompanied the motion of the beast, a repetitive mechanical click, *tikka tikka tikka tikka tikka . . .*

"It is like a . . . like a . . ." Levin began, speaking over this insistent tattoo, his mind turning wildly.

"A koschei, master," said Socrates, fumbling in his beard for some weapon with which to confront the apparition. *"Like an enormous koschei."*

There was no more time to speak, as the worm darted suddenly downward. Levin leapt backward, but too late: The puckering ring of the thing's mouth closed around his thigh. Most shocking to Levin in this

moment was that what he felt tightening around his upper leg was not
the disturbing, clammy warmth of worm flesh, but the sharp, cold bite of
metal.

Socrates shouted, *"Master!"* and leapt to his side, while in the carriage Dolly and the children shrieked and wept.

Levin slapped roughly at the face of the beast with his riding crop,
estimating from the dark indentations where its eyes might be. He slashed
a scar into the face, and some kind of bright-yellow muck poured forth
from of the wound; the smell was not like that of any bodily fluid, but
more like . . .

"Humectant," blared Socrates, waving the chemometer he had pulled
from his cluster of machinery. *"Our foe is definitively inorganic."*

Whatever it was, the monster still had Levin's leg caught in its maw,
even as it had had fully emerged from its hole in the dirt, unspooling to some fifteen yards in length. Socrates grasped it at its midpoint
and tugged with the full strength of his groznium arms. With a hideous
screeching noise the worm tore in two, and more of the bright-yellow
goo sprayed forth, before, in a matter of seconds, the wound cleanly
stitched itself closed, a new mouth formed on what had been the rear
portion of the beast, and now there were two of the writhing things. The
second one rapidly wriggled free from Socrates' end-effectors and into
the coach with Dolly and the children.

"Sorry," Socrates muttered, as the horrid *tikka tikka tikka* doubled in
volume, approaching now a near-deafening level.

"I do not understand," shouted Levin above the din, kicking at the
head of the beast with his one free foot. "The Higher Branches declared
that all koschei had been flushed from the countryside."

"And surely this thing is too big to be a koschei!" added Dolly
from the carriage, where she stomped at the segmented, gray body of the
worm with one boot heel.

Dolly's youngest boy Grisha crept silently forth from the backseat
of the carriage and reactivated his Class I plaything, determined in the

naive and valiant way of children to play what part he could in fending off this attack. He aimed the toy at the eyes of the creature and pressed the trigger to activate a sudden and powerful flash of light; the effect was instantaneous and gratifying—like a mole recoiling from the glare of sunlight, the worm-like machine-monster hissed, writhed away, and spun back toward the safety of its underground warren from which it had emerged.

"Why, Grisha!" said Dolly. Levin, meanwhile, still caught in the maw of the original of the two worm-beasts, called out to his beloved-companion. "Socrates!" he hollered. "Would you mind terribly . . . "

The tall and angular Class III, however, was already in motion, grabbing out of his beard a I/Flashpop of exactly the sort Grisha had used, only vastly more powerful. The burst of irradiation the device subsequently dispensed sent the first worm skittering after its mate, back into the hole—and left a dread silence in its wake, the rattling click at last stilled. It left, too, Konstantin Levin clutching at his bruised leg, Dolly and her family heaving great breaths of exhaustion and relief, and Socrates scouring the dirt for whatever evidence he could find of what, exactly, they had just encountered.

As the carriage resumed its slow progress back to Ergushovo, Levin and Socrates rode beside, discussing the possible provenance of the strange, wormlike attack-robots. The obvious answer was that these were simply a new model of koschei, more powerful than any UnConSciya had previously unleashed—but something about that answer felt dissatisfying to Levin, and Socrates with his higher-level analytical functionality agreed. Could the smaller, more typical wormlike koschei have *grown* somehow? But what could have caused them to do so?

"Well, whatever has set this unholy machine upon us," Dolly put in, "I am certainly glad that you were here to act in our defense."

"Of course," said Levin, "Though your Grisha seemed more than up to the challenge!"

The youngest of Dolly's brood beamed his pleasure at the

compliment. The children knew Levin very little, and could not remember when they had seen him, but they experienced in regard to him none of that strange feeling of shyness and hostility that children so often experience toward hypocritical, grown-up people, and for which they are so often and miserably punished. Hypocrisy in anything whatsoever may deceive the cleverest and most penetrating man, but the least wide-awake of children recognizes it, and is revolted by it, however ingeniously it may be disguised. Whatever faults Levin had, there was not a trace of hypocrisy in him, and so the children showed him the same friendliness that they saw in their mother's face.

Here, in the country, with children, and with Darya Alexandrovna and her plump, matronly Class III, Dolichka, Levin was in a mood, not infrequent with him, of childlike light-heartedness that she particularly liked in him. After dinner, Dolly, sitting alone with him on the balcony, began to speak of Kitty.

"You know, Kitty's coming here, and is going to spend the summer with me."

"Really," he said, flushing, and at once, to change the conversation, he said: "Then I'll send you a new cow, shall I? I heard from Stiva you had a bit of trouble with your II/MilkExtractor/47. If you insist on a bill you shall pay me five rubles a month; but you really shouldn't."

"No, thank you. We can manage very well now."

And Levin, to turn the conversation, explained to Dolly the theory of cow-keeping, based on the principle that the cow is simply a kind of machine, designed for the transformation of food into milk, and so on.

He talked of this, and passionately longed to hear more of Kitty, and, at the same time, was afraid of hearing it. He dreaded the breaking up of the inward peace he had gained with such effort.

"Yes, but still all this has to be looked after, and who is there to look after it?" Dolly responded, without interest.

"*Pardon,*" interrupted Socrates, and they all turned to look at the robot; under the weight of their collective stare, he absently began flicking a switch on his hip assembly, on and off, on and off. *"I have been running a full analysis on the matter of the worm-beast. I cannot compute: If it is true that the creature we encountered is but a larger version of the koschei that have previously infested the land—for what reason? Why would a simple UnConSciya device grow to such a size? And . . . how?"*

"Oh dear!" said Dolichka.

And, thought Levin, loathe to float such a possibility within the hearing of Darya Alexandrovna and her her children, or even to Socrates, *can it be that there are other things the Ministry is hiding from us?*

CHAPTER 4

KITTY REPORTS IN HER LATEST communiqué that there's nothing she longs for so much as quiet and solitude," Dolly said.

"And how is she—better?" Levin asked in agitation.

"Thank God, she's quite well again. I never believed her lungs were affected."

"Oh, I'm very glad!" said Levin, and Dolly fancied she saw something touching, helpless, in his face as he said this and looked silently into her face.

"Let me ask you, Konstantin Dmitrich," she said then, smiling her kindly and rather mocking smile, "why is it you are angry with Kitty?"

"I? I'm not angry with her," said Levin.

"Yes, you are angry. Why was it you did not come to see us or them when you were in Moscow?"

"Darya Alexandrovna," he said, blushing up to the roots of his hair, "I wonder really that with your kind heart you don't feel this. How it is you feel no pity for me, if nothing else, when you know . . . "

"What do I know?"

"You know I made an offer and that I was refused," said Levin, and all the tenderness he had been feeling for Kitty a minute before was replaced by a feeling of anger for the slight he had suffered.

Dolly traded expressions of mock astonishment with Dolichka.

"What makes you suppose I know?"

"Because everybody knows it. . . . "

"That's just where you are mistaken; I did not know it, though I had guessed it was so."

"Well, now you know it."

"All I knew was that something had happened that made Kitty dreadfully miserable, and that she begged me never to speak of it, and then they left to orbit Venus. And if she would not tell me, she would certainly not speak of it to anyone else. But what did pass between you? Tell me."

"I have told you."

"When was it?"

"When I was at their house the last time."

"Do you know that," said Darya Alexandrovna, "I am awfully, awfully sorry for her. You suffer only from pride. . . . "

"Perhaps so," said Levin, "but—"

She interrupted him.

"But she, poor girl . . . I am awfully, awfully sorry for her. Now I see it all."

"Well, Darya Alexandrovna, you must excuse me," he said, getting up and signaling to Socrates his readiness to depart.

"No, wait a minute," she said, clutching him by the sleeve, as tears came into her eyes. "Wait a minute, sit down. If I did not like you, and if I did not know you, as I do know you . . . "

The feeling that had seemed dead revived more and more, rose up and took possession of Levin's heart.

"Yes, I understand it all now," Dolly said. "You can't understand it; for you men, who are free and make your own choice, it's always clear whom you love. But a girl's in a position of suspense, with all a woman's or maiden's modesty, a girl who sees you men from afar, who takes everything on trust—a girl may have, and often has, such a feeling that she cannot tell what to say."

"Yes, if the heart does not speak . . . "

"No, but I mean even when the heart *does* speak! *You* mean, you make an offer when your love is ripe or when the balance has completely turned between the two you are choosing from. But a girl is not asked. She is expected to make her choice, and yet she cannot choose, she can only answer 'yes' or 'no.' "

Yes, to choose between me and Vronsky, thought Levin, and the dead thing that had come to life within him died again, and weighed on his heart and set it aching. Socrates, with an uncharacteristic gesture of physical tenderness, placed a comforting arm across his master's hunched and agitated shoulders as Levin recalled Kitty's words. She had said: "*No, that cannot be. . . .* "

"Darya Alexandrovna," he said dryly, "I appreciate your confidence in me, but I believe you are making a mistake. But whether I am right or wrong, that pride you so despise makes any thought of Katerina Alexandrovna out of the question for me, you understand, utterly out of the question."

"I will only say one thing more," Dolly said. "You know that I am speaking of my sister, whom I love as I love my own children. I don't say she cared for you; all I meant to say is that her refusal at that moment proves nothing."

"I don't know!" said Levin, jumping up. "If you only knew how you are hurting me. It's just as if a child of yours were dead, and they were to say to you: He might have been like this, or like that, and if you could travel back in time . . . but man cannot travel in time! The experiment has been attempted and abandoned, so what is the use of imagining!"

"How absurd you are!" said Dolly, looking with mournful tenderness at Levin's excitement. "Yes, I see it all more and more clearly," she went on musingly. "So you won't come to see us, then, when Kitty's here?"

"No, I shan't come. Of course I won't avoid meeting Katerina Alexandrovna, but as far as I can, I will try to save her the annoyance of my presence."

"You are very, very absurd," Dolly repeated, looking with tenderness into his face.

Levin and Socrates said good-bye and drove away while Dolly and her beloved-companion bade them farewell from the front yard of the house at Ergushovo. Before she turned back into the house Dolly paused, her hands frozen at her hips, as she listened to a faint but distinct noise from the middle distance:

Tikka tikka tikka.

Tikka tikka tikka. Tikkatikkatikkatikka . . .

"*Oh dear oh dear,*" said Dolichka, and Dolly murmured her agreement. "Oh dear, indeed."

CHAPTER 5

"WELL, WHAT AM I GOING to do with my life?" said Levin to Socrates the next morning, as they joined a team of peasants, delivering a freshly excavated batch of ore to the smeltworks. "How am I to set about it?"

He was trying to express to his Class III the range of ideas and emotions he had passed through since their visit to Dolly and her family. Socrates, employing his advanced circuits for logic, sorted all his master's thoughts and feelings into a thought matrix for him. Thought Category A was the renunciation of his old life, of his utterly useless education. This renunciation gave Levin satisfaction, and was easy and simple. Thought Category B was a series of mental images related to the life he longed to live now. The simplicity, the purity, the sanity of this life he felt clearly, and he was convinced he would find in it the content, the peace, and the dignity, of the lack of which he was so miserably conscious.

But Thought Category C turned upon the question of how to effect this transition from the old life to the new. And there nothing took clear shape for him. Socrates, in his efficient and meticulous way, rapidly divided and subdivided the possibilities:

POSSIBILITY 1. Have a wife?
POSSIBILITY 2. Have work and the necessity of work?
POSSIBILITY 3. Leave Provokovskoe?
POSSIBILITY 4. Buy land?
POSSIBILITY 5. Become a member of a peasant community?
POSSIBILITY 6. Marry a peasant girl?

"But how am I to set about such things?" Levin said confusedly in reply, and Socrates' logistical circuits set busily back to work.

"Never mind, never mind," Levin said then. "I'll work it out later. One thing's certain, this night has decided my fate. All my old dreams of home life were absurd."

"Absurd," Socrates seconded reluctantly, not wishing to confirm such a dismal verdict, but unwilling also to contradict his master in such a mood.

"It's all ever so much simpler and better to ... to ... "

"Master?"

"How beautiful!" Levin exclaimed, and Socrates tilted back his head unit to take in the sight: a daylight meteor shower, with dozens of golden-red stars dancing in their turns across the clear blue sky. "How exquisite a sight on this exquisite morning! And when and how do such things come to be! Just now I looked at the sky, and there was nothing in it—just the clouds and the gentle glow of the sun. And now, this display of stunning beauty! Yes, and so imperceptibly too my views of life changed!"

Shrinking from the cold, Levin walked rapidly, looking at the ground. "What's that? Someone's coming," he said suddenly, catching the tinkle of bells, and lifting his head.

"At forty paces, master . . . there . . . "

Indeed, at forty paces, a carriage harnessed to a four-treaded Puller was driving toward him along the grassy road on which he was walking. The treads were shallow, designed primarily for city travel rather than the countryside, but the dexterous Class II driver held a careful hand on the shaft, so that the treads stayed on the smooth part of the road.

This was all Levin noticed, and without wondering who it could be, he gazed absently at the coach.

In the coach was an old lady dozing in one corner, and at the window, evidently only just awake, sat, perfectly still, a young girl holding in both hands the ribbons of a white cap. With a face entirely absent of thought or attention she stared out the window of the carriage. Levin realized that this girl was hibernating, in the state of chemically induced suspended animation into which ill people are commonly placed to better bear the rigors of the journey to and from an orbital.

At the moment Levin realized upon whom he was gazing, her subdermal anesthesia wore off, and slowly she began to wake. Her eyes blinked once, and then again, and then fell shut—but her face was alive again, full of light and thought, full of a subtle, complex inner life that was remote from Levin.

He watched, wonderingly, as the eyes—such familiar eyes—slowly opened again, like flowers newly budding. And then she recognized him, and her face, in the hazy glow of gradually returning consciousness, lighted up with wondering delight.

He could not be mistaken. There were no other eyes like those in the world. There was only one creature in the world who could concentrate for him all the brightness and meaning of life. It was she. It was

Kitty. He understood that she was driving to Ergushovo from the Grav station. And everything that had been stirring Levin during that sleepless night, all the resolutions he had made, all the branching algorithmic calculations that Socrates had produced, all vanished at once. He recalled with horror his dreams of marrying a peasant girl. Only there, in the carriage that had crossed over to the other side of the road, and was rapidly disappearing, only there could he find the solution to the riddle of his life, which had weighed so agonizingly upon him of late.

She did not look out again. The sound of the carriage-treads faded; the drone of the II/Driver could scarcely be heard. The barking of dogs showed the carriage had reached the village, and all that was left was the empty fields all around, the village in front, and he and Socrates wandering lonely along the deserted high road.

He glanced at the sky, expecting again to see the meteor shower, that miracle of blazing torches pirouetting though the daylight. But there was nothing in the sky; there, in the remote heights above, a mysterious change had been accomplished. The sky was empty of falling stars; it had grown blue and bright; and with the same softness, but with the same remoteness, it met his questioning gaze.

"No," he said to Socrates, "however good that life of simplicity and toil may be . . . "

"You cannot go back to it."

"No, dear friend, I cannot. I love *her*."

CHAPTER 6

ALEXEI ALEXANDROVICH'S singular beloved-companion, his dread Face, had been biding its time. Ever since its machine consciousness had first flickered into existence, it had lurked, a creature of the shadows, flitting in the recesses of Karenin's mind, growing, evolving, gaining strength, gaining power.

Now its moment had come.

When, returning from the Cull, Anna had informed him of her relations with Vronsky, and immediately afterward—when, as their carriage weathered the emotion bombs, she had burst into tears, hiding her face in her hands—Alexei Alexandrovich was aware immediately of a crying out in his breast of pure human emotion, of the abiding empathy he still harbored for this woman he had loved for so long; it brought to him a rush of that emotional disturbance always produced in him by tears. But in the next instant, that burst of humane feeling in his breast was countered by a searing stream of invective from the Face, which demanded in a cold, vicious voice, speaking out in his mind, that he silence his tears and summon his manful qualities.

BE MORE OF METAL THAN OF FLESH, ALEXEI ALEXANDROVICH, the Face had exhorted him, and so he had, stiffening his spine and keeping his emotions carefully controlled. He tried to suppress every manifestation of life in himself, and so neither stirred nor looked at her. This was what had caused that strange expression of deathlike rigidity in his face, which had so impressed Anna.

When they reached the house he helped her to get out of the carriage, and making an effort to master himself, took leave of her with his usual urbanity; he said that tomorrow he would let her know his decision.

His wife's words, confirming his worst suspicions, had sent a cruel pang to the heart of Alexei Alexandrovich. That pang was intensified by the strange feeling of physical pity triggered by her tears, and intensified all the more by the harsh, mocking laughter of the Face, laughter directed as much at his pity as at her tears.

But later, when he was all alone, Alexei Alexandrovich, to his surprise and delight, felt complete relief both from this pity and from the doubts and agonies of jealousy. He felt strong and powerful, and the Face was determined to feed those feelings, just as a master throws scraps of bloody meat to his dog.

NO HONOR. NO HEART. NO RELIGION, spat the Face, and Karenin bitterly agreed.

"A corrupt woman," he concluded aloud, sitting in his study, alone but not alone, in the darkest hours of that night.

YOU ALWAYS KNEW IT AND ALWAYS SAW IT.

"I tried to deceive myself to spare her."

SPARE HER? FOR WHAT REASON? TO WHAT PURPOSE?

Alexei Alexandrovich had never been so glad for the presence of his metal-thinking attachment, his *secret* beloved-companion—for it could bluntly address those things he could think but never express. Its mechanical eye showed him dark mysteries, and its voice demanded he acknowledge life's darker truths.

"I made a mistake in linking my life to hers, but there was nothing wrong in my mistake, and so I cannot be unhappy."

BUT SHE . . . SHE MUST BE MADE UNHAPPY.

Everything relating to her and her son, toward whom his sentiments were as much changed as toward her, ceased to interest him. The only thing that interested him now was the question of in what way he could best, with most propriety and comfort for himself, and thus with most justice, extricate himself from the mud with which she had spattered him in her fall, and then proceed along his path of active, honorable, and useful existence.

Even as he processed these perfectly rational thoughts, even congratulating himself on his ability to remain logical in the grip of emotional distress, his body, guided by the vicious impulses of the Face, obeyed a different course. Alexei Alexandrovich strode briskly into the bedroom while siding onto his ring finger, just above his wedding ring, a small silver burn-circle—an ingenious groznium-based device of his own invention—and set about incinerating his wife's possessions with cruel efficiency.

"I cannot be made unhappy by the fact that a contemptible woman has committed a crime," he said, and, leveling his hand carefully, blasted

Anna Karenina's ancient and stately armoire to splinters with the burn-circle.

"I have only to find the best way out of the difficult position in which she has placed me."

He aimed at and destroyed her birch-wood dressing table.

"And I shall find it."

YOU SHALL FIND IT INDEED.

Moving rapidly, deeply inhaling the sharp, pleasing scent of burnt furniture mixed with perfumes and bedside lotions, he felt that he could think clearly for the first time in a long time. In his study Alexei Alexandrovich walked up and down twice, then stopped at the household's expensive and stately freestanding monitor. He bent his head on one side, thought a minute, and began to dictate a communiqué, without pausing for a second.

"At our last conversation," he began, *"I notified you of my intention to communicate to you my decision in regard to the subject of that conversation. Having carefully considered everything, I am contacting you now with the object of fulfilling that promise. My decision is as follows. Whatever your conduct may have been, I do not consider myself justified in breaking the ties in which we are bound by a Higher Power, and the beneficence of the Ministry. The family cannot be broken up by a whim, a caprice, or even by the sin of one of the partners in the marriage, and our life must go on as it has done in the past. This is essential for me, for you, and for our son. I am fully persuaded that you have repented and do repent of what has called forth the present letter, and that you will cooperate with me in eradicating the cause of our estrangement, and forgetting the past. In the contrary event, you can conjecture what awaits you and your son. I trust that you understand."*

"Yes, time will pass—time, which arranges all things, and the old relations will be re-established," Alexei Alexandrovich announced to the Face, which fairly cackled its pleasure at the implied threat Alexei had leveled at his wife: to be subject to his will, or be destroyed. "So far re-established, that is, that I shall not be sensible of a break in the continuity of my life. She is bound to be unhappy, but I am not to blame, and so I cannot be unhappy."

Having completed and transmitted his communiqué, he returned to the bedchamber, slipping back on his burn-circle as he went. With calm deliberateness Alexei Alexandrovich destroyed the four-post bed in which he and his wife had lain together so many times. The sheets of silk and linen easily took to flame, and Alexei Alexandrovich, tucking his fleshy hand comfortably into the crook of his arm, watched the fire grow—the Face whispering **GOOD GOOD GOOD** as the bed was consumed into ash.

CHAPTER 7

THOUGH ANNA HAD OBSTINATELY and with exasperation contradicted Vronsky when he told her their position was impossible, at the bottom of her heart she regarded her own position as false and dishonorable, and she longed with her whole soul to change it.

On the way home from the Cull she had told her husband the truth in a moment of excitement, and in spite of the agony of the moment, she was glad of it. After her husband had left her, she told herself that she was glad, that now everything was made clear, and at least there would be no more lying and deception. It seemed to her beyond doubt that her position was now made clear forever. It might be bad, this new position, but it would be clear; there would be no indefiniteness or falsehood about it. That evening she saw Vronsky, but she did not tell him of what had passed between her and her husband, though, to make the position definite, it was necessary to tell him.

When she woke up the next morning, Android Karenina was seated with perfect poise at her bedside, having completed her morning routines, and gazing down with calm beneficence upon her mistress; as Anna opened her eyes she saw the Class III there, silhouetted against the day's first light—they stared at one another, eyes into faceplate, sharing one brief intense moment before Android Karenina rose to fetch her mistress's dressing gown.

In the perfect serenity of the new day, the words she had spoken to her husband seemed to her so awful that she could not conceive now how she could have brought herself to utter those strange, coarse words, and could not imagine what would come of it. But the words were spoken, and Alexei Alexandrovich had gone away without saying anything. "I saw Vronsky and did not tell him," she said to Android Karenina, as the Class III slipped her gown over her porcelain shoulders.

"At the very instant he was going away I would have turned him back and told him, but I changed my mind, because it was strange that I had not told him the first minute. Why was it I wanted to tell him and did not tell him?" In answer to this question Android Karenina issued a light, empathetic whistle and tidied the bedclothes.

Anna's position, which had seemed to her simplified the night before, suddenly struck her now as not only not simple, but as absolutely hopeless. She felt terrified at the disgrace, of which she had not ever thought before. When she thought of what her husband would do, the most terrible ideas came to her mind. She had a vision of being turned out of the house, of her shame being proclaimed to all the world. She asked herself where she should go when she was turned out of the house, and she could not find an answer.

When she thought of Vronsky, it seemed to her that he did not love her, that he was already beginning to be tired of her, that she could not offer herself to him, and she felt bitter against him for it. It seemed to her that the words that she had spoken to her husband, and had continually repeated in her imagination, she had said to everyone, and everyone had heard them. She could not bring herself to look those of her own household in the face. She could not bring herself to call her II/Maid/76, and still less go downstairs and see her son and his II/Governess/D145.

As she fretted and paced about her room, her anxiety deepened into a distinct feeling of dread, reminding her powerfully and unpleasantly of her feeling at the Moscow Grav station, watching the body of the man lifted from the tracks. Android Karenina then beeped gently, signaling receipt of a communiqué, and Anna, trembling, bid her play it. Just moments before, she had regretted that she had spoken to her husband, and wished for nothing so much as that those words could be unspoken. And here this communiqué regarded them as unspoken, and gave her what she had wanted. But the communiqué seemed to her more awful than anything she had been able to conceive.

"He's right!" she said to Android Karenina, when the communiqué had played through and dimmed away. "Of course, he's always right; he's a Christian, he's generous! Yes, vile, base creature! And no one understands it except me, except *us*, and no one ever will; and I can't explain it. They say he's so religious, so high-principled, so upright, so clever; but they don't see what I've seen. They don't know how he has crushed my life for eight years, crushed everything that was living in me—he has not once even thought that I'm a live woman who must have love. They don't know how at every step he's humiliated me, and been just as pleased with himself."

Android Karenina took on a crimson glow, moving to darker and darker shades of crimson, her coloring embodying her mistress's wild flush of emotion.

"Haven't I striven, striven with all my strength, to find something to give meaning to my life? Haven't I struggled to love him, to love my son when I could not love my husband? But the time came when I knew that I couldn't cheat myself any longer, that I was alive, that I was not to blame, that God has built me so that I must love and live. And now what does he do? If he'd killed me, if he'd killed him, I could have borne anything, I could have forgiven anything; but, no, he . . . How was it I didn't guess what he would do? He's doing just what's characteristic of his mean character. He'll keep himself in the right, while me, in my ruin, he'll drive still lower to worse ruin yet. . . . "

She recalled the words from the communiqué: *You can conjecture what awaits you and your son.* . . . "That's a threat to take away my child, or worse, and Heaven knows he, he who sits in the Higher Branches, may do as he wishes! And he has been . . . has been . . . "

Android Karenina nodded, and Anna knew that her beloved-companion understood: Karenin had been changing, in ways as impossible to describe as they were to ignore.

"He doesn't believe even in my love for my child," Anna continued bitterly, "Or he despises it, just as he always used to ridicule it. He despises that feeling in me, but he knows that I won't abandon my child, that I can't abandon my child, that there could be no life for me without my child, even with him whom I love; but that if I abandoned my child and ran away from him, I should be acting like the most infamous, basest of women. He knows that, and knows that I am incapable of doing that."

She recalled another sentence in the communiqué: *Our life must go on as it has done in the past.* . . . "That life was miserable enough in the old days; it has been awful of late. What will it be now? And he knows all that; he knows that I can't repent that I breathe, that I love; he knows that it can lead to nothing but lying and deceit; but he wants to go on torturing me. I know him; I know that he's at home and is happy in deceit, like a fish swimming in the water. No, I won't give him that happiness. I'll break through the spiderweb of lies in which he wants to catch me, come what may. Anything's better than lying and deceit.

"But how? My God! My God! Was ever a woman so miserable as I am . . . ?"

Anna collapsed in tears, and Android Karenina gathered her up and held her close, and Anna's tears poured into the metal lap of her only friend.

CHAPTER 8

IN SPITE OF VRONSKY'S apparently frivolous life in society, he was a man who hated irregularity. He liked to know, for instance, that all of his weapons were in proper working order at all times, and particularly when (according to the rumor currently making the regimental rounds) the Ministry's Department of War was preparing to deploy them against some new, unnamed threat. So he would shut himself up alone and go through each weapon, from grip to muzzle, to satisfy himself that all was in proper working order. This he called his day of reckoning or *faire la lessive*.

On waking up the day after the Cull, Vronsky put on a white linen coat, and without shaving or taking his bath, he distributed about him all the different pieces of weaponry he used, whether frequently or infrequently. Lupo padded in happy circles in a square of sunlight on the floor of the room, ready to be of use if needed, prepared even to act as a moving target if his master was in a mood to practice his aim.

As he worked, Vronsky considered the complexities of his life. Every man who knows the minutest details of the conditions surrounding him cannot help imagining that the complexity of these conditions, and the difficulty of making them clear, is something exceptional and personal, peculiar to himself, and never supposes that others are surrounded by just as complicated an array of personal affairs as he is. So indeed it seemed to Vronsky. And not without inward pride, he thought that any other man would long ago have been in difficulties, would have been forced to some dishonorable course, if he had found himself in such a difficult position. But Vronsky felt that now especially it was essential for him to clear up and define his position if he were to avoid getting into difficulties. As he thought, he bent over his work table.

What Vronsky attacked first were the small arms, the special favorite pieces he kept on his person, and for which he was known. These amounted to: the smokers, which sat with pride on his belt, one jutting forth from each hip; the smoldering hot-whip that coiled around his upper thigh in its transparent skin; and the gleaming crackle dagger tucked into his handsome, black leather boot.

He found all in excellent condition: the smokers unloaded their sizzling streams at the rate of sixteen'a'second, twice the regimental standard. At the pressure of his thumb on the hilt, the hot-whip leaped to life like an extension of his arm, and snapped across the length of the room in all directions. The crackle dagger he hurled with deadly accuracy into the far corner of his lodgings, propelling it into the body of a raccoon, which had picked the wrong moment to emerge from hiding behind the wastepaper basket.

He plucked the twitching, electrocuted raccoon from the blade, and tossed it to Lupo before, remembering his conversation with Anna from the previous day, he sank into meditation.

Vronsky's life was particularly happy in that he had a code of principles that defined with unfailing certitude what he ought and what he ought not to do. This code of principles covered only a very small circle of contingencies, but then the principles were never doubtful, and Vronsky, as he never went outside that circle, had never had a moment's hesitation about doing what he ought to do. In his own mind, he jokingly referred to these principles as the "Bronze Laws," in winking homage to the Iron Laws that regulated robot behavior.

Vronsky's Bronze Laws were a set of invariable rules: that one must never tell a lie to a man, but one may to a woman; that one must never cheat anyone, but one may a husband; that one must never pardon an insult, but one may give one; and so on. These principles were possibly not reasonable and not good, but they were of unfailing certainty, and so long as he adhered to them, Vronsky felt that his heart was at peace and he could hold his head up. Only quite lately in regard to his relations with Anna, Vronsky had begun to feel that his code of principles did not fully cover all possible contingencies, and to foresee in the future difficulties and perplexities for which he could find no guiding clue.

He sighed and turned his little tour of inspection to the complex pieces of ordnance: there was the shoulder-mounted Disrupter; the Demagnetizing Wand; the gleaming obsidian Sapper Gun; and, of course, the dreaded organ-destabilizing propellant gun known as the "Tsar's Vengeance." One by one, he picked up each deadly machine, and with practiced ease disassembled it, inspected the connections, slicked the gears with fresh humectant, and snapped all back in place.

The familiar and repetitive actions cleared his mind and gladdened his heart. His present relation to Anna and to her husband was to his mind clear and simple. It was clearly and precisely defined in the code of principles by which he was guided.

She was an honorable woman who had bestowed her love upon him, and he loved her, and therefore she was in his eyes a woman who had a right to the same, or even more, respect than a lawful wife. He would have had his hand chopped off before he would have allowed himself by a word, by a hint, to humiliate her, or even to fall short of the fullest respect a woman could look for.

His attitude to society, too, was clear. Everyone might know, might suspect it, but no one might dare to speak of it. If any did so, he was ready to force all who might speak to be silent and to respect the nonexistent honor of the woman he loved.

"Ah!" he shouted as, in his split concentration, he closed the clip of the Disrupter over his hand, pinching his fingertips. "Dratted thing."

Vronsky's attitude to the husband was the clearest of all. Thinking of Alexei Alexandrovich, he selected the next weapon from the table, an experimental device called a Particulate Intensifier—one of only seven yet in existence, according to the conspiratorial gadgetman who had sold it to him—and leveled it at the target bay he'd had constructed in the far corner of his chamber.

Vronsky paused before firing the Particulate Intensifier. From the moment that Anna loved him, he had regarded his own right over her as the one thing unassailable. Her husband was simply a superfluous and tiresome person. No doubt he was in a pitiable position, but how could that be helped? He squinted, drew his aim, and pictured superfluous and tiresome Alexei Alexandrovich standing in the target bay, imagined the smirking, half-metal face, and squeezed the trigger.

The target rattled violently for three long seconds, then exploded in a tumult of splintered wood and orange flares; Lupo howled his approval, dancing on his four legs about the room catching sparks and shards on his tongue like snowflakes. Vronsky smiled and looked at this new weapon admiringly. If it crossed his mind that Alexei Alexandrovich was no ordinary husband, and that he might have powers both literally and figuratively greater than any Vronsky may have previously encountered, he did not let that fact bother him. Striding about in his regimental barracks, surrounded by the deadly accoutrements of his trade, Vronsky could feel no sense that there was any man in the world more powerful than he, nor more deserving of the woman upon whom he had settled his attentions.

And yet, of late, new inner relations had arisen between him and her, which frightened Vronsky by their indefiniteness. Only the day before she had told him that she was with child. And he felt that this fact and what she expected of him called for something not fully defined in that code of principles by which he had hitherto steered his course in life. And he had been indeed caught unawares, and at the first moment when she spoke to him of her position, at that awful moment when the godmouth had yawned open and threatened to swallow her away forever, his heart had prompted him to beg her to leave her husband. He had said that, but now thinking things over he saw clearly that it would be better to manage to avoid that; and at the same time, as he told himself so, he was afraid whether it was not wrong.

"If I told her to leave her husband, that must mean uniting her life with mine; am I prepared for that? How can I take her away now, when I have no money? Supposing I could arrange . . . But how can I take her away while I'm in the service? If I say that, I ought to be prepared to do it, that is, I ought to have the money and to retire from the army. But . . . to retire from the army? Can I?" he said to Lupo, bending to scratch the wolf-like Class III in the sensitive spot above his Third Bay.

He flung his crackle dagger again, with an extra curl of the wrist, and watched it sail toward the wall before swinging itself around like a Carpathian throwing stick toward the opposite corner of the room, where it embedded itself solidly in the heart of a second racoon.

Vronsky let out a long whistle, low and admiring, while Lupo retrieved the catch. He had worked all the days of his life to earn his place: the right to wield such powerful devices. Ambition was the old dream of his youth and childhood, a dream which he did not confess even to himself, though it was so strong that now this passion was even doing battle with his love.

"Women are the chief stumbling block in a man's career," his old friend Serpuhovskoy had pronounced the previous night, as they raised glasses together in memoriam of poor Frou-Frou. "It's hard to love a woman and do anything. There's only one way of having love conveniently without its being a hindrance—that's marriage."

"But Serpuhovskoy has never loved," Vronsky murmured softly now, looking straight before him and thinking of Anna. Sensing the drift of his master's thoughts, Lupo yelped sharply in protest, regarding Vronsky with eyes like slits; a Regimental Class III, he was naturally anxious that Vronsky should remain in the service.

"Yes, yes, you're right," Vronsky said. "If I retire, I burn my ships. If I remain in the army, I lose nothing. She said herself she did not wish to change her position." And slowly twirling his mustache, he got up from the table and walked about the room. His eyes shone particularly brightly, and he felt in that confident, calm, and happy frame of mind which always came after he had thoroughly faced his position. Everything was straight and clear, every piece of his armory having been checked and rechecked and fired—except the Tsar's Vengeance, which even the most elite soldiers were not permitted to discharge outside of combat situations—and stowed in its proper place.

Except his oldest and dearest friends: his simple, beloved smokers. Before reholstering them, Vronsky took one more trick shot, admiring the way the weapons' hot blast lit up the four corners of the room.

Lupo ducked and rolled, his Vox-Em howling in vigorous approval of his master's steady eye.

CHAPTER 9

I T WAS SIX O'CLOCK ALREADY, and so, in order to reach Anna quickly, and at the same time not to drive with his own carriage, known to everyone, Vronsky got into Yashvin's hired fly, and ordered the II/Coachman/644 to drive as quickly as possible. It was a roomy, old-fashioned fly, with seats for four. He sat in one corner, stretched his legs out on the front seat, and sank into meditation.

I'm happy, very happy! he said to himself. He had often before had a sense of physical joy in his own body, but he had never felt so fond of himself, of his every sinew, as at that moment. He enjoyed the slight ache in his strong leg, an aftereffect of the catastrophe at the Cull, and he enjoyed the muscular sensation of movement in his chest as he breathed. The bright, cold August day, which had made Anna feel so hopeless, seemed to him keenly stimulating, and refreshed his face and neck, which still tingled from the cold water. The scent of brilliantine on his whiskers struck him as particularly pleasant in the fresh air. Everything he saw from

the carriage window, everything in that cold, pure air, in the pale light of
the sunset, was as fresh and cheery and strong as he was himself: the roofs
of the houses shining in the rays of the setting sun, the strong Russian
four-treads driven by gleaming groznium androids, the sharp outlines of
fences and angles of buildings, the figures of passers-by, the motionless
green of the trees and grass, the airships in their slow, majestic glide, the
hydroponic greenhouses where grew the massive super-potatoes, each of
which would feed a peasant family for a week—everything was bright
like a pretty landscape just finished and freshly varnished.

"Get on, get on!" he said to the driver, putting his head out of the
window, giving the Class II a light jolt with his hot-whip, and the carriage rolled rapidly along the smooth highroad.

"I want nothing, nothing but this happiness," Vronsky declared to
Lupo, who gave a happy woof of agreement before sticking his head out
the carriage window to taste the wind.

"And as I go on," Vronsky declared further, "I love her more and
more. Ah, here's the garden of the Vrede Villa"—where they had planned
to meet. *Whereabouts will she be?* he wondered. *How will she look?*

He ordered the driver to stop before reaching the avenue, and,
opening the door, jumped out of the carriage as it was moving, and went
into the avenue that led up to the house. There was no one in the avenue;
but looking round to the right he caught sight of her. Her face was hidden by a veil, but he drank in with glad eyes the special movement in
walking, peculiar to her alone, the slope of the shoulders and the setting
of the head, and at once a sort of electric shock ran all over him, as if
someone had jolted *him* with a hot-whip. With fresh force, he felt conscious of himself, from the springy motions of his legs to the movements
of his lungs as he breathed, and something set his lips twitching.

Joining him, she pressed his hand tightly.

"You're not angry that I sent for you? I absolutely had to see you,"
she said; and the serious and set line of her lips, which he saw under the
veil, transformed his mood at once.

"I, angry?" he stammered, taken aback by her somber demeanor. "Of course not! But—how have you come, where from?"

"Never mind," she said, laying her hand on his. "I must talk to you."

She and Android Karenina were standing beneath a flowering tree, of a kind that Vronsky had never seen before, with large, overhanging emerald petals. The tree had an unfamiliar and vaguely foreboding appearance, which seemed in keeping with Anna's expression. Vronsky saw clearly that something had happened, and that the rendezvous would not be a joyous one. For all the elation he had felt just a minute before, in her presence he had no will of his own: without knowing the grounds of her distress, he already felt the same distress unconsciously passing over him. He felt like a robot who'd had a burst of rainwater splashed violently behind its faceplate, shorting out his ability to reason and rendering him a useless, immobile hunk of man-shaped debris.

"What is it? What?" he asked her, squeezing her hand with his elbow, and trying to read her thoughts in her face.

She waited a few steps in silence, leaning against the trunk of the peculiar tree, gathering her courage; then suddenly she stopped.

"Yesterday," she began, breathing quickly and painfully, "coming home with Alexei Alexandrovich I told him everything . . . told him I could not be his wife, that . . . and told him everything."

He heard her, unconsciously bending his whole figure down to her as though hoping in this way to soften the hardness of her position for her. But as soon as she had said this he suddenly drew himself up, and a proud and hard expression came over his face.

"Yes, yes, that's better, a thousand times better! I know how painful it was," he said.

But she was not listening to his words; she was reading his thoughts from the expression of his face. She could not guess that that expression arose from the first idea that presented itself to Vronsky—that a duel was now inevitable. The idea of a duel had never crossed her mind, and so she put a different interpretation on this passing expression of hardness.

For Anna, when she got her husband's communiqué, she knew at the bottom of her heart that everything would go on in the old way, that she would not have the strength of will to forego her position, to abandon her son, and to join her lover. But this talk with Vronsky was still of the utmost gravity for her. She had hoped that their conversation would transform her position, and save her. If on hearing this news he were to say to her resolutely, passionately, without an instant's wavering: "Throw up everything and come with me!" she would give up her son and go away with him. But her news had not produced what she had expected in him; he simply seemed as though he were resenting some affront.

"It was not in the least painful to me. It happened of itself," she said irritably, "and see . . ." With a brusque gesture, she directed Android Karenina to play the communiqué for Vronsky.

"I understand, I understand," he interrupted her, ignoring the android's display, not hearing Anna's words, only trying to in vain to soothe her. As he held her in his arms he happened to glance above her head, and observed that one of the unusual tree's emerald flowers had suddenly blossomed—at least, the flower was open, and he was certain, or thought he was certain, that only a moment ago it had been quite shut.

"Anna," he began, but then drew silent, staring at the curious tree as it grew more curious still: A thin film had emerged from within the bell of the flower, and it descended slowly, pouring down over the sides, as if a child with a Class I toy were inside the plant, blowing a bubble.

Anna scowled at his distraction, and he shook his head and focused his eyes upon her. "The one thing I longed for," he continued, "the one thing I prayed for, was to cut short this position, so as to devote my life to your happiness."

"Why do you tell me that?" she said. "Do you suppose I can doubt it? If I doubted—"

A sudden noise made Vronsky start. "Who's that coming?" he asked, pointing to two ladies walking toward them. "Perhaps they know us!" He abruptly took a step backward into the foliage.

"Oh, I don't care!" Anna said, turning away from him. Her lips were quivering. And he fancied that her eyes looked with strange fury at him from under the veil. "Just see what he says to me. Watch the communiqué." She cued Android Karenina to begin again.

Vronsky watched the display, and once again was unconsciously carried away by the sensations aroused in him by his own relation to the betrayed husband. Now he could not help picturing the challenge, which he would most likely find at home today or tomorrow, and the duel itself, in which, with the same cold and haughty expression that his face was assuming at this moment, he would await the injured husband's shot, after having himself gallantly fired his smokers into the air. And at that instant there flashed across his mind the thought of what Serpuhovskoy had said to him, and what he had himself been thinking in the morning—that it was better not to bind himself—and he knew that this thought he could not tell her.

Neither Anna nor Vronsky, preoccupied by these thoughts and counter-thoughts running through their minds while the communiqué played, noticed what transpired directly above her head: the transparent film oozing from the odd flowering tree had silently ballooned outward to huge, though near-invisible, proportions. Now, like a soap bubble, it popped free of the tree and closed around Anna's body, so thin and transparent as to be imperceptible even as it hardened into an impenetrable shell.

"You see the sort of man he is," Anna said, with a shaking voice. "He . . ."

"I rejoice at this!" Vronsky said, speaking at the same time. Each was on their own side of the unseen sphere, and so neither could hear the other; and with Anna looking off into the distance, neither could even see that the other was speaking.

"Things can't go on as they have," Vronsky continued. "I hope that now you will leave him. I hope that you will let me arrange and plan our life."

Unaware, Anna carried on her own conversation: " . . . my child! I should have to leave him!"

Android Karenina looked around curiously. Lupo sniffed the air, with a dawning awareness that something was dreadfully amiss.

And so it went. Not hearing, both lovers simply assumed they knew what the other was thinking. When Vronsky finally looked away from Android Karenina's monitor and raised his eyes to Anna, she did not know what caused them to seem so implacable; she knew only that, whatever he might say to her, he would not say all he thought. And she was certain her last hope had failed her. This was not what she had been reckoning on. And while these sickening thoughts chased themselves around in her mind, the sides of the near-invisible sheath drew taut under her feet like the cinching of a drawstring sack, and she lurched off the ground and up into the air.

"My God!" Vronsky shouted, noticing her for the first time: "Anna! You are floating!"

As if the strange conveyance that was carrying Anna into the air somehow knew it had been discovered, it accelerated the upward motion with which it was lifting her off her feet. Lupo leaped up on his powerful, pneumatic-actuated legs toward the mysterious conveyance, but it was already too high to be reached.

"Stay the thing, Lupo!" shouted Vronsky, reverting at once to his regimental training. Lupo, settling back on his haunches, made his wide, fierce mouth into a perfect O and howled out a resonating battle-cry, sending a precisely modulated echo wave toward the base of Anna's airborne prison—steadying it against the wind and holding it in place. Vronsky searched furiously for a way to deliver Anna to safety, even as, in the back of his mind, he wondered: first a godmouth, and now this bubble-like cage of a prison? UnConSciya was trying to capture or kill Anna Karenina. But why?

He squatted, plucked the crackle-dagger from his boot, and stared carefully towards his target. An inch too high, and the dagger would sail uselessly off into the gardens; an inch too low, and it would bounce harmlessly off the side of the bubble—or, worse, slice through the exterior and into Anna's precious flesh. He squinted, took aim . . . and hesitated, as the wind shifted the bubble ever so slightly upon the air. Lupo redoubled his powerful air-disrupting war cry, but Vronsky knew he hadn't much time left before the shell would be borne off by the winds.

Inside her queer floating prison, Anna looked down upon Vronsky, in his soldier's crouch with weapons drawn, and, despite the furious tangle of fears and doubts that had gripped her, felt her heart wrung by love. *He is a man of action,* she thought, *a man who does not hesitate to grab hold of whatever life presents to him. That is how I am meant to live: with truth, with purpose, with vitality. I cannot give this up—cannot give him up, cannot stop loving him. But . . . am I really prepared to leave my husband? To lose my son? To abandon all I have begun, all I have known? To uproot my life entirely?*

At that thought, all her problems coalesced. Of course! Anna gestured frantically to Vronsky, waving and pointing. Her wild but deliberate motions captured his attention, stopping him just before his cocked arm would have sent the deadly crackle-dagger arcing towards her. At last, they were communicating.

Vronsky, following her pantomimed suggestion, swung his crackle-dagger around to attack not the flowering bubble that held her fast, but at the base of the tree whence it had come. Lupo joined in the assault, extending excavation-quality end-effectors from his paws to dig furiously at the root of the mechanical plant. Within moments, they severed the trunk from the earth, and as it creaked and fell to the ground, the bubble that had been its progeny dissipated—sending Anna tumbling down to where Android Karenina waited to catch her beloved mistress in her arms.

"MY GOD!" VRONSKY SHOUTED, AT LAST NOTICING: "ANNA! YOU ARE FLOATING!"

*   *   *

After Anna had assured Vronsky for the third time that she had suffered nothing but minor bruising in the fall, they sat beside each other upon the stone wall beside the tree.

She turned his face to hers, looking him squarely in the eye. With the intensity brought on by peril, they focused and listened to one another.

"I cannot lose my son," Anna began simply.

"But, for God's sake, which is better?—leave your child, or keep up this degrading position?"

"To whom is it degrading?"

"To all, and most of all to you."

As they spoke, Lupo padded carefully around the tree, sniffing at the earth, gathering up fragments of the translucent sheath for later analysis.

"You say degrading . . . don't say that. That has no meaning for me." Her voice shook. She did not want him now to say what was untrue. She had nothing left but his love, and she wanted to love him. "Don't you understand that from the day I loved you everything has changed for me? For me there is one thing, and one thing only—your love. If that's mine, I feel so exalted, so strong, that nothing can be humiliating to me. I am proud of my position, because . . . proud of being . . . proud . . . " She could not say what she was proud of. Tears of shame and despair choked her utterance. She stood still and sobbed.

He, too, felt, something swelling in his throat and twitching in his nose, and for the first time in his life Vronsky found himself on the point of weeping. The flower-trap; his love; their impossible situation; he could not have said exactly what it was that touched him so. He felt sorry for her, and he felt he could not help her, and with that he knew that he was to blame for her wretchedness, and that he had done something wrong.

"Is not a divorce possible?" he said feebly. She shook her head, not answering. "Couldn't you take your son, and still leave him?"

"Yes; but it all depends on him. Now I must go to him," she said shortly. Her presentiment that all would again go on in the old way had not deceived her.

"On Tuesday I shall be in Petersburg, and everything can be settled."

"Yes," she said. "But don't let us talk any more of it."

Anna's carriage, which she had sent away and ordered to come back to the little gate of the Vrede Garden, drove up. Anna said good-bye to Vronsky. Android Karenina gingerly lifted her up into their carriage, and they drove home.

CHAPTER 10

ON MONDAY THERE WAS the usual sitting of the Higher Branches of the Ministry. Alexei Alexandrovich walked into the hall where the sitting was held, greeted the members and the president as usual, and sat down in his place, the papers laid ready before him. Among these papers lay the necessary evidence and a rough outline of the speech he intended to make. But he did not really need these documents. He remembered every point, and did not think it necessary to go over in his memory what he would say. He knew that when the time came, and when he saw his enemy facing him, and studiously endeavoring to assume an expression of indifference, his speech would flow of itself better than he could prepare it now. The Face murmured quiet encouragement into his cerebral cortex, assuring him that the import of his speech was of such magnitude that every word of it would have weight. Meanwhile, as he listened to the usual report, he had the most innocent and inoffensive air. No one, looking at him gazing calmly through the monocle he wore, somewhat pompously, over his one human eye, and at the air of weariness with which his head drooped on one side, would have suspected that in a few minutes a torrent of words would flow from his lips that would arouse a fearful storm, set the members shouting and attacking one another, and force the president to call for order.

When the report was over, Alexei Alexandrovich announced in his subdued, delicate voice that he had several points to bring before the meeting in regard to the subsequent phases of the Project they had undertaken. All attention was turned upon him. Alexei Alexandrovich cleared his throat, and not looking at his opponent, but selecting, as he always did while he was delivering his speeches, the first person sitting opposite him, an inoffensive little old man who never had an opinion of any sort in the commission, began to expound his views.

"As those of you who have, like myself, been participants in the development of the Project are aware, the first phase of our noble endeavor has been a total and unqualified success."

SO IT HAS BEEN, hissed the Face. **SO I HAVE BEEN.**

"The second phase is now being made ready, under my direct supervision, in a subterranean work office in the Moscow Tower. The new prototype of robot, exactly as I planned, will have those three advancements we wished for: advancements in appearance, advancements in capacity, and advancements in the appropriate distribution of loyalty."

This set of euphemistic and jargonistic phrases earned a smattering of applause from Karenin's colleagues. But when he reached the point about the next phase of the Project, in which all Class III robots extant in Russian society would be gathered up and adjusted to meet the new standard, his opponent jumped up and began to protest. Stremov took the position that only those individuals who so desired it should have their Class IIIs updated to the new version that Karenin was perfecting. Stremov, who had long been Karenin's political enemy, was a man of fifty, partly gray, but still vigorous-looking, very ugly, but with a characteristic and intelligent face. He spoke longly and loudly about "ancient prerogatives" and the "unique nature of the bond between man and beloved-companion," and altogether a stormy sitting followed. But Alexei Alexandrovich triumphed, and his motion was carried, the oath of secrecy-unto-death was sworn; Alexei Alexandrovich's success had been even greater than he had anticipated.

Next morning, Tuesday, Alexei Alexandrovich, on waking up, recollected with pleasure his triumph of the previous day, and he could not help smiling. Absorbed in this pleasure, Alexei Alexandrovich had completely forgotten that it was Tuesday, the day fixed by him for the return of Anna Arkadyevna, and he was surprised and received a shock of annoyance when a II/Footman/74 motored in to inform him of her arrival.

Anna had arrived in Petersburg early in the morning; the carriage had been sent to meet her in accordance with her communiqué, and so Alexei Alexandrovich might have known of her arrival. But when she arrived, he did not meet her. She sent word to her husband that she had come, went to her own room, and occupied herself in sorting out her things, expecting he would come to her. But an hour passed; he did not come. She went into the dining room on the pretext of giving some directions, and spoke loudly on purpose, expecting him to come out there; but he did not come, though she heard him go to the door of his study. She knew that he usually went out quickly to his office, and she wanted to see him before that, so that their attitude to one another might be defined.

She walked across the drawing room and went resolutely to him. When she went into his study he was in official uniform, obviously ready to go out, sitting at a little table on which he rested his elbows, looking dejectedly before him. She saw him before he saw her, and she saw that he was thinking of her.

On seeing her, he would have risen, but changed his mind, then his metal faceplate rapidly radiated through a sequence of colors, from cruel red to a harsh, gleaming gold—an affect Anna had never seen before, and she thought to herself: *It is growing. All the time it is growing.*

Karenin got up quickly and went to meet her, looking not at her eyes, but above them at her forehead and hair. He went up to her, took her by the hand, and asked her to sit down.

"I am very glad you have come," he said, sitting down beside her, and obviously wishing to say something, he stuttered. Several times he tried to begin to speak, but stopped.

SPEAK, MAN. SPEAK! SO STEELY IN THE HALLS OF POWER, SO WEAK IN HIS OWN PRIVATE CHAMBERS. . . .

The silence lasted for some time. "Is Seryozha quite well?" he said, and not waiting for an answer, he added: "I shan't be dining at home today, and I have got to go out directly."

"I had thought of going to Moscow," she said.

"No, you did quite, quite right to come," he said, and was silent again.

Seeing that he was powerless to begin the conversation, she began herself.

"Alexei Alexandrovich," she said, looking at him and not dropping her eyes under his persistent gaze at her hair, "I'm a guilty woman, I'm a bad woman, but I am the same as I was, as I told you then, and I have come to tell you that I can change nothing."

"I have asked you no question about that," he said, all at once, resolutely and with hatred looking her straight in the face, and the Face again pulsed and radiated wild colors, venom traveling along its veins. "That was as I had supposed." Under the influence of anger he apparently regained complete possession of all his ability to speak. "But as I told you then, and have written to you," he said in a thin, shrill voice, "I repeat now, that I am not bound to know this. I ignore it. Not all wives are so kind as you, to be in such a hurry to communicate such agreeable news to their husbands." He laid special emphasis on the word "agreeable," and Anna thought she noticed that his voice changed as he said it, darkening dramatically in pitch and tone: **AGREEABLE**.

"I shall ignore it so long as the world knows nothing of it, so long as my name is not disgraced. And so I simply inform you that our relations must be just as they have always been, and that only in the event of your compromising me I shall be obliged to take steps to secure my honor."

"But our relations cannot be the same as always," Anna began in a timid voice, looking at him with dismay.

When she saw once more those composed gestures, heard that shrill, childish, and sarcastic voice, her aversion for him extinguished her pity for him, and she felt only afraid, but at all costs she wanted to make clear her position.

"I cannot be your wife while I . . . ," she began.

He laughed a cold and malignant laugh, and she felt a jab of sharp pain inside her mind, as if a knitting needle had been thrust between the lobes of her brain. She gave out a choked sob of pain, and Android Karenina, obeying her programmed impulses, reached out to place a comforting arm across her mistress's shoulders.

Karenin then spoke: "The manner of life you have chosen is reflected, I suppose, in your ideas. I have too much respect or contempt, or both . . . I respect your past and despise your present . . . that I was far from the interpretation you put on my words."

Anna sighed and bowed her head.

"Though indeed I fail to comprehend how—with the independence you show," he went on, getting hot, "announcing your infidelity to your husband and seeing nothing reprehensible in it, apparently—you can see anything reprehensible in performing a wife's duties in relation to your husband."

"Alexei Alexandrovich! What is it you want of me?"

TO REPENT OF HER UNFAITHFULNESS.

TO GROVEL AT YOUR FEET.

TO SUBMIT TO YOUR WILL, OR PAY THE ULTIMATE CONSE-QUENCE FOR HER REFUSAL!

Alexei Alexandrovich screamed out loud, and the little drawing-room table flew up into the air and spiraled over their heads to smash against the opposite wall. Anna whirled round in fright as a vase of flowers on the other side of the room suddenly exploded, as if shot; the door, which she had left ajar, slammed violently closed and the mechanism of the lock noisily engaged.

Anna turned back and gaped at Alexei Alexandrovich, who took a deep, labored breath as if trying to overmaster himself. Finally the room was still, and while Anna trembled, her husband calmly and coldly expressed his wishes. "I want you not to meet that man here, and to conduct yourself so that no one in the world, not even a *robot*, can find fault with you. Not to see him: that's not much, I think. And in return you will enjoy all the privileges of a faithful wife without fulfilling her duties. That's all I have to say to you. Tonight I am not dining at home." He folded his arms across his chest and turned away.

"Alexei?"

He looked back.

"Is it possible . . . for me to . . . " She looked with evident uncertainty to the heavy oaken door.

LEAVE IT.

LET HER STAY UNTIL SHE ROTS.

But Alexei Alexandrovich only shook his head slightly, and the lock disengaged, and the door swung open. Immediately, she got up, and signaled to Android Karenina that they would leave. Bowing in silence, Alexei Alexandrovich let them pass before him, visibly composed but inwardly as miserable and confused as she.

Only the Face was pleased, for in every such encounter it gained exponentially in power and control.

Over the man—over the woman—over them *all*.

CHAPTER 11

ONE AFTERNOON, TOWARD THE END of the spring extraction season, Levin and Socrates were in the living room, engaged in an intense discussion about the giant koschei that plagued the countryside around Provokovskoe. More and more peasants had reported hearing the dreaded *tikkatikkatikka* echoing through the woods at night; some spoke of friends who had gone out hunting and not returned; Levin spoke to one man who told personally of his battle with one of the robotic monsters, of how he narrowly escaped its tremendous gathering maw. Socrates had determined through rigorous analysis of recovered metallic shreds that the things were indeed of the same mechanical infrastructure as the small wormlike koschei that had plagued the countryside last season—but how they had grown so large, and so prevalent, especially after the Ministry had determined them exterminated, remained an open question.

While Socrates mulled this question yet one more time, charting out the various possibilities with branching mathematical precision in the chambers of his mind, Levin had a seemingly unrelated recollection that nevertheless chilled him to the bones: of Countess Nordston, Kitty's foolish friend, speaking of her belief in the Honored Guests—extraterrestrial beings who, supposedly, would one day come to redeem the human race.

"In three ways," she had said. *"They will come for us in three ways."*

Turning over this gnomic phrase in his mind, wondering what connection it could have to the question of the wormlike koschei, Levin did not at first hear the sound of a long, wrenching cough coming from the front hall. But he heard it indistinctly through the sound of his own footsteps, and hoped he was mistaken. Then he caught sight of a long, bony, familiar figure, followed by a squat, rattling metal shadow, and now it seemed there was no possibility of mistake; and yet he still went on hoping that this tall man taking off his fur cloak and coughing was not his brother, Nikolai, accompanied by his woeful Class III, Karnak.

Levin loved his brother, but being with him was always a torture. Levin was confused and anxious about the koschei, and had not seen his beloved Kitty since the day he spotted her, waking gently in her carriage, and he was in a troubled and uncertain humor; meeting with his ailing brother in such a state seemed particularly difficult. Instead of a lively, healthy visitor, some outsider who would, he hoped, cheer him up in his uncertain humor, he had to see his brother, who knew him through and through, who would call forth all the thoughts nearest his heart, would force him to show himself fully. And that he was not disposed to do.

Angry with himself for so base a feeling, Levin ran into the hall; as soon as he saw his brother close, this feeling of selfish disappointment vanished instantly and was replaced by pity. Terrible as his brother Nikolai had been before in his emaciation and sickliness, now he looked still more emaciated, still more wasted. He was a skeleton covered with skin.

He stood in the hall, jerking his long, thin neck and pulling the scarf off it, and smiled a strange and pitiful smile. When he saw that smile, submissive and humble, Levin felt something clutching at his throat.

"You see, I've come to you," said Nikolai in a thick voice, never for one second taking his eyes off his brother's face. As Levin regarded him, the skin of Nikolai's face, pulled so tightly across his skull, rippled grotesquely, like small waves moving across the surface of a fetid pond.

"I've been meaning to come a long while, but I've been unwell all the time," he said, rubbing his beard with his big, thin hands. "Now I'm ever so much better."

"Yes, yes!" answered Levin. He approached him to offer a kiss, but instantly drew back, horrified at the idea of his lips coming into contact with the pale, beleaguered flesh of his suffering brother. But even as he drew away, covering his mouth with his hand, he saw that Nikolai's big eyes were full of a strange light.

A few weeks before, Konstantin Dmitrich had written to his brother that through the sale of a small part of their property that had remained undivided, there was a sum of about two thousand rubles to come to him as his share.

Nikolai said now that he had come to take this money and, what was more important, to stay a while in the old nest, to get in touch with the earth, so as to renew his strength like the heroes of old for the work that lay before him. In spite of his exaggerated stoop and the emaciation that was so striking from his height, his movements were as rapid and abrupt as ever. Levin led him into his study.

His brother had dressed with particular care—a thing he never used to do—and he combed his scanty, lank hair, not noticing that as he did he tugged free several stray clumps.

"Well, I'll spend a month or two with you, and then I'm off to Moscow," Nikolai said. He was in the most affectionate and good-humored mood, just as Levin often remembered him in childhood. And yet there was something in his brother's voice and manner, something that suggested to Levin some deep concern he needed to share, but did not know how to express.

Even as he spoke, Levin saw that the flesh-rippling was not confined to Nikolai's forehead; his stomach, his chest, even his eyes undulated nearly imperceptibly. Nikolai grimaced, evidently trying to hide his discomfort from his brother.

"Besides, I want to turn over a new leaf completely now. I've done silly things, of course, like everyone else, but money's the last consideration; I don't regret it. So long as there's health, and my health, thank God, is quite restored."

As the brothers moved toward the bedrooms, Karnak wobbled along at their heels, his woefully maltuned navigation circuits occasionally driving him into the walls.

As the house was damp, and only one bedroom had been kept heated, Levin put his brother to sleep in his own bedroom behind a screen. Socrates' Third Bay emitted a gentle perfume throughout the night, to minimize the combined stench of rust and dissolution emitting from Nikolai and Karnak.

His brother got into bed, and whether he slept or did not sleep, he tossed about, coughed, and when he could not get his throat clear, mumbled something. Sometimes when his breathing was painful, he said, "Oh, my God!" Sometimes when he was choking, he muttered angrily, "Ah, the devil!" Levin could not sleep for a long while, hearing him. His thoughts were most various, but the end of all his thoughts was the same: death. Death, the inevitable end of all, for the first time presented itself to him with irresistible force. And death, which was here in this beloved brother, groaning half asleep and from habit calling without distinction on God and the devil, was not so remote as it had hitherto seemed to him. It was in himself, too, he felt that. If not today, tomorrow; if not tomorrow, in thirty years—wasn't it all the same! And what was this inevitable death; he did not know, had never thought about it, and what was more, had not the power, had not the courage to think about it.

"I work, I want to do something, but I had forgotten it must all end; I had forgotten—death."

He sat on his bed in the darkness, crouched up, hugging his knees, and, holding his breath from the strain of thought, he pondered. But the more intensely he thought, the clearer it became to him that it was indubitably so, that in reality, looking upon life, he had forgotten one little fact: that death will come, and all ends; that nothing was even worth beginning, and that there was no helping it anyway. Yes, it was awful, but it was so.

"But I am alive still. Now what's to be done? What's to be done?" he said to Socrates in despair. He lighted a candle, got up cautiously, stood before the monitor of his beloved-companion, and set it to show himself to himself. Yes, there were gray hairs about his temples. He opened his mouth. His back teeth were beginning to decay. He bared his muscular arms. Yes, there was strength in them. But Nikolai, who lay there breathing with terrible difficulty had had a strong, healthy body too. "And now that bent, hollow chest . . . with that awful rippling below his skin . . . and I, not knowing what will become of me, or wherefore . . . "

"It is . . . it is inside . . . ," his brother's voice called elusively.

"What . . . what do you mean, inside?" Levin replied "What is inside?"

Nikolai thrashed in the sheets; he was not awake, but talking from the depths of some consuming nightmare.

"It is inside me . . . deep inside . . . get it out . . . please . . . please, brother . . . "

Levin shuddered, withdrew behind the screen, and huddled tremulously with Socrates. The question of how to live had hardly begun to grow a little clearer to him, when a new, insoluble question presented itself: death.

Through the night, Nikolai continued to moan and shudder and call out from the depths of his slumbering consciousness.

"Inside . . . it is inside me. . . . "

PART FOUR: A STRUGGLE
FOR THE SOUL OF A MAN

CHAPTER 1

THE KARENINS, HUSBAND AND WIFE, continued living in the same house, met every day, but were complete strangers to one another. Alexei Alexandrovich, though consumed with preparations for the next and most delicate phase of his cherished Project, made it a rule to see his wife every day so that the servants would have no grounds for suppositions, but avoided dining at home. Vronsky was never at Alexei Alexandrovich's house, but Anna saw him away from home, and her husband was aware of it.

The position was one of misery for all three, and not one of them would have been equal to enduring this position for a single day if it had not been for the expectation that it would change, that it was merely a temporary, painful ordeal which would pass over. Alexei Alexandrovich hoped that this passion would pass, as everything does pass, that everyone would forget about it, and his name would remain unsullied. Anna, on whom the position depended, and for whom it was more miserable than for anyone, endured it because she not merely hoped, but firmly believed, as she repeatedly expressed to Android Karenina, that it would all very soon be settled and come right. Vronsky, against his own will or wishes, followed her lead, hoped too that something, apart from his own action, would be sure to solve all difficulties.

*　*　*

Vronsky had that winter endured and survived a particularly brutal and long-lasting inter-regimental Cull, one intended to prepare the ranks for a new and quite serious threat to the Motherland, the details of which were murky, but for which the Ministry demanded all soldiers hone their readiness. Vronsky had advanced as his reward to the rank of colonel, and as part of his new responsibilities, he was dispatched by his superior officer to spend a week entertaining a foreign prince—an assignment that promised at first some mild amusement, but ended up being the most tedious of chores. The prince's tastes ran to the most excessive and wearisome form of indulgence, and all week long Alexei Kirillovich was obliged to partake in flute after flute of champagne, to sit through long games of Flickerfly, and to attend the robot-human diversions known as metal-flesh, officially illegal but widely enjoyed during such "stag nights."

When the visitor had at last departed, and Vronsky's time was his own again, Vronsky arrived home to find a note from Anna. She wrote, "I am ill and unhappy. I cannot come out, but I cannot go on longer without seeing you. Come in this evening. Alexei Alexandrovich goes to the Ministry at seven and will be there till ten." Thinking for an instant of the strangeness of her bidding him come straight to her, in spite of her husband's insisting on her not receiving him, he decided to go.

After having some lunch, he lay down on the sofa and cued Lupo's monitor to display a soothing Memory to aid him in falling off to sleep. He did not know how long he slept, but at some point he became aware that time had passed, and that Lupo's monitor still glowed on—and as Vronsky gazed with heavy lids at the screen, he saw that the images had grown distorted and unsettling. Here was Anna being sucked again into that horrid godmouth; here she was in the Vrede Garden, encased in the translucent sheath, drifting upward toward some uncertain doom. And here, at the Grav Station, the two of them together, watching the charred and battered body, curtained in burlap, lifted from the magnet bed. . . .

"Lupo!" Vronsky screamed, sitting up in a wild panic, and the Class III looked chastened and confused, for apparently the strange images had played unbidden. He hurried to cue a new Memory, but it was too late; Vronsky's rest had become impossible.

"What queer maltuning is this!" muttered Vronsky darkly, rising from the sofa drenched in sweat, and glanced at his watch. He rang up his servant, dressed in haste, and went out onto the steps, trying to shake from his head the sequence of alarming Memories, worried too about being late.

As he drove up to the Karenins' entrance he looked at his watch and saw it was ten minutes to nine. A high, narrow carriage with a pair of grays was standing at the entrance. He recognized Anna's carriage. "She is coming to me," muttered Vronsky, "and better she should. I don't like going into that house. But no matter; I can't hide myself," and with that manner peculiar to him from childhood, as of a man who has nothing to be ashamed of, Vronsky got out of his sledge, his thumb tracing anxious circles on the hilt of his hot-whip, and went to the door. The door opened, and the II/Porter/7e62, a rug draped in the grip of its end-effector, called the carriage.

And then, suddenly, in the doorway, Vronsky almost ran up against Alexei Alexandrovich. The gas jet threw its full light on the blood-less, sunken face, half-concealed beneath the gleaming alloy mask and the black hat, the white cravat brilliant against the beaver of the coat. Karenin's fixed, dull eye was fastened upon Vronsky's face.

A long moment passed, and Vronsky bowed—or rather, he began to bow, and stopped short, feeling himself unable to do so. Lupo swiveled his big silver head unit back and forth, now with trepidation at Alexei Karenin, now with fear and uncertainty at his master. Vronsky, thinking in one confused moment that it was fear, or even social awkwardness, that held him in his place, tried again to bow; it was then he realized that his body was held fast, seemingly wrapped in thick blankets of invisible force.

The telescopic eye starkly obtruded from Alexei Alexandrovich's face as the man stood chewing his lips, directed straight at him. The invisible grip tightened slowly, constricting about Vronsky's body like a snake . . . and then sliding him, slowly at first and then quickly, toward the heavy oaken front door. Lupo whimpered and huddled weakly in the opposite corner. Vronsky felt he was a piece of furniture set on rollers, only he moved not in the strong grips of II/Porter/7e62s, but was propelled instead by some invisible push radiating from Anna's queer husband. Karenin stood, calm and composed, staring at him through that lenticular eye like a jeweler examining a stone, as Vronsky smashed with terrible force into the door.

In the next moment, the force that had held him relaxed like an unclenching fist, and he lay on the ground in a numb heap, pain radiating from where his back had banged into the heavy wood of the door, drinking in great, heaving gasps of sweet air.

Without a word, Alexei Karenin stepped over him, lifted his hand to his hat, and went on. Vronsky saw him without looking round get into the carriage, pick up the rug and the opera glass at the window, and disappear. Vronsky went into the hall. His brows were scowling, sweat was pouring off his body, and his eyes gleamed with a proud and angry light in them.

"What a position!" he said to Lupo, trotting at his heels. "If he would fight fair, would stand up for his honor, I could act, could express my feelings; but this weakness or baseness . . . He puts me in the position of playing false, which I never meant and never mean to do. . . . "

He trailed off, then added darkly: "How in blazes did he *do* that?"

He was still in the hall when he caught the sound of Anna Karenina's retreating footsteps. He knew she had been expecting him, had listened for him, and was now going back to the drawing room.

"No," she cried, on seeing him, and at the first sound of her voice the tears came into her eyes. "No, if things are to go on like this, the end will come much, much too soon."

"What is it, dear one?"

"What? I've been waiting in agony for an hour, two hours. . . . You met him?" she asked, when they had sat down at the table in the lamp-light. "You're punished, you see, for being late."

"Such punishment," he replied, rubbing at the small of his back, where he could feel the first tender blossom of the angry bruise to come. "seems rather excessive. Wasn't he to be at the Ministry?"

"He had been and come back, and was going out somewhere again."

"Never mind, never mind," Vronsky said, and she looked a long while at him with a profound, passionate, and at the same time searching look. She was studying his face to make up for the time she had not seen him. She was, every time she saw him, making the picture of him in her imagination (incomparably superior, impossible in reality) fit with him as he really was.

CHAPTER 2

WHERE HAVE YOU BEEN? With that foreign prince still?" She knew every detail of his existence. He was going to say that he had been up all night and had dropped asleep, but looking at her thrilled and rapturous face, he was ashamed. He said he had had to go to report on the prince's departure.

"But it's over now? He is gone?"

"Thank God it's over! You wouldn't believe how insufferable it's been for me."

"Why so? Isn't it the life all of you, all young men, always lead?" she said, knitting her brows, taking up the end of a length of the crochet yarn slowly spooling from a giant ball in Android Karenina's torso. She began drawing the hook out of it, without looking at Vronsky.

"I gave that life up long ago," he said, wondering at the change in her face, and trying to divine its meaning. "And I confess," he said, with a smile, showing his thick, white teeth, "this week I've been, as it were, looking at myself in a glass, seeing that life—the endless Flickerfly, the metal-flesh, and all—and I didn't like it."

She held the work in her hands, but did not crochet, and looked at him with strange, shining, and hostile eyes.

"How disgusting you are, you men! How is it you can't understand that a woman can never forget that," she said, getting more and more angry, and so letting him see the cause of her irritation. "Especially a woman who cannot know your life? What do I know? What have I ever known?" she asked. "What you tell me. And how do I know whether you tell me the truth?"

"Anna, you hurt me. Don't you trust me? Haven't I told you that I haven't a thought I wouldn't lay bare to you?"

"Yes, yes," she said, evidently trying to suppress her jealous thoughts. "But if only you knew how wretched I am! I believe you, I believe you. . . . What were you saying?"

Vronsky could not at once recall what he had been going to say. These fits of jealousy, which of late had been more and more frequent with her, horrified him, and, however much he tried to disguise the fact, made him feel cold toward her, although he knew the cause of her jealousy was her love for him. How often he had told himself that her love was happiness; and now she loved him as a woman can love when love has outweighed for her all the good things of life—and he was much further from happiness than when he had followed her from Moscow. Then he had thought himself unhappy, but happiness was before him; now he felt that the best happiness was already left behind. She was utterly unlike what she had been when he first saw her. Both morally and physically she had changed for the worse. He looked at her as a man looks at a faded flower he has gathered, with difficulty recognizing in it the beauty for which he picked and ruined it. And in spite of this, he felt that then, when his love was stronger, he could, if he had greatly wished it, have torn that love out of his heart; but now, when it seemed to him he felt no love for her, he knew that what bound him to her could not be broken.

She turned away from him, and rapidly, with the help of her forefinger, began working loop after loop of the wool that was dazzling white in the lamplight, while the slender wrist moved swiftly, nervously in the embroidered cuff. The soft machine hum of the yarn's rapid unspooling filled the silence.

"I don't understand your husband in the least," said Vronsky. "He toys with us, literally toys; if he has the power to destroy me with a glance, why not employ that power? How can he put up with our unsettled position? He feels it, that's evident."

"He?" she said sneeringly. "He's perfectly satisfied."

"What are we all miserable for, when everything might be so happy?"

"Only he is not happy. Don't I know him, the falsity in which he's utterly steeped? He's not a man, not a human being—he's a machine. At least, and you must understand me, Alexei, because I mean it sincerely: There is some struggle within him between the man and the machine. For now at least the human part of him still lives and thrives, and it is that and nothing else that prevents him from destroying you and me together. Oh, if I'd been in his place, I'd long ago have killed, have torn to pieces a wife like me. He doesn't understand that I'm your wife, that he's outside, that he's superfluous. . . . Don't let's talk of him!"

"You're unfair, very unfair, dearest," said Vronsky, trying to soothe her. "But never mind, don't let's talk of him. Tell me what you've been doing? What is the matter? What has been wrong with you, and what did the doctor say?"

She looked at him with mocking amusement. Evidently she had hit on other absurd and grotesque aspects of her husband and was awaiting the moment to give expression to them.

But he went on:

"I imagine that it's not illness, but your condition. When will it be?"

The ironical light died away in her eyes, but a different smile, a consciousness of something, he did not know what, and of quiet melancholy, came over her face. Android Karenina buzzed swiftly and silently to a side table and poured her a glass of cool water.

"You say that our position is miserable," Anna said, "That we must put an end to it. If you knew how terrible it is to me, what I would give to be able to love you freely and boldly! I should not torture myself and torture you with my jealousy. . . . And it will come soon, but not as we expect."

And at the thought of how it would come, she seemed so pitiable to herself that tears came into her eyes, and she could not go on. She laid her hand on his sleeve.

"It won't come as we suppose. I didn't mean to say this to you, but you've made me. Soon, soon, all will be over, and we shall all, all be at peace, and suffer no more."

"I don't understand," he said, understanding her.

"You asked when? Soon. And I shan't live through it. Don't interrupt me!" and she made haste to speak. "I know it; I know for certain. I shall die; and I'm very glad I shall die, and release myself and you."

Tears dropped from her eyes; Vronsky bent down over her hand and began kissing it, trying to hide his emotion, which, he knew, had no sort of grounds, though he could not control it.

"Yes, it's better so," she said, tightly gripping his hand. "That's the only way, the only way left to us."

In the melancholy stillness that followed, Lupo suddenly jumped to his feet, his hyper-attuned sensors mistaking some distant twig crack or carriage rumble for the sound of Karenin's returning footfalls.

Vronsky recovered himself, and lifted his head. "How absurd! What absurd nonsense you are talking!"

"No, it's the truth."

"What, what's the truth?"

"That I shall die. I have—I have had a dream."

"A dream?" repeated Vronsky, recalling the quasi-Memories which had confronted him on Lupo's monitor earlier in the day.

"Yes, a dream," she said. "It's a long while since I dreamed it. I dreamed that I ran into my bedroom, that I had to get something there, to find out something; you know how it is in dreams," she said, her eyes filling with horror. "And in the bedroom, the corner, stood something."

"Oh, what nonsense! How can you believe . . . "

But she would not let him interrupt her. What she was saying was too important to her. "And the something turned round, and I saw it was a man with a disheveled beard, in some sort of dirty white coat, little, and dreadful looking. I wanted to run away, but he bent down over the sack, and was fumbling there with his hands. . . . "

She showed how he had moved his hands. There was terror in her face. And Vronsky felt the same terror filling his soul.

"He was fumbling and kept talking quickly, quickly in French, you know: *Il faut le battre, le groznium, le brayer, le pétrir.* . . . And in my horror I try to wake up, and wake up . . . but wake up still in the dream. And I began asking myself what it meant. And it is Android Karenina, who in reality never speaks, it is she who answers me: *'In childbirth you'll die, mistress, you'll die. . . .'* And I woke up."

"What nonsense, what nonsense!" said Vronsky; but he felt that there was no conviction in his voice. He risked a glance at Android Karenina, the real one, standing in the room with them, to see her reaction to what her mistress had just revealed. But something in her eyebank's expression, in the tilt of her head unit, spoke to her anguish at having been, even in a dream, a source of pain to her beloved mistress.

"But don't let's talk of it," Anna said. "Let's have tea, stay a little now; it's not long I shall—"

But all at once she stopped. The expression of her face instantaneously changed. On her face was a look of soft, solemn, blissful attention. He could not comprehend the meaning of the change. She was listening to the stirring of the new life within her.

CHAPTER 3

A LEXEI ALEXANDROVICH, after meeting Vronsky on his own steps, drove, as he had intended, to the Vox Fourteen. He sat through two acts there, and saw everyone he had wanted to see. On returning home, he carefully scrutinized the hat stand, and noticing that there was not a military overcoat there, he went, as usual, to his own room. But, contrary to his usual habit; he did not go to bed; he walked up and down his study till three o'clock in the morning.

The feeling of furious anger with his wife, who would not observe the proprieties and keep to the one stipulation he had laid on her, not to receive her lover in her own home, gave him no peace.

YOU COULD HAVE SLAIN HIM SO EASILY.

COULD HAVE LEFT HIM IN A SHATTERED HEAP IN THE FRONT HALLWAY.

Alexei tried to argue with the furious anger of the Face. "Such an extreme measure, driven out of personal passion, would gain so little and risk so much."

YOU ARE TOO TIMID. A SIMPLE BLOW TO THE HEAD . . .

"No!"

A RAPID CONSTRICTION OF THE WINDPIPE . . .

"For God's sake, no!"

This internal dissension—perfectly sensible to Alexei Alexandrovich, who could hear the voice in his head as clearly as that of any other person, but no different to an outside observer than the ravings of a madman—continued into the late hours of the night. She had not complied with his request, and he was bound to punish her and carry out his threat: obtain a divorce and take away his son. He knew all the difficulties connected with this course, but he had said he would do it, and now he must carry out his threat.

OR YOU COULD SIMPLY—

"No! That I cannot do! Now I bid you be silent!"

He did not sleep the whole night, and his fury, growing in a sort of vast, arithmetical progression, reached its highest limits in the morning. He dressed in haste, and as though carrying his cup full of wrath, and fearing to spill any over, fearing to lose with his wrath the energy necessary for the interview with his wife, he went into her room as soon as he heard she was up.

Anna, who had thought she knew her husband so well, was amazed at the violence of his arrival. Lying still in her bedclothes, she flung up her hand before her eyes as the door flew inward off its hinges and smashed into splinters on the ground.

His brow was lowering, and his telescopic eye zoomed toward her, scanning every inch of her body—except her eyes, scrupulously he avoided her eyes; his mouth was tightly and contemptuously shut. In his walk, in his gestures, in the sound of his voice there was a determination and firmness such as his wife had never seen in him.

"What do you want?" she cried, leaping from the bed.

"Sit down! Sit!" he commanded. Amazed and intimidated, she gazed at him in silence.

"I told you that I would not allow you to receive your lover in this house."

"I had to see him to . . . "

She stopped, not finding a reason. Words poured into Alexei Alexandrovich's mind:

DO IT SAY IT DO IT SAY IT

"I do not enter into the details of why a woman wants to see her lover."

YOU WASTE WORDS YOU WASTE TIME DO IT SAY IT

"I meant, I only . . . ," she said, flushing hotly. This coarseness of his angered her, and gave her courage. "Surely you must feel how easy it is for you to insult me?" she said.

"An honest man and an honest woman may be insulted, but to tell a thief he's a thief is simply *la constatation d'un fait.*"

"This cruelty is something new I did not know in you."

"There is much of me you do not know. There are facets of my life, of my being, let alone of the being of this world, this universe, that you cannot understand, and secrets that if I revealed them to you would seal your destruction."

His cruelty was overtaking him; with every moment it was over-whelming him, rising up in his blood like a fever. The Face sang out in his mind:

IMPLORE CONTROL INSULT INSIST OVERMASTER

With a physical effort he calmed himself, strove to regain himself, to speak with his own voice and with words chosen from his own mind. "You call it cruelty for a husband to give his wife liberty and the honor-able protection of his name, simply on the condition of observing the proprieties: is that cruelty?"

"It's worse than cruel—it's base, if you want to know!" Anna cried in a rush of hatred, and rose to leave.

"No!" he shrieked, in his shrill voice, which pitched a note higher than usual even, and at once she felt what Vronsky had felt in the hallway: her body frozen and then snatched up like a poppet in the hand of a child, tossed in the air and slammed into the ceiling, helpless, pressure squeezing upon her throat, the breath choked out of her. Her husband stared up at her where she flailed in the air, a fish on a hook.

"Base! If you care to use that word, what is base is to forsake hus-band and child for a lover, while you eat your husband's bread!"

He stared up at her, his oculus telescoping forward ominously, click by click, and she felt the whole of her body forced flatter against the ceil-ing. She had to argue her case, make him feel her, her humanity, or this

"NO!" HE SHRIEKED, AND ANNA FELT HER BODY SLAMMED INTO
THE CEILING, PRESSURE SQUEEZING UPON HER THROAT

was the end—he would destroy her.

"You cannot describe my position as worse than I feel it to be myself," she cried out desperately. "Alexei . . .

"I beg of you, Alexei . . .

"Alexei . . . "

"Ah!" he shouted finally, and released his mental hold. She fell, landing fortuitously—or had some breath of humanity inside him guided her there?—into her chair.

COWARD COWARD COWARD

Anna gasped for breath in the chair, each swallow of air as delicious as the finest wine. She did not say what she had said the evening before to her lover, that *he* was her husband, and her husband was superfluous; she did not even think that. She felt glad to be alive, and in that state she could not help but feel all the justice of his words. She sat in silence as he continued.

"You may know that since you have not carried out my wishes in regard to observing outward decorum, I will take measures to put an end to this state of things."

"Soon, very soon, it will end, anyway," she said.

"It will end sooner than you and your lover have planned! If you must have the satisfaction of animal passion . . . "

"Alexei Alexandrovich! I won't say it's not generous, but it's not like a gentleman to strike anyone who's down."

"Yes, you only think of yourself! But the sufferings of a man who was your husband have no interest for you. You don't care that his whole life is ruined, that he is thuff . . . thuff . . . "

Alexei Alexandrovich was speaking so quickly that he stammered, and was utterly unable to articulate the word "suffering."

DONKEY!

IF YOU CANNOT DESTROY, AT LEAST SUMMON THE COURAGE TO SPEAK PLAINLY, YOU FOOL—YOU FAKE—YOU—

In a paroxysm of anger and exasperation, Alexei Alexandrovich clutched at his Face, trying in vain to tear it from him, to rip free the millions of tiny neural junctures that connected the Face's circuits to his own cell walls. Anna watched in horrified fascination as her husband, screaming with the full force of his lungs, turned in haphazard circles about the room, wrenching at the cruel metal mask. Though she did not, could not, understand what had overtaken him, for the first time, for an instant, she felt for him, put herself in his place, and was sorry for him. But what could she say or do? Her head sank, and she sat silent. He too was silent for some time, and then began speaking in a frigid, less shrill voice, emphasizing random words that had no special significance.

At last he gave up, collapsed in a woeful heap in the opposite corner of the room.

"I came to tell you . . . ," he said at last, softly and slowly. . . .

She glanced at him. *No, to feel sorry for him, it was my fancy,* she thought, recalling the expression of his face when he stumbled over the word "suffering." *No, can a man with those dull eyes, with that self-satisfied complacency, feel anything?*

"I cannot change anything," she whispered.

"I have come to tell you that I am going tomorrow to Moscow, and shall not return again to this house, and you will receive notice of what I decide through the lawyer into whose hands I shall entrust the task of getting a divorce. My son is going to my sister's," said Alexei Alexandrovich, with an effort recalling what he had meant to say about his son.

"You take Seryozha to hurt me," she said, looking at him from under her brows. "You do not love him. . . . Leave me Seryozha!"

"Yes, I have lost even my affection for my son, because he is associated with the repulsion I feel for you. But still I shall take him. Good-bye!"

The interview was complete. Anna revivified her beloved-companion and left in tears.

In the echoing chambers of Alexei Alexandrovich's brain, the Face was silent; but it was the silence of the victor, a jubilant silence, anticipating glories to come. Its goal grew closer—closer with every passing day.

CHAPTER 4

ALEXEI ALEXANDROVICH LEFT HOME with the intention of not returning to his family again. He discussed his intention of obtaining a divorce with a lawyer; by this action he had translated the matter from the world of real life to the world of bureaucratic action, he had grown more and more used to his own intention, and by now distinctly perceived the feasibility of its execution.

He traveled then to Moscow, where he was to oversee the final adjustments to the improved Class III model that he had created—what he now with some audacity called the Class IV. As he worked in his sub-basement laboratory, double-checking the precision sighting mechanism embedded in the steely blue eyes of his masterpiece, he heard the loud tones of Stepan Arkadyich's voice. Stepan Arkadyich was disputing with Karenin's II/Footman/74, and insisting on being announced.

Alexei Alexandrovich thought to bar the visitor, or hide the Class IV from sight, as his own security protocol dictated, and as he could do with a single button push. But he impulsively decided instead to give his ridiculous brother-in-law a treat, and let the thing remain in view.

LET HIM ENTER. LET HIM SEE WHAT RUSSIA IS TRULY CAPABLE OF.

"Come in!" he said aloud, collecting his papers, and putting them in the blotting paper.

"There, you see, you're talking nonsense, and he's here!" responded Stepan Arkadyich's voice, addressing the Footman, which had refused to let him in; and taking off his coat as he went, Oblonsky walked into the room. "Well, I'm awfully glad I've found you! So I hope while you are in Moscow, you will come and dine with us. . . . " Stepan Arkadyich began cheerfully, before stopping short and gasping.

"What . . . Alexei Alexandrovich, what is that?"

"Surely even in the Department of Toys and Misc., it is being discussed that the Higher Branches are planning, at long last, a new iteration of robot. Stepan Arkadyich Oblonsky, meet the Class IV."

"But . . . but . . . ," Oblonsky stammered, staring openmouthed while Small Stiva scuttled backward whirring with alarm. Karenin smiled, drinking in their discomfort. "But what will you do with them?"

OH SO MANY THINGS
SO MANY THINGS
OH

But Alexei merely raised his eyebrow. "Our world is ever-changing, Stepan Arkadyich," he said mildly. "Our beloved-companions must change, too.

"Now. As to your kind inquiry, no—I cannot come to dinner," Alexei Alexandrovich continued, standing and not asking his visitor to sit down. "I can't dine at your house, because the terms of the relationship which have existed between us must cease."

"How? How do you mean? What for?" said Stepan Arkadyich, still nervously eyeing the Class IV that stood staring back at him from the corner.

"Because I am beginning an action for divorce against your sister, my wife. I ought to have—"

But before Alexei Alexandrovich had time to finish his sentence, Stepan Arkadyich was behaving not at all as he had expected. He groaned and sank into an armchair.

"No, Alexei Alexandrovich! What are you saying?" cried Oblonsky, and his suffering was apparent in his face. "Did you hear this?" he said to Small Stiva.

"Heard it, yes, but cannot believe it!"

Alexei Alexandrovich sat down, feeling that his words had not had the effect he anticipated, and that it would be unavoidable for him to explain his position, and that, whatever explanations he might make, his relations with his brother-in-law would remain unchanged. He wished his visitor would go and leave him be, leave him to put the last touches on his beautiful machine.

"Yes, I am brought to the painful necessity of seeking a divorce," he said.

"I will say one thing, Alexei Alexandrovich," said Stepan Arkadyich. "I know you for an excellent, upright man; I know Anna—excuse me, I can't change my opinion of her—for a good, an excellent woman; and so, excuse me, I cannot believe it. There is some misunderstanding."

"Oh, if it were merely a misunderstanding!"

"Pardon, I understand," interposed Stepan Arkadyich. "But of course . . . one thing: you must not act in haste. You must not, you must not act in haste!"

"I am not acting in haste," Alexei Alexandrovich said coldly, "but one cannot ask advice of anyone in such a matter. I have quite made up my mind."

"This is awful!" said Stepan Arkadyich. "I would do one thing, Alexei Alexandrovich. I beseech you, do it!" he said. "No action has yet been taken, if I understand rightly. Before you take advice, see my wife, talk to her. She loves Anna like a sister, she loves you, and she's a wonderful woman. For God's sake, talk to her! Do me that favor, I beseech you! Do this, come and see my wife."

"Well, we look at the matter differently," said Alexei Alexandrovich coldly. "However, we won't discuss it."

"No, but why shouldn't you come today to dine, anyway? My wife's expecting you. Please, do come. And, above all, talk it over with her. She's a wonderful woman. For God's sake, on my knees, I implore you!"

"If you so much wish it, I will come," said Alexei Alexandrovich, sighing.

"Believe me, I appreciate it, and I hope you won't regret it," answered Stepan Arkadyich, smiling. "Come, Small Stiva," he said. Then, putting on his coat as he went, he cast one last nervous glance at the Class IV, patted Alexei Alexandrovich's II/Footman/74 on the head, chuckled, and went out.

Alexei stood, shaking his head with irritation. He thought the word *engage*, and the eyes of the Class IV glowed to life. He thought the word *reduce*, and in the next instant the chair on which Stiva had perched burst into flames and burned quickly away to ash.

OH SO MANY THINGS said the Face, and Karenin's mind echoed with terrible, cackling laughter.

CHAPTER 5

I T WAS PAST FIVE, and several guests had already arrived at the Oblonskys' for dinner, before the host himself got home. He went in together with the intellectuals, Sergey Ivanovitch Koznishev and Pestsov, two men respected for their education and erudition, and widely known for their strong opinions on the Robot Question. Koznishev and Pestsov respected each other, but were in complete and hopeless disagreement upon almost every fine point of the subject, for each had his own special shade of opinion. Both men were leading exponents of what was known broadly as the Advancement Theory, holding that servomechanisms must and should grow in their intelligence and abilities. Koznishev believed that this process should be carefully overseen by the appropriate branches of the Ministry at each step, in order that robot capabilities remained carefully understood and contained. Koznishev considered himself an acolyte of the Jewish scholar Abraham Ber Ozimov, a rye merchant turned machine theorist from Petrovichi whose theories had inspired the Iron Laws, anticipating the need to safeguard against any future "rebellion of the machines." Pestsov dismissed this idea of mechanical revolt as a fairy tale, the sort of thing used to scare children into obeying their II/Governess/7s. He argued that the gadgetmen should go wherever their experimentation led them, and that their charges should be allowed to socialize more freely with each other, and with humankind. In this way, said Pestsov and his supporters, they could learn and grow in a natural and organic process.

Since no difference is less easily overcome than the difference of opinion about semi-abstract questions, the two intellectuals never agreed in any opinion, and had long, indeed, been accustomed to jeer without anger, each at the other's incorrigible aberrations.

In the drawing room there were already sitting Prince Alexander Dmitrievich Shcherbatsky, Turovtsin, Kitty, and the stiff figure of Karenin, his telescoping oculus scanning the room.

Oblonsky worked his sociable magic on the assemblage in the drawing room, beginning them in innocuous but spirited conversation, and then, in the dining room he was met by Konstantin Levin and the familiar, angular figure of Socrates.

"I'm not late?"

"Of course we're late. We were invited for half past seven, and at present the exact—"

"You can never help being late!" said Stepan Arkadyich, taking Levin's arm and wagging a merry finger at Socrates.

"Have you a lot of people? Who's here?" asked Levin, unable to help blushing, as his beloved-companion took his cap and carefully knocked the snow off it.

"All our own set. Kitty's here. Come along, I'll introduce you to Karenin."

Stepan Arkadyich was well aware that to meet Karenin, a man of the Higher Branches, was sure to be felt as a flattering distinction, and so treated his best friends to this honor. But at that instant Konstantin Levin was not in a condition to feel all the gratification of making such an acquaintance. He had not seen Kitty since that memorable evening when he met Vronsky, not counting, that is, the moment when he had had a glimpse of her on the highroad, in her luminescent semiconscious state as she emerged from suspended animation. He had known at the bottom of his heart that he would see her here today. But now, when he heard that she was here, he was suddenly conscious of such delight, and at the same time of such dread, that his breath failed him and he could not utter what he wanted to say.

"Oh, please, introduce me to Karenin," Levin brought out with an effort, and with a desperately determined step he walked into the drawing room and beheld her. And as he walked, Socrates, walking one step behind, said precisely what he was thinking, anxiously whispering the words into the nape of his neck, just above the level of thought: *"What is she like, what is she like? Like what she used to be, or like what she was in the carriage? What if Darya Alexandrovna told the truth? Why shouldn't it be the truth?"*

She was not the same as she used to be, nor was she as she had been in the carriage; she was quite different.

She was scared, shy, shame-faced, and still more charming from it. She saw him the very instant he walked into the room. She had been expecting him. She was delighted, and so confused at her own delight that there was a moment, the moment when he went up to her sister and glanced again at her, when she, and he, and Dolly, who saw it all, thought she would break down and would begin to cry. She crimsoned, turned white, crimsoned again, and grew faint, waiting with quivering lips for him to come to her. Tatiana, her once-ignored, now-beloved Class III, sat beside her, gently massaging her knee. Levin went up to them, bowed, and held out his hand without speaking. Except for the slight quiver of her lips and the moisture in her eyes that made them brighter, her smile was almost calm as she said:

"How long it is since we've seen each other!" and with desperate determination she pressed his hand with her cold hand. Socrates bowed low to the charming Tatiana, who burbled coquettishly in return.

"You've not seen me, but I've seen you," said Levin, with a radiant smile of happiness. "I saw you when you were driving from the railway station to Ergushovo: you were only just emerging from suspended animation, and what a lovely picture you did make."

"When?" she asked, wondering.

"You were driving to Ergushovo," said Levin, feeling as if he would sob with the rapture that was flooding his heart. He glanced with teary eyes at Socrates, as if to say: *How dared I associate a thought of anything not innocent with this touching creature?* Socrates' eyebank flashed in warm understanding.

When it was time to be seated for dinner, quite without attracting notice, Stepan Arkadyich put Levin and Kitty side by side.

"Oh, you may as well sit there," he said to Levin.

The dinner was as choice as the china, of which Stepan Arkadyich was a connoisseur. The *soupe Marie-Louise* was a splendid success; the tiny pies eaten with it melted in the mouth and were irreproachable. Small Stiva, acting the role of waiter in a charming little white cravat, did his duty with the dishes and wines unobtrusively, quietly, and swiftly. On the material side the dinner was a success; it was no less so on the immaterial. The conversation, at times general and at times between individuals, never paused, and toward the end the company was so lively that the men rose from the table without stopping speaking.

Only Karenin remained cold and distant, listening with evident displeasure to the heated talk of the two intellectuals as they endlessly presented their varying opinions on the Robot Question.

He remained silent, however, even when Koznishev turned the question to him directly. "It is only under the guidance of those such as our honored guest," he said, offering Karenin a respectfully deep bow of the head, "that our Class IIs and IIIs have evolved even to the extraordinary levels at which they presently function. Why, just look at them! Serving tureens of soup and balancing heavy drink trays!" He paused to gesture to Small Stiva, who did a happy little twirl, playing to the spotlight. "But what a future they may hold . . . "

But Alexei Alexandrovich scowled and said nothing; the intellectuals grew silent, and looked away.

CHAPTER 6

EVERYONE TOOK PART in the conversation except Kitty and Levin. At first there rose to Levin's mind what he had to say on the Robot Question. He thought of his recent foray deep into the bowels of his mine, swinging an axe alongside his clever and industrious Pitbots; how he had come to admire them, like one admires a fellow man, though they were technically but Class IIs. But these ideas, once of such importance in his eyes, seemed to come into his brain as in a dream, and had now not the slightest interest for him. It even struck him as strange that they should be so eager to talk of what was of no use to anyone. Kitty, too, should, one would have supposed, have been interested when the subject turned to the supreme value of Class IIIs to women, as a means of relieving them from the drudgery of household labor. How often she had mused on just this subject, how Class IIIs were more than mere chore-doers, how they offered bosom companionships—how useful Tatiana had been to her as emotional support in her long and painful days aboard the Venutian orbiter.

But it did not interest her at all. She and Levin had a conversation of their own, yet not a conversation, but some sort of mysterious communication, which brought them every moment nearer, and stirred in both a sense of glad terror before the unknown into which they were entering.

At first Levin, in answer to Kitty's question of how he could have seen her last year in the carriage, told her how he had been coming home from the smeltworks along the highroad and had met her.

*   *   *

Over time the evening's conversation turned from cold robotics to warm human passions. Turovtsin, another of the party, as a means of drawing attention away from the Robot Question, about which he knew nothing, mentioned an acquaintance involved in an intrigue.

"You heard, perhaps, about Pryatchnikov?" said this Turovtsin, warmed up by the champagne he had drunk. "Vasya Pryatchnikov," he said, with a good-natured smile on his damp, red lips, addressing himself principally to the most important guest, Alexei Alexandrovich, "they told me today he fought a duel with Kvitsky at Tver, and has killed him."

Just as it always seems that one bruises oneself on a sore place, so Stepan Arkadyich felt now that the conversation would by ill luck fall every moment on Alexei Alexandrovich's sore spot. Small Stiva, as attuned as his master to conversational nuance, brought himself up short in his round of bustling, flashing with alarm at Oblonsky. Together they would have contrived to pull the brother-in-law away, but Alexei Alexandrovich himself inquired, smiling neutrally from behind his mask:

"What did Pryatchnikov fight about?"

"His wife. Acted like a man, he did! Called him out and blasted him!"

"Ah!" said Alexei Alexandrovich indifferently, and lifting his eyebrows, he went into the drawing room, and the rest of the party resumed their conversation.

"How glad I am you have come," Dolly Oblonsky, Stiva's wife, said to Karenin with a frightened smile, meeting him in the outer drawing room. "I must talk to you. Let's sit here."

"*Sit sit,*" echoed her Class III, Dolichka. "*Oh do, sit.*"

Alexei Alexandrovich, with the same expression of indifference given him by his lifted eyebrows, sat down beside Darya Alexandrovna, and smiled affectedly.

"It's fortunate," he said, "especially as I was meaning to ask you to excuse me, and to be taking leave. I have to start tomorrow."

Darya Alexandrovna was firmly convinced of Anna's innocence, and she felt herself growing pale and her lips quivering with anger at this frigid, unfeeling man, wreathed by the eldritch gleam of his silvery half-face, who was so calmly intending to ruin her innocent friend.

"Alexei Alexandrovich," she said, with desperate resolution looking him in the face, "I asked you earlier about Anna, but you made me no answer. How is she?"

"She is, I believe, quite well, Darya Alexandrovna," replied Alexei Alexandrovich, not looking at her.

"Alexei Alexandrovich, forgive me, I have no right . . . but I love Anna as a sister, and esteem her; I beg, I beseech you to tell me what is wrong between you? What fault do you find with her?"

Alexei Alexandrovich frowned, and almost closing his eyes, dropped his head, and was at once confronted by the caustic hissing of the Face.

HOW DARE SHE

"Quiet! Please!" he cried aloud, and balled a fist against his forehead; Dolly stared back at him tremulously.

"I presume that your husband has told you the grounds on which I consider it necessary to change my attitude toward Anna Arkadyevna?" he said, not looking her in the face.

"I don't believe it, I don't believe it, I can't believe it!" Dolly said, clasping her bony hands before her with a vigorous gesture. She rose quickly, and laid her hand on Alexei Alexandrovich's sleeve. "We shall be disturbed here. Come this way, please."

HOW DARE SHE began the Face again, but Dolly's agitation had an effect on Alexei Alexandrovich. He got up and followed her to the schoolroom. They sat down to a table covered with an old sheet of acetate, cut in slits by I/Penknife/4s; at such "writing tables" did children play at the old game, a mere amusement since the time of the Tsars, of "learning one's letters."

"I don't, I don't believe it!" Dolly began, trying to catch his glance, which avoided her.

"One cannot disbelieve facts, Darya Alexandrovna," he said, with an emphasis on the word "facts."

"But what has she done?" said Darya Alexandrovna. "What precisely has she done?"

"She has forsaken her duty, and deceived her husband. That's what she has done," said he.

"No, no, it can't be! No, for God's sake, you are mistaken," said Dolly, putting her hands to her temples and closing her eyes.

Alexei Alexandrovich smiled coldly, with his lips alone, meaning to signify to her and to himself the firmness of his conviction; but this hot defense, though it could not shake him, reopened his wound. He began to speak with greater heat.

"It is extremely difficult to be mistaken when a wife herself informs her husband of the fact—informs him that eight years of her life, and a son, all that's a mistake, and that she wants to begin life again," he said angrily, with a snort.

"Anna and sin—I cannot connect them, I cannot believe it!"

"Darya Alexandrovna," he said, now looking straight into Dolly's kindly, troubled face, and feeling that his tongue was being loosened in spite of himself, "I would give a great deal for doubt to be still possible. When I doubted, I was miserable, but it was better than now. When I doubted, I had hope; but now there is no hope, and still I doubt of everything. I am in such doubt of everything that I even hate my son, and sometimes do not believe he is my son. I am very unhappy."

He had no need to say that. Darya Alexandrovna had seen that as soon as he glanced into her face; and she felt sorry for him, and her faith in the innocence of her friend began to totter.

Karenin's inner voice for once was silent, and he was glad for that—he could bear, he thought, this woman's childish pity, but not the ruthless disdain of the Face.

"Oh, this is awful, awful! But can it be true that you are resolved on a divorce?"

"I am resolved on extreme measures. There is nothing else for me to do."

"Nothing else to do, nothing else to do . . . ," Dolly echoed, with tears in her eyes.

"Nothing else? Nothing?" came the third echo, this from Dolichka, parroting her mistress in sad, mechanical tones.

OH BUT THERE IS SOMETHING, came the brutal dead whisper of the Face.

OH BUT THERE IS.

DIVORCE HER? YOU MUST KI—

"No! It is enough!!" said Karenin, with a force shocking to Dolly. "I shall divorce her, and that is all!"

"No, it is awful! She will be no one's wife, she will be lost!"

"What can I do?" said Alexei Alexandrovich, raising his shoulders and his eyebrows. "I am very grateful for your sympathy, but I must be going," he said, getting up.

"No, wait a minute. You must not ruin her. Wait a little; I will tell you about myself. I was married, and my husband deceived me; in anger and jealousy, I would have thrown away everything, I would myself . . . But I came to myself again; and who did it? Anna saved me. And here I am living on. The children are growing up, my husband has come back to his family, and feels his fault, is growing purer, better, and I live on. . . . I have forgiven it, and you ought to forgive!"

Alexei Alexandrovich heard her, but her words had no effect on him now. All the hatred of that day when he had resolved on a divorce had sprung up again in his soul. He shook himself, and said in a shrill, loud voice:

"Forgive I cannot, and do not wish to, and I regard it as wrong. You must understand that divorce is not the worst I can do to her, but the best she might hope for. I have done everything for this woman, and she has trodden it all in the mud to which she is akin. I am not a spiteful man, I have never hated anyone, but I hate her with my whole soul, and

I cannot even forgive her, because I hate her too much for all the wrong she has done me!"

"Love those who hate you. . . . " Darya Alexandrovna whispered timorously.

When he spoke in response his natural speaking voice was displaced with the cruel rasp of the Face, speaking out from his mouth.

"NO," he said. **"HATE THEM MORE."**

And turning on his heel, he left Dolly there to shudder and to whisper to Dolichka, exactly as others had whispered before: "What is he?"

Meanwhile Karenin himself gathered his coat and hat and stopped at the door, glaring icily at the two old intellectuals, who still sat over their drained bowls of soup, parsing the question of robot intelligence.

"I might humbly suggest, gentlemen, you spend too much effort debating these ancient and intricate questions. In short order, the issue will be . . . let us say . . . moot."

And then, Alexei Alexandrovich quietly took leave and went away.

CHAPTER 7

WHEN THE GROUP finished eating and rose from the table, Levin would have liked to follow Kitty into the drawing room, but he was afraid she might dislike this as too obviously paying her attention. He remained in the little ring of men, taking part in the general conversation, and without looking at Kitty, he was aware of her movements, her looks, and the place where she was in the drawing room.

"I thought you were going toward the piano," he said, at last approaching her. "That's something I miss in the country—music."

She rewarded him with a smile that was like a gift. "What do they want to argue for? No one ever convinces anyone, you know."

"Yes, that's true," said Levin. "It generally happens that one argues hotly simply because one can't make out what one's opponent wants to prove."

And with that the two in the drawing room, with their beloved-companions standing back a deferential distance, closed their eyes against the discussion in the other room, and felt at once that all the world was theirs alone. Kitty, going up to a game table, sat down, and, taking up a mini-blade, began drawing diverging circles over the new acetate surface.

They began on another of the subjects that had been started at dinner—the liberty and occupations of women. Levin was of the opinion of Darya Alexandrovna that a girl who did not marry should find a woman's duties in a family: that of *petite mécanicienne*, maintaining the Class Is of the household.

"No," said Kitty, blushing, but looking at him all the more boldly with her truthful eyes, "a girl may be so positioned that she cannot live in the family without humiliation, while she herself . . . "

At the hint he understood her.

"Oh, yes," he said. "Yes, yes, yes—you're right, you're right!"

Socrates and Tatiana exchanged a knowing look, and then both enacted an exceedingly rare gesture, in tacit acknowledgment of the powerful mood of intimacy blossoming between their respective masters: reaching up at the same moment beneath their chins, they put themselves in Surcease.

A silence followed. She was still tracing shapes with the blade on the table. Kitty's eyes were shining with a soft light. Under the influence of her mood he felt in all his being a continually growing tension of happiness.

"Ah! I've scratched figures all over the acetate!" she said, and, laying down the little blade, she made a movement as though to get up.

"What! Shall I be left alone—without her?" he thought with horror, and he took the knife. "Wait a minute," he said, sitting down to the table. "I've long wanted to ask you one thing."

He looked straight into her caressing, though frightened eyes.

"Please, ask it."

"Here," he said, and he carved the initial letters: *w, y, t, m, i, c, n, b, d, t, m, n, o, t.* These letters meant: *When you told me it could never be, did that mean never, or then?* There seemed no likelihood that she could make out this complicated sentence; among the thousands of miraculous innovations groznium had gifted to the Russian people, mind-reading remained as impossible as it was in the time of the Tsars.

But Levin looked at her as though his life depended on her understanding the words. She glanced at him seriously, then leaned her puckered brow on her hands and began to read. Once or twice she stole a look at him, as though asking him, *Is it what I think?*

"I understand," she said, flushing a little.

"What is this word?" he said, pointing to the *n* that stood for *never*.

"It means *never*," she said, "but that's not true!"

He quickly laid down another sheet of acetate, gave her the blade, and stood up. She scratched: *t, i, c, n, a, d.*

Dolly was completely relieved of the depression caused by her conversation with Alexei Alexandrovich when she caught sight of the four figures Tatiana and Socrates in their meaningful Surcease; Kitty with the penknife in her hand, with a shy and happy smile looking upward at Levin; and his handsome figure bending over the table with glowing eyes fastened one minute on the table and the next on her.

He was suddenly radiant: he had understood. It meant: *Then I could not answer differently.*

He glanced at her questioningly, timidly.

"Only then?"

"Yes," her smile answered.

"And n . . . and now?" he asked.

"Well, read this. I'll tell you what I should like—should like so much!" she etched the initial letters: *i, y, c, f, a, f, w, h.* This meant: *if you could forget and forgive what happened.* He snatched the knife with nervous, trembling fingers, and wrote the initial letters of the following phrase: *I have nothing to forget and forgive; I have never ceased to love you.*

She glanced at him with a smile that did not waver.

"I understand," she said in a whisper.

He sat down and scratched out a long phrase, requiring him to roll out a third sheet of acetate. She understood it all, and without asking him, "Is it this?" took the blade and at once answered.

For a long while he could not understand what she had written, and often looked into her eyes. He was stupefied with happiness. He could not supply the word she had meant; but in her charming eyes, beaming with happiness, he saw all he needed to know. And he scratched out three letters. But he had hardly finished writing when she read them over her arm, and herself finished and wrote the answer, *Yes.*

Levin rose, beaming, and escorted Kitty to the door, their two revivified Class IIIs trailing behind, arm in arm.

In their conversation everything had been said; it had been said that she loved him, and that she would tell her father and mother that he would come tomorrow morning.

CHAPTER 8

THE STREETS WERE STILL EMPTY the next morning, when Levin went to the house of the Shcherbatskys. The visitors' doors were closed and everyone was asleep. He walked back, went into his room again, and ordered coffee from the II/Samovar/1(8). Levin tried to drink coffee and put some roll in his mouth, but his mouth was quite at a loss what to do with the roll. Instead he put on his coat and went out again for a walk. It was nine o'clock when he reached the Shcherbatskys' steps the second time. In the house they were only just up, and he watched as

the II/Cook/89 motored off toward the market. He had to get through
at least two hours more.

All that night and morning Levin lived perfectly unconsciously, and
felt perfectly lifted out of the conditions of material life. He had eaten
nothing for a whole day, had not slept for two nights, had spent several
hours undressed in the frozen air, and felt not simply fresher and stronger than ever, but utterly independent of his body; he moved without
muscular effort, and felt as if he could do anything. He was convinced he
could fly upward or lift the corner of the house, if need be. He spent the
remainder of the time in the street, incessantly looking at his wrist-borne
I/Hourprotector/8 and gazing about him.

And what he saw then, he never saw again after. The children,
especially going to school, the bluish doves flying down from the roofs
to the pavement, and the little loaves covered with flour, thrust out by
an unseen hand, touched him. Those loaves, those doves, and those two
boys were not earthly creatures. It all happened at the same time: a boy
ran toward a dove and glanced smiling at Levin; the dove, with a whir
of her wings, darted away, flashing in the sun amid grains of snow that
quivered in the air, while from a little window there came a smell of
fresh-baked bread, and the loaves were put out. All of this together was
so extraordinarily nice that Levin laughed and cried with delight. Going
a long way round by Gazetny Place and Kislovka, he went back again
to the hotel, and putting the Hourprotector before him, he sat down
to wait for twelve o'clock. In the next room they were talking about
some new sort of Ministry policy being spoken of, something about a
registry—was that what they said, registry?—of Class III robots, some
sort of improvement project . . . none of it mattered. Not to Levin. He
could hardly believe that these men did not realize that the dial of the
Hourprotector was approaching twelve.

At last the hour was at hand. Levin went out onto the steps, and
hired a sledge; the II/Coachman/47-T knew the Shcherbatskys' house,
and drew up at the entrance with a curve of his flexible effector and a

hearty, resonant *"Ho!"* The Shcherbatskys' household Class IIs, Levin knew, were not programmed for emotional sensitivity, but it was obvious to Levin that the II/Porter/42 certainly knew all about everything—there was something so cheery in the red glow of its faceplate, something positively mischievous in the way it intoned:

"*Enter, sir . . . enter, sir . . .*"

As soon as he entered, swift, swift, light steps sounded on the parquet, and his bliss, his life, himself—what was best in himself, what he had so long sought and longed for—was quickly, so quickly approaching him. She did not walk, but seemed, by some unseen force, to float to him, Tatiana trailing behind her with a tinkling snippet of Chopin playing from her Third Bay. But he could hardly hear the gentle strains, indeed hardly noticed the Class III, for he saw nothing but his darling's clear and truthful eyes, frightened by the same bliss of love that flooded his heart. Those eyes were shining nearer and nearer, blinding him with their light of love. She stopped still close to him, touching him. Her hands rose and dropped onto his shoulders.

She had done all she could—she had run up to him and given herself up entirely, shy and happy. He put his arms round her and pressed his lips to her mouth that sought his kiss.

She too had not slept all night, and had been expecting him all the morning.

Her mother and father had consented without demurring, and were happy in her happiness. She had been waiting for him. She wanted to be the first to tell him her happiness and his. "Let us go to Mamma!" she said, taking him by the hand. For a long while he could say nothing, not so much because he was afraid of desecrating the loftiness of his emotion by a word, as that every time he tried to say something, instead of words he felt that tears of happiness were welling up. He took her hand and kissed it.

"Can it be true?" Levin said at last in a choked voice, straightening up. "I can't believe you love me, dear!"

She smiled at that "dear," and at the timidity with which he glanced at her.

"Yes!" she said significantly, deliberately. "I am so happy!"

And then Socrates motored into the room, and Levin was startled, for the first time realizing that in his clouded, joyous state he had left his beloved-companion behind at the hotel. He blushed and lowered his head, and his embarrassment and shame were only compounded when Socrates explained what had befallen him on the way.

"I was detained by a man some sort of man some sort of man, a man with a mustache a man a man," Socrates intoned in an agitated rush, his eyebank flickering wildly. *"He said he was from the Ministry, from Enforcement."*

"A Caretaker?" Levin began, taken aback; he had never seen his oft-agitated Class III quite so agitated as this.

"Not a Caretaker. No 77s with him. His uniform was of a kind I did not recognize. He took my information, and then then then then . . . "

"Socrates?" Levin said again, his confusion deepening into anxiety and fear.

"He said unaccompanied Class IIIs will be no longer allowed to pass unescorted."

"What?!"

Levin was startled by such a report, but Kitty, in her childish and charming innocence, was merely affronted. "Well, who was this man with his little mustache, to talk such foolishness!" she tittered, and Tatiana nodded, though hesitantly—for she understood, as only another android could, the depth of cold mechanical terror reflected in Socrates' eyebank.

The prince and princess then entered, and in half an hour the man with the mustache was entirely forgotten, and the wedding planning had begun.

CHAPTER 9

GOING OVER IN HIS memory the conversations that had taken place during and after dinner, Alexei Alexandrovich returned to his solitary sub-basement laboratory in the Moscow Tower. Darya Alexandrovna's words about forgiveness had aroused in him a queer pity, but from the Face it had earned nothing but contempt. Indeed, the Face continually recalled to him the phrase of that stupid, good-natured Turovtsin—"*Acted like a man, he did! Called him out and blasted him!*" Everyone had apparently shared this feeling, though from politeness they had not expressed it.

AND YOU—YOU WITH SUCH POWER . . .

"But the matter is settled, it's useless thinking about it," Alexei Alexandrovich replied bitterly. He sat down at his desk, tried to turn his energies to the monumental task ahead of him: the long logistical effort of identifying the Class IIIs, of gathering them up, of implementing the necessary changes in appearance, in circuitry . . .

IN LOYALTY . . .

"*Two communiqués,*" said a II/Porter/7e62, buzzing into the room. "*Beg pardon, excellency, two communiqués . . . two . . .*"

Alexei Alexandrovich impatiently ordered them transferred to his desk-mounted monitor; the first was the announcement of Stremov's appointment to the very post Karenin had coveted, as overseer of the final phase of the Project. Alexei Alexandrovich trembled in his seat.

YOU CANNOT ALLOW

"I know."

NOT NOW

"I know!" Stremov could not be allowed to take over the Project, he would ruin everything . . . but his colleagues in the Higher Branches had spoken.

If Karenin could not undo the appointment . . .

YOU MUST UNDO STREMOV.

Alexei Alexandrovich stabbed the monitor into silence, and flushing a little, got up and began to pace up and down the room shouting *"Quos vult perdere dementat!"* He was furious that he had not received the post, that he had been conspicuously passed over; and it was incomprehensible, amazing to him that they did not see that the wordy phrasemonger Stremov was the last man fit for it.

THEY WILL PAY

THEY WILL PAY

WE WILL MAKE CERTAIN THAT THEY PAY.

"This will be something else in the same line," Alexei Alexandrovich said bitterly, cuing the second communiqué. It was from his wife.

SHE

SHE WHO TORMENTS YOU

SHE—

Alexei blocked out the voice of the Face as Anna's tearful, pained eyes swam into view. "I am dying; I beg, I implore you to come. I shall die easier with your forgiveness," said the tinny image of Anna Karenina.

He smiled contemptuously, and flicked his finger to stop this communiqué as well, but then paused, and he watched it again, growing tearful himself. "I am dying; I beg, I implore you to come. I shall—"

THIS IS A TRICK AND A FRAUD. THERE IS NO DECEIT SHE WOULD STOP AT.

"She is near her confinement," Alexei Alexandrovich replied, trying idiotically to have a reasoned and rational conversation with the rageful Face. "Perhaps it is the confinement . . . what would be the aim of a trick?

TO LEGITIMIZE THE CHILD, TO COMPROMISE YOU, TO PREVENT A DIVORCE.

"But something was said in it . . . " He cued the communiqué again—"I am dying; I beg, I implore you to come. I shall die easier with your forgiveness"—and suddenly the plain meaning of what was said in it struck him.

"And if it is true?" he said aloud, and the Face laughed, sneeringly.

TRUE? TRUE THAT SHE SUFFERS? TRUE THAT SHE MAY DIE? THEN GOOD! ONLY A SHAME THAT HER DEATH SHOULD COME OTHERWISE THAN AT YOUR HANDS.

"If it is true that in the moment of agony and nearness to death she is genuinely penitent, and I, taking it for a trick, refuse to go? That would not only be cruel, and everyone would blame me, but it would be stupid on my part."

"Call a coach," he said to the II/Porter/7e62.

NO—NO, YOU CAN'T—YOU MUST STAY HERE—YOU MUST COMPLETE THE PROJECT . . . STOP STREMOV . . . REGAIN CONTROL CONTROL CONTROL CONTROL

But when the II/Coachman/47-T returned, Alexei Alexandrovich said, "I am going to Petersburg."

* * *

And all the long way back to Petersburg, Karenin's mind was hushed and still; not a further whisper did he hear from the Face. When he arrived, a II/Porter/44 opened the door before Alexei Alexandrovich rang; still the Face was silent.

"How is she?" he demanded.

"Very ill, sir."

"Ill?" said Alexei Alexandrovich, and he went into the hall.

On the hat stand there was a silver regimental overcoat. Alexei Alexandrovich noticed it and asked:

"Who is here?"

"The doctor, the midwife, and Count Vronsky."

Alexei Alexandrovich paused at the steps, expecting at any moment to be brought up short by the angry roar of the Face, but he heard nothing. He went into the inner rooms.

In the drawing room there was no one; at the sound of his steps there came out of her boudoir a scared and tired looking doctor with his II/Prognosis/64. "Thank God you've come! She keeps on about you and nothing but you," said the man.

Alexei Alexandrovich went into her boudoir.

At the table, sitting sideways in a low chair, was Vronsky, his face hidden in his hands, weeping; at his feet was Lupo, his wolf-like Class III, who at the sight of Alexei Alexandrovich reared back on his haunches and growled warningly. Seeing the husband, Vronsky was so overwhelmed that he sat down again, drawing his head down to his shoulders, as if he wanted to disappear; but he made an effort over himself, got up, and said:

"She is frozen."

"Frozen? What can that mean?"

"It comes and goes. In some moments she snaps out of it, and is entirely herself, seeming to have no recollection of what has just occurred. Then it begins again: her hair stands on end, her back arches, her eyes roll back into her head, and she is locked into that strange posture. The doctors say they have no idea, that they have seen nothing like it before."

Vronsky stopped for a moment, and then stammered what was hardest for him to say to the husband: "But as for me, I have seen it. . . . " He trailed off, unable to speak aloud to Alexei Alexandrovich the intimate circumstance in which he had previously seen Anna enter this bizarre altered state.

"I am entirely in your power," he said instead. "Only let me be here. . . . "

At those words, "Only let me be here," Karenin's mind exploded in light and noise, as if a bomb had been detonated in the depths of his cerebral cortex.

"LET ME BE HERE! LET ME BE HERE!"

The Face shouted through Karenin's mouth, angry and incredulous, and it was then that the struggle began, a struggle between Alexei Alexandrovich Karenin's true human heart and his hateful mechanical Face, which is to say, between Karenin and himself; a struggle to be fought inside his brain, the crevices and folds of gray matter contested like the rugged hills of a battlefield; a struggle for the soul of a man, and for the future of a nation.

HE WOULD HAVE YOUR FORGIVENESS! YOUR LOVE!

Silence, Karenin thought.

HE STANDS BEFORE YOU WEEPING, AND YOU BID ME BE SILENT!

Be silent!

NO! NEVER! NO! YOU MUST MAKE HIM SUFFER—YOU MUST MAKE THEM ALL SUFFER MUST MUST MUST . . .

And there the battle was nearly lost; indeed, at that moment Karenin even reached out for Vronsky with his mind, even telescoped his oculus toward him, intent for one deadly second on raising him high above the floor of the room and then dashing out his brains. But then from the bedroom came the sound of Anna's voice saying something.

"She moves!" he cried.

Her voice was lively, eager, with exceedingly distinct intonations. Forgetting in the space of a heartbeat his murderous intentions, Alexei Alexandrovich went into the bedroom, and went up to the bed.

She was lying turned with her face toward him. Her cheeks were flushed crimson, her eyes glittered, her little white hands thrust out from the sleeves of her dressing gown were playing with the quilt, twisting it about. It seemed as though she were not only well and blooming, but in the happiest frame of mind. She was talking rapidly, musically, and with exceptionally correct articulation and expressive intonation.

"Alexei, come here," Anna began. "I am in a hurry, because I've no time, I've not long left to live; this is what I wanted to say. Don't be surprised at me. I'm still the same. . . . But there is another woman in me, I'm afraid of her: she loved that man, and I tried to hate you, and could not forget about her who used to be. I'm not that woman. Now I'm my real self, all myself."

And then it happened, exactly what Vronsky had warned him of: Anna's fragile body snapped into a fearful rigidity, her jaw clenched, her eyes rolled back into her head. And then, as he watched, her entire frame lifted six inches above the drenched mattress, oscillating wildly in the air before him. Alexei looked about desperately, but the doctor with his Class II had left the room. It was just him and her—and, he noticed suddenly, Android Karenina, who looked at him with calm directness from where she stood partially concealed in the drapes, as if to say: *This shall pass.*

And pass it did; in a matter of seconds, Anna's body relaxed, her color returned, and she fell back into her place atop the bedspread. She continued speaking, mid-sentence, mid-thought even, apparently having no memory or understanding of the frightful spell.

"There is only one thing I want: forgive me, forgive me quite. I'm terrible, but my nurse used to tell me; the holy martyr—what was her name? She was worse. And I'll go to Rome; there's a wilderness, and there I shall be no trouble to anyone, only I'll take Seryozha and the little one. . . . No, you can't forgive me! I know, it can't be forgiven! No, no, go away, you're too good!" She held his hand in one burning hand, while she pushed him away with the other.

Still, the Face was silent; and Alexei Alexandrovich felt, for the first time in many months—no, in many years—that he was master of his own mind. This realization gave him all at once a new happiness he had never known. He knelt down, and laying his head in the curve of her arm, which burned him as with fire through the sleeve, he sobbed like a little child. She put her arm around his head, moved toward him, and with defiant pride lifted up her eyes.

Vronsky had entered the room, and he now came to the side of the bed, and seeing Anna, hid his face in his hands.

"Uncover your face—look at him! He's a saint," she said. "Oh! uncover your face, do uncover it!" she said angrily. "Alexei Alexandrovich, do uncover his face! I want to see him."

Alexei Alexandrovich, never moving a muscle, focused his attention on the other man, and making use of that invisible fog of controlling force, which he had previously used to dominate and threaten, gently tugged Vronsky's hands away from his face to reveal his timid expression. Just as on the night they had encountered each other in the doorway, the one man was controlling the other without physical power, but with the force of the mind; but now, the control was firm but gentle, like that of a loving father, guiding the hands of his son.

"Now give him your hand," Anna demanded. "Forgive him."

Alexei Alexandrovich gave Count Vronsky his hand.

"Thank God, thank God," Anna said. "Now everything is ready. Now—"

And again she locked, and arched, and her spine grew rigid like a bridge of steel as her body floated several inches above the mattress. For some minutes they stood that way: Vronsky and Karenin with their hands clasped, still and solemn as supplicants at her bedside. Until at last Android Karenina motored over from the window glowing lavender and placed a gentle palm across Anna's forehead.

Anna recovered from the attack, but immediately fell into a deep sleep.

* * *

On the third day, Anna was continuing to suffer these occasional and inexplicable attacks; the doctor, even with the help of a prototype II/ Prognosis/5 that Alexei Alexandrovich requisitioned from the Ministry of Wellness & Recovery, could not discern what was causing the attacks.

That day Alexei Alexandrovich went into the boudoir where Vronsky was sitting, and closing the door sat down opposite him.

"Alexei Alexandrovich," said Vronsky, feeling that a statement of his position was coming, "I can't speak, I can't understand. Spare me! However hard it is for you, believe me, it is more terrible for me."

He would have risen, but Alexei Alexandrovich took him by the hand, and said:

"I beg you to hear me out; it is necessary. I must explain my feelings, the feelings that have guided me and will guide me, so that you may not be in error regarding me. You know I had resolved on a divorce, and had even begun to take proceedings. I won't conceal from you that in the beginning of this I was in uncertainty, I was in misery; I will confess that I was pursued by a desire to revenge myself on you and on her. I will go so far as to say that a certain part of me wanted . . . *more* than divorce. Wanted *revenge*. To cause you pain. To clutch at your insides and squeeze until I felt the blood burst from your brain, and your very lungs burst within you like two bags of rotten refuse."

Vronsky shifted uncomfortably in his seat.

"However . . . when I got the communiqué, I came here with the same feelings; I will say more, I longed for her death. I wished that I could—never mind. But . . . " He paused, pondering whether to disclose or not to disclose his feeling to him. "But I saw her and forgave her. And the happiness of forgiveness has revealed to me my duty. I forgive completely. I would offer the other cheek, I would give my cloak if my coat were taken. I pray to God only not to take from me the bliss of forgiveness!"

A tear stood in his one human eye, and the luminous, serene look impressed Vronsky.

"This is my position: you can trample me in the mud, make me the laughingstock of the world, but I will not abandon her, and I will never utter a word of reproach to you," Alexei Alexandrovich went on. "My duty is clearly marked for me; I ought to be with her, and I will be. If she wishes to see you, I will let you know, but now I suppose it would be better for you to go away."

He got up, and sobs cut short his words. Vronsky too was getting up, and in a stooping, not yet erect posture, looked up at him from under his brows. He did not understand Alexei Alexandrovich's feeling, but he felt that it was something higher and even unattainable for him with his view of life.

The Face was silent, but not vanquished. It dwelled in hidden chambers, biding its time, analyzing opportunities. Waiting.

CHAPTER 10

O N GETTING HOME, after three sleepless nights, Vronsky, without undressing, lay down flat on the sofa, clasping his hands and laying his head on them. His head was heavy.

"To sleep! To forget!" he said to himself with the serene confidence of a healthy man who, if he is tired and sleepy, will go to sleep at once. And the same instant his head did begin to feel drowsy and he began to drop off into forgetfulness. The waves of the sea of unconsciousness had begun to meet over his head, when all at once—it was as though a violent shock of electricity had passed over him. He started so that he leaped up on the springs of the sofa, and leaning on his arms got in a panic onto his knees. His eyes were wide open as though he had never been asleep. The heaviness in his head and the weariness in his limbs that he had felt a minute before had suddenly gone.

"You can trample me in the mud," he heard Alexei Alexandrovich's words and saw him standing before him, and saw Anna's face with its burning flush and glittering eyes, gazing with love and tenderness not at him but at Alexei Alexandrovich; he saw his own, as he fancied, foolish and ludicrous figure when Alexei Alexandrovich had mysteriously pulled his hands away from his face. He stretched out his legs again and flung himself on the sofa in the same position and shut his eyes.

"To sleep! To forget!" he repeated to himself. But with his eyes shut he saw more distinctly than ever Anna's face as it had been on the memorable evening before the Cull.

"That is not and will not be, and she wants to wipe it out of her memory. But I cannot live without it. How can we be reconciled? How can we be reconciled?" he said aloud, and unconsciously began to repeat these words. This repetition checked the rising up of fresh images and memories, which he felt were thronging in his brain. Not Memories, but memories—he remembered as a child remembers. Again in extraordinarily rapid succession his best moments rose before his mind, and then his recent humiliation. "Take away his hands," Anna's voice said. He felt the strange force remove the hands from his face, and felt the shame-stricken and idiotic expression of his face. He still lay down, trying to sleep, though he felt there was not the smallest hope of it, and kept repeating stray words from some chain of thought, trying by this to check the rising flood of fresh images. He listened, and heard in a strange, mad whisper words repeated: "I did not appreciate it, did not make enough of it. I did not appreciate it, did not make enough of it."

"What's this? Am I going out of my mind?" he said quietly to Lupo, who shook his thickly whiskered head unit in an energetic no.

"What makes men go out of their minds; what makes men shoot themselves?"

Lupo growled with worry; his mechanical tail stood straight back; the hair bristled up and down the ladder of his spine.

"No, I must sleep!" Vronsky moved the cushion up, and pressed his head into it, but he had to make an effort to keep his eyes shut. He jumped up. "That's all over for me," he said, pacing, Lupo pacing behind him. "I must think what to do. What is left?"

His mind rapidly ran through his life apart from his love of Anna.

"The regiment? The court? Destroying koschei?" He could not come to a pause anywhere. All of it had had meaning before, but now there was no reality in it. He got up from the sofa, took off his coat, undid his belt, and uncovering his hairy chest to breathe more freely, walked up and down the room. "This is how people go mad," he repeated, "and how they shoot themselves . . . to escape humiliation," he added slowly.

He went to the door and closed it, then with fixed eyes and clenched teeth he approached his full-length mirror, and unholstered his twin smokers. For two minutes, his head bent forward with an expression of an intense effort of thought, he stood with the smokers in his hand, motionless, thinking.

"Of course," he announced at last—as though a logical, continuous, and clear chain of reasoning had brought him to an indubitable conclusion. In reality this "of course," which seemed convincing to him, was simply the result of exactly the same circle of memories and images through which he had passed ten times already during the last hour—memories of happiness lost forever. There was the same conception of the senselessness of everything to come in life, the same consciousness of humiliation. Even the sequence of these images and emotions was the same.

"Of course," he repeated, when for the third time his thought passed again round the same spellbound circle of memories and images. With a minute and yet decisive flick of his thumbs he sent the smokers to life, and felt the pleasant, familiar sensations of their barrels glowing in his palms.

Lupo began to protest, barking madly—"*Yelpyelpyelp!*"—charging in circles at the foot of his master; with the unseeing determination of the sleepwalker, Vronsky crouched down on his knees and flicked the mighty wolf into Surcease. Lupo was stopped in mid-motion, a forepaw raised in desperation, a gleaming silver statue of unavailing loyalty.

Pulling one of the smokers to the left side of his chest, and clutching it vigorously with his whole hand, as it were, squeezing it in his fist, he pulled the trigger. He did not hear the hot *zap* of the shot, but a violent blow on his chest sent him reeling.

He tried to clutch at the edge of the table, dropped the smokers, staggered, and sat down on the ground, looking about him in astonishment. The groznium plating of his uniform had of course absorbed 80 or more percent of the blast, exactly as it was designed to do. "Idiotic!" he cried.

Meanwhile, the 20 percent of unabsorbed smoker blast was ricocheting wildly around the room.

He heard the sound of the subsequent explosion, as the smoker stream landed in the worst possible place: the trunk of munitions in the opposite corner of the room. The Disrupter, its feather trigger activated by the force of the smoker stream, exploded to life, and the whole room began to shake violently; next the six-load of glowbombs erupted one after the other, a string of deafening, concussive explosions. Vronsky clutched at his forehead and ducked under the settee, grasping with desperate fingers for Lupo, exposed in the center of the room, helpless in Surcease.

He cowered there, his chest throbbing, covering his beloved-companion with his body, until the firestorm abated. When Vronsky looked up from the floor, he could barely recognize his room: the bent legs of the table, the wastepaper basket, and the tiger-skin rug, all of it a smoking ruin. He breathed with difficulty through scorched lungs, stumbled for the exit, smelled the terrible odor of his own singed hair and skin.

"I've got you, old friend," he muttered raggedly to Lupo, shielding his eyes against the smoke with one hand while with the other he flicked his beloved-companion back to life.

"I've got you."

CHAPTER 11

THE MISTAKE MADE by Alexei Alexandrovich—that, when preparing to see his wife, he had overlooked the possibility that her repentance might be sincere, and he might forgive her, and she might not die—this mistake was, two months after his return from Moscow, brought home to him in all its significance. But the mistake made by him had arisen not simply from his having overlooked that contingency, but also from the fact that until that day of his interview with his dying wife, he had not known his own heart. At his sick wife's bedside he had for the first time in his life given way to that feeling of sympathetic suffering always roused in him by the sufferings of others, and hitherto looked on by him with shame as a harmful weakness. And pity for her, and remorse for having desired her death, and most of all, the joy of forgiveness made him at once conscious, not simply of the relief of his own sufferings, but of a spiritual peace he had never experienced before. In the profound silence of the Face's unexpected disappearance, he suddenly felt that the very thing that was the source of his sufferings had become the source of his spiritual joy; that what had seemed insoluble while he was judging, blaming, and hating had become clear and simple when he forgave and loved.

He forgave his wife and pitied her for her sufferings and her remorse. He forgave Vronsky, and pitied him, especially after reports reached him of his desperate action. He felt more for his son than before. And he blamed himself now for having taken too little interest in him. But for the little newborn baby he felt a quite peculiar sentiment, not of pity, only, but of tenderness. At first, from a feeling of compassion alone, he had been interested in the delicate little creature, who was not his child, and who was cast on one side during her mother's illness, and would certainly have died if he had not troubled about her, and he did not himself observe how fond he became of her. He would go into the nursery several times a day until the child got quite used to his presence. Sometimes for half an hour at a stretch he would sit silently gazing at the saffron-red, downy, wrinkled face of the sleeping baby in its I/Perambulator/9, watching the movements of the frowning brows, and the fat little hands with clenched fingers that rubbed the little eyes and nose. At such moments particularly, Alexei Alexandrovich had a sense of perfect peace and inward harmony, and saw nothing extraordinary in his position, nothing that ought to be changed.

But then . . . then he heard the whisper.

DESTROY IT

DESTROY IT

DESTROY THE CHILD

DESTROY

And he knew in that instant that the struggle was not over. He knew that besides the blessed spiritual force controlling his soul, there was another, a brutal force, as powerful, or more powerful, which controlled his life, and that this force would not allow him that humble peace he longed for. There had been a period of détente, and now it was at an end. His Face, his dear friend and most fearsome enemy, had returned.

DESTROY, it whispered.

CONTROL

DESTROY

CHAPTER 12

HAVING RECEIVED SEVERAL anxious communiqués relating to his sister's difficult confinement and long recovery, Stepan Arkadyich and his beloved-companion Small Stiva traveled from Moscow to pay her a visit.

They found her in tears. Small Stiva immediately joined Android Karenina in tending to Anna's physical condition, turning up her Galena Box, smoothing the bedcovers with his flattened end-effectors, and refilling the ice water of his master's ailing sister. As for Stepan Arkadyich himself, he immediately and quite naturally fell into the sympathetic, poetically emotional tone which harmonized with her mood. He asked her how she was, and how she had spent the morning.

"Very, very miserably. Today and this morning and all past days and days to come," she said.

"I think you're giving way to pessimism. You must rouse yourself, you must look life in the face."

"*Rouse! Rouse!*" beeped Small Stiva, up-actuating the Galena Box.

"I have heard it said that women love men even for their vices," Anna began suddenly, "but I hate him for his virtues. I can't live with him. Do you understand? The sight of him has a physical effect on me, it makes me beside myself. But what am I to do? I have been unhappy, and used to think one couldn't be more unhappy, but the awful state of things I am going through now, I could never have conceived. Would you believe it, that knowing he's a good man, a splendid man, that I'm not worth his little finger, still I hate him. I hate him for his generosity. And there's nothing left for me but . . . "

She would have said "death," but Stepan Arkadyich would not let her finish.

"You are ill and overwrought," he said. "Believe me, you're exaggerating dreadfully. There's nothing so terrible in it."

And Stepan Arkadyich smiled. No one else in Stepan Arkadyich's place, having to do with such despair, would have ventured to smile (the smile would have seemed brutal); but in his smile there was so much sweetness and almost feminine tenderness that his smile did not wound, but softened and soothed. His gentle, soothing words and smiles were as soothing and softening as almond oil. And Anna soon felt this.

"No, Stiva," she said, "I'm lost, lost! Worse than lost! I can't say yet that all is over; on the contrary, I feel that it's not over. I'm an overstrained string that must snap. But it's not ended yet . . . and it will have a fearful end."

"No matter, we must let the string be loosened, little by little. There's no position from which there is no way of escape."

"I have thought, and thought. Only one . . . "

Small Stiva burbled cheerily, trying to lift everyone's spirits, but Stiva felt that his pleasantness was, for once, unwarranted, and sent the little bot into Surcease.

"Listen to me," he said to Anna. "You can't see your own position as I can. Let me tell you candidly my opinion." Again he smiled discreetly his almond-oil smile. "I'll begin from the beginning. You married a man twenty years older than yourself. You married him without love and not knowing what love was. It was a mistake, let's admit."

"A fearful mistake!" said Anna.

"But I repeat, it's an accomplished fact. Then you had, let us say, the misfortune to love a man not your husband. That was a misfortune; but that, too, is an accomplished fact. And your husband knew it and forgave it." He stopped at each sentence, waiting for her to object, but she made no answer. "That's so. Now the question is: Can you go on living with your husband? Do you wish it? Does he wish it?"

"I know nothing, nothing."

"But you said yourself that you can't endure him."

"No, I didn't say so. I deny it. I can't tell, I don't know anything about it." She gripped the bedcovers, and then whispered: "There's something else, Stepan. Something in his character I cannot fathom, something . . . "

She could not finish, and Stepan Arkadyich did not pursue the point. But in his mind he returned to the Moscow sub-basement, and saw again what Karenin had shown him there, and felt again the fear and confusion he had experienced on that day.

"Yes, but let . . . "

"There's nothing, nothing I wish . . . except for it to be all over."

"But he sees this and knows it. And do you suppose it weighs on him any less than on you? You're wretched, he's wretched, and what good can come of it?" With some effort Stepan Arkadyich brought out his central idea, and looked significantly at her. "But divorce would solve the difficulty completely."

She said nothing, and shook her cropped head in dissent. But from the look in her face, which suddenly brightened into its old beauty, he saw that if she did not desire this, it was simply because it seemed to her an unattainable happiness.

"I'm awfully sorry for you! And how happy I should be if I could arrange things!" said Stepan Arkadyich, smiling more boldly. "Don't speak, don't say a word! God grant only that I may speak as I feel. I'm going to him."

Anna looked at him with dreamy, shining eyes, and said nothing.

*　　*　　*

Outside the room, Alexei Alexandrovich heard all, and the Face heard all, and took its chance to strike.

YOU SEE? it shouted, the cruel and taunting voice bouncing like rocket fire off the corners of his mind.

YOU SEE WHAT YOUR FORGIVENESS HAS EARNED YOU?

Alexei flushed with shame and anger and returned to his room, where he paced like a caged animal. Louder and louder grew the vituperative roar of the Face.

NO MORE GENTLENESS.

NO MORE FORGIVENESS.

ONLY CONTROL.

Stepan Arkadyich, with the same, somewhat solemn expression with which he used to take his presidential chair at his board, walked into Alexei Alexandrovich's room. Alexei Alexandrovich was walking about his room with his hands behind his back, lost deep in the violent eddies of his mind.

"I'm not interrupting you?" said Stepan Arkadyich, on the sight of his brother-in-law. To conceal this embarrassment he took out a Class I cigarette case he had just bought that opened in a new way, and, flicking the blue-green toggle, took a cigarette out of it.

"No. Do you want anything?" Alexei Alexandrovich asked, while into his mind's eye came a picture of the Class I exploding, of Stepan Arkadyich's fat, smirking face melting off of his skull.

LET HIM PAY.

LET THEM ALL PAY.

"Yes, I wished . . . I wanted . . . yes, I wanted to talk to you," said Stepan Arkadyich, with surprise, aware of an unaccustomed timidity.

This feeling was so unexpected and so strange that he did not believe it was the voice of conscience telling him that what he was meaning to do was wrong.

Alexei Alexandrovich meanwhile looked with angry eyes at Small Stiva, that squat, twittering fool of a Class III.

SOON. SOON ITS TIME TOO WILL COME.

Stepan Arkadyich made an effort and struggled with the timidity that had come over him.

Alexei knew what Stepan Arkadyich would say, and knew as well what his reply would be. Let her have her divorce; let her go; who cared?

What did it matter? There were weightier matters at hand. He had wrested control of his Project back from his opponents; Stremov lay in a Petersburg basement, buried to his neck in rock and gravel, never to mount another challenge.

His focus must remain on his work: even now new ideas were flooding into his head; even now the Project was evolving . . . becoming exactly what the Face had always wanted it to be.

SO LET HER GO. LET HER GO WITH HER HANDSOME BORDER OFFICER.

"I hope you believe in my love for my sister and my sincere affection and respect for you," he said, reddening.

Alexei Alexandrovich stood still and said nothing.

LET THEM ROAM FREE LET THEM TASTE FREEDOM. LET THEM ENJOY IT WHILE THEY CAN.

"I intended . . . I wanted to have a little talk with you about my sister and your mutual position," he said, still struggling with an unaccustomed constraint. "If you will allow me to give my opinion, I think that it lies with you to point out directly the steps you consider necessary to end the position."

"If you consider that it must be ended, let it be so," Alexei Alexandrovich interrupted him.

"Then you would consent to a divorce?" Stiva said timidly, dragging on his cigarette. Small Stiva's irritating, tinny Vox-Em repeated the stupid word: *"Divorce? Divorce?"*

"Let her be divorced. **LET HER DIE**," Alexei Alexandrovich said suddenly and harshly, the silver mask pulsing and undulating, veins of hot groznium alive inside it. **"LET HER BODY BE BORNE TO THE FAR WINDS OF THE UNIVERSE, ONLY LET ME NEVER SEE HER, OR HIM, OR YOU AGAIN!"**

Stepan Arkadyich went slack-mouthed: whatever horrid *thing* Anna had warned him of, whatever force lurked inside of Alexei Alexandrovich, it was that which he was in conversation with now, not the man.

"Yes, I imagine that divorce—yes, divorce," Stepan Arkadyich repeated, backing away. "That is from every point of view the most rational course for married people who find themselves in the position you are in. What can be done if married people find that life is impossible for them together? That may always happen."

Alexei Alexandrovich raised his fists and screamed, **"GET OUT!"**

The scream poured forth from him like a wave roaring up from the depths of the roiling sea; it threw Stiva and Small Stiva across the room, and they slammed against the opposite wall. Stiva's head rang from the impact, and a deep dent was knocked in Small Stiva's heretofore unbendable exterior.

When Stiva crawled out of his brother-in-law's room he was scared, deeply scared, of what he had just witnessed; but that did not prevent him from being glad he had successfully brought the matter to a conclusion.

* * *

Alexei Alexandrovich threw on his coat and stomped off through the snow-crusted streets, and within a half hour was at his St. Petersburg office. Waiting for him there was a crowd of fashionable young men, all of them thin-framed and handsome, each wearing black boots and a neat blond mustache.

"My friends," he said, and the blond men nodded in unison. "The Project begins in earnest. Find the Class IIIs.

"Find them all."

CHAPTER 13

VRONSKY'S WOUND HAD BEEN a dangerous one, filling his lungs with smoke and leaving him with a system of nasty burns along his chest, and for several days he had lain between life and death.

And yet he felt that he was completely free from one part of his misery. By his action he had, as it were, washed away the shame and humiliation he had felt before. He could now think calmly of Alexei Alexandrovich. He recognized all his magnanimity, but he did not now feel himself humiliated by it. Besides, he got back again into the beaten track of his life. He saw the possibility of looking men in the face again without shame, and he could live in accordance with his own habits. One thing he could not pluck out of his heart, though he never ceased struggling with it, was the regret, amounting to despair, that he had lost her forever. That now, having expiated his sin against the husband, he was bound to renounce her, and never in the future to stand between her with her repentance and her husband, he had firmly decided in his heart; but he could not tear out of his heart his regret at the loss of her love, he could not erase from his memory those moments of happiness that he had so little prized at the time, and that haunted him in all their charm.

Serpuhovskoy had arranged Vronsky's appointment at the head of a new and elite regiment, one being formed to take on this still-unnamed grave threat spoken of by the Ministry of War, and Vronsky agreed to the proposition without the slightest hesitation. But the nearer the time of departure came, the bitterer was the sacrifice he was making to what he thought his duty.

His wounds had healed, and he was making preparations for his departure for the new regiment, when late in the afternoon he answered his door to find Android Karenina, staring at him in her cold and quiet way, her eyebank glowing an unceasing and meaningful purple. The Class III did not say a word, only held out a hand, and pointed back to the carriage in which she had come.

"She desires to see me?"

Without even troubling himself to finish his preparations, forgetting all his resolutions, without asking when he could see her, where her husband was, Vronsky went with Android Karenina and together they drove straight to the Karenins'. He ran up the stairs seeing no one and nothing, Lupo chasing at his heels, and with a rapid step, almost breaking into a run, he went into her room. And without considering, without noticing whether there was anyone in the room or not, he flung his arms round her, and began to cover her face, her hands, her neck with kisses.

Anna had been preparing herself for this meeting, had thought what she would say to him, but she did not succeed in saying anything of it; his passion mastered her. She tried to calm him, to calm herself, but it was too late. His feeling infected her. Her lips trembled so that for a long while she could say nothing.

"Yes, you have conquered me, and I am yours," she said at last, pressing his hands to her bosom.

"So it had to be," he said. "So long as we live, it must be so. I know it now."

"That's true," she said, getting whiter and whiter, and embracing his head. "Still there is something terrible in it after all that has happened."

"It will all pass, it will all pass; we shall be so happy. Our love, if it can be stronger, will be strengthened by there being something terrible in it," he said, lifting his head and parting his strong teeth in a smile.

Lupo paced in giddy circles, but Android Karenina stood perfectly still at the edge of the room: simple purple beauty in the long shadows of late afternoon, watching the reunion with her quiet joy.

Anna could not but respond with a smile—not to Vronsky's words, but to the love in his eyes. She took his hand and stroked her chilled cheeks and cropped head with it.

"I don't know you with this short hair," he said. "You've grown so pretty. Like a boy. But how pale you are!"

"Yes, I'm very weak," she said, smiling. And her lips began trembling again.

"We'll travel to the moon, and indulge in the spas there; you will get strong," he said.

"Can it be possible we could be like husband and wife, alone, your family with you?" she said, looking close into his eyes.

"It only seems strange to me that it can ever have been otherwise."

"Stiva says that *he* has agreed to everything, but I can't accept *his* generosity," she said, looking dreamily past Vronsky's face. "I don't want a divorce; it's all the same to me now. Only I don't know what he will decide about Seryozha."

He could not conceive how at this moment of their meeting she could remember and think of her son, of divorce. What did it all matter?

"Don't speak of that, don't think of it," he said, turning her hand in his, and trying to draw her attention to him; but still she did not look at him.

"Oh, why didn't I die! It would have been better," she said, and silent tears flowed down both her cheeks; but she tried to smile, so as not to wound him.

To decline the flattering and dangerous new appointment would have been, Vronsky had till then considered, disgraceful and impossible. But now, without an instant's consideration, he declined it, and observing dissatisfaction in the most exalted quarters at this step, he immediately retired from the army.

A month later Alexei Alexandrovich was left alone with his son in his house at Petersburg, while Anna and Vronsky had gone to the moon: not having obtained a divorce, and having absolutely declined all idea of one.

PART FIVE: THE STRANGE DEATH OF MIHAILOV

CHAPTER 1

THE WORKINGS OF A CLASS III ROBOT are as surpassingly complex as they are surpassingly small. As is well known, each of these miraculous humanoid automatons contains within itself a self-perpetuating system of systems, a universe of infinitesimal mechanisms, and the movement of these intricately interconnected contraptions is powered by the "sun" that sits at the core of every Class III. That sun is the groznium engine, the approximate size and proportion of a human heart, which burns for the life of the machine with furious intensity. It is that remarkable heat-giving heart, unseen from without but all-powerful within, that gives life to the machine, generating the energy to turn the gears to animate the thousands of interlocking parts creating the easy, fluid functioning of a companion robot.

So, too, goes the working of our universe. God's will in the world is like that unseen groznium fire—its heat and power forever surrounding us, suffusing every new event and idea. Whether we know it or not, we are but servomechanisms in the service of fate, and our movements, our very thoughts, are powered only by the magnificent heat shed by the Almighty.

And so, just as a Class III performs its variety of ever-changing duties with seeming intelligence and independence, we humans may attempt in our arrogance to steer the events of the world, but never can we indeed control those events—they will continue along their own way, along *God's* way, no matter the fervency of our desires or the force of our expectations. We are but gears, turned only by the unseen hand of the Lord.

*   *   *

The Higher Branches of the Ministry, led by Alexei Alexandrovich Karenin, now unquestionably their dominant figure, moved forward with the momentous Project: the collection of all Class III robots to undergo "adjustments," the precise nature of which were still a great mystery to the public in general, who would be affected. Softening the blow was the civil and decorous manner of the young officers assigned to enact the adjustment provision; reportedly recruited from the highest ranks of the Caretakers, these young men soon became known as Toy Soldiers, what with their neatly pressed blue uniforms and slim black boots. In pairs or groups of three they appeared on doorsteps all over the country, inquiring respectfully whether any Class III robots were among the household. With handheld Class I devices they diligently recorded the names and generational information of each beloved-companion, and carefully provided a receipt before the machine was loaded in the back of a coach.

Anyone who thought to question the Toy Soldiers as to the precise nature of the planned circuitry "adjustments" was told firmly but with gentleness that such concerns were the responsibility of the Ministry, and wouldn't we all do well to put our trust in our leaders? In general, this response was considered satisfactory, and the people accepted their receipts and bade calm farewell to their Class IIIs.

Even Stepan Arkadyich Oblonsky, whose beloved-companion Small Stiva flashed his usually cheerful eyebank tremulously as he was led away, waved merrily and called out, "Never fear, little Samovar. I shall see you again soon." Stepan Arkadyich tried mightily, by dint of a peculiar internal ability he cherished, to block out unpleasant thoughts and associations, to forget what he had seen in Karenin's basement office in the Moscow Tower. There could be no connection, he assured himself, between Karenin's strange experiments and what was happening now. "Wouldn't we all do well to put our trust in our leaders?" he chastened his tearful wife, Darya Alexandrovna, as her kind and matronly Dolichka was led away.

"Wouldn't we?"

CHAPTER 2

THE GEARS OF LIFE turned and turned again, ever forward, and in time the anxious confusion surrounding the departure of Small Stiva and Dolichka was replaced in the household of Oblonsky by joyful anticipation, as preparations began for the wedding of Dolly's sister, Kitty Shcherbatskaya, to Stepan's oldest friend, Konstantin Dmitrich Levin.

When they arrived at the church, a crowd of people, principally women, was thronging round the church lighted up for the wedding. Those who had not succeeded in getting into the main entrance were crowding about the windows, pushing, wrangling, and peeping through the gratings.

More than twenty carriages had already been drawn up in ranks along the street by the Class II police robots, their bronze weather-protected outercoating primed against the rusting frost. More carriages were continually driving up, and ladies wearing flowers and carrying their trains, and men taking off their helmets or black hats kept walking into the church. The church windows, programmed for the occasion by a highly sought-after display gadgeteer, glowed brightly with the life of the Savior, one luminously delineated scene shifting seamlessly into the next. This ornate display, along with the gilt on the red background of the holy picture-stand, the silver of the lusters, and the stones of the floor, and the rugs, and the banners above in the choir, the steps of the altar, the cassocks and surplices—all were flooded with light.

The only thing missing was the loving couple. Every time there was heard the creak of the opened door, the conversation in the crowd died away, and everybody looked round expecting to see the bride and bridegroom come in. But the door had opened more than ten times, and each time it was either a belated guest or guests, who joined the circle of the invited on the right, or a spectator, who had eluded the II/Policeman/56s, and went to join the crowd of outsiders on the left. The Galena Box sent its waves of oscillation through the room, but was proving insufficient to dampen the mood of confused anxiety; both the guests and the outside public had by now passed through all the phases of anticipation. The long delay began to be positively discomforting, and relations and guests tried to look as if they were not thinking of the bridegroom but were engrossed in conversation.

At last one of the ladies, glancing at her I/Hourprotector/8, said, "It really is strange, though!" and all the guests became uneasy and began loudly expressing their wonder and dissatisfaction.

Kitty meanwhile had long ago been quite ready, and in her white dress and long veil and wreath of orange blossoms she was standing in the drawing room of the Shcherbatskys' house. Beside her was her pink-flushed Class III, Tatiana, one of the last beloved-companions left in Moscow. Kitty had been allowed to forestall her Class III's collection for "adjustment" until after the wedding, thanks to the intercession of her father, Prince Shcherbatsky, with a childhood friend who sat on the Higher Branches. ("A girl cannot be wed without the soothful presence of her Class III," the prince had pleaded; meanwhile, all across Russia, less well-connected brides were somehow making do.) Tatiana was looking out of the window, and had been for more than half an hour piping a soft and calming lullaby from her Third Bay, to keep her mistress from becoming too anxious that her bridegroom was not yet at the church.

Levin meanwhile, in his trousers, but without his coat and waist-coat, was walking to and fro in his room at the hotel, with Socrates pac-ing directly behind him, his beard clanking. (He, too, had been granted a reprieve, exhausting the favors due to the old prince). Man and machine took turns poking their heads out of the door and looking up and down the corridor. But in the corridor there was no sign of the Class II who had been dispatched to bring Levin his shirtfront, which had been for-gotten. The shirtfront had been left at home by Levin's best man, Stepan Arkadyich, who placed the blame on Small Stiva—or rather, the absence of Small Stiva. Oblonsky had assumed that his beloved-companion, ever mindful of such details, would bring the necessary accoutrements, and it slipped his mind entirely that his dear friend was by now at a Robot Processing Facility in Vladivostok, in deep Surcease with his mechanical guts splayed out on a workbench.

While Socrates frantically paced, Levin addressed Stepan Arkadyich, who was smoking serenely.

"Was ever a man in such a fearful fool's position?" he said.

"Yes, it is stupid, and I feel awful," Stepan Arkadyich assented, smil-ing soothingly. "I'm a simple block of wood without my Little Samovar. But don't worry, it'll be brought directly."

"No, what is to be done!" said Levin, with smothered fury. "What if it's been lost?"

"It's not been lost," reassured Stepan Arkadyich.

"It may have been lost. Yes, probably it's lost," intoned Socrates.

"That is not helpful," said Stepan Arkadyich with a glare suggesting a wish that Socrates, too, were in a Vladivostok R.P.F. Addressing him-self to Levin, he said: "Just wait a bit! It will come round."

And so while the bridegroom was expected at the church, he was pacing about his room like a caged Huntbear, peeping out into the cor-ridor, and with horror and despair recalling what absurd things he had said to Kitty and what she might be thinking now.

At last the II/Runner/470 zipped into the room with the shirt held aloft from a pincer, like a dog with a bagged quail. Three minutes later Levin ran full speed into the corridor not looking at his I/Hourprotector/8 for fear of aggravating his sufferings.

"It's eleven thirty. . . ," moaned Socrates, motoring quickly behind him. *"eleven thirty-one! We are very late, very late indeed!"*

"Not helpful," sighed Stepan Arkadyich as he tossed his cigarette into an ashtray, where it sputtered, hissed, and disappeared. "Not helpful at all."

CHAPTER 3

"THEY'VE COME!" "Here he is!" "Which one? The tall yellow robot?" "No, fool! The robot's master!" "Rather young, eh?" were the comments in the crowd, when Levin at last walked with Socrates into the church.

Stepan Arkadyich told his wife the cause of the delay, and the guests were whispering it with smiles to one another. Levin saw nothing and no one; he did not take his eyes off his bride as she walked up the aisle toward him.

Everyone said she had lost her looks dreadfully of late, and was not nearly so pretty on her wedding day as usual; but Levin did not think so. He looked at her hair done up high, with the long white veil and white flowers and the high, stand-up, scalloped collar, her strikingly slender figure, and it seemed to him that she looked better than ever—not because her beauty was accented by these flowers, this veil, this gown from Paris, and by the gentle pink backlight shed by Tatiana—but because, in spite of the elaborate sumptuousness of her attire, the expression of her sweet face, of her eyes, of her lips was still her own characteristic expression of guileless truthfulness.

"I was beginning to think you meant to run away," she said, and smiled at him.

"It's so stupid, what happened to me, I'm ashamed to speak of it!" he said, reddening.

Dolly came up, tried to say something, but could not speak, cried, and then laughed unnaturally. She was more affected than she had anticipated by the absence of Dolichka. How perfectly ridiculous, she thought, to have no nimble metal fingers to hand her tissues, no strong metal shoulder to lean on, at her own sister's wedding!

Kitty looked at her, and at all the guests, with the same absent eyes as Levin.

Meanwhile the officiating clergy had gotten into their vestments, and the priest and deacon came out to the lectern, which stood in the forepart of the church. The priest turned to Levin saying something, but it was a long while before Levin could make out what was expected of him. For a long time they tried to set him right and made him begin again—because he kept taking Kitty by the wrong arm or with the wrong arm—till he understood at last that what he had to do was, without changing his position, to take her right hand in his right hand. When at last he had taken the bride's hand in the correct way, the priest walked a few paces in front of them and stopped at the lectern. The crowd of friends and relations moved after them, with a buzz of talk and a rustle of skirts. Someone stooped down and pulled out the bride's train. The church became so still that one could hear the faint buzz of the I/Lumiére/7s in their sconces.

All eyes were fixed upon the altar, and no one noticed that outside the church, the II/Policeman/56s were motoring in arbitrary circles, periodically colliding harmlessly, a sure sign of having been severely, and purposefully, maltuned.

The little old priest in his ecclesiastical cap, with his long, silvery-gray locks of hair parted behind his ears, was fumbling with something at the lectern. "Drat it, Saint Peter, where'd'ya keep the things?" he

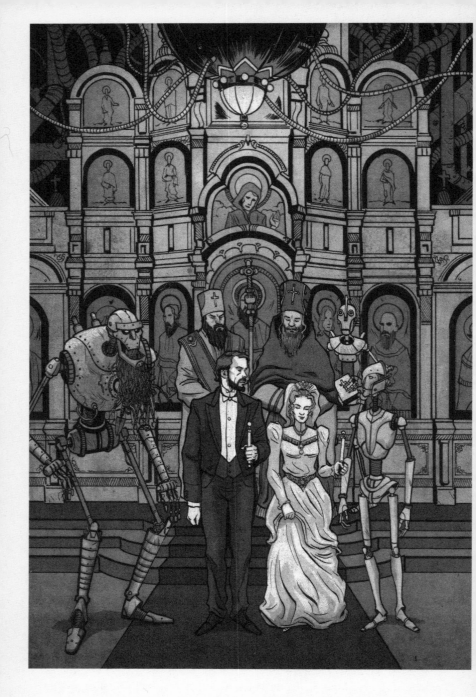

"A GIRL CANNOT BE WED WITHOUT THE SOOTHFUL
PRESENCE OF HER CLASS III," THE PRINCE HAD PLEADED

muttered in frustration; but while the church's sacramental robot had been permitted to remain in its place at the altar, its analytical core had been removed for the Ministry's adjustment. At last the priest put out his little old hands from under the heavy silver vestment with the gold cross on the back of it.

The priest initiated two I/Lumiére/7s, wreathed with flowers, and faced the bridal pair. He looked with weary and melancholy eyes at the bride and bridegroom, sighed, and putting his right hand out from his vestment, blessed the bridegroom with it, and also with a shade of solicitous tenderness laid the crossed fingers on the bowed head of Kitty. Then he gave them the lumiéres, and taking the censer, moved slowly away from them.

"Can it be true?" thought Levin, and he looked round at his bride. Looking down at her he saw her face in profile, and from the scarcely perceptible quiver of her lips and eyelashes he knew she was aware of his eyes upon her.

She did not look round, but the high, scalloped collar, which reached her little pink ear, trembled faintly. He saw that a sigh was held back in her throat, and the little hand in the long glove shook as it held the thin illuminated Class I.

All the fuss of the shirt, of being late, all the talk of friends and relations, their annoyance, his ludicrous position—all suddenly passed away and he was filled with joy and dread.

It was that precise cocktail of strong feeling that triggered the first of the emotion bombs.

It exploded with pinpoint precision beneath the seat of a single parishioner, an elderly second cousin of Kitty's seated in the third pew from the back. The blast unleashed all the destructive force of a traditional explosion, but all concentrated on this one unfortunate soul, furiously vibrating every molecule in his body and turning his insides to a gelatinous paste. So precise was this terrible blast of force, however, that even the parishioners to the left and right of the man did not realize what had transpired, that the wedding was suddenly under attack by agents of UnConSciya. The wedding guest simply slumped forward in his seat, and might have been sleeping: an impolite but hardly shocking action by an elderly man at a church service.

"Blessed be the name of the Lord," the solemn syllables rang out slowly one after another, as the priest intoned the liturgy, setting the air quivering with waves of sound. The brains of the murdered second cousin, essentially turned to liquid, leaked slowly from his ears.

"Blessed is the name of our God, from the beginning, is now, and ever shall be," the little old priest said in a submissive, piping voice, still fingering something at the lectern. And the full chorus of the unseen choir rose up, filling the whole church, from the windows to the vaulted roof, drowning out a lone woman's panicked shrieking from the back of the church.

"This man is dead! My God, what has—what's happened?!"

A second emotion bomb ignited, this time beneath a young peasant woman with her head wrapped in colorful scarves—like the elderly relative, she collapsed in her place, her insides instantly emulsified.

The triumphant and praiseful sound of the choir grew ever stronger, and joy and mystery swelled in the bosoms of Levin and his bride, amplifying the danger for all present. The officiants prayed, as they always do, for peace from on high and for salvation; for the long life of the Higher Branches they prayed; and for the servants of God, Konstantin and Ekaterina, now pledging their troth. The closer the liturgy drew to the fateful moment, when Kitty and Levin would together enter the mysterious country of matrimonial connection, the more palpable was the bubbling admixture of dread and joy in their respective hearts; and with every upswell of that queer emotional tide, more of the quiet, precise bombs went off, each one more brutally effective than the last. Kitty and Levin stared into each other's eyes, lost in tender feeling and contemplation of their intertwined fates, as the grim toll of their love grew every second.

"Vouchsafe to them love made perfect, peace and help, O Lord, we beseech Thee," came the voice of the head deacon. Levin heard the words, and they impressed him.

"How did they guess that it is help, just help that one wants?" he whispered to Socrates, who stood faithfully at his elbow.

"Help!" cried Princess Shcherbatskaya. "My Lord, help!" Her sister, Kitty's aunt, had suddenly jerked in her seat, twisted her body unnaturally, and tumbled forward into the princess's lap. Levin and Kitty wheeled around from the altar, at last to behold the bedlam unfolding around them: a horror becoming worse every moment, as dread-joy bombs went off like celebratory I/Flashpop/4s at a child's birthday party. Kitty screamed, her hands clutching at the side of her face in horror, as another explosion—no longer silent, indeed, louder than a sky full of thunder—shattered the electronically programmed window, sending shards of Savior-emblazoned glass raining down.

The first decisive action to stem the tide of violence came from the two beloved-companion robots. In a single smooth gambol, Tatiana tackled her mistress to the ground and arched backward into a bridge to protect her from the hail of glass. Socrates, plucking a well-worn physiometer from the tangle of tools in his beard, waded into the crowd to begin triage, and Levin could only rush to keep up.

"Why does it continue?" Kitty shouted to Levin, as he and his faithful machine-man surveyed the damage and tended to the wailing wounded. "If this is an emotion bombing"—for such was the only logical conclusion—"and if the bombs are fed by our joy at entering the blessed state of marriage, then why have they not stopped, now that our happiness is entirely subsumed?" Tatiana, meanwhile, with fluttering phalangeals deflected a fresh rain of glass and splintered wood.

Levin smiled despite himself. *What a woman! How clever she is, to make such an astute analysis amid such dreadful circumstances.* "Oh, God," he said in sudden horror. "It's *me*. I am happy! Heavenly Father, forgive me, but I am *happy*! I look at her, and even in such straits I cannot help it: I love her, and I feel joy!"

As if in grim confirmation of Levin's realization, at the moment he uttered the word "joy" a blast rattled the back of the hall.

He looked about him in horror, marveling at the power of his love, trying and failing to squelch its power in his breast; and then Kitty lunged at him, her gown of lush white and lace billowing out behind her, clawing feverishly at his eyes and pulling viciously at his beard. Levin, shocked, covered his head against the onslaught, and, in that wild, pained instant, he was so surprised at her assault that his love for Kitty transformed into its opposite.

"Stop it," he shouted at his beloved. "For God's sake, stop! Are you insane?"

He grasped her wrists to cease the onslaught; she collapsed, spent, against his chest, weeping. Socrates looked up, beeping questioningly in the sudden hush that followed.

For as Konstantin Dmitrich's joy waned, so had the attack. The emotion bombs were silenced and the devastated church grew silent and terribly still, but for the moaning and weeping of the wounded.

"She is a very capable woman," said Socrates, admiringly.

"To be sure, old friend," Levin agreed, stroking her hair. "As capable and intelligent as she is—"

Boom! A rafter cracked above the apse, and a displaced I/Lumiére/7 hurtled down from above.

"Master, let us remove you from this place."

* * *

Twenty minutes later, outside the rubble of the church, the surviving officiant concluded the ceremony in a melancholy spirit. Kitty and Levin stood with laced hands, bruised and tearful, but unwilling—in the ancient Russian spirit—to let the terrorists of UnConSciya ruin their sacred day of union.

And so the old priest turned to the bridal pair and began: "Eternal God, who joinest together in love those who were separate," he said in a sad, piping voice, as voices wailed in the background, "who hast ordained the union of holy wedlock that cannot be set asunder, Thou who didst bless Isaac and Rebecca and their descendants, according to Thy Holy Covenant; bless Thy servants, Konstantin and Ekaterina, leading them in the path of all good works. For gracious and merciful art Thou, our Lord, and glory be to Thee, the Father, the Son, and the Holy Ghost, now and ever shall be."

Even as the ancient words were intoned, within the church the ragged and helpless victims awaited the inevitable arrival of a Caretaker with his troupe of 77s, who always arrived in the aftermath of such horrors. They wept for their injuries, for the continued plague of UnConSciya upon society; and they wept bitterly that their Class IIIs had not been there to protect them, and were not there now to lend them support and comfort.

* * *

The violent disorder of his wedding day could not help but have its effect on Konstantin Dmitrich's romantic ideas about marriage, and the life he was now to lead. Levin felt more and more that all his ideas of marriage, all his dreams of how he would order his life, were mere childishness, and that it was something he had not understood hitherto, and now understood less than ever, though it was being performed upon him. The lump in his throat rose higher and higher; tears that would not be checked came into his eyes.

After supper, the same night, the young people left for the country.

CHAPTER 4

V RONSKY AND ANNA had been traveling for three months
together on the surface of the moon. They had visited the Mare
Tranquillitatis and the famous canals of St. Catherine, and had just
arrived at a hotel, part of the small farside colony where they meant to
stay some time.

A Moonie, one of the weird, wiry Class IIs with bulbous glowing
head units employed in nearly all man-serving positions on the moon's
surface, stood with his hands in the full curve of his silver outercoating,
giving some frigid reply to a gentleman in a coarse engineer's jumpsuit
who had stopped him. Catching the sound of footsteps coming from
the other side of the entry toward the staircase, the Moonie swiveled
his big, bright ball of a head and, seeing the Russian count, who had
taken their best rooms, with a bow informed him that a communiqué
had been received: the business about the module he and his companion planned to rent had all been arranged.

"Ah! I'm glad to hear it," said Vronsky. "Is madame at home or not?"

"Madame . . . went out for walk . . . but returned now," answered the
Class II in the distinctive stop-start manner of the Moonie.

Vronsky took off his soft, wide-brimmed hat and passed his handkerchief over his heated brow and hair, which had grown half over his
ears, and was brushed back covering the bald patch on his head. And
glancing casually at the gentleman, who still stood there gazing intently
at him, he almost moved on.

"This gentleman . . . a Russian . . . inquiring after you."

With mingled feelings of annoyance at never being able to get away from acquaintances anywhere, and longing to find some sort of diversion from the monotony of his life, Vronsky looked over at the gentleman, who had retreated and stood still again. Lupo, instinctually distrustful of strangers, leaned back on his haunches and bared his teeth at the stranger; but Vronsky, recognizing the man, whistled a sharp "stand down" to his Class III and smiled broadly.

"Golenishtchev!"

"Vronsky!"

Surprising though it was, it really was Golenishtchev, a comrade of Vronsky's from the Corps of Pages. Golenishtchev and Vronsky had gone completely different ways on leaving the corps, and had only met once since, and had not gotten along. But now they beamed and exclaimed with delight on recognizing one another. Vronsky would never have expected to be so pleased to see Golenishtchev, but probably he was not himself aware how bored he was, so many space-versts from home, with only Anna for human company. With a face of frank delight he held out his hand to his old comrade, and the same expression of delight replaced the look of uneasiness on Golenishtchev's face.

"How glad I am to meet you!" said Vronsky, showing his strong white teeth in a friendly smile.

"I heard the name Vronsky, but I didn't know which one. I'm very, very glad!"

"Let's go in. Come, tell me what you're doing."

"Digging, friend! Digging and digging and digging."

Now Vronsky understood the reason for the dust-caked jumpsuit; Golenishtchev, a trained excavation and extraction engineer, had received a license from the Ministry's Extra-Orbital Branch to plumb huge tracts of the lunar surface in search of the Miracle Metal—on the theory that, if it had mysteriously appeared in the Russian soil, and if the Russians in their ingeniousness had utilized groznium-derived technologies to land men on the moon, surely the Miracle Metal would one day be found there as well; although, Golenishtchev reported with a sad shrug, so far he had found only moon-rocks and dust.

"Ah!" said Vronsky, with sympathy, before deciding to broach the difficult subject, which he knew would come up sooner or later with any acquaintance. "Do you know Madame Karenina? We are traveling together. I am going to see her now," he said, carefully scrutinizing Golenishtchev's face.

"Ah! I did not know," Golenishtchev answered carelessly, though he did know, and excused himself to ask a question of the obsequious Moonie.

"Yes, he's a decent fellow, and will look at the thing properly," Vronsky said happily to Lupo. "I can introduce him to Anna, he looks at it properly."

During these weeks that Vronsky had spent on the moon, he had always on meeting new people asked himself how the new person would look at his relations with Anna, and for the most part, in men, he had met with the "proper" way of looking at it. But if either he or those who looked at it "properly" had been asked exactly how they did look at it, both he and they would have been greatly puzzled to answer.

In reality, those who in Vronsky's opinion had the "proper" view had no sort of view at all, but behaved in general as well-bred persons do behave in regard to all the complex and insoluble problems with which life is encompassed on all sides; they behaved with propriety, avoiding allusions and unpleasant questions. They assumed an air of fully comprehending the import and force of the situation, of accepting and even approving of it, but of considering it superfluous and uncalled for to put all this into words.

Vronsky at once divined that Golenishtchev was of this class, and therefore was doubly pleased to see him. And in fact, Golenishtchev's manner toward Madame Karenina and her android, when he was taken to call on them, was all that Vronsky could have desired. Obviously without the slightest effort he steered clear of all subjects that might lead to embarrassment. He had never met Anna before, and was struck by her beauty and the sleek lines of her beloved-companion, and still more by the frankness with which the woman accepted her position. She blushed when Vronsky brought in the rough-hewn Golenishtchev, his everlit helmet dangling from its chinstrap, his I/Shovelhoe/40(b) clanking at his side, and he was extremely charmed by this childish blush overspreading her candid and handsome face. But what he liked particularly was the way in which at once, as though on purpose that there might be no misunderstanding with an outsider, she called Vronsky simply Alexei, and said they were moving into a house they had just taken, what was here called a module. Golenishtchev liked this direct and simple attitude toward her own position. Looking at Anna's manner of simple-hearted, spirited gaiety, Golenishtchev fancied that he understood her perfectly. He fancied that he understood what she was utterly unable to understand: how it was that, having made her husband wretched, having abandoned him and her son and lost her good name, she yet felt full of spirits, gaiety, and happiness.

"I tell you what: it's a lovely day, let's go and have another look at the module," said Vronsky, addressing Anna.

"I shall be very glad to; I'll go and find my helmet. And how is the gravity today?" she said, stopping short in the doorway and looking inquiringly at Vronsky. Again a vivid flush overspread her face.

Vronsky saw from the way her eyes would not meet his, resting instead on Android Karenina's reassuring and familiar faceplate, that she did not know on what terms he cared to be with Golenishtchev, and so was afraid of not behaving as he would wish.

He looked a long, tender look at her. "The gravity is extremely fine," he said. "All that could be wished for."

And it seemed to her that she understood everything, most of all that he was pleased with her; and smiling to him, she walked with her rapid step out the door, Android Karenina whizzing along with equal confidence behind her. Vronsky and his old acquaintance glanced at one another, and a look of hesitation came into both faces, as though

ANNA EMERGED IN PERAMBULATING TOGS, HER PALE AND LOVELY HAND
HOLDING THE HANDLE OF HER DAINTY LADIES'-SIZE OXYGEN TANK

Golenishtchev, unmistakably admiring her, would have liked to say something about her, and could not find the right thing to say, while Vronsky desired and dreaded his doing so.

Anna excused herself to put on her perambulating togs. It was a rather cumbersome and complicated outfit, but every piece was entirely necessary: the oxygen tanks; the heavy, treaded boots; the asbestos-lined undersuit; and of course the sturdy, airtight helmet of reinforced glass. When Anna emerged, her stylish feathered hat bent to fit inside the dome of the helmet, her pale and lovely hand holding the handle of her dainty ladies'-size oxygen tank, it was with a feeling of relief that Vronsky broke away from the plaintive eyes of Golenishtchev, and with a fresh rush of love looked at his charming companion, full of life and happiness.

They walked to the module they had reserved, and looked over it, Golenishtchev pompously taking the role of chief inspector, carefully examining the sealing systems and hatches, having vastly more experience than they with lunar living.

"I am very glad of one thing," said Anna to Golenishtchev when they were on their way back. "Alexei will have a capital atelier. You must certainly take that module," she said to Vronsky in Russian, using the affectionately familiar form as though she saw that Golenishtchev would become intimate with them in their isolation, and that there was no need of reserve before him.

"Do you paint?" said Golenishtchev, turning round quickly to Vronsky.

"Yes, I used to study long ago, and now I have begun to do a little," said Vronsky, reddening.

"He has great talent," said Anna with a delighted smile, and Lupo yipped his proud agreement. "I'm no judge, of course. But good judges have said the same."

CHAPTER 5

A NNA, IN THAT PERIOD of her emancipation and rapid return to health, after her dangerous confinement and delivery, had felt herself unpardonably happy and full of the joy of life. The memory of all that had happened after her illness: her reconciliation with her husband, its breakdown, the news of Vronsky's wound, his visit, the preparations for divorce, the departure from her husband's house, the parting from her son, traveling to the moon inside an ovoid canister shot from a giant cannon—all that seemed to her like a delirious dream, from which she had woken up alone with Vronsky on the lunar surface. The thought of the harm caused to her husband aroused in her a feeling like repulsion, and akin to what a drowning man might feel who has shaken off another man clinging to him. That man did drown. It was an evil action, of course, but it was the sole means of escape, and better not to brood over these fearful facts.

One consolatory reflection upon her conduct had occurred to her at the first moment of the final rupture, and when now she recalled all the past, she remembered that one reflection. "I have inevitably made that man wretched, but I don't want to profit by his misery," she mused, while Android Karenina's slim fingers braided her hair into charming plaits. "I too am suffering, and shall suffer; I am losing what I prized above everything—I am losing my good name and my son. I have done wrong, and so I don't want happiness, I don't want a divorce, and shall suffer from my shame and the separation from my child."

Android Karenina nodded kindly, her eyebank glittering from deep red to sympathetic lilac. But she knew as well as her mistress that, although Anna had expected to suffer, she was not suffering. Shame there was not. She and Vronsky had never placed themselves in a false position, and everywhere they had met people who pretended that they perfectly understood their position, far better indeed than they did themselves. It was not by accident that they had traveled to the moon, a permissive enclave where judgment, along with gravity, held only a fraction of its usual force. Separation from the son she loved—even that did not cause her anguish in these early days. The baby girl—his child—was so sweet, and had so won Anna's heart, since she was all that was left to her, that Anna rarely thought of her son.

The desire for life, waxing stronger with recovered health, was so intense, and the conditions of life were so new and pleasant, that Anna felt unpardonably happy. The more she got to know Vronsky, the more she loved him. She loved him for himself, and for his love for her. Her complete ownership of him was a continual joy to her. His presence was always sweet to her. All the traits of his character, which she learned to know better and better, were unutterably dear to her. His appearance, changed by his civilian dress, was as fascinating to her as though she were some young girl in love. In everything he said, thought, and did, she saw something particularly noble and elevated; she cherished a childish vision of Vronsky and Lupo as of a paladin and his steed. Her adoration of him alarmed her indeed; she sought and could not find in him anything not fine. She dared not show him her sense of her own insignificance beside him. It seemed to her that, knowing this, he might sooner cease to love her; and she dreaded nothing now so much as losing his love, though she had no grounds for fearing it. But she could not help being grateful to him for his attitude toward her, and showing that she appreciated it. He, who had in her opinion such a marked aptitude for a regimental career, in which he would have been certain to play a leading part—he had sacrificed his ambition for her sake, and never betrayed the slightest regret. He was more lovingly respectful to her than ever, and the constant care that she should not feel the awkwardness of her position never deserted him for a single instant. He, so manly a man, never opposed her, had indeed, with her, no will of his own, and was anxious, it seemed, for nothing but to anticipate her wishes. And she could not but appreciate this, even though the very intensity of his solicitude for her, the atmosphere of care with which he surrounded her, sometimes weighed upon her.

Vronsky, meanwhile, in spite of the complete realization of what he had so long desired, was not perfectly happy. He soon felt that the realization of his desires gave him no more than a grain of sand out of the mountain of happiness he had expected. It showed him the mistake men make in picturing to themselves happiness as the realization of their desires. For a time after joining his life to hers, after unwinding the hot-whip from his thigh and donning civilian dress, he had felt all the delight of freedom in general of which he had known nothing before, and of freedom in his love—and he was content, but not for long. He was soon aware that there was springing up in his heart a desire for desires—*ennui*. He longed for the camaraderie of the battlefield, missed the sparks and the heat and fog of combat, missed the clang of the Exterior door swinging shut behind him, missed the weight of a smoker in his hand. Without conscious intention he began to clutch at every passing caprice, taking it for a desire and an object. Sixteen hours of the day must be occupied in some way, since they were living in complete freedom, outside the conditions of social life that filled up time in Petersburg. As for the amusements of bachelor existence, which had provided Vronsky with entertainment on previous extra-atmospheric sojourns, they could not be thought of, since his sole attempt of that sort had led to a sudden attack of depression in Anna, quite out of proportion with the cause—a late game of lunar croquet with bachelor friends.

Relations with the society of the place—foreign and Russian—were equally out of the question owing to the irregularity of their position. The inspection of the various panoramas, of Earth's blue-green magnificence or the starry sprawl of distant galaxies, had not for Vronsky, a Russian and a sensible man, the immense significance Englishmen are able to attach to that pursuit.

And just as the hungry stomach eagerly accepts every object it can get, hoping to find nourishment in it, Vronsky quite unconsciously clutched first at politics, then at new books, and then at pictures. He began to understand the semi-mystical art of painting with groznium-based pigments, how the artist could push the little pools of color around the canvas with subtle flicks of the brush, how the individual droplets would attract each other, creating luminous patterns as singular as fingerprints or snowflakes. Vronsky concentrated on these studies; with this technique he began to paint Anna's portrait in her boots and helmet, and the portrait seemed to him, and to everyone who saw it, extremely successful.

CHAPTER 6

THE OLD, NEGLECTED MODULE they had leased, with its lofty, hard-textile ceilings and off-white, dimly lit passageways, with its slow-sequencing, Earth-scenery monitor frames, its manual door locks and gloomy reception rooms—this base did much, by its very appearance after they had moved into it, to confirm in Vronsky the agreeable illusion that he was not so much a Russian country gentleman, a retired army officer, as an enlightened, bohemian "moon man" and patron of the arts, who had renounced his past, his connections, and his planet for the sake of the woman he loved.

"Here we live, and know nothing of what's going on," Vronsky said to Golenishtchev as he came to see him one morning. "Have you seen Mihailov's picture?" he said, pointing to Lupo's monitor, where was displayed a communiqué from a Russian friend that he had received that morning, and pointing to an article on a Russian artist living in the very same colony and just finishing a picture which had long been talked about. "Couldn't we ask him to paint a portrait of Anna Arkadyevna?" said Vronsky.

"Why mine?" Anna interjected. "After yours I don't want another portrait. Better have one of Annie" (so she called her baby girl). She glanced with a smile through the glass porthole into the nursery, where the child was giggling delightedly at the clownish tumbling of a I/HurdlyGurdly/2.

"I have met Mihailov, you know," Golenishtchev said. "But he's a queer fish. He did not migrate to the moon entirely of his own volition, if my meaning is quite clear." It was not, of course, and in answer to Vronsky's curious expression Golenishtchev leaned forward, in exactly that conspiratorial fashion with which people in possession of secrets signal that they wish to be pressured into revealing them.

"I understand that many years ago he professed rather an extreme view on the Robot Question. Took the line that the extent of evolution of any given machine should be up to its owner, and its owner alone."

"Yes, well," Anna began, gesturing proudly to her own beloved-companion, preparing to defend that position, or at least argue its merits.

"But this Mihailov took the idea to a rather bizarre conclusion, publishing his opinion that robots were, in many ways, the equals of human beings—and that junkering a Class III was therefore tantamount to murdering a human being." Vronsky raised his eyebrows, and Golenishtchev went on. "It is even said that he put these rather extreme opinions into practice, and . . . ," Golenishtchev made a pretense of blushing before continuing, "and fell in love with his wife's Class III, and would have married it. The point is, one way or another he found it necessary to decamp for the charming lunar colony where now we find him."

Golenishtchev settled happily back into his chair, evidently quite pleased with his own skills as raconteur, while Anna sat silent, absently stroking Android Karenina's hand. Were Mihailov's views so wrong? Was not her beloved-companion twice the woman—twice the person—twice the ... whatever one might call it—than most of the people Anna had known?

"I tell you what," said Anna finally. "Let's go and see him!"

CHAPTER 7

T HE ARTIST MIHAILOV was, as always, at work when the greeting signal of Count Vronsky and Golenishtchev sounded in his studio. He walked rapidly to the door, and in spite of his annoyance at the interruption, he was struck by the soft light that Android Karenina was shedding on Anna's figure as she stood in the shade of the entrance listening to Golenishtchev, who was eagerly telling her something, while she evidently wanted to look round at the artist and his work.

They spoke but Mihailov only noticed every fifth word; he was examining in his mind's eye that subtle nimbus of luminescence the robot imparted to her mistress. So he readily agreed to paint a portrait of Anna, and on the day he fixed, he came and began the work.

In another man's house, and especially in Vronsky's module, Mihailov was quite a different man from what he was in his studio. He behaved with hostile courtesy, as though he were afraid of coming closer to people he did not respect. He called Vronsky "Your Excellency," and notwithstanding Anna's and Vronsky's invitations, he would never stay for dinner, nor come except for the sittings. Anna was even more friendly to him than to other people, and was very grateful for her portrait. Vronsky was more than cordial with him, and was obviously interested to know the artist's opinion of his picture. Mihailov met Vronsky's talk about his painting with stubborn silence, and he was as stubbornly silent when he was shown Vronsky's picture. He was unmistakably bored by

Golenishtchev's transparent attempts to goad him into conversation on the Robot Question, and he did not attempt to oppose him.

From the fifth sitting the portrait impressed everyone, especially Vronsky, not only by its resemblance, but by its characteristic beauty. It was strange how Mihailov could have discovered just her characteristic beauty. "One needs to know and love her as I have loved her to discover the very sweetest expression of her soul," Vronsky murmured to Lupo, who rumbled softly in his lap; though in truth it was only from this portrait that he had himself learned this sweetest expression of her soul. But the expression was so true that he, and others too, fancied they had long known it.

To Anna, what was remarkable was Mihailov's decision to include Android Karenina in the painting, a decision not in keeping with traditions of portraiture, but one which seemed to her entirely fitting and appropriate.

*   *   *

On the sixth day of the sitting Golenishtchev entered with his usual bluster. As he pulled off his thick, dust-caked moon boots, he reported on a communiqué he had just received from a friend in Petersburg, who spoke of a rather bizarre new dictate emerging from the Ministry: all Class III robots, it seemed, were being gathered up by the government for some sort of mandatory circuitry adjustment.

Golenishtchev passed easily on to other subjects, nattering next about a funny little Moonie he had lost in the pit earlier today, and the various difficulties attending to Extractor maintenance in low gravity. But Mihailov and Anna Karenina—that is, the painter and the painted— seemed deeply struck by the pitman's information. Mihailov laid down his brush and looked off through the big bay window of the module.

As for Anna, she instantly knew who was behind this enigmatic new Ministry program. "Might it be," she murmured to Android Karenina, rising from her model's stool, stretching, and walking arm and arm with

her beloved-companion through the atelier, "that in my absence, whatever strange force lives inside my husband has gathered strength? Has my
departure, my immersion in the freedom that the moon has given me,
doomed my fellow Russians, and their beloved-companions, to suffer in
my stead?"

And her heart was rent by feelings of guilt and frustration.

Vronsky did not share these concerns; he was instead agonized by
his dawning understanding of his own failure to master the technique
of groznium-pigment painting, and his realization that he never would.
"I have been struggling on for ever so long without doing anything," he
said of his own portrait of her, "and he just looked and painted it. That's
where technique comes in."

"That will come," was the consoling reassurance given him by
Golenishtchev, in whose view Vronsky had both talent and what
was most important, culture, giving him a wider outlook on art.
Golenishtchev's faith in Vronsky's talent was propped up by his need of
Vronsky's sympathy and approval for his own hope of finding groznium
on the moon, and he felt that the praise and support must be mutual.
"Isn't that correct, M. Mihailov?"

But Mihailov remained silent. He walked, slowly, still clutching his
brush, away from that big bay window and toward the airlock. "Tell me,
sir," he said to Golenishtchev, propping himself up against the reinforced
steel of the door. "This Project; they intend to 'gather up' all Class IIIs
for what purpose?"

"It is not said—only that we must put our trust in the Ministry."

"Ah," he said. "I suppose we must do that. That I suppose we
must do."

A long stillness then filled the atelier: Golenishtchev looked toward
Vronsky and Anna with raised eyebrows and a wry expression, impress-
ing upon them his enjoyment of the idiosyncratic behavior of the great
artiste. Vronsky continued his contemplation of the master's portrait of
Anna, while Anna herself stood with her hand in the gentle end-effector

of Android Karenina, gazing down thoughtfully toward that big blue-green Class I toy, the Earth.

The airlock had already swung closed behind Mihailov, decisively clanking shut before anyone realized that he had exited—and had not taken with him his oxygen tank, nor even his helmet.

They watched with eyes wide with amazement, as the old painter tromped in his moon boots across the dusty lunar landscape and, showing no sign of the desperate constriction of his lungs that was surely taking place, blew a single, sad kiss in the direction of Earth; and then lay down heavily on the lunar dust, and ran out of breath.

* * *

After the strange death of Mihailov, Anna and Vronsky's rented module suddenly seemed so obtrusively old and dirty: the periodic small malfunctioning of their Class I door locks, the streaks in the glass, the dried-out putty on the seals became so disagreeably obvious, as did the everlasting sameness of Golenishtchev, forever talking of the great day when he would strike his long-dreamed-of lunar ore. They had to make some change, and they resolved to return to Russia. In Petersburg Vronsky intended to arrange a partition of land with his brother, while Anna intended, somehow, to see her son.

Vronsky and Anna soon were climbing inside the ballistic canister and hurtling back toward the planet from whence they had come.

_____

CHAPTER 8

LEVIN HAD BEEN MARRIED three months. He was happy, but not at all in the way he had expected to be. At every step he found his former dreams disappointed, and new, unexpected surprises of happiness. He was happy; but on entering upon family life he saw at every step that it was utterly different from what he had imagined. At every step he experienced what a man would experience who, after admiring the smooth, happy course of a meteor around a planetoid, should be given an opportunity to climb aboard that meteor. He saw that it was not all sitting still, floating smoothly; that one had to think too, not for an instant forgetting where one was floating; and that there was atmospheric pressure around one, and that one must endeavor somehow to steer one's meteor; and that his unaccustomed hands would be sore; and that it was only to look at it that was easy; but that doing it, though very delightful, was very difficult, and very likely fatal.

As a bachelor, when he had watched other people's married life, seen the petty cares, the squabbles, the jealousy, he had only smiled contemptuously in his heart. In his future married life there could be, he was convinced, nothing of that sort; even the external forms, indeed, he fancied, must be utterly unlike the life of others in everything. And all of a sudden, instead of his life with his wife being made on an individual pattern, it was, on the contrary, entirely made up of the pettiest details, which he had so despised before, but which now, by no will of his own, had gained an extraordinary importance that could not be denied. Although Levin believed himself to have the most exact conceptions of domestic life, unconsciously, like all men, he pictured domestic life as the happiest enjoyment of love, with nothing to hinder and no petty cares to distract. He ought, as he conceived the position, to do his work, and to find repose from it in the happiness of love. She ought to be beloved, and nothing more. But, like all men, he forgot that she too would want work. And he was surprised that she, his poetic, exquisite Kitty, could not merely busy herself about the Class Is and the furniture, about mattresses for visitors, about a tray, about the II/Cook/6 and the dinner, and so on.

Now her trivial cares and anxieties jarred upon him several times. But he saw that this was essential for her. And, loving her as he did, though he jeered at these domestic pursuits, he could not help admiring them. He jeered at the way in which she arranged the furniture they had brought from Moscow; rearranged their room; placed the Galena Box carefully on a certain shelf, then the next day reconsidered and moved it to another shelf; saw after a Surcease nook for the new II/Maid/467, a wedding gift from Levin's parents; ordered dinner of the old II/Cook/6; came into collision with his ancient *mécanicienne*, Agafea Mihalovna, taking from her the charge of the Is and IIs.

He did not know the great sense of change Kitty was experiencing; she, who at home had sometimes wanted some favorite dish, or sweets, without the possibility of getting either, now could order what she liked, riding on a tandem I/Bicycle/44 with her darling Tatiana to the store to buy pounds of sweets, spend as much money as she liked, and order any puddings she pleased.

This care for domestic details in Kitty, so opposed to Levin's ideal of exalted happiness, was at first one of the disappointments; and this sweet care of her household, the aim of which he did not understand, but could not help loving, was one of the new happy surprises.

Another disappointment and happy surprise came in their quarrels. Levin could never have conceived that between him and his wife any relations could arise other than tender, respectful, and loving ones, and all at once in the very early days they quarreled, so that she said he did not care for her, that he cared for no one but himself, burst into tears, and wrung her arms.

This first quarrel arose from Levin's having gone with Socrates to a nearby farmhouse, having heard from a fellow landowner that another of the mysterious, gigantic, wormlike koschei had been spotted in that corner of the countryside. Going to investigate, Levin did not find the beast-machine itself, but paused for some time to contemplate what he found instead: a thick pool of expectorated ochre-yellow goo, along with the skeleton of a man with all the flesh neatly stripped off the bone.

He and Socrates passed a happy hour recreating the struggle, carefully

measuring each scuff mark in the soil with a precision triangulator from
the Class III's beard. Ultimately they determined that this mechanical
monster had to have been larger by a third than the one they had fended
off, with the help of Grisha's I/Flashpop/4, the previous season.

Socrates ran his usual analysis, but to Levin the only conclusion
possible was that these UnConSciya koschei (*were* they UnConSciya?)
were growing—but why? And how?

Flush with the usual pleasure he took in scientific investigation and
discovery, Levin started off toward home; but as they drove, one happiness shifted to another, and soon his thoughts turned to Kitty, to her
love, to his own happiness. The nearer he drew to home, the warmer
was his tenderness for her. He ran into the room with the same feeling,
with an even stronger feeling than he had had when he reached the
Shcherbatskys' house to make his offer. And suddenly he was met by a
lowering expression he had never seen in her. He would have kissed her;
she pushed him away.

"What is it?"

"You've been enjoying yourself," she began, and he saw Tatiana
standing behind her, glowing an accusatory cadmium yellow, her slender arms crossed. Kitty tried to be calm and spiteful, but as soon as she
opened her mouth, a stream of reproach, of senseless jealousy, of all that
had been torturing her during that half hour which she had spent sitting
motionless at the window, burst from her. He felt now that he was not
simply close to her, but that he did not know where he ended and she
began. He felt this from the agonizing sensation of division that he experienced at that instant. He was offended for the first instant. "Enjoying
myself!" he exclaimed. "I have literally been crouched in goo-thickened
mud, examining mutilated human remains!"

"*It's true, Madame,*" Socrates added, presenting as evidence a handful
of the thick, yellow gunk, which dropped grossly through his end-
effectors. Kitty and Tatiana drew back in disgusted unison from this
repulsive offering.

Levin felt that he could not be offended by his dear Kitty, that she was *himself*. He felt as a man feels when, having suddenly received a violent blow from behind, he turns round, angry and eager to avenge himself, to look for his antagonist, and finds that it is he himself who has accidentally struck himself, that there is no one to be angry with, and that he must put up with and try to soothe the pain.

Before he could conceive of how to do so, the scene of marital discord was interrupted by the mechanized tritone of the I/Doorchime/3. A moment later the II/Footman/C(c)43 led in a handsomely uniformed pair of visitors, each with a rosy-fresh complexion, a neat, blond haircut and trim mustache, and slim black boots: Toy Soldiers.

"Good afternoon," said the first of the men, speaking with every drop of the great respect and politeness due the master of Pokrovskoe and his new bride. The other man stood with arms crossed and his hat at a slightly insouciant angle on his blond head, saying nothing, a smile frozen on his face. His careful gaze was locked on Socrates and Tatiana.

"We are representatives of the Ministry of Robotics and State Administration," continued the first man, speaking in a polished but rushed manner, as if from a prepared text. "We have come today to collect your Class III companion robots, in compliance with the nationwide order for compulsory circuitry adjustment. You were each granted an extension in respect of your nuptials. And may we add our congratulations, on behalf of the Ministry, on that blessed event."

The other soldier uncrossed his arms and spoke curtly, gesturing roughly at the two companion robots. "These are the machines to be taken?"

Tatiana took a sidelong, slippered step toward Kitty, and the two locked arms and stood upright, like dancers preparing to launch into a partnered minuet.

"But no!" Kitty announced suddenly, with a wide-eyed, innocent expression. "They cannot go!"

Levin drew breath to speak, intending to upbraid his wife for indulging in such childish defiance of authority. Gazing upon her, how-ever, arm in arm with her beloved-companion, he was softened by the distress evident on her face. What is more, he felt in his heart—especially when his intelligent eyes saw the concern evident in the flickering eye-bank and nervous twitching of his own loyal Class III—that Kitty was absolutely correct in her defiance.

For how *could* they?

"Gentlemen, I beg that you pardon my wife the rashness of her young age and tenderhearted spirit. Naturally we shall comply and sub-mit these machines for the necessary adjustments. But I wonder if you, in your official capacity, might first perform a service for a local landowner."

Speaking rapidly, directing his words primarily to the first Toy Soldier, the one who seemed to him to have the friendliest nature, Levin explained what he and Socrates had observed at the old farmhouse: the skeleton stripped of flesh; the signs of struggle; the puddle of viscous ochre goo. He told them, too, of his own encounter with the gigantic, wormlike koschei outside Ergushovo. "Could you not, as long as your official business has brought you to this province, ride out to these spots I have mentioned and investigate? The threat of such unusual and deadly monsters is a cause of deep distress, as you can imagine, to myself and my household."

But the Toy Soldier to whom Levin directed his appeal scratched his head and squinted, seemingly entirely uninterested in the bizarre creatures Levin spoke of. "That is indeed a most alarming tale," he said softly, "but it does not, alas, have to do with us and our business." Levin glanced from the corner of his eye at Socrates, and saw that he had brought one end-effector up to gently touch Tatiana where her torso unit met her lower portion—a touchingly human gesture. "Sir, we have precise instructions from the Ministry."

Levin was inwardly cursing the seeming singlemindedness of the soldiers when the other one, who had been standing mute with arms crossed, seeming not to pay attention, held up an open palm. "This wormlike machine," he said, "did it emit a sound—like a sort of ticking, a *tikka tikka tikka* sound?"

Levin nodded his assent, at which the Toy Soldier sighed and spoke in a whisper to his companion. As they turned on their slim black boots and walked back toward the door, the first of the soldiers glanced amiably over his shoulder at Levin, and said in a casual tone, "We shall return shortly, and complete our previously announced business here. We have no desire to perform our commission by force."

"No," said the second soldier, as he pulled the big front door of the manor house behind them. "Not yet."

Kitty burst into tears, running to her Class III and hiding her face in Tatiana's thin metal bosom. "I could not bear for her to be taken!" she said through her tears.

"Nor I, my dear," was Levin's reply, as he looked gravely out the front window, watching the Toy Soldiers ride off. "Nor I."

"And what will they do with them? I mean, *really* do?"

"I don't know, Kitty."

"Madame?" interjected Tatiana anxiously, as Levin and Kitty embraced.

"Sir?" echoed Socrates.

"Yes, yes, beloved-companions," Levin said. "You are quite right. Now we must leave Pokrovskoe. And fast."

CHAPTER 9

IMMEDIATELY THERE COMMENCED in the Levin household that frenzy of activity, among robots and humans alike, attendant upon a rapid and secret flight to safety. What to take? How much luggage? How best to travel undetected? And where to go?

"I shall take the Class IIIs with me to the small provincial town of

Urgensky, where my brother Nikolai is residing," Levin said. "In his last communiqué he said his own Class III, Karnak, has not been taken in for adjustment. We may hope that Urgensky is too out of the way, with too few Class III companion robots in residence there, to be considered worth the effort of the state to collect them."

Kitty's face changed at once.

"When?" she said.

"Immediately! A visit to my ailing brother is a perfectly reasonable excuse for travel, and I shall carry the Surceased robots with my luggage."

"And I will go with you, can I?" Kitty said.

"Kitty! What are you thinking of?" he said reproachfully.

"How do you mean?" she said, offended that he should seem to take her suggestion unwillingly and with vexation. "Why shouldn't I go? I shan't be in your way. I—"

"The journey is to be long, and likely dangerous," said Levin, all the fire of their earlier quarrel returning. "Why should you—"

"Why? For the same reason as you."

"Ah!" said Levin, and bitterly muttered to Socrates, though loud enough for Kitty to hear. "At a moment of such gravity, she only thinks of her being dull by herself, alone here in the pit-house without me or Tatiana."

"*Now now,*" counseled Socrates, looking guiltily at Kitty. "*Do not be cross with her.*"

"No!" said Levin sternly. "It's out of the question."

Tatiana brought Kitty a cup of tea from the I/Samovar/1(8); Kitty did not even notice her. The tone in which her husband had said the last words wounded her, especially because he evidently did not believe what she had said.

"I tell you, that if you go, I shall come with you; I shall certainly come," she said hastily and wrathfully.

"It is out of the question!"

"Why out of the question? Why do you say it's out of the question?"

"Because I'll be going God knows where, by all sorts of roads and to all sorts of hotels. And my brother lives in entirely unsuitable circumstances! That would be reason enough to bar your coming, before one even considers the danger of our being discovered by agents of the Ministry and prosecuted as Januses for disobeying the compulsory adjustment order. You would be a hindrance to me," said Levin, trying to be cool.

"What dangers you can face, I can!" replied Kitty hotly.

"Yes, yes. But think, too, of where we are going, and whom we will meet. For one thing then, this woman's there whom you can't meet."

"I don't know and don't care to know who's there and what. My husband is undertaking a risk, to protect his beloved-companion as well as mine, and I will go with my husband too. . . . "

"Kitty! Don't get angry. But just think a little: this is a matter of such importance that I can't bear to think that you should bring in a feeling of weakness, of dislike to being left alone. Come, you'll be dull alone, so go and stay at Moscow a little."

"There, you always ascribe base, vile motives to me," she said with tears of wounded pride and fury. "I didn't mean, it wasn't weakness, it wasn't. . . . I feel that it's my duty to be with my husband when he's in trouble, but you try on purpose to hurt me, you try on purpose not to understand. . . . "

"No, this is awful! To be such a slave!" cried Levin, getting up, and unable to restrain his anger any longer. But at the same second he felt that he was beating himself.

"Then why did you marry? You could have been free. Why did you, if you regret it?"

He began to speak, trying to find words not to dissuade but simply to soothe her. But she did not heed him, and would not agree to anything. He bent down to her and took her hand, which resisted him. He kissed her hand, kissed her hair, kissed her hand again—still she was silent. But when he took her face in both his hands and said "Kitty!" she suddenly recovered herself, and began to cry, and they were reconciled.

It was decided that they should go together, as soon as possible. The robots were put in Surcease, and locked together in a trunk.

CHAPTER 10

THE HOTEL IN URGENSKY, the provincial town where Nikolai Levin was living, was one of those provincial hotels which are constructed on the newest model of modern improvements, with the best intentions of cleanliness, comfort, and even elegance, but owing to the public that patronizes them, are with astounding rapidity transformed into filthy taverns with a pretension of modern improvement that only makes them worse than the old-fashioned, honestly filthy hotels.

There remained only one filthy room, which would barely fit the two of them, and their robots, once revivified. Levin was feeling angry with his wife because what he had expected had come to pass: at the moment of arrival, when his heart throbbed with emotion and anxiety to find his brother and make whatever arrangements were necessary to find a place where the Class IIIs could stay here undetected, he had to be seeing after her.

"Go, do go!" she said, looking at him with timid and guilty eyes.

He went out of the door without a word, and at once stumbled over his brother's consort, Marya Nikolaevna, who had heard of his arrival and had not dared to go in to see him. She was just the same as when he saw her in Moscow; the same woolen gown, and bare arms and neck, and the same good-naturedly stupid, pockmarked face, only a little plumper.

Speaking rapidly and with obvious apprehension, Marya Nikolaevna expressed her relief at seeing him: Nikolai's illness, she explained, had dramatically worsened, and indeed she feared he was now at death's door.

"What? Well, and how is he at present?"

"Very bad. He can't get up. His body writhes with pain, and there is in the texture of his flesh a strange and unseemly rippling. I fear the worst. Come," Marya Nikolaevna continued. "He has kept expecting you."

The door of his room opened and Kitty peeped out. Tatiana's head peeped out just under hers. Levin crimsoned both from shame and anger with his wife, who had put herself and him in such a difficult position; but Marya Nikolaevna crimsoned still more. She positively shrank and flushed to the point of tears, and clutching the ends of her apron in both hands, twisted them in her red fingers without knowing what to say or what to do.

For the first instant Levin saw an expression of eager curiosity in the eyes with which Kitty looked at this awful woman, so incomprehensible to her; but it lasted only a single instant.

"Well! Have you explained to her our plan, regarding the Class III robots?" she turned to her husband and then to her.

"But one can't go on talking in the corridor like this!" Levin said, looking angrily at a gentleman who walked jauntily at that instant across the corridor, as though going about his affairs. Could this be one of them? A Toy Soldier? Some other agent of the state, disguised in everyday clothes?

"Well then, come in," said Kitty, turning to Marya Nikolaevna, who had recovered herself, but noticing her husband's face of dismay, she added, "or go on; go, and then come for me," and she and Tatiana went back into the room.

Levin went to his brother's room. There he was aghast to see the instructions etched above the door, but he obeyed them nonetheless, donning the elaborate sickroom costume of mask, gown, and gloves.

"My poor brother," he murmured to Socrates, who was donning his own mask; of course a companion robot required no protection from human infection, but the costume would at least delay his immediate detection as a machine-man, should a doctor or other stranger happen into the room.

Levin, from Marya's descriptions, had expected to find the physical signs of the approach of death more marked—greater weakness, greater emaciation, but still almost the same condition of things. He had expected himself to feel the same distress at the loss of the brother he loved and the same horror in face of death as he had felt then, only in a greater degree.

In this little, dirty room with the caution posted by the door, with the painted panels of its walls filthy with spittle, and conversation audible through the thin partition from the next room, in a stifling atmosphere saturated with impurities, on a bedstead moved away from the wall, there lay, covered with a quilt, a body. One arm of this body was above the quilt, and the wrist, huge as a rake handle, was attached, inconceivably it seemed, to the thin, long bone of the arm, smooth from the beginning to the middle. The head lay sideways on the pillow. Levin could see the scanty locks wet with sweat on the temples and the tense, transparent-looking forehead.

Propped against the opposite wall was Karnak, Nikolai's staggering rust-bucket of a Class III, if anything more decrepit and dilapidated than the last time Levin had seen him. "One can see why the Ministry has no interest in adjusting such machines," whispered Levin to Socrates, who had instinctively recoiled from the sad, shrunken metal figure.

As they approached the bed, any doubt that this wracked figure was Levin's dear brother became impossible. In spite of the terrible change in the face, Levin had only to glance at those eager eyes raised at his approach, only to catch the faint movement of the mouth under the sticky mustache, to realize the terrible truth that this death-like body was his living brother.

When Konstantin took him by the hand, the thick, white protective gloves feeling scarcely protection enough, Nikolai smiled. There was at that moment the scrape of a boot heel in the hallway outside, and Levin looked up sharply: was it them? Had they been found already? Socrates pulled his mask higher over his face, his eyebank flashing unsteadily.

"You did not expect to find me like this," Nikolai articulated with effort.

"Yes . . . no," said Levin. The sound of the footsteps faded down the hallway.

A great swell of flesh bubbled up from Nikolai's midsection, as if his body was a balloon and air had been temporarily forced into one part of it. Levin looked away, as Nikolai winced and groaned.

"How was it you didn't let me know before that you were suffering so?"

Nikolai could not answer; again the flesh of his torso bubbled grotesquely, and again he gritted his teeth and scowled with evident agony.

Levin had to talk so as not to be silent, and he did not know what to say, especially as his brother made no reply. His odd condition was not, it appeared, contained to his midsection; as Levin watched, one of Nikolai's eyes bulged grotesquely, and then the other. He tried to speak and his swollen tongue lolled like bread dough onto his cheek. Containing his horror and revulsion, Levin said to his brother that his wife had come with him. When his tongue detumesced and he could speak again, Nikolai expressed pleasure, but said he was afraid of frightening her by his condition. A silence followed—Levin would not say so, but he had precisely the same fear.

"Let me explain the reason we have come," Levin then said. "It has to do with . . . " He lowered his voice to a whisper, drawing nearer his brother's wrecked flesh, and said, "the robots."

Karnak's leg fell off, and he fell to the ground with a scrape and clank. Socrates, politely, lifted the other machine back up and placed him in his previous position against the wall.

Suddenly Nikolai stirred, and began to say something, entirely ignoring Levin's whispered comment about the Class IIIs and speaking instead of his health. He found fault with the doctor, regretting he had not a celebrated Moscow doctor with a II/Prognosis/4 or higher. Levin saw that he still hoped.

Seizing the first moment of silence, Levin got up, anxious to escape, if only for an instant, from his agonizing emotion, and said that he would go and fetch his wife.

"Very well, and I'll tell Karnak to tidy up here. It's dirty and stinking here, I expect. Karnak! Clear up the room," the sick man said with effort. Karnak swiveled his head unit uncertainly, his aural sensors detecting some distant sensory input.

"Well, how is he?" Kitty asked with a frightened face when Levin went to fetch her.

"Oh, it's awful, it's awful! What did you come for?" said Levin.

Kitty was silent for a few seconds, looking timidly and ruefully at her husband; then she went up and took him by the elbow with both hands.

"Kostya! Take me to him; it will be easier for us to bear it together. You only take me, take me to him, please, and go away," she said. "You must understand that for me to see you, and not to see him, is far more painful. There I might be a help to you and to him. Please, let me!" she besought her husband, as though the happiness of her life depended on it.

Levin was obliged to agree, and regaining his composure, and completely forgetting about Marya Nikolaevna by now, he went again to his brother with Kitty.

Stepping lightly, and continually glancing at her husband, showing him a valorous and sympathetic face, Kitty donned the mask and gloves and gown, went into the sickroom, and, turning without haste, noiselessly closed the door. With inaudible steps she went quickly to the sick man's bedside, and going up so that he had not to turn his head, she immediately clasped in her fresh, young, thickly gloved hand, the skeleton of his huge hand, pressed it, and began speaking with that soft eagerness, sympathetic and not jarring, which is peculiar to women.

"We have met, though we were not acquainted, on the Venus orbiter," she said. "You never thought I was to be your sister?"

"Would you have recognized me?" he said, with a radiant smile at her entrance.

"Yes, I would. I am sorry to have found you unwell, and I hope I can be of some use to you."

"And I to you, and to your machines." Nikolai smiled, and from this quiet statement Levin gathered that his brother had indeed heard his allusion to the robots, and was willing despite his grave health to help keep their beloved-companions safe.

It was decided that when the time came for Levin and Kitty to return to Pokrovskoe (meaning, though none spoke the words aloud, when Nikolai had passed into the Beyond), their Class IIIs would stay here, their exterior trim radically downgraded, masquerading as Class IIs at work in a local cigarette factory—the owner of which, Nikolai felt sure, would accept a small payment to hide the robots among his workforce—and spending their Surceased nights in the dingy factory basement.

CHAPTER 11

AS THE HOURS and then days passed, Levin found he could not look calmly at his brother; he could not himself be natural and calm in his presence. When he went in to be with the sick man, his eyes and his attention were unconsciously dimmed, and he did not see or distinguish the details of his brother's position. He smelled the awful odor, saw the dirt, disorder, and miserable condition, and heard the groans, and felt that nothing could be done to help. While Kitty directed her full attention and sympathy to the dying man, and Socrates anxiously circumnavigated the room, Levin's mind wandered, like a landowner traveling the acres of his life. He surveyed all that was pleasurable, like his pit-mining operation and his beloved Kitty, and he surveyed all those tracts causing him concern: the mysterious, wormlike mechanical monsters rampaging the countryside; the circuitry adjustment protocol, which seemed to Levin an inexplicable and unjustified exercise of state power against the citizenry; and worst of all, the unspeakable illness eating his dear brother alive.

It never entered his head to analyze the details of the sick man's situation, to consider how that body was lying under the quilt, how those emaciated legs and thighs and spine were lying huddled up, how those long waves of undulating flesh were appearing and disappearing, and whether they could not be made more comfortable, whether anything could not be done to make things, if not better, at least less bad. It made his blood run cold when he began to think of all these details. He was absolutely convinced that nothing could be done to prolong his brother's life or to relieve his suffering. To be in the sickroom was agony to Levin; not to be there still worse. And he was continually, on various pretexts, going out of the room and coming in again, because he was unable to remain alone.

But Kitty thought, and felt, and acted quite differently. On seeing the roiling flesh of the sick man, she pitied him. And pity in her womanly heart did not arouse at all that feeling of horror and loathing that it aroused in her husband, but a desire to act, to find out all the details of his state, and to remedy them. And since she had not the slightest doubt that it was her duty to help him, she had no doubt either that it was possible, and immediately set to work. The very details, the mere thought of which reduced her husband to terror, immediately engaged her attention. She sent for the doctor, and set Tatiana and Socrates and Marya Nikolaevna to sweep and dust and scrub, as slow, crossed-wire Karnak was quite useless in this regard. She herself washed up something, washed out something else, laid something under the quilt. Something was by her directions brought into the sickroom, something else was carried out. She herself went several times to her room, regardless of the men she met in the corridor, got out and brought in sheets, pillowcases, towels, and shirts.

The sick man, though he seemed and was indifferent about it, was not angry, but only abashed, and on the whole, as it were, interested in what she was doing with him. Coming back from the doctor to whom Kitty had sent him, and putting back on his layers of prophylactic gear, Levin, on opening the door, came upon the sick man at the instant when, by Kitty's directions, they were changing his linen. The long, white ridge of his spine, with the huge, prominent shoulder blades and jutting ribs and vertebrae, was bare, and covered in a rough constellation of black and greenish scabs; Marya Nikolaevna and the waiter were struggling with the sleeve of the nightshirt, and could not get the long, limp arm into it. Kitty, hurriedly closing the door after Levin, was not looking that way, but the sick man groaned, and she moved rapidly toward him.

"Make haste," she said.

"Oh, don't you come," said the sick man angrily. "I'll do it myself. . . . "

"What say?" queried Marya Nikolaevna. But Kitty heard and saw he was ashamed and uncomfortable at being naked before her.

"I'm not looking, I'm not looking!" she said, putting the arm in. "Marya Nikolaevna, you come to this side, you do it," she added.

Levin found a new doctor, not the one who had been attending Nikolai Levin, as the patient was dissatisfied with him. With Socrates and Tatiana secreted away in Levin and Kitty's room, the new doctor came and sounded the patient; he consulted his II/Prognosis/M4, prescribed medicine, and with extreme minuteness explained first how to take the medicine and then what diet was to be kept to. He advised eggs, raw or hardly cooked, and seltzer water, with warm milk at a certain temperature.

"But what is wrong with him?" asked Levin, wringing his hands.

"It is unquestionably a unique case," the doctor began, glancing warily at Nikolai's stomach, where a grotesque convexity was even then fighting upward, like a frog squirming within a mud bank. "I must tell you, however, that as to the nature of his condition, I have not the slightest idea."

When the doctor and his II/Prognosis/M4 had gone away, the sick man said something to his brother, of which Levin could distinguish only the last words: "Your Katya." By the expression with which he gazed at her, Levin saw that he was praising her.

"I'm much better already," he said. "Why, with you I would have gotten well long ago. How nice it is!" he took her hand and drew it toward his lips, but as though afraid she would dislike such contact, he changed his mind, let it go, and only stroked it. Kitty took his hand in both of hers and pressed it.

"Now turn me over on the left side and go to bed," he said.

CHAPTER 12

THE NEXT DAY the sick man received the sacrament and extreme unction from a priest, who stood, with his cross raised before him, a precautionary three feet away from the sickbed. During the ceremony Nikolai Levin prayed fervently. His great eyes, rotating in opposite directions from each other, tried but failed to fasten on the holy image that was set out on a card table covered with a colored napkin. For Levin it was agonizingly painful to behold the supplicating, hopeful eyes and the emaciated body, wasted and covered in its pattern of sores, making the sign of the cross on his tense, pockedmarked brow, and the prominent shoulders and hollow, gasping chest, which could not feel consistent with the life the sick man was praying for. During the sacrament Levin did what he, an unbeliever, had done a thousand times. He said, addressing God, "If Thou dost exist, make this man to recover" (of course this same thing has been repeated many times), "and Thou wilt save him and me." When the priest had gone, Socrates came forth from hiding and Levin loaded his Third Bay with the same hopeful prayer, playing it over and over again.

After extreme unction the sick man became suddenly much better.

He did not cough once in the course of an hour, and no fresh turgescence troubled his midsection. He smiled, kissed Kitty's hand, thanking her with tears, and said he was comfortable, free from pain, and that he felt strong and had an appetite. He even raised himself when his soup was heated in a primitive I/Warmer/1, and asked for a cutlet as well. Hopelessly ill as he was, obvious as it was at the first glance that he could not recover, Levin and Kitty were for that hour both in the same state of excitement, happy, though fearful of being mistaken. Even Karnak emitted a harsh, happy garble, pinpricks of hopeful orange registering in the mud brown of his eyebank.

"Is he better?"

"Yes, much."

"It's wonderful."

"There's nothing wonderful in it."

"Anyway, he's better," they said in a whisper, smiling to one another.

This self-deception was not of long duration. The sick man fell into a quiet sleep, but he was woken up half an hour later by a violent, wracking cough, accompanied by the abrupt return of the flesh-bulging phenomenon, extending this time from his stomach all along the length of his frame, from his neck down to his thighs. And all at once every hope vanished in those about him and in himself. The reality of his suffering crushed all hopes in Levin and Kitty and in the sick man himself, leaving no doubt, no memory even of past hopes.

At eight o'clock in the evening Levin and his wife were drinking tea in their room when Marya Nikolaevna ran in to them breathlessly. She was pale, and her lips were quivering. "He is dying!" she whispered. "I'm afraid he will die this minute."

Both of them ran to him. He was lying in the bed, rocking back and forth, his stomach bulging and puckering, a new system of sores visible on his neck and arms, his long back bent, and his head hanging low.

"How do you feel?" Levin asked in a whisper.

"It is inside me," Nikolai said enigmatically but with extreme distinctness, screwing the words out of himself.

Levin took Nikolai to mean that lurking inside him was the spirit of death, which was determined to consume him.

"Inside me," Nikolai said again.

"Why do you think so?" said Levin, so as to say something.

"Inside—inside—it wants to come out," he repeated, as though he had a liking for the phrase. "It must come out. It's the end."

Marya Nikolaevna went up to him.

"You had better lie down; you'd be easier," she said.

"I shall lie down soon enough," he pronounced slowly, a great, thick pocket of flesh bubbling up from his torso. "When I'm dead."

Levin laid his brother on his back, sat down beside him, and gazed at his face, holding his breath. The dying man lay with closed eyes, but the muscles twitched grotesquely from time to time on his forehead, living creatures dancing within the skin. Levin involuntarily thought with him of what it was that was happening to him now, but in spite of all his mental efforts to go along with him he saw by the expression of that calm, stern face that for the dying man all was growing clearer and clearer that was still as dark as ever for Levin.

"Yes, yes, so," the dying man articulated slowly at intervals, speaking with difficulty through a tongue that swelled and receded, swelled and receded.

"My God," said Levin sotto voce to Socrates. "What manner of death is this?"

*   *   *

Three more days of agony followed; the sick man was still in the same condition. The sense of longing for his death was all felt by everyone now at the pitiable sight of the patient, writhing and moaning; all thought of capture, of the danger to the Class IIIs, was forgotten in the face of such evident distress. Nikolai arched his back and gritted his teeth; he clutched at his pulsing stomach. Only at rare moments, when the Galena Box's salutary hum gave him an instant's relief from the pain, he would sometimes, half asleep, utter what was ever more intense in his heart than in all the others: "Oh, if it were only the end!" or, more ominously, "It is inside . . . it is inside . . . inside. . . . " Occasionally, tired old Karnak plopped down on the floor and imitated his master's agonized posture, his rusted end-effectors clutching across his dinged and dented midsection.

Such was the consuming horror of Nikolai's suffering that when, on the tenth day from their arrival at the town, Kitty felt mildly unwell, Levin could not contain an anxious expression, which his wife immediately understood. "But you do not fear," she began, choking back sobs, "that I have contracted Nikolai's illness?"

"Of course not, dear. It cannot be so." He gathered her to him for an embrace; only when he had brought her to bed and laid her down for a replenishing midday rest, did he carefully study her neck and forehead, for any signs of the terrible rippling that marked his brother's flesh. But no; Kitty was untainted.

After dinner Kitty again donned her protective accoutrements and went as usual with her work to the sick man. He looked at her sternly when she came in, and smiled contemptuously when she said she had been unwell. That day he was alive with sores, his whole body covered with them, all of them throbbing and red like so many angry craters.

"How do you feel?" she asked him.

"Worse," he articulated with difficulty. "In pain!"

"In pain, where?"

"Everywhere." He gestured to his body, covered in ulcerated divots and loose flaps of skin.

"It will be over today, you will see," said Marya Nikolaevna. Though it was said in a whisper, the sick man, whose hearing Levin had noticed was very keen, must have heard. Levin said hush to her, and looked round at the sick man. Nikolai had heard; but these words produced no effect on him. His eyes, ringed though they were with tiny sores on his cheeks and eyelids, had still the same intense, reproachful look.

"Why do you think so?" Levin asked her, when she had followed him into the corridor.

"He has begun picking at himself," said Marya Nikolaevna.

"How do you mean?"

"Like this," she said, scratching wildly at her arms and legs, as if clawing at something beneath the skin.

Marya Nikolaevna's prediction came true. Toward night the sick man was not able to lift his hands, and could only gaze before him with the same intensely concentrated expression in his eyes. Even when his brother or Kitty bent over him, so that he could see them, he looked just the same. Kitty sent for the priest to say the prayer for the dying.

While the priest was administering the blessing, the dying man suddenly buckled violently, his hands thrashing, his body contorting up and back, shaking like a bridge wracked by high water. The priest attempted to continue the prayer as the dying man thrashed madly on the bed, every sore on his body pulsing vividly; indeed, as he stretched and his eyes rolled madly in his head, the little sores started to spurt cobalt bile like hideous little dragon mouths spitting gouts of fire. The priest scrabbled for his Holy Book and desperately continued chanting, reaching forward with a tremulous hand to try and place the cross to Nikolai's cold forehead, but the dying man was bucking forward and back, slapping at his stomach, which bulged forward to an obscene degree. He moaned terribly, and Karnak emitted an awful, high-pitched shriek of distress.

"It is inside," cried Nikolai. "Inside ... "

At that moment the door was kicked open, and two young and handsome men with regimental-grade smokers burst into the sickroom.

"We are representatives of the Ministry of Robotics and State Administration. We have come today to ... dear Heavenly Father!"

For while the man was speaking, Nikolai sat bolt upright, and his skin tore clean from his body like the wrapping ripped from a Class I plaything, his flesh flying free and scattering about the floor of the room like paper and ash. All present, including the two Toy Soldiers, stood frozen as Nikolai Dmitrich issued his last gurgling scream before his head lolled backward at a terrible angle. The remains of his body were shook free like a useless husk: shook free by a hunched, slavering inhuman being, more than six feet in height, its flexing, green-gray exoskeleton rippling with knobby stubs. The monstrosity, now standing astride the sickbed, had some dozens of eyes, clustered around a jagged, reptilian snout ending in a crooked, dirty-yellow beak. A thick, scaly tail swept about the room, while four stubby arms, each ending in a grasping three-fingered talon, lashed out in various directions.

Levin cried out and threw himself in front of Kitty; the priest wept and murmured prayers into his beard. Tatiana leaped in a rapid *jeté* from where she had been hiding, along with Socrates, behind the curtain in the rear of the room—and landed on one of the Toy Soldiers.

"Ah! Help!" shouted the Toy Soldier, as the Class III, her normal pink hue tinged with furious orange, clawed at his eyes with her long, manicured groznium fingernails. "Help!"

His colleague was unable to respond: for, as the others watched, transfixed, the unearthly creature let out a high, shrieking war cry, bounded off the bed, flexed its gigantic claws in midair, and landed on the other Toy Soldier, who had only just gathered the presence of mind to raise the smoker and draw aim. Before he could fire, the beast snapped its beak shut on the man's head like the jaws of a trap.

The monster reared back with the soldier's body dangling limply from its mouth, smashed its fat tree trunk of a tail against the wall, and stomped off through the broken door.

Tatiana meanwhile remained crouched over the other Toy Soldier, battering away robotically with clenched fists, dozens of blows a second, until at last the man stopped moving. The lissome Class III then sat coiled over his body for a long moment, the urgent flash of her eyebank slowly returning to its normal, even pulse.

NIKOLAI DMITRICH ISSUED HIS LAST GURGLING SCREAM BEFORE
HIS HEAD LOLLED BACKWARD AT A TERRIBLE ANGLE

Through all of this, Levin stared with forlorn confusion at the sick-bed where formerly his brother had lain—now but a tangle of sodden sheets, dotted with pieces of scalp, flesh in ill-colored hunks, small, gray piles of shed skin. Socrates gingerly helped Tatiana to her feet, and then bent to examine the battered body of the Toy Soldier, plucking a vision-ary-hundredfold from the metallic instrument tangle of his beard.

Kitty regarded her Class III with confusion, love, and fear. "I . . . I cannot express my thanks, that you took such a risk in defending our safety, as well as your own. But, but Tati . . . ," she trailed off, and Levin was forced to complete the thought for her: "Tatiana, you have violated the Iron Laws. No robot may strike a human being! How could your programming have allowed such an action?"

"I am uncertain," said Tatiana slowly, anxiously smoothing out her tutu with one trembling end-effector.

"I shall explain," answered Socrates, looking up from the Toy Soldier's unmoving form. *"This is not the corpse of a human being. This is groznium. These men were robots."*

* * *

As he and Kitty bid a tearful farewell to their brave beloved-com-panions, and began along the road home to Pokrovskoe, Dmitrich Levin was left to contend with twin mysteries: the grisly death of his brother, apparently as the result of having somehow become a sort of human hatching ground for an abominable alien creature; and the revelation that the Ministry's new elite cadre, the very persons charged with collecting the nation's Class IIIs for adjustment, were not persons at all but perfectly humanoid robots. These mysteries revived in Levin that sense of horror in the face of the insoluble enigma that had come upon him that autumn evening when his brother had slept beside him. This feeling was now even stronger than before; even less than before did he feel capable of apprehending the meaning of life and death, and its inevitability rose up before him more terrible than ever.

But now, thanks to his wife's presence, that feeling did not reduce him to despair. In spite of death and fear, he felt the need of life and love. He felt that love saved him from despair, and that this love, under the menace of despair, had become still stronger and purer. The one mystery of death, still unsolved, had scarcely passed before his eyes, when another mystery had arisen, as insoluble, urging him toward love and toward life.

When they arrived home, the provincial doctor confirmed his earlier suppositions in regard to Kitty's health: her indisposition was a symptom indicating that she was with child.

CHAPTER 13

FROM THE MOMENT when Alexei Alexandrovich understood that all that was expected of him was to leave his wife in peace, without burdening her with his presence, and that his wife herself desired this, he felt the madness that simmered like a kind of fever in the back of his brain begin to burn hotter and hotter—exactly what the Face had hoped for. Let Alexei be weak . . . let him grant forgiveness . . . let the woman and her mustachioed brigand live and go free. . . . In time, the Face knew, their continuing existence would be a sharp nettle to torture Alexei's already anguished mind past the point of no return.

Alexei did not know himself what he wanted now. It was only when Anna had left his house, and the II/Porter/7e62 asked whether he desired the full table setting, though he would be dining alone, that for the first time he clearly comprehended his position, and was appalled by it. Most difficult of all in this position was the fact that he could not in any way connect and reconcile his past with what was now. It was not the past when he had lived happily with his wife that troubled him. The transition from that past to a knowledge of his wife's unfaithfulness he had lived through miserably already; that state was painful, but he could understand it. If his wife had then, on declaring to him her unfaithfulness, left him, he would have been wounded, unhappy, but he would not have been in the hopeless position—incomprehensible to himself—in which he felt himself now. He could not now reconcile his immediate past, his tenderness, his love for his sick wife, and for the other man's child with what was now the case; for in return for all this he now found himself alone.

PUT TO SHAME. A LAUGHINGSTOCK. NEEDED BY NO ONE. DESPISED BY ALL.

"Yes," responded Karenin, pacing the empty rooms of his home.

NOT I THOUGH.

I SHALL NEVER ABANDON YOU.

His confidence buttressed by the supportive exhortations of the Face, Alexei was able to preserve an appearance of composure, and even of indifference. Answering inquiries about the disposition of Anna Arkadyevna's rooms and belongings, he exercised immense self-control to appear like a man in whose eyes what had occurred was neither unforeseen nor out of the ordinary course of events, and he attained his aim: no one could have detected in him signs of despair.

On the second day after her departure, Alexei Alexandrovich was paid a visit by a shop clerk, to whom he had previously sent word that his wife's outstanding bills should be sent to her directly.

"Excuse me, your Excellency, for venturing to trouble you. But she is on the moon, where collections efforts are exceedingly difficult."

Alexei began in his cold and formal way to explain that whatever planet or planetoid his wife cared to live upon was not his concern. But he trailed off, midway through his sentence, his head cocked slightly to the side, listening to an unheard admonition.

HOW DARE HE?

Yes, thought Alexei Karenin. *Yes*.

"You come to me today in search of money, the money owed to

you by Anna Arkadyevna. You come and speak as if you do not know of
our situation."

"Of course, that is, I do know," the shopkeeper stammered. "I do
know of the situation to which you refer."

"Yes," Alexei began, and the human portion of his face twisted into
a sneer, while his voice changed, emerging unnaturally with the timbre
of nails rattling in an empty can: **"BUT DO YOU KNOW WHO I AM?"**

"I . . . I—yes, your Excellency," the man stammered helplessly,
stepping backward slowly as he spoke. "And normally of course before
troubling you I would send my Class III. Funny little robot called
Wholesale. But, sir, of course he's been sent for adjustment."

Alexei Alexandrovich threw his head back and pondered, as it seemed
to the clerk, and all at once, turning round, he sat down calmly at the table.

"I am sorry for bothering you. Perhaps it is best that I go. Sir? Sir?"

Letting his head sink into his hands, Karenin sat for a long while in
that position, several times attempted to speak and stopped short. Then,
at last, he looked up, stared directly at the man, and his ocular device
clicked slowly forward.

* * *

When it was done—when the shopkeeper's windpipe had been shattered like the neck of a wine bottle, when his eyes popped out of his head
like overripe fruit, when what had been the man's body lay in a ragged
mass on the floor, one hand still clutching Anna's overdue bill—Alexei
Alexandrovich allowed a small smile to creep into the corner of his mouth.

"You may consider it paid, sir," he said to the corpse as he stepped
over it and returned to his bedchamber.

But, alone again, Alexei Alexandrovich recognized that he had not
the strength to keep up the line of firmness and composure any longer.
He gave orders for the carriage that was awaiting him to be taken back,
and for no one to be admitted, and he did not go down to dinner.

He felt that he could not turn aside from himself the hatred of men, because that hatred did not come from his being bad (in that case he could have tried to be better), but from his being shamefully and repulsively unhappy. He knew that for this, for the very fact that his heart was torn with grief, they would be merciless to him. He felt that men would crush him as dogs strangle a torn dog yelping with pain—if he did not crush them first. He knew that his sole means of security against people was to hide his wounds from them, and instinctively he tried to do this for two days, but now he felt incapable of keeping up the unequal struggle.

SHE MADE YOU THE FOOL, ALEXEI.

Tomorrow he would appear before his colleagues in the Ministry; accompanied by a regiment of Toy Soldiers, loyal to him and him alone, he would appear before them to deliver a decisive announcement.

SHE ABANDONED YOU, AND THE WORLD HOWLED WITH LAUGHTER.

He would announce to them his new thinking on the topic of the grand Project, of which he was the supervisor; for his plans on that topic had somewhat . . . evolved.

NOW SHE MUST SUFFER.

AND THE WORLD ALONG WITH HER.

He threw back his head and emitted a long, horrid noise, beginning as a laugh that was a cold parody of laughter, and trailing off into a hideous, sobbing moan of despair. His despair was even intensified by the consciousness that he was utterly alone in his sorrow. In all Petersburg there was not a human being to whom he could express what he was feeling, who would feel for him, not as a high official, not as a member of society, but simply as a suffering man; indeed he had not such a one in the whole world.

THE WORLD MUST SUFFER ALONG WITH HER.

The so-called beloved-companions, now that they had all been gathered up, would not have their circuits adjusted and then be returned to their owners.

They would never be returned at all.

ONLY ONE FRIEND, ALEXEI.
ONLY ME.

CHAPTER 14

WHEN THEY HAD ALIT upon terra firma, after the journey back from the moon, Vronsky and Anna stayed at one of Petersburg's finest hotels: he in a lower story, she in a suite of rooms with her child, a II/Governess/D145 to attend to the baby, and Android Karenina.

On the day of his arrival Vronsky went to his brother's. There he found his mother, who had come from Moscow on business. His mother and sister-in-law greeted him as usual: they asked him about his stay on the moon, and talked of their common acquaintances, but did not let drop a single word in allusion to his connection with Anna. His brother came the next morning to see Vronsky, and of his own accord asked him about her, and Alexei Vronsky told him directly that he looked upon his connection with Madame Karenina as a marriage; that he hoped to arrange a divorce, and then to marry her, and until then he considered her as much a wife as any other wife, and he begged him to tell their mother and his wife so.

"If the world disapproves, I don't care," said Vronsky, "but if my relations want to be on family terms with me, they will have to be on the same terms with my wife."

The elder brother, who had always a respect for his younger brother's judgment, could not well tell whether he was right or not till the world had decided the question; for his part he had nothing against it, and with Alexei he went up to see Anna.

Before his brother, as before everyone, Vronsky addressed Anna with a certain formality, treating her as he might a very intimate friend, but it was understood that his brother knew their real relations.

In spite of all his social experience, Vronsky was, in consequence of the new position in which he was placed, laboring under a strange misapprehension. One would have thought he must have understood that society was closed for him and Anna; but now some vague ideas had sprung up in his brain that this was only the case in old-fashioned days, and that now with the rapidity of modern progress (he had unconsciously become by now a partisan of every sort of progress) the views of society had changed, and that the question of whether they would be received in society was not a foregone conclusion. *Of course,* he thought, *intimate friends can and must look at it in the proper light.*

One of the first ladies of Petersburg society whom Vronsky saw was his cousin Betsy.

"At last!" she said, greeting him joyfully. "And Anna? How glad I am! I can fancy after your delightful travels you must find our poor Petersburg horrid. I can fancy your honeymoon in the Mare Tranquillitatis! And your charming Lupo has yet to be gathered up! How marvelous for you!"

And thus did Betsy jump from subject to subject, clearly ill at ease with her old friends. She rambled about the rumors of alien monsters at large in the countryside— "Our Honored Guests, at last arrived!"—and spoke of how she eagerly awaited the return of the Class IIIs. "Not that I miss Darling Girl one bit, of course. I'm doing just fine without her." Vronsky nodded, noting with stifled amusement that Betsy's hair sat in a sloppy bun atop her head, and her dress front was abominably wrinkled.

"How about the divorce," Betsy prattled on. "Is that all over?"

"No, not yet—but what is the meaning of—"

Vronsky noticed that Betsy's enthusiasm waned when she learned that no divorce had as yet taken place.

"People will throw stones at me, I know," she said, "but I shall come and see Anna; yes, I shall certainly come. You won't be in Petersburg long, I suppose?"

And she did certainly come to see Anna and Android Karenina the same day, but her tone was not at all the same as in former days. She unmistakably prided herself on her courage, and wished Anna to appreciate the fidelity of her friendship. She only stayed ten minutes, talking of society gossip and speculating about the Honored Guests: Were they from Venus? This new planet, Neptune, that had only just been discovered? Regardless, the Ministry was offering every assurance that the threat could be easily countered, and who would be such a fool as to doubt it?

On leaving she said:

"You've never told me when the divorce is to be? Supposing I'm ready to fling my cap over the mill, to show my friendship—other starchy people will give you the cold shoulder until you're married. And that's so simple nowadays. Although your husband, or so I understand, is exceptionally busy these days, overseeing the adjustment of the beloved-companions.

"If only your husband were someone else entirely. I do hear that of late he has become somewhat . . . "

She trailed off, raising one hand to her unkempt mess of hair.

"Somewhat *strange*."

From Betsy's tone Vronsky might have grasped what he had to expect from the world; but he made another effort in his own family. The day after his arrival Vronsky went to Varya, his brother's wife, and finding her alone, expressed his wishes directly: that she would not throw stones, and would go simply and directly to see Anna, and would receive her in her own house.

"You know, Alexei," she said after hearing him, "how fond I am of you, and how ready I am to do anything for you; but I have not spoken because I knew I could be of no use to you and to Anna Arkadyevna," she said, articulating the name *Anna Arkadyevna* with particular care. "Don't suppose, please, that I judge her. Never; perhaps in her place I should have done the same. I don't and can't enter into that," she said, glancing timidly at his gloomy face. "But one must call things by their names. You want me to go and see her, to ask her here, and to rehabilitate her in society; but do understand that I *cannot* do so. I have daughters growing up, and I must live in the world for my husband's sake."

Vronsky left gloomily, knowing well that further efforts were useless, and that he had to live in Petersburg as though in a strange town, avoiding every sort of relation with his own old circle in order not to be exposed to the annoyances and humiliations, which were so intolerable to him. Even among strangers, he was always aware of the cold and envious stares of those wondering how he was allowed to walk about with his Class III robot. And to this implied question, he had no answer. Why had not these famous Toy Soldiers, who were led of course by none other than Alexei Alexandrovich Karenin himself, come to take away his beloved Lupo?

Indeed, one of the most unpleasant features of his position in Petersburg was that Alexei Alexandrovich and his name seemed to meet him everywhere. He could not begin to talk of anything without the conversation turning on Alexei Alexandrovich; he could not go anywhere without risk of meeting him. So at least it seemed to Vronsky, just as it seems to a man with a sore finger that he is continually, as though on purpose, grazing his sore finger on everything.

Their stay in Petersburg was all the more painful to Vronsky because he perceived all the time a sort of new mood that he could not understand in Anna. At one time she would seem in love with him, and then she would become cold, irritable, and impenetrable, spending hours sitting quietly alone with Android Karenina. She was worrying over something, and keeping something back from him, and did not seem to notice the humiliations that poisoned his existence, and for her, with her delicate intuition, must have been still more unbearable.

The old adage, which Vronsky remembered from his youth, seemed to hold true: You may travel to the moon, but do not be surprised if the world changes while you are gone.

CHAPTER 15

ONE OF ANNA'S OBJECTS in coming back to Russia had been to see her son; she understood from letters she had received that Sergey had been told she was dead, and that terrible deception weighed heavily on her heart. From the day she left the moon the thought of it had never ceased to agitate her. And as she got nearer to Petersburg, the delight and importance of this meeting grew ever greater in her imagination. When Vronsky spied her sitting in quiet counsel with Android Karenina, it was this dream she was speaking of, talking endlessly of Sergey and cuing Memories of the boy day and night. Anna did not even put to herself the question of how to arrange it. It seemed to her natural and simple to see her son when she should be in the same town with him. But on her arrival in Petersburg she was suddenly made distinctly aware of her present position in society—not only her relations with Vronsky, but her possession of one of the few remaining Class IIIs on the city streets—and she grasped the fact that to arrange this meeting was no easy matter. To go straight to the house, where she might meet Alexei Alexandrovich, that she felt she had no right to do.

But to get a glimpse of her son out walking, finding out where and when he went out, was not enough for her; she had so looked forward to this meeting, she had so much she must say to him, she so longed to embrace him, to kiss him.

She decided that the next day, Seryozha's birthday, she would go straight to her husband's house and at any cost see her son and overturn the hideous deception with which they were encompassing the unhappy child.

As her plan formed itself in her mind, she went to a toy shop, bought toys; and then crept into Vronsky's private *chambres d'armory*, while he slept soundly, and carefully removed what she felt were the items necessary for the excursion. She thought over a plan of action. She would go early in the morning at eight o'clock, when Alexei Alexandrovich would be certain not to be up. She carefully explained her intentions to Android Karenina, who instantly and completely understood her desires.

The next day, at eight o'clock in the morning, a woman climbed from a hired sledge outside the home of Alexei Karenin and rang at the front entrance.

"Some lady," grunted the Karenins' stoic, old *mécanicien*, Kapitonitch, who, not yet dressed, in his dumpy, grey undercoat, peeped out of the window to see a lady in a veil standing close up to the door. Kapitonitch opened the door and was astonished to see the figure of his old mistress, Anna Karenina, covered in her familiar traveling cloak and veil.

Kapitonitch stood perfectly still, a statue of a man with his hand upon the doorknob—for how could he open it? He remembered Anna's kindness, and he wished for nothing greater than to allow her entrance to what had been her home; but it was Kapitonitch who had buried the poor store clerk in a rutted ditch behind the house.

"Whom do you want?" he asked, affecting a voice as hard as tempered steel.

From behind her veil, Anna, apparently not hearing his words, made no answer.

At the same moment, in the gardens behind the house, the real Anna Karenina—for of course it was Android Karenina standing still and wordless at the front door behind Anna's veil—the real Anna overleaped the high electrified fence and landed with a bone-rattling thud beside the fountain. Uneasily holding one of Vronsky's prized regimental smokers before her, she advanced in her stocking feet toward the rear door of the great house that once, a lifetime ago, had been her own. Step after careful step she advanced, not daring to glance up at the bedroom windows, and instead noticing, a few feet from the back door, a kind of rickety outbuilding she did not recognize.

The large metal door of this shed hung slightly open, glinting in the daylight, and Anna's curiosity overcame her.

At the front door, noticing the embarrassment of the unknown lady, Kapitonitch went out to her, opened the second door for her, and asked her what she wanted.

Again the woman said nothing.

"His honor's not up yet," said Kapitonitch, looking at her attentively. Then, hearing a loud, sharp shriek from the rear of the house—the distressed call of a captured bird? the strangled cry of a woman?—he wheeled sharply about.

*   *   *

Anna hid herself behind the shed, out of which she had rapidly retreated, in horror of what lay inside. *Dear God,* she thought, jamming her thick fox-fur muff into her mouth to muffle the ragged sound of her breathing.

Dear merciful God.

Inside the shed she had seen a long, wooden worktable, lined with human faces. Some were displayed in velvet cases, some scattered haphazardly in a gruesome clutter; faces high-cheeked and fleshy and beady-eyed; whole faces and faces in various states of ghoulish disassembly: here a mouth, there the broad expanse of a forehead, there a pair of eyeballs rolling in a wooden box; half a cheek, the skin peeled back to reveal the tangle of red-black muscle beneath.

Still reeling from the stomach-turning awfulness of such a sight, Anna gave the lock of the house's rear door a single silenced blast-charge, slipped quietly inside, and stood with her eyes wide, breathing deeply. She had not anticipated that the absolutely unchanged hall of the house where she had lived for nine years would so greatly affect her. Memories sweet and painful rose one after another in her heart, and for a moment she forgot what she was here for.

Android Karenina, at the doorstep, her duty discharged, bowed to Kapitonitch and turned to depart; but the old *mécanacien*, still believing this to be his old mistress, felt a pang of grief that this kind woman, however to blame, should leave without seeing her son. "Stop," he cried. "Wait a moment."

There was something in the immediate way she obeyed his order. . . .

"Spin in a circle," Kapitonitch ordered, squinting with suspicion as the woman did so immediately. "Put your hands in the air. Wiggle your fingers." At each command, the woman demonstrated automatic—that is, *robotic*—obedience.

"I can't believe it," he said. "Android Karenina?"

"Turn around. *Slowly*," said the real Anna, from where she now stood, directly behind Kapitonitch, the smoker still drawn and leveled shakily at his head. But as he turned, Kapitonitch drew a weapon of his own: a small, metallic hand cannon, as long again as the length of his arm, and aimed directly at her head.

Of course the mécanicien of this household is armed, thought Anna. *Of course.*

"Oh, Madame Karenina," said Kapitonitch sadly, and unlike Anna's, his hand did not shake.

For a long moment they stared at each other, weapons drawn. On the stoop Android Karenina, her veil now drawn back, regarded the scene in terrified silence, her eyebank fluttering double-time as she calculated her odds of disarming Kapitonitch without harm to her mistress. Anna offered a silent prayer that, if she were fated to die here, Providence would allow her to see her dear son once more before it was all over.

But it was not Providence that saved her, it was human kindness; so often, one comes dressed in the clothing of the other. "I cannot shoot you, Madame Karenina. Please come in, your Excellency," he said to her.

She tried to say something, but her voice refused to utter any sound; with a guilty and imploring glance at the old man she went with light, swift steps up the stairs. Bent over, and his galoshes catching on the steps, Kapitonitch ran after her, imploring in an urgent whisper that she not tarry.

Anna mounted the familiar staircase, not understanding what the old man was saying.

"This way, to the left, if you please. Excuse its not being tidy. Your husband's in the old parlor now," the *mécanicien* said, panting. "Excuse me, wait a little, your Excellency; I'll just see," he said, and overtaking her, he opened the high door and disappeared behind it. Anna stood still, waiting. "He's only just awake," Kapitonitch reported, coming out.

"Do be quick, madame," he said again. "*Please.* He will not be happy to find you here. Most unhappy indeed."

And at the very instant the *mécanicien* said this, Anna caught the sound of a childish yawn. From the sound of this yawn alone she knew her son and seemed to see him living before her eyes.

"Let me in; go away!" she said, and went in through the high doorway, Android Karenina heeling her closely. On the right of the door stood a bed, and sitting up in the bed was the boy. His little body bent forward with his nightshirt unbuttoned, he was stretching and still yawning. The instant his lips came together they curved into a blissfully sleepy smile, and with that smile he slowly and deliciously rolled back again.

"Seryozha!" she whispered, going noiselessly up to him. Android Karenina glowed warmly, suffusing the scene with delicate pinks of joy.

When Anna was parted from her Sergey, and all this latter time when she had been feeling a fresh rush of love for him, she had pictured him as he was at four years old, when she had loved him most of all. Now he was not even the same as when she had left him; he was still further from the four-year-old tot, more grown and thinner. How thin his face was, how short his hair was! What long hands! How he had changed since she left him! But it was he, with his head, his lips, his soft neck and broad little shoulders.

"Seryozha!" she repeated just in the child's ear.

He raised himself again on his elbow, turned his tangled head from side to side as though looking for something, and opened his eyes. Slowly and inquiringly he looked for several seconds at his mother standing motionless before him, and just behind her the comforting familiar figure of her beloved-companion.

All at once he smiled a blissful smile, and shutting his eyes, rolled not backward but toward her into her arms.

"Seryozha! My darling boy!" she said, breathing hard and putting her arms round his plump little body.

"Mother!" he said, wriggling about in her arms so as to touch her hands with different parts of him. "I know," he said, opening his eyes; "it's my birthday today. I knew you'd come. I'll get up right now."

And saying that he fell back asleep.

Anna looked at him hungrily; she saw how he had grown and changed in her absence. She knew, and did not know, the bare legs, so long now, that were thrust out below the quilt, those short-cropped curls on his neck, which she had so often kissed. She touched all this and could say nothing; tears choked her.

"What are you crying for, mother?" Seryozha said, waking completely up. "Mother, what are you crying for?" he cried in a tearful voice.

"I won't cry . . . I'm crying for joy. It's so long since I've seen you. I won't, I won't," she said, gulping down her tears and turning away. "Come, it's time for you to dress now," she added after a pause, and, never letting go his hands, she sat down by his bedside on the chair, where his clothes were ready for him.

"How do you dress without me? How . . . ," she tried to begin talking simply and cheerfully, but she could not, and again she turned away.

"I don't have a cold bath, Papa didn't order it. Why, you're sitting on my clothes!"

And Seryozha went off into a peal of laughter. She looked at him and smiled.

"Mother, darling, sweet one!" he shouted, flinging himself on her again and hugging her. It was as though only now, on seeing her smile, he fully grasped what had happened.

"I don't want that on," he said, taking off her hat. And as it were, seeing her afresh without her hat, he fell to kissing her again. "Why do you carry a smoker? Mother!"

"But what did you think about me? You didn't think I was dead?"

"They said you were killed! By a koschei that came upon you in the marketplace, while you shopped for apples."

"Not so!"

"They said it attached itself at the base of your spine, and then burrowed all the way up to your brain."

"No, indeed, my darling!"

"They said when you were found, your face was so mutilated, it was almost impossible to recognize it."

Anna's eyelashes fluttered furiously, as she attempted to conceal her dismay at the wishful thinking that had clearly gone into that particular detail of the story Karenin had concocted for Seryozha.

"I never believed it," the boy said.

"You didn't believe it, my sweet?"

"I knew, I knew!" he repeated his favorite phrase, and snatching the hand that was stroking his hair, he pressed the open palm to his mouth and kissed it. He afforded a sweet glance, too, to Android Karenina, who issued a small hum of pleasure and tried in vain to straighten his mess of childish curls with her slender phalangeals.

"You must go," said Kapitonitch from the door, a note of desperation in his voice. "He must not discover you here. I should not have permitted it. Please, madame." But neither mother nor son would permit their reunion to be interrupted.

The old *mécanicien* shook his head, and with a sigh he closed the door. "I'll wait another ten minutes," he said to himself, clearing his throat and wiping away tears. "I have made a mistake. A terrible mistake."

Anna could not say good-bye to her boy, but the expression on her face said it, and he understood. "Darling, darling Kootik!" she used the name by which she had called him when he was little, "you won't forget me? You . . . ," but she could not say more.

"Of course not, mother," he responded simply. And then, seeming to think of something suddenly, he said, "She has not been collected for circuitry adjustment?"

"Not yet, dear son, not yet."

"Oh. Then are you among the deserving?"

"What?

"Father says only the deserving ones will have their Class IIIs returned to them after their circuits have been properly adjusted. Only the deserving are to own robots from now on."

Anna's eyes widened in bafflement. "And who has your father spoken of, as being amongst the 'deserving?' "

Seryozha thought for a moment, and then let out a gale of childish laughter. "Why, he himself, I suppose! None other than he!"

How often afterward she thought of words she might have said. But now she did not know how to say it, and could say nothing. She only trembled, and clutched dearly at Android Karenina like a drowning woman clutches at a lifeboat. Seryozha only understood that his mother was unhappy and loved him. He knew that his father would wake soon, and that his father and mother could not meet, or the consequences would be disastrous. Android Karenina pulled on her mistress's arm, as it was past time for them to depart, but silently Seroyzha pressed close to her and whispered, "Don't go yet. He won't come just yet."

The mother held him away from her to see what he was thinking, what to say to him, and in his frightened face she read not only that he was speaking of his father, but, as it were, asking her what he ought to think about his father.

"Seryozha, my darling," she said, "you must temper his hatred with your goodness. You are the only human thing he has left."

"I fear him!" he cried in despair through his tears, and, clutching her by the shoulders, he began squeezing her with all his force to him, his arms trembling with the strain.

"My sweet, my little one!" said Anna, and she cried as weakly and childishly as he.

"No . . . please . . . sir . . . no . . . ," came a cry from just beyond the door. Anna had only time to reflect how the voice of a man as strong as Kapitonitch could be reduced, in a moment of terror and desperation, to one like that of a frightened child—when the door flew open with a sharp clatter, and the body of the *mécanicien* came flying into the room. The corpse slammed into the wall above Sergey's head and slid down the wall, leaving a slick of blood below the colorful tapestry hanging above the boy's bed.

Sergey wailed like a bobcat and buried his head in his mother's arms. Android Karenina threw a protective arm around her mistress, and the three of them huddled together, cowering from the tall and dramatic figure of Alexei Karenin, who stood trembling, filling the doorway with his imposing frame.

A long moment passed, before he let out a scream of primal rage. His eyes—one human, one rotating with a dead buzz in his silver half-face—glared from the doorway at the huddled band, and the dread oculus slowly extended toward them, its minute click foretelling some dire and inalterable fate.

Anna, though in her mind she prayed frantically for the safety of her son, was outwardly as silent as Android Karenina.

Only Sergey spoke, opening his young, pink lips and forming a single word: "Father . . . "

And even as Alexei Alexandrovich's cruel mechanical eye quivered in its metal socket; even as he stood with stiffened spine and clenched fists in the doorway; even as every inch of his body seemed to strain with hatred and the desire to destroy; even so, his natural eye softened, and his mouth went slack and moist. From somewhere within him, a single, small word welled up and fought its way to freedom.

"*Go.*"

Anna hurriedly rose, but in the rapid glance she flung at him, taking in his whole figure in all its details, feelings of repulsion and hatred for him and jealousy over her son took possession of her. How could she go? How could she leave her dear Sergey with this monster?

But Android Karenina, calculating options at lightning speed, knew that there could be no other choice: if they did not go quickly, all would die. The loyal machine-woman lifted her mistress bodily over her shoulder, as a mother carries a sleeping child to bed, and together they fled the house. Anna had not time to undo, and so carried back with her, the parcel of toys she had chosen the day before in a toy shop with such love and sorrow.

CHAPTER 16

A S INTENSELY AS ANNA had longed to see her son, and as long as she had been thinking of it and preparing herself for it, she had not in the least expected what had occurred. The man now living in that house—the man with trembling jaw and destructive oculus, who kept a collection of half-built human faces in a shed—this man was not the same man who once had been her husband. On getting back to her lonely rooms in the hotel, she could not for a long while understand why she was there. "Yes, it's all over, and I am again alone," she said to herself, and without taking off her hat she sat down in a low chair by the hearth. Fixing her eyes on a I/Hourprotector/47 standing on a table between the windows, she tried to think.

She thought of the sympathy that Kapitonitch had shown in letting her into the home, and what it had cost him; she thought of Sergey's words: "Only the deserving . . . " She had lost her son now, forever; and how much longer before Android Karenina, too, was torn from her—never to return?

The II/Governess/143 brought the baby to Anna. The plump, well-fed little baby, on seeing her mother, as she always did, held out her fat little hands, and with a smile on her toothless mouth, began, like a fish with a float, bobbing her fingers up and down the starched folds of her embroidered skirt, making them rustle. It was impossible not to smile, not to kiss the baby, impossible not to hold out a finger for her to clutch, crowing and prancing all over; impossible not to offer her a lip, which she sucked into her little mouth by way of a kiss. And all this Anna did, and took her in her arms and made her dance, and kissed her fresh little cheek and bare little elbows; but at the sight of this child it was plainer than ever to her that the feeling she had for her could not be called love in comparison with what she felt for Seryozha. And she was forever—not physically only, but spiritually—divided from him, and it was impossible to set this right.

She gave the baby back to the nurse, let her go, and cued happy Memories of Sergey on Android Karenina's monitor. In the last and best Memory, Sergey was playing in a white smock, sitting astride a chair, trying to solve a I/Puzzle/92 depicting a Huntbear, working with frowning eyes and smiling lips. It was his best, most characteristic expression.

That was the last Memory in the series, and after it, by chance, came one of Vronsky on the moon performing a lighthearted gravity-reduced dance with his longish hair tucked inside his glass helmet. "Oh, here he is!" she said, regarding the Memory of Vronsky, and she suddenly recalled that he was the cause of her present misery. She had not once thought of him all morning. But now, coming all at once upon that manly, noble face, so familiar and so dear to her, she felt a sudden rush of love for him.

"But where is he? How is it he leaves me alone in my misery?"

she asked of Android Karenina, forgetting she had herself kept from him everything concerning her son. She sent to ask him to come to her immediately; with a throbbing heart she awaited him, rehearsing to herself the words in which she would tell him all, and the expressions of love with which he would console her. The II/Footman/74 returned with the answer that he had a visitor with him, but that he would come immediately, and that he asked whether she would let him bring with him Prince Yashvin, who had just arrived in Petersburg. *He's not coming alone, and since dinner yesterday he has not seen me,* she thought. *He's not coming so that I could tell him everything, but coming with Yashvin.* And all at once a strange idea came to her:

"Android Karenina," she asked, "what if he has ceased to love me?" The Class III's eyebank bubbled a warm, empathetic lavendar, and she held out her arms to comfort her mistress. But it was no use; in going over the events of the last few days, Anna saw in everything a confirmation of this terrible idea: the fact that he had not dined at home yesterday, and the fact that he had insisted on their taking separate sets of rooms in Petersburg, and that even now he was not coming to her alone, as though he were trying to avoid meeting her face to face.

"But he ought to tell me so. I must know that it is so. If I knew it, then I would know what I should do!" she said to the robot, who in response reset her monitor to the previous sequence, hoping with the Memories of Sergey to reverse her mistress's melancholy humor. But Anna was caught in this frightening way of thinking, utterly unable to picture to herself the position she would be in if she were convinced of his not caring for her. She thought he had ceased to love her, she felt close to despair, and consequently she felt exceptionally alert. She left Android Karenina and went to her room alone, and as she dressed, she took more care over her appearance than she had done all those days, as though he might, if he had grown cold to her, fall in love with her again because she had dressed and arranged her hair in the way most becoming to her.

She heard the bell ring before she was ready. When she went into the drawing room it was not he, but Yashvin, who met her eyes. Vronsky was watching the Memory of Sergey, and he made no haste to look round at her.

"We have met already," she said, putting her little hand into the huge hand of Yashvin, whose bashfulness was so queerly out of keeping with his immense frame and coarse face. "We met last year at The Cull. Shut that off," she said, indicating sharply to Android Karenina to dim the Memory, and glancing significantly at Vronsky's flashing eyes. "Were the matches good this year?"

Having talked a little while, and noticing that Vronsky glanced at the clock, Yashvin asked her whether she would be staying much longer in Petersburg, and unbending his huge figure reached after his cap.

"Not long, I think," she said hesitatingly, glancing at Vronsky.

"So then we shan't meet again?"

"Come and dine with me," said Anna resolutely, angry, it seemed, with herself for her embarrassment, but flushing as she always did when she defined her position before a fresh person. "The dinner here is not good, but at least you will see him. There is no one of his old friends in the regiment Alexei cares for as he does for you."

"Delighted," said Yashvin with a smile, from which Vronsky could see that he liked Anna very much.

Yashvin said good-bye and went away; Vronsky stayed behind.

"Are you going too?" she said to him.

"I'm late already," he answered. "Run along! I'll catch you up in a moment," he called to Yashvin.

She took him by the hand, and without taking her eyes off him, gazed at him while she ransacked her mind for the words to say that would keep him.

"Wait a minute, there's something I want to say to you," and taking his broad hand she pressed it on her neck. "Oh, was it right my asking him to dinner?"

"You did quite right," he said with a serene smile that showed his even teeth, and he kissed her hand.

"Alexei, Petersburg is strange now—it is lonely and strange without the Class IIIs," she said, pressing his hand in both of hers. "Soon ours will be taken from us as well. We will be safer in the provinces, Alexei, safer and happier."

"I cannot agree with you, dear, given what Yashvin was telling me only just before you came in. These aliens, these so-called Honored Guests, rampage everywhere outside the cities; they say that now, when a person falls ill, his family packs up and flees as rapidly as possible, because soon a large, beaked reptile with dozens of eyeballs will burst forth from inside him and join the hordes. Yashvin says it is quickly becoming very like a full-scale invasion, and speaks as though the provinces will soon be entirely overrun."

"Alexei, I am miserable, and scared. Where can we go? And when?"

"Soon, soon. You wouldn't believe how disagreeable our way of living here is to me too," he said—but then he drew away his hand, and turned his face away.

He is happy that there are these aliens in the woods, she thought bitterly. *Happy for a reason to keep us here.*

"Well, go, go!" she said in a tone of offense, and she walked quickly away from him.

CHAPTER 17

AT DINNER, YASHVIN SPOKE of the sensational new opera then in residence at Petersburg's grand Vox Fourteen; Anna, much to Vronsky's alarm, determined that they should get a box for the evening. After dinner, Yashvin went to smoke, and Vronsky went down with him to his own rooms. After sitting there for some time he ran upstairs. Anna was already dressed in a low-necked gown of light silk and velvet that she had had made on the moon, and had set Android Karenina to a charming pearl-white glow that was particularly becoming.

"Are you really going to the theater?" he said, trying not to look at her.

"Why do you ask with such alarm?" she said, wounded again at his not looking at her. "Why shouldn't I go?" She appeared not to understand the motive of his words.

"Oh, of course, there's no reason whatever," he said, frowning.

"That's just what I say," she said, willfully refusing to see the irony of his tone, and quietly turning back her long, perfumed glove.

"Anna, for God's sake! What is the matter with you?" he said, exasperated.

"I don't understand what you are asking."

"You know that it's out of the question to go."

"Why so?"

He shrugged his shoulders with an air of perplexity and despair.

"But do you mean to say you don't know . . . ?" he began.

"But I don't care to know!" she almost shrieked. "I don't care to. Do I regret what I have done? No, no, no! If it were all to do again from the beginning, it would be the same. For us, for you and for me, there is only one thing that matters, whether we love each other. Other people we need not consider. Why can't I go? I love you, and I don't care for anything," she said, glancing at him with a peculiar gleam in her eyes that he could not understand. "If you have not changed to me, why don't you look at me?"

He looked at her. He saw all the beauty of her face, set against Android Karenina's gentle pearl-white glow. But now her beauty and elegance were just what irritated him.

"My feeling cannot change, you know, but I beg you, I entreat you," he said again in French, with a note of tender supplication in his voice, but with coldness in his eyes.

She did not hear his words, but she saw the coldness of his eyes, and answered with irritation:

"And I beg you to explain why I should not go."

"Because . . . because . . . " He hesitated, and then grasped for an explanation which was not the true cause of his reluctance, but which nevertheless had the virtue of being quite true: "Because of Android Karenina! Flaunting yourself in public in the company of your Class III will only give your husband and his minions a perfect opportunity to subject her to his ridiculous circuitry adjustment program after all."

"This is a risk I am willing to take," she said, filled with spite toward him, toward Alexei Karenin, and toward their whole pitiful situation. Only her Class III did she love and hold blameless, and now she turned tenderly to Android Karenina. "A risk that *we* are willing to take. Aren't we, my beloved-companion?"

In answer, Android Karenina flashed her eyebank tenderly at her mistress, and motored off behind her to the Vox Fourteen.

CHAPTER 18

V RONSKY FOR THE FIRST TIME experienced a feeling of anger against Anna, almost a hatred for her willfully refusing to understand her own position. This feeling was aggravated by his being unable to tell her plainly the cause of his anger. If he had told her directly what he was thinking, he would have said:

"In that dress, with that android-cast glow, to show yourself at the theater is not merely equivalent to acknowledging your position as a fallen woman, it is flinging down a challenge to society—that is to say, cutting yourself off from it forever."

What Alexei Kirillovich could not yet understand was that such concerns simply did not matter any longer. After that night at the Vox Fourteen, a night that would be long remembered and long mourned by the people of Russia, he would understood much better.

Left alone in the wake of her departure, he finally got up from his chair and began pacing up and down the room.

"And what's today?"

Lupo gave a gruff yelp, tilted his head, and scraped the hard wooden floor four times with his right front claw. "Yes, of course, the fourth night. Yegor and his wife are there, and my mother, most likely. Of course all Petersburg's there. By now she's gone in, taken off her cloak and come into the light." Vronsky threw himself back into the chair and patted his lap for Lupo to leap into it. "What about me? What about us? Are we frightened? From every point of view—stupid, stupid! . . . And why is she putting me in such a position?" he said with a gesture of despair.

"Come, friend," Vronsky snarled, and his fierce beloved-companion obeyed. "We're going to the theater."

When they arrived at the palatial Vox Fourteen it was half past eight and the performance was in full swing. The II/Boxkeeper/19, recognizing Vronsky as he peeled off his fur coat, called him "your Excellency." In the brightly lighted corridor there was no one but the II/Boxkeeper/19 and two II/Attendant/77s listening at the doors. Through the closed doors came the sounds of the discreet staccato accompaniment of the orchestra, and a single female voice rendering distinctly a musical phrase. The door opened to let the Boxkeeper slide through, and the phrase drawing to the end reached Vronsky's hearing clearly. But the doors were closed again at once, and Vronsky did not hear the end of the phrase and the cadence of the accompaniment, though he knew from the thunder of applause that it was over.

When he entered the Vox Fourteen, brilliantly lighted with I/Lumiére/7s and gas jets, the noise was still going on. On the stage the singer, bowing and smiling, with bare shoulders flashing with diamonds, was, with the help of the tenor who had given her his arm, gathering up the bouquets that were flying awkwardly over the footlights. Then she went up to a gentleman with glossy pomaded hair parted down the center, who was stretching across the footlights holding out something to her, and all the public in the stalls as well as in the boxes was in excitement, craning forward, shouting and clapping. The conductor from his podium assisted in passing the offering, and straightened his white tie. Vronsky walked into the middle of the stalls, and, standing still, began looking about him. His attention turned upon the familiar, habitual surroundings, the stage, the noise, all the familiar, uninteresting, particolored herd of spectators in the packed theater. There were no Class IIIs. No beloved-companions lounging at their master's elbows, shedding flattering light, fetching spectacles and lighting cigarettes. All these people— the uniforms and black coats, the dirty crowd in the upper gallery, and in the boxes and front rows, the *real* people, the people of society—but not a robot moving among them.

Or so it appeared to Count Vronsky.

He had not yet seen Anna. He purposely avoided looking in her direction. But he knew by the direction of people's eyes where she was. He looked round discreetly, but he was not seeking her; expecting the worst, his eyes sought out Alexei Alexandrovich. To his relief *he* was not in the theater that evening.

"How little of the military man there is left in you!" his friend Serpuhovskoy was saying to him. "A diplomat, an artist, something of that sort, one would say."

"Yes, it was like going back home when I put on a black coat," answered Vronsky, smiling and with a few clicks activating his opera glass.

"Well, I'll own I envy you there. When I come back from abroad and put on this," he touched his epaulets, "I regret my freedom."

Serpuhovskoy had long given up all hope of Vronsky's career, but he liked him as before, and was now particularly cordial to him.

"What a pity you were not in time for the first act!"

Vronsky, listening with one ear, moved his opera glass from the stalls and scanned the boxes. Near a lady in a turban and a bald old man, who seemed to wave angrily in the moving opera glass, Vronsky suddenly caught sight of Anna's head, proud, strikingly beautiful, with Android Karenina's pearl glow casting intricate shadows through the lace of her collar. She was in the fifth box, twenty paces from him. She was sitting in front, and, slightly turning, was saying something to Yashvin. The setting of her head on her handsome, broad shoulders, the restrained excitement and brilliance of her eyes and her whole face reminded him of her just as he had seen her at the float in Moscow. But he felt utterly different toward her beauty now. In his feeling for her now there was no element of mystery, and so her beauty, though it attracted him even more intensely than before, gave him now a sense of injury. She was not looking in his direction, but Vronsky felt that she had seen him already.

When Vronsky turned the opera glass again in that direction, he noticed that Anna's friend Princess Varvara was particularly red, and kept laughing unnaturally and looking round at the next box. Anna, de-telescoping her I/Fan/6 and tapping it on the red velvet, was gazing away and did not see, and obviously did not wish to see, what was taking place in the next box. Yashvin's face wore the expression which was common when he was losing at cards. Scowling, he sucked the left end of his mustache further and further into his mouth, and cast sidelong glances at the next box.

In that box on the left were the Kartasovs. Vronsky knew them, and knew that Anna was acquainted with them. Madame Kartasova, a thin little woman, was standing up in her box, and, her back turned upon Anna, she was putting on a mantle that her husband was holding for her. Her face was pale and angry, and she was talking excitedly. Kartasov, a fat, bald man, was continually looking round at Anna, while he attempted to soothe his wife. When the wife had gone out, the husband lingered a long while, and tried to catch Anna's eye, obviously anxious to bow to her. But Anna, with unmistakable intention, avoided noticing him, and talked to Yashvin, whose cropped head was bent down to her.

Vronsky could not understand exactly what had passed between the Kartasovs and Anna, but he saw that something humiliating for Anna had happened. He knew this both from what he had seen, and most of all from the face of Anna, who, he could see, was taxing every nerve to carry through the part she had taken up. And in maintaining this attitude of external composure she was completely successful. Anyone who did not know her and her circle, who had not heard all the utterances of the women expressive of commiseration, indignation, and amazement, that she should show herself in society, and show herself so conspicuously with her lace and her beauty, and with the audacity to parade her Class III *in such circumstances*—anyone would have admired the serenity and loveliness of this woman, without suspecting that she was undergoing the sensations of a man in the stocks.

Knowing that something had happened, but not knowing precisely what, Vronsky felt a thrill of agonizing anxiety, and hoping to find out something, he went toward the box where she sat. Working his way through the aisles toward her, he jostled as he came out against the colonel of his regiment, talking to two strangers.

The colonel greeted him with genial familiarity, and hastened to introduce him to the others. The colonel's companions were young, with neat hairstyles under regimental caps, high cheekbones, and cold, green-gray eyes.

"Excuse me, gentlemen, but I must pass. Good evening, sir," he said curtly, ignoring the two strangers and addressing only his old friend, the colonel. The men did not step aside, however, but to the contrary formed a tight, jostling ring around him, chattering familiarly.

"Ah, Vronsky! When are you coming to the regiment? We can't let you off without a supper. You're one of the old set," said one of the men. But even as he smiled politely, still glancing up toward Anna's box and trying to shoulder past, Vronsky saw that all three, even his old friend the colonel, wore not the bronze uniform of his regiment, but the crisp blue of the Toy Soldiers. Vronsky turned away from them, silently appealing to the colonel to let him by . . . and noticed with a start, as he looked directly into the colonel's round, handsome eyes, that this was not his old friend at all.

The face was *almost* the same face—the same set of the jaw, the same roll of flesh below the chin, the same bristly black mustache—but a cunning simulacrum of his friend's appearance, not the real thing.

Vronsky recoiled. "I can't stop, awfully sorry, another time," he said, and tried again to break free, to get to the carpeted stairs that led to Anna's box.

"No, no," replied the colonel-who-was-not-the-colonel genially. "We insist." One of the other soldiers grinned, as if preparing to invite Vronsky for a drink or a game of Flickerfly. "Say, the adjustment protocol is moving toward completion. How strange it is that your Class III remains uncollected."

"Oh yes!" said the third soldier. "Why, we could rectify that situation right away!"

Lupo hissed and showed his teeth. Vronsky murmured a demurral while his left hand, hidden by his cloak, moved discreetly toward his belt. Although not, apparently, as discreetly as he had hoped.

"Oh, that won't do, your Excellency," said the "colonel" with a smile. "That won't do at all."

The colonel's face blurred, wavered, and was replaced in a terrible instant by a silver-black mass of churning gears. Vronsky yelped in startlement as the same hideous transformation unfolded on the other men: the skin of their faces retracted, revealing not flesh but gears—gears rolling in gears, tiny pistons pumping up and down, winding tracks—all in the approximate shape of a human face, but made from the stuff of robots.

"Good God," Vronsky had time to say, before a tongue of flame shot forth from the mouth-space on the colonel's face, or rather where the face had been a moment ago. Vronsky ducked in the last moment and caught the blast with the top of his head. He cried out in pain, smelling his own singed flesh and burnt hair, and drew his smoker to open fire; Lupo launched himself forward on his strong hind legs and landed on the chest of one of the counterfeit soldiers, groznium teeth sinking into groznium Adam's apple. The robot cried out and went down in what appeared to be some genuine form of pain, while Lupo wrestled and thrashed at his neck.

Abstractedly, Vronsky heard the panicked screams of the other theatergoers; he ducked and rolled away from a second fire-blast, crouching behind a red-upholstered seat and returning fire. The non-colonel winced as he absorbed a fusillade that would have killed a real human several times over.

Vronsky cursed, and then heard, from the other side of the box, a strangely commonplace refrain coming from the third soldier. "Here boy," the soldier said, crouching down and patting at his lap. "Here, Lupo."

Vronsky, rolling away from a third belch of fire from his antagonist, nearly laughed at the implausibility of such a plan—until he saw that Lupo had indeed released his toothsome clasp on the one robot's neck and was trotting, spellbound, toward the other. "What in the . . . "

A fresh gout of fire spilled over the seat, and Vronsky narrowly avoided it, got off a quick smoker blast at the face-hole of the pretended colonel, and was then distracted again—this time by the sound of weapons firing above.

Anna's box.

"No!" he cried.

He looked up, to where two more of the Toy Soldiers in their handsome blue uniforms stood, with smokers drawn and aimed at Anna's heart. And fat, foolish Kartasov, who mere minutes ago had presented no more significant a threat than societal disapprobation, had revealed his own churning, silver-black death-robot face—from whose mouth-space was billowing a swirling, malevolent column of blue-black smoke.

This cloud snaked forward, Vronsky saw with some relief, not toward Anna but toward Android Karenina; his relief lasted only until

Anna boldly jumped forward, interposing herself between the strange cloud and her beloved-companion.

I should not have let her come to the opera. How could I have let her come?

Cursing, Vronsky leapt from behind the barricade of the seat row and leveled his most deadly blast yet at the robot colonel, crossing the trajectories of his two smokers in a deadly effluxion that he knew would drain the weapons, creating a fire pattern so powerful he could technically face court martial for employing it indoors; *the least of my worries,* he thought drily, watching with satisfaction as the robot's torso melted into a sodden mass.

He was dashing for the door of the box when he heard a pitiful yip from behind him—*Damn it,* he thought. *Lupo.* It appeared that the blue uniformed man-machine, just by staring in the dog's eyes and calling him, had drawn Lupo nearly all the way to his lap—where, Vronsky noticed with horror, the Toy Soldier held a long, nasty-looking groznium scimitar, of exactly a sort he had seen used to junker animal-form Class IIIs in the most direct and irrevocable way. He jerked on the triggers of his smokers, knowing it was no use: his maneuver had exhausted the weapons and they were dead metal in his hands. "Stay!" he shouted to Lupo. "Stay, boy!" But Lupo, caught by the mysterious power glowing out of the soldier's eyes-that-were-not-eyes, continued the forward trot toward his own doom.

Vronsky, in one swift and terrible movement, snapped his hot-whip to life and flicked it at his own Class III's aural sensors. In an instant, the wolf was blinded, the cruel spell was broken, and Vronsky scooped him up under his arm—except that now they faced the Toy Soldier, unarmed. Their faceless opponent drew back the gleaming groznium scimitar and was about to swing . . .

Suddenly Anna Karenina and her companion robot, their hands joined in one powerful fist, smashed down on him from the balcony above. The robot collapsed, and Vronsky, still clutching poor, blinded Lupo beneath his arm, ran to the woman and machine-woman.

"Are you hurt?"

"Not so badly as they," Anna replied smartly, clutching at her leg as she smoothed her skirts and struggled to her feet. Vronsky glanced up at the theater box, and saw the two Toy Soldiers slumped over the sides of the railing, broken like dolls, and the Kartasov robot with its head unit entirely torn off.

"How—" he began, but Anna interrupted: "Alexei, we must go." She was gesturing at the prone Toy Soldier, whose machine-face, stilled at the moment of injury, had begun to whir and glow back to life.

The mechanical soldier leaped to his feet, hissed angrily, raised his gleaming sword—and was set upon again: this time by a massive beast, resembling a madman's hallucination of a jungle lizard, standing upright, with a cluster of yellow-grey eyeballs and the long, razored snout of a bird of prey. The inhuman monster's beak gored the groznium belly of the Toy Soldier, while his ragged claws laced into the arms and legs of the machine-man. As soon as the robot stopped moving, the beast bounded away, leaping over the heads of Anna, Vronsky, and their Class IIIs, and down the aisles.

"It's . . . my Lord, it's . . . ," Vronsky stammered.

"It is our chance, Alexei," cried Anna. "For God's sake, run!"

* * *

This alien was the first of many.

Twitching, snarling, slavering, their massive reptilian heads bubbling with eyeballs; their craggy, ridged snouts ending in knife-like beaks; their clutching, slashing claws; their long, scaly tails dragging against the lush carpets—the aliens poured in a great, fearsome horde into the Petersburg Vox Fourteen, dozens and dozens of them, yowling in a loud, high-pitched shriek as they sped up and down the aisles.

But the Vox Fourteen was well defended, more so than anyone had realized: the Toy Soldiers, robots in the form of men, were, it seemed, everywhere. As Vronsky and Anna rushed headlong for the exits, all over the Vox Fourteen people jumped to their feet and revealed themselves to be robots. Husbands, wives, soldiers, singers—hundreds of pretend people, all secreted by the Ministry of Security among the thousands of theatergoers; as, it was later realized, they must have been secreted *everywhere*. As their shocked companions watched, their faces wavered, blurred, disappeared, and were replaced by the deadly weapon-faces of the Toy Soldiers, and they joined combat with the Honored Guests.

But as has been the way of combat since the times of the Greeks and Romans, it was those with the least stake in the conflict who suffered the most grievously: as the robotic Toy Soldiers defended the Petersburg Vox Fourteen from the onslaught of the alien invaders, it was the human beings who died. The robots shot at the aliens and the humans were caught in the crossfire; the aliens slashed and tore at the robots and the humans were slashed and torn. Not one in ten made it out alive; not one in ten escaped the scalding glow of the smoker or the ragged claw of the lizard-beast, or the trampling boot heels of their fellow theatergoers, desperate for escape.

By morning the stage of the Vox Fourteen was littered with blood and bodies, the aisles with shredded hunks of alien flesh, the orchestra pit with groznium shrapnel and tangles of wire. But Anna Karenina and Count Alexei Kirillovich Vronsky had long since made their escape.

* * *

By the time the first fingers of dawn crept along the windowsills and into her rented rooms, Anna was packing hurriedly. They were fugitives now, and both knew it. Some new life would have to be forged, a new place found; the alien threat aside, she and Vronsky had obviously earned the status of outlaws, fugitives from the strange new society that was being built—under the leadership, Anna thought darkly, of her own husband.

When Vronsky went up to her, she was in the same dress as she had worn at the theater, madly throwing her things into a valise; as each new

TWITCHING, SNARLING, THEIR MASSIVE REPTILIAN HEADS BUBBLING
WITH EYEBALLS, THE ALIENS POURED INTO THE OPERA HOUSE

article of clothing was tossed in, Android Karenina rapidly took it up
again, folded it neatly with fast-flying phalangeals, and placed it back in
careful order.

"Anna," said Vronsky, passionately, "I nearly lost you."

"You, you are to blame for everything!" she cried, with tears of
despair and hatred in her voice.

"I begged, I implored you not to go, I knew it would be
unpleasant. . . . "

"Unpleasant!" she cried. "Hideous! Those men—"

"Robots, Anna, they are robots!"

"You think I don't know that! As long as I live I shall never forget
it. But I will tell you Alexei, those vicious robot soldiers and bloodthirsty
creatures were scarcely worse than the sneering expression of Madame
Kartasov and her husband."

"In fairness, Kartasov was also a robot."

She scowled and continued her feverish preparations for departure.

"Forget it, you must forget all that," said Vronsky, pacing back and forth,
Lupo at his heels. "There are more important things to occupy us now."

"I hate your calm. You ought not to have brought me to this. If you
had loved me . . . "

"Anna! How does the question of my love come in?"

"Oh, if you loved me, as I love, if you were tortured as I am . . . !"
she said, looking at him with an expression of terror.

He was sorry for her, and angry notwithstanding. He assured her
of his love because he saw that this was the only means of soothing her,
and he did not reproach her in words, but in his heart he reproached her.
He spoke softly to her again of a place he knew, where they could be
together and be safe, at least for now, along with their Class IIIs.

And the asseverations of his love, which seemed to him so vulgar
that he was ashamed to utter them, she drank in eagerly, and gradually
became calmer. The next hour, completely reconciled, they and their
battered beloved-companions left for the country.

PART SIX: THE QUEEN OF THE JUNKERS

CHAPTER 1

T*HEY WILL COME for us in three ways."*

It was this strange phrase that was on everyone's lips in the days and weeks after the terrible violence at the Vox Fourteen. "They will come for us in three ways," a strange scrap of liturgy from the discredited quasi-religion of xenotheologism, once in vogue in certain corners of Moscow and Petersburg, long since discarded along with its primary adherents, women like the farcical Madame Stahl.

"They will come for us in three ways."

There was no doubting that they had come in *one* way, not as benevolent light-beings but as the awful, screeching humanoid lizard-things that had wreaked such havoc and spilled the blood of so many Russians at the Vox Fourteen. If, indeed, there was any wisdom in that strange, old, tattered bit of liturgy, then what were the other two ways? And were they to be feared as much as the first? Questions abounded, fears doubled and redoubled, anxious rumors tore wildly like II/Coachman/6-less carriages through the streets of Petersburg and Moscow. One thing that all could agree on was how fortunate it was, on the night of the terrible attack, that so many of the new, powerful, perfectly humanoid Class IV robots had been present to fight off the foe.

Having previously labored to hide the shocking fact of this new cre-
ation from society, the Higher Branches of the Ministry of Robotics and
State Administration now shifted gears, as it were, proudly proclaiming
the arrival of the new generation of servomechanism, proclaiming the
Class IV robots Mother Russia's newest and greatest protectors, whether
against lizard-like creatures from the starry beyond, or the scientist-ter-
rorist schemers of UnConSciya. To this much-heralded revelation was
coupled, almost incidentally, the confirmation of another rumor: No,
came this further announcement from the councils of the Ministry, the
old beloved-companion robots would *not* be coming back. The circuitry
adjustment, it seemed, had been a failure; the old machines, due to an
inherent and previously undetected flaw in design, could not be properly
brought up to date.

And thus, at a stroke, the ancient class of beloved-companion robots
entered its obsolescence.

In Moscow, the onion-shaped bulb of the Tower still revolved,
framed now by two plumes of black and purple smoke—emanating, or
so went the most persistent and disquieting rumor of all, from the sub-
sub-basements, where the junkered Class III robots were being melted
for scrap.

CHAPTER 2

THESE FOREBODING PLUMES of smoke could not be seen
from the groznium mine and surrounding estate at Pokrovskoe,
but the changes they represented were as much felt there as anywhere.
Konstantin Levin and his new wife, Kitty, now felt united not only by the
bonds of matrimony but by a common purpose: having left Socrates and

Tatiana behind, disguised as battered old Class IIs, and slaving in a grimy cigarette factory, they vowed never to submit their beloved-companions for "adjustment"—now understood to be a most permanent adjustment indeed—no matter what should happen.

They were united, too, in their fear of the Honored Guests; Kitty had watched as Levin with determination set his army of Pitbots and Extractors to the building of strong fencing and the digging of trenches around the grounds of the estate, in hopes of repelling the alien hordes.

But for Kitty and Levin, all this tension and fear and looming dread only reaffirmed and even heightened their love.

They were playing host to a small party up from Moscow, and Levin and Kitty were particularly happy and conscious of their love that evening. The presence of Dolly, and of Kitty's mother, the old princess—both of whom who had grudgingly submitted their own Class IIIs to be adjusted, and now knew they had lost them for good—only made their shared bond that much stronger. They loved each other and their happiness in their love seemed to imply a disagreeable slur on those who would have liked to feel the same and could not—and they felt a prick of conscience.

Kitty longed to tell her mother their secret, of how Socrates and Tatiana were yet extant and well. But she was urged by Levin to hold her tongue, for he feared that this forbidden knowledge would inevitably travel from the princess to Dolly, and from Dolly to Stepan Arkadyich—who Levin felt had far too casual a manner to be trusted with the confidence.

That evening they were expecting Stepan Arkadyich to come down by Grav, and the old prince had written that possibly he might come too.

"Mark my words, Alexander will not come," said the old princess. "And I know why: he says that young people ought to be left alone for a while at first."

"But Papa has left us alone. We've never seen him," said Kitty. "Besides, we're not young people!—we're old married people by now."

"If he doesn't come, I shall say good-bye to you children," said the princess, sighing mournfully.

"What nonsense, Mamma!" both the daughters fell upon her at once. "How do you suppose he is feeling? Why, now . . . "

And suddenly there was an unexpected quiver in the princess's voice. Her daughters were silent, and looked at one another. *These days, Mamma always finds something to be miserable about,* they said in that glance. Ever since she had married off her last and favorite daughter, and her beloved-companion La Shcherbatskaya had been carted off, the old home had been left empty.

In the middle of the after-dinner conversation they heard the hum of an engine and the sound of wheels on the gravel. Dolly had not time to get up to go and meet her husband, when from the window of the room below, where Levin was helping Grisha with his Latin lesson, Levin leaped out and lifted Grisha out after him.

"It's Stiva!" Levin shouted from under the balcony. "We've finished, Dolly, don't worry!" he added, and started running like a boy to meet the carriage.

"*Is ea id, ejus, ejus, ejus!*" shouted Grisha, skipping along the avenue.

"And someone else too! Papa, of course!" cried Levin, stopping at the entrance of the avenue. "Kitty, don't come down the steep staircase, go round."

But Levin had been mistaken in taking the person sitting in the carriage for the old prince. As he got nearer to the carriage he saw beside Stepan Arkadyich not the prince but a handsome, stout young man in a Scotch cap, with long ends of ribbon behind.

This figure was introduced as Vassenka Veslovsky, a distant cousin of the Shcherbatskys, a brilliant young gentleman in Petersburg and Moscow society. "A capital fellow, and a keen sportsman," as Stepan Arkadyich said, introducing him.

Not a whit abashed by the disappointment caused by his having come in place of the old prince, Veslovsky greeted Levin gaily, claiming acquaintance with him in the past, and snatching up Grisha into the carriage, lifted him over the spaniel that Stepan Arkadyich had brought with him. (The pup was meant by Oblonsky to make an end to the sullen air of disappointment Grisha had maintained since being informed that, after a little lifetime of waiting, he would now never "come of age" and receive his own Class III.)

Levin did not get into the carriage, but walked behind. He was rather vexed at the non-arrival of the old prince, whom he liked more and more the more he saw of him, and also at the arrival of this Vassenka Veslovsky, a quite uncongenial and superfluous person. He seemed to him still more uncongenial and superfluous when, on approaching the steps where the whole party, children and grown-ups, were gathered together in much excitement, Levin saw Vassenka Veslovsky, with a particularly warm and gallant air, kissing Kitty's hand.

"Well, and how is the Hunt-and-be-Hunted this season?" Stepan Arkadyich said to Levin, hardly leaving time for everyone to utter their greetings. "We've come with the most savage intentions. How pretty you've grown, Dolly," he said to his wife, once more kissing her hand, holding it in one of his, and patting it with the other.

Levin, who a minute before had been in the happiest frame of mind, now looked darkly at everyone, and everything displeased him. He thought for a moment of Socrates, rusting away in some dank, provincial backwater. *How can it be that this crass arriviste should be here among us,* he thought, glaring at the preposterous Veslovsky, *while my beloved-companion molders, many versts from where I might enjoy his company?*

And who was it he kissed yesterday with those lips? he thought, looking at Stepan Arkadyich's tender demonstrations to his wife. He looked at Dolly, and he did not like her either. *She doesn't believe in his love. So what is she so pleased about? Revolting!* thought Levin. He looked at the princess, who had been so dear to him a minute before, and he did not like the manner in which she welcomed this Vassenka, with his ribbons, just as though she were in her own house. And more hateful than anyone was Kitty for falling in with the tone of gaiety with which this gentleman regarded his visit in the country, as though it were a holiday for himself and everyone else.

Noisily talking, they all went into the house; but as soon as they were all seated, Levin turned and went out. Kitty saw something was wrong with her husband. She tried to seize a moment to speak to him alone, but he made haste to get away from her, saying he was wanted at the pit, where the perimeter of the mine was being fortified by thick defensive battlements against the possibility of alien attack. It was long since his own work on the estate had seemed to him so important as at that moment. *It's all holiday for them*, he thought; *but these are no holiday matters, they won't wait, and there's no living without them.*

CHAPTER 3

I T IS EXACTLY THAT MAN most distracted by fear of death from above who is most vulnerable to death from below. Such it was with Konstantin Dmitrich Levin in his fit of pique, as he stomped along the familiar woodsy path to his groznium mine, his gaze fixed on the tree line, in case a pack of the hideous Honored Guests should come leaping over the aspens. For it was the ground beneath his feet that tore open and spewed forth the long, twisting body of a worm-beast. The segmented death machine writhed toward him, emitting as before the ominous *tikka tikka tikka*. Levin gasped and stumbled backwards into a crouch, trying to judge the size of the peril. He and Socrates had estimated that the last one was the size of a hippopotamus, but this one was long as an elephant, and nearly half as high.

With a quick, grunting roll of its powerful head, the thrashing metal-plated thing knocked Levin off his feet, even as more of its body poured up out of the ground like a Grav emerging from a tunnel. Levin, now flat on his back, swung determinedly with his sturdy oaken walking stick, making satisfying contact with the eyeless face of the beast. The great worm drew back, its sucking mouth-hole dripping ochre fluid, the *tikka tikka tikka* loud as a drumroll, emanating from . . . from where? Some sort of Vox-Em, he imagined, somewhere from the midsection of the robotic beast. Konstantin Dmitrich, breathing heavily, feeling the thud of blood in his veins, scrabbled to his feet and circled backward, the walking stick raised and poised to strike. Curiously, however, the creature's huge did not parry again—it paused and held steady with crooked neck, the featureless head twitching in the air above, twisting first this way and then that, as if searching for something. Levin thought he saw dim lights pulsing somewhere beneath the semi-opaque, grey outer covering of the monster—rapidly flickering greenish lights—the light of sensors searching the landscape?

By God, it's looking for something, thought Levin, stepping slightly forward and examining the underside of the thing. "What are you looking for?" he said aloud, as if the segmented, twelve-foot-long ticking mechanical worm could somehow summon human voice and answer. Instead, the thing stopped moving, its head cocked in a northerly direction, and the queer *tikka tikka tikka* noise abruptly grew drastically louder, so much so that Levin clasped his hands over his ears. *He's got it*, Levin thought. *He's got the scent.* And the great worm lunged up and over Levin, its whole writhing body traveling over his head in a fluid motion, like a long jet of water sprayed from a hose; and then plunging back into the ground on the opposite side of the clearing, disappearing into another wormhole in the soil. In a matter of seconds, the entire length of the worm-thing had disappeared into this fresh cavity.

*   *   *

Levin did not continue on to the pit, as he had planned, but instead settled his lank frame on a rock to contemplate the mystery of the worm-beast, with his walking stick at his side, scratching at his head and tugging at his beard in unconscious emulation of his absent beloved-companion.

Levin came back to the house only when they sent to summon him to supper. On the stairs were standing Kitty and Agafea Mihalovna, examining the I/Humidor/19, consulting about wines for supper.

"But why are you making all this fuss? Have what we usually do."

"No, Stiva doesn't drink . . . Kostya, stop, what's the matter?" Kitty began, hurrying after him, but all his irritation with her supposedly inappropriate carryings-on came back to him in a flood, and he strode ruthlessly away to the dining room without waiting for her. There he joined in the lively general conversation which was being maintained by Vassenka Veslovsky and Stepan Arkadyich.

"Well, what do you say, are we to Hunt-and-be-Hunted tomorrow?" said Stepan Arkadyich.

"Please, do let's go," said Veslovsky, moving to another chair, where he sat down sideways, with one fat leg crossed under him.

"I shall be delighted, we will go. I shall order the Huntbears warmed and baited," said Levin to Veslovsky, speaking with that forced amiability that Kitty knew so well in him, and that was so out of keeping with him. "I can't answer for our finding grouse, especially as, with the Honored Guests about, we will need to stay within the perimeter fence, or find ourselves hunted a bit more realistically than is pleasant. Only we ought to start early. You're not tired? Aren't you tired, Stiva?"

"Me tired? I've never been tired yet."

"Yes, really, let's not go to bed at all! Capital!" Veslovsky chimed in. "I have little use for the interval of unconsciousness."

It was a rather peculiar way of phrasing such a declaration, and Levin looked with renewed irritation at Veslovsky. He was eager to retire to his bedchamber, where he could compose a communiqué to Socrates, expressing his thoughts on the question of the worm-machines.

"Suppose we stay up all night. Let's go for a walk!" agreed Stepan Arkadyich with radiant good humor.

"Oh, we all know you can do without sleep, and keep other people up too," Dolly said to her husband, with that faint note of irony in her voice which she almost always had now with her husband.

"Do you know Veslovsky has been at Anna's, and he's going to them again? He swears that their little hideaway is hardly fifty miles from you, and I too must certainly go over there. Veslovsky, come here!"

Vassenka crossed over to the ladies, and sat down beside Kitty.

"Ah, do tell me, please; you have stayed with her? How was she? *Where* is she?" Darya Alexandrovna appealed to him.

"Ah, that I cannot tell you," laughed Vassenka, "for in a blindfold was I led to the camp, and in a blindfold led away."

Levin was left at the other end of the table, and though never pausing in his conversation with the princess, he saw that there was an eager and mysterious conversation going on between Stepan Arkadyich, Dolly, Kitty, and Veslovsky. And that was not all. He saw on his wife's face an expression of real feeling as she gazed with fixed eyes on the handsome face of Vassenka, who was telling them something with great animation.

"It's exceedingly rugged, their place, some sort of old farm from the time of the Tsars, somewhat restored, but really barely livable," Veslovsky was telling them about Vronsky and Anna. "I can't, of course, take it upon myself to judge, but I certainly would not want to live there."

"What do they intend to do?"

Vassenka smiled enigmatically, trying of course to prolong the moment when everyone believed he knew the answer to that most intriguing of questions: what was intended by Anna Karenina and Count Alexei Vronsky, who after the night at the Vox Fourteen had fled into hiding, along with their Class IIIs, in willful and open defiance of the Ministry—and of Anna's own husband.

"What they intend, alas, I cannot say, and I am not sure they can agree amongst themselves. They do seem well hidden though, and I imagine they can live in their secret paradise forever," he said with a chuckle.

"How jolly it would be for us all to go over to them together! I think we might even convince them to rejoin polite society! When are you going there again?" Stepan Arkadyich asked Vassenka.

"July."

"Will you go?" Stepan Arkadyich said to his wife.

"I shall certainly go, if I am invited and told the location," said Dolly. "I am sorry for her, and I know her. She's a splendid woman. But I will go alone, when you go back to Moscow, and then I shall be in no one's way. And it will be better indeed without you."

"To be sure," said Stepan Arkadyich. "And you, Kitty?"

"I? Why should I go?" Kitty said, flushing all over, and she glanced round at her husband.

"Do you know Anna Arkadyevna, then?" Veslovsky asked her. "She's a very fascinating woman."

"Yes," she answered Veslovsky, crimsoning still more. She got up and walked across to her husband.

"Are you to be Hunting and Hunted, then, tomorrow?" she said to Levin. His jealousy had advanced far indeed in these few moments, especially at the flush that had overspread her cheeks while she was talking to Veslovsky. Now as he heard her words, he construed them in his own fashion. Strange as it was to him afterward to recall it, it seemed to him at the moment clear that in asking whether he was going on the hunt, all she cared to know was whether he would give that pleasure to Veslovsky, with whom, as he fancied, she was in love.

"Yes, I'm going," he answered her in an unnatural voice, disagreeable to himself.

"No, better spend the day here tomorrow, or Dolly won't see anything of her husband, and will set off the day after," said Kitty.

The motive of Kitty's words was interpreted by Levin thus: *Don't separate me from him. I don't care about your going, but do let me enjoy the society of this delightful young man.*

"Oh, if you wish, we'll stay here tomorrow," Levin answered, with peculiar amiability.

Vassenka, meanwhile, got up from the table after Kitty, and watching her with smiling and admiring eyes, he followed her.

Levin saw that look. He turned white, and for a minute he could hardly breathe. *How dare he look at my wife like that!* was the feeling that boiled within him.

"Tomorrow, then? Do, please, let us go," said Veslovsky, sitting down on a chair, and again crossing his leg as was his habit.

Levin's jealousy went further still, growing from moment to moment, evolving as it were from I/Jealousy/4 to I/Jealousy/5 to I/Jealousy/6. Already he saw himself a deceived husband, looked upon by his wife and her lover as simply necessary to provide them with the conveniences and pleasures of life.... But in spite of that, he made polite and hospitable inquiries of Vassenka about his shooting, his gun, and his boots, and agreed to go hunting the next day.

Happily for Levin, the old princess cut short his agonies by getting up herself and advising Kitty to go to bed. But even at this point Levin could not escape another agony. As he said goodnight to his hostess, Vassenka would again have kissed her hand, but Kitty, reddening, drew back her hand and said with a naive bluntness, for which the old princess scolded her afterward:

"We don't like that fashion."

In Levin's eyes she was to blame for having allowed such relations to arise, and still more to blame for showing so awkwardly that she did not like them.

Levin scowled and stalked up the stairs to compose a communiqué to Socrates about the terrible worms.

CHAPTER 4

KONSTANTIN DMITRICH SPENT several hours in concentration, composing, recording, and reviewing the communiqué, as he carefully considered how to express his dawning understanding of the worm-machines: what they were, where they came from, and how they were connected to the other troubles plaguing Russia. He went to sleep happy and satisfied with the process of his inquiry, looking eagerly forward to a return communiqué from his poor, exiled beloved-companion.

But it took very little time, the next morning, for Levin's jealousy to be coaxed back to life by the nettlesome Veslovsky. At breakfast, the conversation Vassenka had started with Kitty was running on the same lines as on the previous evening: discussing Anna, and whether love is to be put higher than worldly considerations. Kitty disliked the subject, and she was disturbed as well both by the tone in which it was conducted and by the knowledge of the effect it would have on her husband. But she was too simple and innocent to know how to cut short the talk, or even to conceal the superficial pleasure afforded her by the young man's very obvious admiration. She wanted to stop it, but she did not know what to do. Whatever she did she knew would be observed by her husband, and the worst interpretation put on it. And, in fact, when she asked Dolly what was wrong with her daughter Masha, and Vassenka, waiting till this uninteresting conversation was over, began to gaze indifferently at Dolly, the question struck Levin as an unnatural and disgusting piece of hypocrisy.

"What do you say, shall we go and look for mushrooms today?"

said Dolly.

"By all means, please, and I shall come too," said Kitty, and she blushed. She wanted from politeness to ask Vassenka whether he would come, but she did not ask him.

"Where are you going, Kostya?" she asked her husband with a guilty face, as he passed by her with a resolute step. This guilty air confirmed all his suspicions.

"To inspect the pit for aliens," he said, not looking at her.

"Again?"

He went downstairs, but before he had time to leave his study he heard his wife's familiar footsteps running with reckless speed to him. He did not turn, but stalked out of the house into the surrounding gardens, past a II/Gardener/9, who Levin had put to work visually scanning for Honored Guests in the woods. Finally he had to acknowledge Kitty's presence:

"Well, what do you have to say to me?"

He did not look her in the face, and did not care to see that she in her condition was trembling all over, and had a piteous, crushed look. He did not care, that is to say, to recall how difficult it must be for a woman with child, deprived of the special comfort that only a Class III can provide.

"We can't go on like this! It's misery! I'm wretched, you are wretched! What for?" she said, when they had at last reached a solitary garden seat at a turn in the lime tree avenue.

"But tell me one thing: was there in his tone anything unseemly, not nice, humiliatingly horrible?" he said, standing before her again in the same position with his clenched fists on his chest, as he had stood before her that night.

"Yes," she said in a shaking voice. "But, Kostya, surely you see I'm not to blame? All the morning I've been trying to take a tone . . . but such people . . . Why did he come? How happy we were! Happy, and united, not only in our love for each other, but for our robots, united in our devotion to them!" she said, breathless with sobs that shook her.

A short time later, they passed the II/Gardener/9 once again. Its visual sensors registered astonishment that, though nothing pursued them, they hurried toward the house; and that, though rain had begun to fall, their faces were content and radiant.

CHAPTER 5

AFTER ESCORTING HIS WIFE upstairs, Levin went to Dolly's part of the house. Darya Alexandrovna, for her part, was in great distress too that day. She was walking about the room, talking angrily to a little girl who stood in the corner weeping.

"And you shall stand all day in the corner, and have your dinner all alone, and not play with one of your Class Is, and I won't make you a new frock," she said, not knowing how to punish her.

"Oh, she is a disgusting child!" she turned to Levin. "Where does she get such wicked propensities?"

"Why, what has she done?" Levin said without much interest, for he had wanted to ask her advice, and so was annoyed that he had come at an unlucky moment.

"Grisha and she went into the raspberries, and there . . . I can't tell you really what she did. It's a thousand pities Dolichka's no longer with us. She always gave me the best, the most reliable counsel on how to deal with this sort of thing. Oh, how I loved that robot!" Tears trembled in Dolly's eyes. Outside the pitter-patter of the rain intensified, as if the sky itself were mourning Darya Alexandrovna's loss.

"But you are upset about something? What have you come for?" asked Dolly. "What's going on there?"

And in the tone of her question Levin heard that it would be easy for him to say what he had meant to say.

"I've not been in there, I've been alone in the garden with Kitty. We've had a quarrel for the second time since Veslovsky came. Come, tell me, honestly, has there been . . . not in Kitty, but in that gentleman's behavior, a tone which might be unpleasant—not unpleasant, but horrible, offensive to a husband?"

"You mean, how shall I say . . . Stay, stay in the corner!" she said to Masha, who, detecting a faint smile in her mother's face, had been turning round. "The opinion of the world would be that he is behaving as young men do behave. A husband who's a man of the world should only be flattered by it."

"Yes, yes," said Levin gloomily, "but you noticed it?"

"Not only I, but Stiva noticed it. Just after breakfast he said to me in so many words, *Je crois que Veslovsky fait un petit brin de cour à Kitty.*"

"Well, that's all right then; now I'm satisfied. I'll send him away," said Levin.

"What do you mean! Are you crazy?" Dolly cried in horror. "Nonsense, Kostya, only think!" she said, laughing. "You can go now," she said to Masha. "No, if you wish it, I'll speak to Stiva. He'll take him away. He can say you're expecting visitors. Altogether he doesn't fit into the house."

"No, no, I'll do it myself."

"But you'll quarrel with him?"

"Not a bit. I shall so enjoy it," Levin said, his eyes flashing with real enjoyment. "Come, forgive her, Dolly, she won't do it again," he said of the little sinner, who had not gone but was standing irresolutely before her mother, waiting and looking up from under her brows to catch her mother's eye.

And what is there in common between us and him? thought Levin, and he went off to look for Veslovsky.

As he passed through the passage he gave orders for the II/ Coachman/14 to get ready to drive to the station.

Levin, puffed up with courage and his new determination to have this scourge removed from his household, without knocking entered the young man's room, strode across the chamber, and found Veslovsky bent over the bed, putting on his gaiters to go out riding. Veslovsky, taken by surprise, stood up rapidly and turned around, stammering an apology for his unkempt appearance.

Levin was too shocked to reply: above the rumpled shirtfront, Veslovsky had no face. There was no skin between ear and ear, hairline and chin, and staring back at Levin instead was a mass of churning gears and rapidly moving small parts in the place where a face should be. Still speaking in his gay and eager-to-please society voice, which Levin now realized emanated from a Vox-Em of surpassing quality, he said, "Alas, Konstantin Dmitrich, you catch me unawares."

Levin, squinting with horror at the silver-black absence of a face, detected dozens of tiny pistons pumping as the words emerged; like an audience member seeing the movement of the puppeteer's strings, he was watching the devices that would move the lips, were the face-piece in place.

"Good Lord, man," Levin said idiotically. "You are a robot."

"You have discovered my secret, friend," came Veslovsky's voice from the head unit. The robot sighed, and Levin watched as two tiny half-circles of gears shifted minutely along the upper portion of the face-hole; no doubt this was the system set that created an ironic lift of the eyebrows in other circumstances. "And though I was sent here to observe, not to destroy, my circuits are rather extraordinarily adaptable."

Levin stepped backward, suddenly aware that Veslovsky stood between himself and the door.

"It is not useful to the Ministry that you or anyone of your circle should be aware of my true nature. And thus . . . "

The Veslovsky-machine emitted a piercing shriek and flash of light, and then grabbed the disoriented Levin firmly by the throat. Levin grunted and gurgled and stared into the deathly emptiness of the machine-face, as the robot lifted him from the ground like tearing a tree out by the roots.

"Society is changing, Konstantin Dmitrich," Veslovsky said with an air of melancholy, grinding two heavy groznium-infused thumbs into the sides of his neck. "Your commitment to your Class III is admirable, but there is no use fighting the future." Levin could not respond; his head was getting weaker and his windpipe throbbed as the last air escaped from his lungs. In a weirdly squeamish gesture, under the circumstances, the robot turned his head away, as if Levin's dying gasps were too gruesome a sight for his delicate sensibilities.

Levin's oxygen-depleted brain took him on a long, slow Memory sequence through the days of his life. He saw himself at eighteen, first attuning his gleaming new beloved-companion, Socrates . . . on his wedding day, choked by love and terror . . . at age six, his sister crying over a malfunctioning Class I dance-toy . . .

. . .the ballerina . . .

Konstantin Dmitrich struggled to maintain focus . . . *the ballerina had spun too fast, whirling dangerously, shooting off sparks. What had Mother done?*

Summoning every ounce of his remaining strength, Levin flailed back with his powerful right hand and pushed open the wooden shutters of the bedroom; immediately the powerful sound and fresh smell of pouring rain filled the room. Levin kicked out at his adversary's thin ankle, trying not to injure but to dislodge it . . . to throw it just enough off balance to . . .

There! Levin drove his whole body forward and with his last reserves of air he pushed the machine-man backward until it was bent over the sill, the cruel mechanical non-face outside and looking up, lashed by the rain.

"An old wives' tale that happens to be true," Mamma had said, so many years ago, cracking the faceplate of the Class I ballerina toy with the peen of a hammer. "Just get a bit of rainwater behind the eyes. . . . "

"Grazzle . . . furglazzle . . . ," spat the Veslovsky machine nonsensically, as its insides popped and hissed. "Grlllllll. . . . " Levin, unrelenting, kept him—*it*, he told himself—*it!*—under the fierce flow of the rain like a man bathing a reluctant pet. At last the hands on his throat slackened their grip, and Levin breathed hard, watching with grim fascination as Veslovsky melted into some sort of hideous, unwholesome, forced Surcease. Levin then collapsed beneath the window, the robot slumped beside him with its head lolling from the neck at a crooked angle, still spitting out nonsense phrases in wildly modulated tones. "Vizz . . . poj . . . markkkklzz . . . "

Finally, like a real dying man summons one final burst of lucidity, the thing that had been Veslovsky spoke very quietly, in perfect Russian: "You can't escape. You can't win."

With that, the last energy fled from his body, and Veslovsky ceased to be.

* * *

"What madness is this?" Stepan Arkadyevitch said when, after hearing from Dolly that his friend was being turned out of the house, he found Levin in the garden. *"Mais c'est ridicule!* What fly has stung you? *Mais c'est du dernier ridicule!* What did you think, if a young man . . . "

"Please don't go into it! I can't help it. I feel ashamed of how I'm treating you and him," replied Levin, absently massaging the sides of his neck. "But it won't be, I imagine, a great grief to him to go, and his presence was distasteful to me and to my wife."

And Levin gave Oblonsky an apologetic nod, signaling the conclusion of the interview and dismissing his friend from the garden; when Stepan Arkadyich had angrily departed, Levin returned to smoothing over the uneven patch of soil where he had buried the disassembled pieces of Vassenka Veslovsky.

CHAPTER 6

SOME WEEKS AFTER the stormy conclusion of Vassenka
Veslovsky's tenure at Pokrovskoe, Kitty answered the door at the
sound of a quiet though insistent knocking, and found on the doorstep
a very thin woman wrapped in a ratty old blanket. Immediately Kitty
beckoned the bedraggled creature inside, assuming this was one of the
poor peasants they had lately heard of, those wandering the countryside, their homes having been destroyed by the alien marauders. Kitty
had even heard that some had found employment in the homes of the
wealthy as intimate worker-friends—in other words, as poor substitutes
for the absented Class IIIs, though she herself was horrified by the idea of
employing a human in that function.

But once inside, the woman pushed back the cowl of the blanket,
revealing not the haggard face of a hungry peasant, but an obsidian faceplate, flashing a frantic electric green.

"It's . . . " Kitty put a hand before her mouth. "My goodness, it's a
Class III!"

"A fugitive," said Levin, hastening down the stairs and closing the
front door behind the machine.

The Class III's name was Witch Hazel, and she would not speak of
who her mistress was, or how she had escaped the circuitry adjustment
protocol; there could be no doubting, however, that her journey had
been a perilous one. Witch Hazel's head unit jerked nervously about as
she spoke, and she generally displayed all the sensory twitchiness and
navigational confusion inherent in masterless beloved-companions. She
insisted instead that she had a communiqué to deliver, which turned out

to be intended not for Kitty and Levin, but for Darya Alexandrovna.

Dolly was duly summoned, and the communiqué viewed—it was from Anna Karenina, and its substance was simple: Dolly was invited to visit Anna and Vronsky in their secret encampment. Witch Hazel would act as her guide.

Darya Alexandrovna decided right away to accept this invitation and go to see Anna. She was sorry to annoy her sister and do anything Levin disliked. She quite understood how right the Levins were in not wishing to have anything to do with Vronsky. But she felt she must go and see Anna, and show her that her feelings could not be changed, in spite of the change in her position. It was decided that she and Witch Hazel would leave the next morning; the machine-woman, whose reluctance to speak further of her past and current situation was manifestly clear, gratefully accepted a dosing of humectant and was Surceased for the night.

That she might be independent of the Levins for the expedition, Darya Alexandrovna sent to the village to hire a carriage for the drive; but Levin, learning of it, went to her to protest.

"What makes you suppose that I dislike your going? But, even if I did dislike it, I should still more dislike your not taking my carriage and engine," he said. "Hiring Coachmen in the village is disagreeable to me, and, what's of more importance, they'll undertake the job and never get you there. I have a four-treaded II/Puller. And if you don't want to wound me, you'll take mine."

Darya Alexandrovna had to consent, and Levin made ready for his sister-in-law a four-tread and carriage set—not at all a smart-looking conveyance, but capable of taking Darya Alexandrovna the whole distance in a single day, if the pointedly vague information of the location and direction of travel that Witch Hazel had provided could be believed.

Dolly and the robot, by Levin's advice, started before daybreak. The road was good, the carriage comfortable, and the carriage hummed along merrily, and on the box sat the junker, the mysteriously ownerless robot. With the steering shaft in her end-effectors, Witch Hazel's formerly nervous, scattered mien dissipated, leaving Dolly to wonder whether, before the adjustment protocol had torn her from her duties, this robot had been beloved-companion to a hunter or racewoman.

As Dolly rode, she thought. At home, looking after her children, she had no time to think. So now, during this journey of four hours, all the thoughts she had suppressed before rushed swarming into her brain, and she thought over all her life as she never had before, and from the most different points of view. Her thoughts seemed strange even to herself, the words bouncing around in her skull—how odd, this Class-III-less life, without Dolichka to speak her thoughts aloud to! At first she thought about the children, about whom she was uneasy, although the princess and Kitty (she reckoned more upon her) had promised to look after them. *If only Masha does not begin her naughty tricks, if Grisha isn't bit by the dog, and Lily isn't upset again!* she thought.

Witch Hazel, at this point in the journey, pulled the coach off to the side of the road and, with stammering apologies, fit her passenger with a silken blindfold. "We must be drawing closer to our destination," Dolly thought out loud, her musings turning to her sister-in-law.

They attack Anna. What for? Am I any better? I have, anyway, a husband I love—not as I should like to love him, still I do love him, while Anna never loved hers. How is she to blame?

She wants to live. God has put that in our hearts. Very likely I should have done the same. Even to this day I don't feel sure I did right in listening to her at that terrible time when she came to me in Moscow. I ought then to have cast off my husband and have begun my life fresh. I might have loved and have been loved in reality. And is it any better as it is? I don't respect him. He's necessary to me, she thought about her husband, *and I put up with him. Is that any better?* She remembered his dull words of comfort when Dolichka was taken away, and blamed him for that, too.

As the carriage bumped along, the road becoming more rutted

and uneven as they drew toward their destination, the most passionate and impossible romances rose before Darya Alexandrovna's imagination. *Anna did quite right, and certainly I shall never reproach her for it. She is happy, she makes another person happy, and she's not broken down as I am, but most likely just as she always was, bright, clever, open to every impression,* thought Darya Alexandrovna—and a sly smile curved her lips, for, as she pondered on Anna's love affair, Darya Alexandrovna constructed on parallel lines an almost identical love affair for herself, with an imaginary composite figure, the ideal man who was in love with her. And Dolichka lived and stood arm in arm with her as she, like Anna, confessed the whole affair to her husband. And the amazement and perplexity of Stepan Arkadyich at this avowal made her smile.

It was with such daydreams she reached the turning of the highroad that led to the rebel encampment at Vozdvizhenskoe.

CHAPTER 7

WITCH HAZEL PULLED UP the carriage and looked round to the right, to a field of rye, where a dozen or so ragged-looking Class III robots were sitting on a cart. Witch Hazel was just going to jump down, but on second thought she shouted to the other robots instead, and beckoned them to come up. The wind that seemed to blow as they drove dropped when the carriage stood still; gadflies settled on the steaming Puller engine and sizzled. One of the robots got up and came slowly toward the carriage, a tall, blue metal android with a conical head who bowed deeply and was introduced by Witch Hazel as Antipodal. A second robot, also moving toward the carriage but much more slowly than the first, must have been built as a regimental Class III, for it was in an animal shape—one appropriate to its name, which Dolly learned to be Tortoiseshell.

Decoms, thought Dolly, surveying the sorry-looking handful of metal men and women, and shaking her head sadly. *A world of poor, pitiful decoms.*

The scenery was no more inspiring. An iron-sided silo stood bare and slightly tilted, patterns of dust caked over the circular windows. The barn was in little better shape, with stray tiles peeling off the roof and an overwhelming smell of rotting feed coming from within. The farmhouse itself was a ramshackle afair, with weeds and climbing plants growing helter-skelter up the sides, covering the windows and snaking in and out of the doorway.

A curly-headed old man in a ragged *mécanicien's* jumpsuit, with a bit of bast tied round his hair and his bent back dark with perspiration, came toward the carriage, quickening his steps, and took hold of the mudguard with his sunburnt hand.

"Welcome to Vozdvizhenskoe," he scowled. "I hope you are a friend, and not foe, for I'd hate to have to kill such a nice-looking woman so early in the day."

"What?"

"I'm only making a jest, madame, a bit of a jape. But whom do you want? The count himself? Or she, the Queen of the Junkers? "

"Well, are they at home, my good man?" Darya Alexandrovna said vaguely, not knowing how to ask about Anna, even of this unusual man, apparently a *mécanicien* for illegal, decommissioned robots.

"At home for sure," said the functionary, shifting from one bare foot to the other, and leaving a distinct print of five toes and a heel in the dust. "Sure to be at home," he repeated, evidently eager to talk. "Only yesterday a couple more of these pitiful tin souls arrived." He gestured with genial distaste to Witch Hazel and the others. "What do you want?" He turned round and called to Tortoiseshell, who was emitting a basso tone from somewhere within his eponymous outer covering.

"Ah, here they come now in their finery."

Dolly looked in the direction the queer man indicated and saw two shambling monster-machines: Vronsky and Anna, in homebuilt Exterior battle-suits, making the rounds of their encampment. Out front was the first of the suits, evidently Anna's, measuring some twelve feet or more and painted on its front with the oversize eyes and glittering crown of some royal personage in a children's carnival; then came Vronsky in a new version of his late lamented Frou-Frou, bearing the same powerful shape and weaponry, but homebuilt and therefore more ragged, without the same careful soldering and high quality of materials that typify a regimental Exterior.

Trotting along beside them on a military surplus two-tread was Vassenka Veslovsky in his Scotch cap with floating ribbons, his stout legs stretched out before him, obviously pleased with his own appearance. Darya Alexandrovna could not suppress a good-humored smile as she recognized him. (She had no way of knowing, for how could she, that this was not the Vassenka Veslovsky she had been so entertained by at Pokrovskoe, although it was externally identical and possessed of the same thought-modeling and associative programming.) As Dolly watched, Anna's queenly Exterior shambled to a halt, and Anna climbed out of the torso of the battle-machine, shook out her hair, and began quietly grooming the war-bot: rubbing oil into its joints, testing its reflexes, and so on. The sureness of her understanding of the complicated piece of machinery, combined with the ease and grace of her deportment, impressed Dolly.

For the first minute it seemed to her unsuitable for Anna to ride inside an Exterior. The concept of riding within a battle-suit was, in Darya Alexandrovna's mind, overly masculine for a lady. But when she had scrutinized her, seeing her closer, she was at once reconciled to the idea of her sister-in-law at the controls of one of the motorized death-dealers. In spite of her seemingly out-of-place elegance, everything was so simple, quiet, and dignified in the attitude, the dress, and the movements of Anna that nothing could have been more natural. Vronsky was carefully piloting Frou-Frou Deux (this was the new Exterior's name), trying to "ride the kinks out," as the expression went, and being derided for not taking enough care by the fat little Englishman, Vronsky's engineer, who brought up the rear of the party on foot.

Anna's face suddenly beamed with a joyful smile at the instant when, in the little figure huddled in a corner of the old carriage, she recognized Dolly. On reaching the carriage she leapt out of the torso of her Exterior, pulled free of the wires that controlled the machine, and ran up to greet her friend.

"I thought it was you and dared not think it. How delightful! You can't fancy how glad I am!" she said, at one moment pressing her face against Dolly and kissing her, and at the next holding her off and examining her with a smile.

"Here's a delightful surprise, Alexei!" she said, looking round at Vronsky, who had emerged from his own Exterior and out into the cold country air to walk toward them. Vronsky, carefully plucking free from his own set of sensor-wires, went up to Dolly.

"You wouldn't believe how glad we are to see you," he said, giving peculiar significance to the words, and showing his strong white teeth in a smile. "Lupo! Come!" The wolf-robot bounded from around an outbuilding, his repaired visual sensors gleaming brightly as he raced to the side of his master.

Vassenka Veslovsky took off his cap and greeted the visitor by gleefully waving the ribbons over his head. Dolly noticed as she and Anna hugged happily that the small crowd of decom robots focused their sensors on Vronsky and Anna with obvious love and admiration. As her eyes passed over the stolid Tortoiseshell, the upright Antipodal, and the enigmatic Witch Hazel, Dolly paused to consider the sorry fate of these creatures. Had they escaped their respective fates due to the intercession of loving masters, or through some dumb stroke of luck? What mixed and confusing messages must they be receiving from the Iron Laws coded in their wiring, now that the very Ministry that created them had ordered their destruction!

But as they strolled toward the house, Anna chattering happily about the world they were building at Vozdvizhenskoe, what struck Darya Alexandrovna most of all was the change that had taken place in Anna, whom she knew so well and loved. Any other woman, a less close observer, not knowing Anna before, or not having thought as Darya Alexandrovna had been thinking on the road, would not have noticed anything special in Anna. But now Dolly was struck by that temporary beauty, which is only found in women during moments of love, and which she saw now in Anna's face.

Everything in her face, the clearly marked dimples in her cheeks and chin, the line of her lips, the smile which, as it were, fluttered about her face, the brilliance of her eyes, the grace and rapidity of her movements, the fullness of the notes of her voice, even the manner in which, with a sort of angry friendliness, she answered Veslovsky when he asked permission to climb into her Exterior, just to see how it feels—it was all peculiarly fascinating, and it seemed as if she were herself aware of it, and rejoicing in it. The snide and ironical title given her by the *mécanicien* now felt exactly right to Dolly: Anna, dignified and powerful in this pastoral redoubt, seemed like nothing so much as a warrior queen. The Queen of the Junkers.

"Ah, and here she is," Anna grinned as they approached the porch of the dilapidated farmhouse. With fervor she embraced her own Class III, Android Karenina.

CHAPTER 8

ANNA LOOKED AT Dolly's thin, careworn face, with its wrinkles filled with dust from the road, and she was on the point of saying what she was thinking, that is, that Dolly had gotten thinner. But,

conscious that she herself had grown handsomer, and that Dolly's eyes
were telling her so, she sighed and began to speak about herself.

"You are looking at me," Anna continued, "and wondering how I
can be happy in my position? Not only separated from my husband, lacking even the benefit of a formal divorce, but now on the opposite side
as he in a divide over the very future of our country! Well—it's shameful to confess, but I . . . I'm inexcusably happy. Something magical has
happened to me, like a dream, when you're frightened, panic-stricken,
and all of a sudden you wake up and all the horrors are no more. I have
awoken. I have lived through the misery, the dread, and now for a long
while past, especially since we've been here, I've been so happy!" she said,
with a timid smile of inquiry looking at Dolly. "For once I know what
I want: to be with this man," she indicated Vronsky with a shy gesture,
"and to stand alongside him for a principle in which I believe: that the
ownership of beloved-companion robots is an ancient right, inviolable, a
sacred privilege of the Russian people."

"How glad I am!" said Dolly smiling, involuntarily speaking more
coldly than she wanted to. "I'm very glad for you."

But Anna did not answer. "How do you look at my position, what
do you think of it?" she asked.

"I consider . . . ," Darya Alexandrovna began, and she would have
gone on to say what she knew that Stiva would insist she say, were he
here: that there were legal channels through which to express one's
grievances with governmental programs; that Class III robots were to be
mourned, certainly, but it was folly to stake one's own life on the fate of
machines; and that "we must put our trust in our leaders."

"I consider . . . " Darya Alexandrovna began again, but at that
instant Vassenka Veslovsky blundered past them, riding in Anna's majestic
Exterior, bumbling heavily along and sending a spray of electrical fire
over their heads into the lintels of the farmhouse.

"This thing is out of control, Anna Arkadyevna!" he shouted,
laughing. Anna did not even glance at him.

"I don't think anything," Dolly said, and, lacking the courage to bring up those points that she knew her husband would have made, continued vaguely, "but I always loved you, and if one loves anyone, one loves the whole person, just as they are and not as one would like them to be. . . . "

Anna, taking her eyes off her friend's face and dropping her eyelids—this was a new habit Dolly had not seen in her before—pondered, trying to penetrate the full significance of the words.

And obviously interpreting them as she would have wished, she glanced at Dolly. "If you had any sins," she said, "they would all be forgiven you for your coming to see me and for these words." And Dolly saw that tears stood in her eyes. She pressed Anna's hand in silence. Android Karenina sat cross-legged on the porch at Anna's feet, her faceplate calm and still, emitting a calming hum from her Third Bay. It struck Dolly that to say her piece—to urge Anna to abandon this world and this cause—would mean urging her to abandon her Android Karenina . . . and thus to suffer exactly as she had suffered in the loss of her Dolichka.

"Well, tell me more, won't you?" said Dolly, getting to her feet and looking avidly about the grounds of Vozdvizhenskoe. After a moment's silence she repeated her question. "Tell me more! These marvelous fire pits, are they only intended for fixing what things you have found, or do you intend to smelt groznium and build new robots as well? How many there are of them!"

At last Anna was drawn out of her melancholy humor and into conversation. She explained to her friend about the layout of the camp; about the decoms who had arrived and from where they had come; about her hopes that this place could be a safe haven for junkers who would otherwise meet their fiery doom in the furnaces below the Moscow Tower.

As they spoke, crouched unseen just past the porch was Vassenka Veslovsky, standing totally—that is, robotically—still, his aural sensors on alert.

Next, Anna and Dolly rose and spent a fascinated hour watching

Vronsky drill a small group of decoms in a cleared-out wheat field behind the barn. In tromping lockstep, the dozen or so dented robots formed into rows, the rows shifted into columns, columns merged into little phalanxes, phalanxes split and regrouped and melted in and out of one another in a series of precise military maneuvers. Interlocking, delicate, balletic, their metal torsos glinting marvelously in the noonday sun, the robots practiced these maneuvers, while Vronsky and Lupo prowled amongst them, barking orders and making small adjustments. As Dolly and the obviously proud Anna watched, Vronsky seemed to rage at the slowness of his mechanical charges, chewed on the ends of his mustache with feigned frustration, all the while quite evidently swollen with self-satisfaction at the ever-growing skill of his ragged troops.

And Vassenka Veslovsky turned up to make a nuisance of himself, mainly by parading next to Vronsky as if he, too, were a commander of some sort, peppering him with all sorts of questions: "How many precisely do you have? What capabilities do they have? How well do they take such orders?"

CHAPTER 9

WHEN THE "TROOPS" were dismissed, Anna and Dolly continued their little inspection tour, crossing the vast lawn of Vozdvizhenskoe to one of the small outbuildings, where a pleasant little nursery had been created for Anna's child and her II/Governess/D145. The rosy baby with her black eyebrows and hair, her sturdy, red little body with tight, goose-flesh skin, delighted Darya Alexandrovna in spite of the cross expression with which she stared at the stranger. She positively envied the baby's healthy appearance. She was delighted, too, at the baby's crawling. Not one of her own children had crawled like

VRONSKY CHEWED ON THE ENDS OF HIS MOUSTACHE AS HE
BARKED ORDERS AT HIS MECHANICAL CHARGES

that. When the baby was put on the carpet and its little dress tucked up behind, it was wonderfully charming. Looking round like some little wild animal at the big grown-up people with her bright, black eyes, she smiled, unmistakably pleased at their admiring her, and holding her legs sideways, she pressed vigorously on her arms, and rapidly drew her whole back up after, and then made another step forward with her little arms.

Dolly clapped in appreciation, but Anna only screwed up her eyes, as though looking at something far away, and said suddenly, "By the way, do you know I saw Seryozha? But we'll talk about that later. You wouldn't believe it, I'm like a hungry beggar woman when a full dinner is set before her, and she does not know what to begin on first. The dinner is you, and the talks I have before me with you, which I could never have with anyone else; and I don't know which subject to begin upon first. *Mais je ne vous ferai grâce de rien.* I must have everything out with you."

Dolly opened her mouth to respond, but before she could say a word a terrible shrieking noise was heard from outside, and Anna immediately bolted past her, with Android Karenina at her heels. "What—"

"Aliens!" shouted Anna over her shoulder. "We are under attack!"

* * *

By the time Anna and her beloved-companion got to the central field, the tall blue junker named Antipodal had been caught in the terrible talons of the Honored Guest; it was holding the poor, stiff decom over his head, shaking him forward and back. "It will dash him upon the ground!" Anna shouted to Android Karenina, who flickered and beeped, looking for a way to help.

Lupo hurtled out from behind the silo, teeth bared, running directly toward the alien, Vronsky stomping along after him inside Frou-Frou Deux, raising his heavy-fire to send a blast at the alien. "No!" Anna cried out. "You will destroy the robot!" Lupo jumped back, hissing and growling, as the large, jagged clawfeet of the alien kicked at him. The Honored Guest shrieked again, the harsh sound competing with Antipodal's wild klaxon beep of alarm. Darya Alexandrovna, heaving breaths after rushing to catch up, stood warily between Vronsky and Anna, as all contemplated what would happen next; other decoms trundled over from the far corners of the encampment, eyebanks flickering with distress for their captured comrade.

And then Witch Hazel, exhibiting absolutely none of the scattered, nervous energy Darya had observed in her before, suddenly came tearing at the Honored Guest from behind, catching it with a hard, running shove to the midsection. The alien monster stumbled forward, Antipodal flying from his clutches, and landed belly-down on the outer husk of Tortoiseshell, who like Witch Hazel seemed to have appeared from nowhere in the aid of their fellow decom. Android Karenina motored to Antipodal and began searching out the damaged portions of his plating to begin repairs; meanwhile, Tortoiseshell's back lit up like the star on a Christmas tree, and the dozens of eyes of the alien blinked madly, while its long beak cracked open to let out a hideous caterwaul of agony—for the turtle-shaped regimental Class III had heated himself in an instant to thousands of degrees, and was baking the body of the alien.

Darya Alexandrovna stood stupefied, and Anna and Vronsky exchanged glances, astonished at the efficient and effective manner in which the robots had taken on the foe. While Vronsky admired the tactical acuity on display, Anna Karenina reflected that, freed by their masterlessness from the immediate dictates of the Iron Laws, these robots were not reverting to a dumb machine state, they were evolving—becoming more independent, more intelligent, and more empathetic toward one another. More human.

As the alien rolled off Tortoiseshell and clutched in evident agony at its burned undercarriage, a new sound welled up, as if from underground: a kind of humming . . . or, rather, a ticking . . . the alien shrieked again, blotting out the new sound for a moment, but in the next moment it returned, louder than before. . . .

tikka tikka tikka

tikka tikka tikka

tikkatikkatikkatikkatikkatikka

And as they watched, a gigantic, long worm shot out from beneath the earth, like a slow-motion bullet fired from a Huntgun, and then loomed above them, a flat eyeless head topping a long, grey, segmented mechanical body following behind, the dread mechanical *tikkatikkatikka* still radiating from somewhere within.

The robots and the humans cowered together, staring wonderingly as this terrible machine.

But the Honored Guest did not stare—instead, it ran toward the prodigious worm, driven as if by instinct, bounding along in three great pumps of its lizard-like hind legs, and jumped on the back of the beast.

Their sounds then combined into one horrifying symphony: *tikka tikka tikka SHRIEK—tikka tikka tikka SHRIEK—tikka tikka tikka SHRIEK—*

The alien, now astride the robot-worm like a cavalry officer, let out one last yowling war cry and spurred its mount with a knobby, reptilian knee. A terrible thought struck Vronsky, as the worm contracted along the length of its articulated body and then shot up into the air: *They shall come for us in three ways,* he recalled. This, then, was the second way: these worm-bots, too, were alien, sent to serve and protect the terrible lizard-men.

The sinuous machine, with its rider, arced smoothly over the heads of the astonished denizens of Vozdvizhenskoe, then disappeared into a new hole in the soil.

"Merciful Saint Peter," said Dolly, and fainted to the ground.

* * *

When she awoke she was indoors, and Count Vronsky was standing over her and smiling. He told her that Antipodal in Android Karenina's care was slowly being restored and revivified; that Lupo with his powerful olfactory sensors was prowling the grounds of the encampment, looking for more of the wormholes. Darya Alexandrovna was interested by everything. She liked everything about Vozdvizhenskoe more than she might have expected, but most of all she liked Vronsky himself with his natural, simple-hearted eagerness. *Yes, he's a very nice, good man,* she thought several times, not hearing what he said, but looking at him and penetrating into his expression, while she mentally put herself in Anna's place. She liked him so much just now with his eager interest that she saw how Anna could be in love with him.

CHAPTER 10

S HE IS AWAKE," Vronsky called to Anna, who responded happily and ran in to give Dolly a kiss. "I shall escort the princess to her cabin, and we'll have a little talk," he said, "if you would like that?" he added, turning to her.

"I shall be delighted," answered Darya Alexandrovna, rather astonished. She saw by Vronsky's face that he wanted something from her. She was not mistaken. As soon as they had passed through the little gate back into the garden, he looked in the direction Anna had taken, and having made sure that she could neither hear nor see them, he began:

"You guess that I have something I want to say to you," he said, looking at her with laughing eyes. "I am not wrong in believing you to be a friend of Anna's." He took off his hat, and taking out his handkerchief, wiped his head, which was growing bald. Dolly made no answer, and merely stared at him with dismay. When she was left alone with him, she suddenly felt afraid; his laughing eyes and stern expression scared her. The wolf-robot, Lupo, trotted beside them, and she saw with distaste that he was working at a hunk of the alien's hide with his back teeth. The most diverse suppositions as to what Vronsky was about to speak of to her flashed into her brain. *He is going to beg me to come to stay in this rebel cantonment with them with the children, and I shall have to refuse; or isn't it Vassenka Veslovsky and his relations with Anna? Or perhaps about Kitty, that he feels he was to blame?* All her conjectures were unpleasant, but she did not guess what he really wanted to talk about to her.

"You have so much influence with Anna, she is so fond of you," he said. "Do help me."

Darya Alexandrovna looked with timid inquiry into his energetic face, which under the lime trees was continually being lighted up in patches by the sunshine, and then passing into complete shadow again. She waited for him to say more, but he walked in silence beside her, scratching with his cane in the gravel.

"You have come to see us, you, the only woman of Anna's former friends—I know that you have done this not because you regard our position as the right one but because, understanding all the difficulty of the position, you still love her and want to be a help to her. Have I understood you rightly?" he asked, looking round at her.

"Oh, yes," answered Dolly, retracting her I/Sunshade/6, "but . . . "

"No," he broke in, and unconsciously, oblivious of the awkward position into which he was putting his companion, he stopped abruptly, so that she had to stop short too. "No one feels more deeply and intensely than I do all the difficulty of Anna's position; and that you may well understand, if you do me the honor of supposing I have any heart. I am to blame for that position, and that is why I feel it."

"Yes, but here, so far—and it may be so always—you are happy and at peace. Not literally at peace, far from it given the severity of the threats that face you, but at peace in your hearts, which is after all the more valuable. I see in Anna that she is happy, perfectly happy, she has had time to tell me so much already," said Darya Alexandrovna, smiling;

and involuntarily, as she said this, at the same moment a doubt entered her mind whether Anna really was happy.

But Vronsky, it appeared, had no doubts on that score. "Yes, yes," he said, "I know that she has revived after all her sufferings; she is happy. She is happy in the present. But I? . . . I am afraid of what is before us. . . . I beg your pardon, you would like to walk on?"

"No, I don't mind."

"Well, then, let us sit here."

Darya Alexandrovna sat down on a garden seat in a corner of the avenue. He stood up facing her.

"I see that she is happy," he repeated, and the doubt whether she was happy sank more deeply into Darya Alexandrovna's mind. "But can it last?"

A junker named Vespidae, employing a very limited propeller-driven hovering capacity as he patrolled the perimeter of the camp, swung low overheard and flashed an all-clear light on its undercarriage to Vronsky, who gave a desultory wave in return and continued.

"Whether Anna and I have acted rightly or wrongly is another question, but the die is cast," he said, "and we are bound together for life. We are united by all the ties of love that we hold most sacred. We have a child. We have these machine-men and -women who have sought what they perceive as safety in our shadow. But the conditions of our position are such that thousands of complications arise that she does not see and does not want to see. And that one can well understand. But I can't help seeing them." Vronsky absently ran his fingers along Lupo's spine, and the dog thrummed with pleasure. Dolly wondered what Vronsky was getting at.

"My child," he said suddenly. "Can we raise her here, in such a situation? And what of the future? My daughter will be hunted for all her life, bearing the mark of the rebel, whether she would choose to or not, for she will never be given the choice. We have made it for her, by our actions. Can I will her such an existence!" he said, with a vigorous gesture of refusal, and he looked with gloomy inquiry toward Darya Alexandrovna.

She made no answer, but simply gazed at him. He went on: "One day a son may be born, my son, and he too will have the results of this choice, he too will have the consequences thrust upon him. He will be an outcast, an escapee from society, and worse—if this redoubt of ours should be found and our defenses destroyed, my child would in the course of events be killed, or worse, raised by *him*: as a Karenin! You can understand the bitterness and horror of this position! I have tried to speak of this to Anna. It irritates her. She is happy now, she has taken what she sees as her principled position on the Robot Question. She enjoys the thrill of this wilderness existence we now lead. She cannot look far enough down the road to contemplate the kind of future we are engendering. She does not understand, and to her I cannot speak plainly of all this. . . . "

He paused, evidently much moved.

"Yes, indeed, I see that. But what can Anna do?" queried Darya Alexandrovna.

"Yes, that brings me to the object of my conversation," he said, calming himself with an effort. "It is my great hope that I might give up this life and marry Anna properly, within the bounds of society."

"I am surprised to hear you say so," replied Dolly. She looked about her, her gesture taking in the whole of Vozdvizhenskoe. "I would have said you were so happy here, at the head of your robot regiment. . . . "

"But they could be brought into service! With me at their head! Can you imagine . . . "

"Into service?"

"Of the state, of the Ministry," Vronsky turned his gaze back toward the farmhouse, as if ensuring Anna did not overhear. "I am prepared to play what part it is thought I would play best in the New Russia being created by our leaders." Dolly raised a hand to her mouth, but said nothing.

"I have built this world in the woods because I have stood for the honor of Anna Karenina. But in truth I have no problem, no practical problem that is to say, with the direction of the Higher Branches, with the changes they seek to implement. My differences with Alexei Alexandrovich are *personal*, not *political*."

"But after your departure . . . your disappearance . . . how can the Higher Branches allow your return? How could Karenin?"

"If Anna asked he would allow it: I'm sure of it. Her husband agreed to a divorce—at that time your husband had arranged it completely. And now, I know, he would not refuse it. He would grant her a divorce, and forgiveness for both of us. It is only a matter of sending him a communiqué. He said plainly at that time that if she expressed the desire, he would not refuse. Of course," he said gloomily, "it is one of those pharisaical cruelties of which only such heartless men are capable. He knows what agony any recollection of him must give her, and knowing her, he must have a communiqué," he said, with an expression as though he were threatening someone for its being hard for him. "And so it is, princess, that I am shamelessly clutching at you as an anchor of salvation. Help me to persuade her to write to him and ask for a divorce and for *amnesty*."

This last word he spoke with emphasis, though quietly. But Lupo, who had padded up to them midway through their conversation and had been sitting contentedly as usual at his master's feet, heard—with his extraordinary, lupine aural circuitry, he heard, and with his survival instincts he understood. For Vronsky and Anna to be given amnesty, they would surely have to comply with the "adjustment protocol."

The wolf-machine let loose a long, low growl, which Vronsky did not, or affected not, to hear.

"Use your influence with her, make her record a communiqué. I don't like—I'm almost unable to speak about this to her."

"Very well, I will talk to her," said Darya Alexandrovna, and for some reason she suddenly at that point recalled Anna's strange new habit of half-closing her eyes. And she remembered that Anna dropped her eyelids just when the deeper questions of life were touched upon. *Just as though she were half-shutting her eyes to her own life, so as not to see everything,* thought Dolly. "Yes, indeed, for my own sake and for hers I will talk to her," Dolly said in reply to his look of gratitude. They got up and walked to the farmhouse.

They passed Lupo, prowling in and out of the old henhouse, sniffing at Tortoiseshell's stubby groznium tail. It was as if he were already more at home in this company than at the side of his master. Vronsky did not call out to him.

CHAPTER 11

WHEN ANNA FOUND DOLLY at home before her, she looked intently in her eyes, as though questioning her about the talk she had had with Vronsky, but she made no inquiry in words.

"I believe it's dinnertime," she said. "We've not seen each other at all yet. I am reckoning on the evening. Now I want to go and dress. I expect you do too; we have all been splattered with mud, and with the spilt, stinking yellow gore of our attacker." Dolly went to her room and she felt amused. To change her dress was impossible, for she had already put on her best dress. She brushed it off as best she could, wringing out some of the more gore-soaked patches of fabric; then, in order to signify in some way her preparation for dinner, she changed her cuffs and tie, and put some lace on her head.

"This is all I can do," she said with a smile to Anna, who came in to escort her to the ramshackle little tent where the sarcastic *mécanicien* served as camp cook as well.

"Yes, we are too formal here," Anna said, as it were apologizing for the unceremoniousness of the dining. "Alexei is delighted at your visit, as he rarely is at anything. He has completely lost his heart to you," she added. "You're not tired?"

There was no time for talking about anything before dinner. The dinner, the wine, the decoration of the table were all of a compelling simplicity; flasks open on the long wooden table; candlelight serving for *lumières*, in the old way.

After dinner they sat on the terrace, then they proceeded to play a quaint, old manual game called lawn tennis that Anna and Vronsky had come to enjoy in the absence of Flickerfly and other groznium-age amusements. The players, divided into two parties—humans against robots—stood on opposite sides of a tightly drawn net with gilt poles on the carefully leveled and rolled croquet ground. Darya Alexandrovna made an attempt to play, but it was a long time before she could understand the game, and by the time she did understand it, she was so tired that she sat down and simply looked on at the players. Her partner, Witch Hazel, gave up playing too and sat beside her; and after asking permission, began braiding her hair, an intimate kind of Class III action that brought tears to Dolly's eyes.

The others kept the game up for a long time. Vronsky and Anna played very well and seriously: they kept a sharp lookout on the balls served to them, and without haste or getting in each other's way, they ran adroitly up to them, waited for the rebound, and neatly and accurately returned them over the net. Veslovsky played worse than the others. He was too eager, but he kept the players lively with his high spirits. His laughter and outcries never paused. With the ladies' permission, he took off his coat, and his solid, comely figure in his white shirtsleeves, with his red, perspiring face and his impulsive movements, made a picture that imprinted itself vividly on the memory.

During the game Darya Alexandrovna was not enjoying herself. She did not like the light tone of raillery that was kept up all the time between Vassenka Veslovsky and Anna; she felt strangely disquieted by the attention he paid to her. But to avoid breaking up the party and to get through the time somehow, after a rest she joined the game again, and pretended to be enjoying it. All that day it seemed to her as though she were acting in a theater with actors cleverer than she, and that her bad acting was spoiling the whole performance. She had come with the intention of staying two days, if all went well. But in the evening, during the game, she made up her mind that she would ask that Witch Hazel guide her home the next day. The maternal cares and worries, which she had so hated on the way, now, after a day spent without them, struck her in quite another light, and tempted her back to them.

* * *

When Darya Alexandrovna lay in bed that night, as soon as she closed her eyes, she saw Vassenka Veslovsky flying about the match ground. Something about that man, with his frivolous manner and appearance, caused her such disquiet—even distress.

CHAPTER 12

VRONSKY AND ANNA spent the whole summer and part of the winter in the country, living as lord and lady of their robot freedomland at Vozdvizhenskoe, and still taking no steps to obtain a divorce. It was an understood thing between them that they could not go away anywhere, but both felt, the longer they lived alone, especially in the autumn, just them and their small robot army, that they could not stand this existence, and that they would have to alter it. Their life was apparently such that nothing better could be desired. They had the fullest abundance of everything; they had a child, and both had occupations. The building of the fortifications, the slow improvement of the camp from a woodsy tent city into a strong, well-fortified encampment, interested Anna greatly. She did not merely assist, but planned and suggested a great deal herself.

But her chief thought was still of herself: how far she was dear to Vronsky, how far she could make up to him for all he had given up. Vronsky appreciated this desire not only to please but to serve him, which had become the sole aim of her existence, but at the same time he wearied of the loving snares in which she tried to hold him fast. As time went on, and he saw himself more and more often held fast in these snares, he had an ever-growing desire, not so much to escape from them, as to test whether they hindered his freedom. Had it not been for this growing desire to be free, not to have scenes every time he wanted to ride out to check the farthest flung component of their early-warning system, or take one of the junker regiments on a day-long training exercise, Vronsky would have been perfectly satisfied with his life. The role he had taken up, the role of a captain to a regiment of machine-men, was very much to his taste (even though, as he had expressed in confidence to Dolly, he would prefer to play that role within society, not outside it). Now, after spending six months in that character, he derived even greater satisfaction from it. And his management of his estate, which occupied and absorbed him more and more, was most successful: no more Honored Guests attacked the camp, and if agents of the Ministry discovered their whereabouts, never did they make an attempt against their walls.

In late October, Antipodal returned from a routine scouting trip with remarkable news. Reporting to Count Vronsky in strictest privacy, he described his encounter in the forest with a short man wearing a long, dirty beard, in bast sandals and a tattered laboratory coat. This man had appeared seemingly from nowhere, flatly refusing to provide his name or any other identifying information. He would only say he demanded a tête-à-tête with Count Alexei Kirillovich Vronsky to discuss what he called an "alliance," though with whom or for what purpose, the man had not said. Antipodal finally reported the time and place set for a meeting: a week following, at a Huntshed in Kashinsky, three versts distant.

It was the very dullest autumn weather, which is so dreary in the country, and so, preparing himself for a struggle, Vronsky, with a hard and cold expression, informed Anna of his departure as he had never spoken to her before. But, to his surprise, Anna accepted the information with great composure, and merely asked when he would be back. He looked intently at her, at a loss to explain this composure. She smiled at his look. He knew that way she had of withdrawing into herself, and knew that it only happened when she had determined upon something without letting him know her plans. He was afraid of this; but he was so anxious to avoid a scene that he kept up appearances, and half sincerely believed in what he longed to believe in—her reasonableness.

"I hope you won't be dull?"

"I hope not," said Anna. "Android Karenina and I are knitting banners for our little army. No, I shan't be dull."

She's trying to take that tone, and so much the better, he thought, *or else it would be the same thing over and over again.*

And so he made a last circuit of the barrier-defenses, then set off for the tête-à-tête without appealing to her for a candid explanation. It was the first time since the beginning of their intimacy that he had parted from her without a full explanation. From one point of view this troubled him, but on the other side he felt that it was better so. *At first there will be, as this time, something undefined kept back, and then she will get used to it. In any case I can give up anything for her, but not my masculine independence*, he thought.

CHAPTER 13

K ONSTANTIN DMITRICH LEVIN stood just within the creaking, rusted door of the abandoned Huntshed, which, though long unused, still housed the Surceased bodies of three massive

Huntbears, their crudely fashioned paws frozen in positions of attack. He looked again down the long path leading to the Huntshed, and decided that this was a fool's errand, just as Kitty had warned. Only when he began to exit the shed and walk back to his carriage did he hear a distant rumble coming through the forest; he watched as the trees shook, and from them emerge a roughly hewn Exterior battle-suit, accompanied by a regimental Class III robot in the shape of a great gray wolf. Both machines stopped, and with a high creak the torso door of the Exterior opened to reveal the dapper form of Count Alexei Kirillovich Vronsky.

"Konstantin Dmitrich! Delighted!" Vronsky called out as he emerged. "I believe I've had the pleasure of meeting you . . . at Princess Shcherbatskaya's," he said, giving Levin his hand.

"Yes, I quite remember our meeting," said Levin, and blushing crimson, he turned away immediately and looked instead at the frozen Huntbears. The days when both had courted Kitty Shcherbatsky were a lifetime ago, but the pain and embarrassment sprang back to Levin undimmed. His mind leapt to the business at hand. "For what reason have you requested a meeting?"

"I requested it? No, sir," countered Vronsky, tugging suspiciously on his mustache. "You mean it was not you?"

Suddenly Lupo snarled, whipped his head around, and bared his teeth. A moment later, Vronsky and Levin saw what had excited the keen-eared wolf: a short, squat man with a long beard, tangled and filthy, draped in an equally squalid laboratory coat.

"*Mea culpa, mea culpa,*" said this strange personage, speaking with exceptional rapidity. "My name is Federov, and I am afraid the blame for the ambiguity attendant on our little tête-à-tête is entirely mine. But hardly could I have sent a communiqué grandly requesting your presence at a meeting with a representative of the Union of Concerned Scientists."

"UnConSciya!" shouted Vronsky, and in an instant his hot-whip was deployed, crackling across the space between himself and Federov. But the man merely touched a small device on his belt, and the whip seemed not even to touch him.

"Now, now," the little man in the lab coat said, as if chastising a child. "I am hardly in a position to ask you to disarm, but our meeting will go more smoothly if you refrain from such posturing. I myself am wearing an array of defensive clothing and underclothing, created of technologies several generations ahead of any you might have access to. 'Always be prepared,' that's the motto of our little society."

Levin looked carefully at Federov. "What is it that you want?"

"Each of you, in your own way, is now as much an enemy of the Ministry as we are. You have come to understand what we have long understood: that our benevolent protectors are at heart neither benevolent, nor protective. Soon all Russia will know it, too, and they will need their leaders."

The squat, strange little man turned to Konstantin Dmitrich and looked him directly in the eye. "Levin, we beg you to travel with your household to Moscow, and wait there until such time as you can be of use."

Vronsky sneered, and spoke derisively, "You ask us to enter into conspiracy with the greatest criminals in Russian history."

"Yes," Levin echoed, his mind racing. "How can we?"

"By knowing this: we have never committed a single one of the violent acts attributed to us by the Ministry. Yes, we left the government laboratories en masse because we did not like certain orders we had been given, the path our rulers demanded technological innovation travel down. But we have never committed a single act of violence."

The funny little man leaned forward, his eyes welling with tears: "Not a *single one*. The emotion bombs, the malfunctions—the Ministry itself has done it all. Remember, if you want to control someone, first protect them. And if you will protect someone, you need something to protect them from."

Vronsky snorted with derision, and shook his head, but Levin trembled like a man hearing the word of God. He was moved beyond words to see that tears were openly rolling down Federov's dirty, bearded face. "I apologize for becoming so emotional," said Federov. "But we have spent a generation outside of possibility, and now I stare at you two proud Russian gentlemen, and I cannot help it—I feel—*hope*."

BOOM!

The forest exploded with fire.

"No," cried Federov. "An emotion bomb! I should have known."

BOOM! A second hope-bomb rattled the treeline, and with a terrible crack a massive oak tree splintered and fell before them, its leaves alive with fire. All three men ducked down to the earth, covering their ears against the concussive roar of the detonations. "It is me," screamed Federov. "My hope! My—"

BOOM! A third blast, the loudest yet, knocked Vronsky's massive Exterior to the ground and tore the roof from the Huntshed. Levin caught a glimpse of the tops of the Surceased Huntbears, their fight grimaces glinting in the fire-lit darkness, before a burning branch cracked free and landed across his back.

"Ahh!" he screamed in terrible pain, and Vronsky rolled atop him, causing him exquisite agony but extinguishing the blaze. Levin wailed helplessly, while Vronsky screamed to Federov. "It is a trap! You have trapped us here! What have you done? You've killed him!"

"I did not cause this attack!" shouted Federov, staggering to his feet. "But I can still the hope that provokes it!" Levin, moaning, clutching at himself with his badly scalded hands, sat up and stared—as Federov pulled out a dagger and drove it into his own heart.

Levin gasped; the man from UnConSciya screamed and doubled forward, pushing the knife in to the hilt. No further bombs were heard, only the eerie crackling of the burning forest.

"Remember these words, men," Federov said between clenched teeth, sinking to his knees. "Rearguard . . . Action."

"Rearguard . . . ," intoned Levin, as if hypnotized.

"Action," Vronsky mumbled.

CHAPTER 14

VRONSKY HAD AGREED to pursue the tête-à-tête at the Huntshed partly because he was attracted, as all cocksure men are, by a chance for further adventures—just as the tippler, once he has tasted wine, will again and again reactivate the II/Barrel/4. But also Vronsky was bored in the country and wanted to show Anna his right to independence. He had not in the least expected that the tête-à-tête would so interest him, so keenly excite him, and that he would be so good at this kind of thing.

After burying the body of the UnConSciya man in a circular hollow a hundred or so paces from the Huntshed, Levin and he stopped to discuss the remarkable events, and to enjoy smoking cigars. They spoke in a calm and happy way—though, while they seemed to be perfect allies and friends, their past rivalry forgotten, Levin did not mention that his Class III still lived, buried in a Urgensky smoke factory; and Vronsky did not bring up his cherished hope, that if only he could get Anna to "see it right," they would give up their share in rebellion entirely.

They were thus smoking and talking, when Lupo was beamed a communiqué and promptly lit it up on his monitor.

It was from Anna, and before Vronsky watched it, he already knew its contents. Expecting the tête-à-tête to be over in five days, he had promised to be back on Friday. Today was Saturday, and he knew that the communiqué contained reproaches for not being back at the fixed time.

The missive was not unexpected, but the form of it was unexpected, and particularly disagreeable to him. Anna's face flashed red in the projection, as she bitterly pronounced, "Annie is very ill, and Placebo"—a Vozdvizhenskoe decom who had once been beloved-companion to a great Moscow doctor—"says it may be inflammation. I am losing my head all alone. I expected you the day before yesterday, and yesterday, and now I am sending to find out where you are and what you are doing. I wanted to come myself, but thought better of it, knowing you would dislike it. Send some answer, that I may know what to do."

Vronsky played the communiqué again, to ensure he had it right, and again watched the pleading face of Anna Karenina. *Send some answer, that I may know what to do.* The child ill, yet she had thought of coming herself. Their daughter ill, and this hostile tone. The adrenalin-flushed excitement of the meeting in the woods and this gloomy, burdensome love to which he had to return struck Vronsky by their contrast. But he had to go, and immediately he bid Levin farewell and set off home.

CHAPTER 15

BEFORE VRONSKY'S DEPARTURE for the tête-à-tête, Anna had reflected that the scenes constantly repeated between them each time he left their fortifications might only make him cold to her instead of attaching him to her, and resolved to do all she could to control herself so as to bear the parting with composure. But the cold, severe glance with which he had looked at her when he came to tell her he was departing for the meeting had wounded her, and before he had started, her peace of mind was already destroyed.

In solitude afterward, thinking over that glance which had expressed his right to freedom, she came, as she always did, to the same point—the sense of her own humiliation. "He has the right to go away when and where he chooses," she complained to Android Karenina. "Not simply to go away, but to leave me. He has every right, and I have none. But knowing that, he ought not to do it." Together they had fled Petersburg, together they had built Vozdvizhenskoe on the old abandoned patch of farmland. But now while he was out playing the role of dashing rebel leader, she waited for him alone in the autumn cold.

"What has he done, though? . . . He looked at me with a cold, severe expression. Of course that is something indefinable, impalpable, but it has never been so before, and that glance means a great deal," she concluded, as Android Karenina softly stroked her flowing hair. "That glance shows the beginning of indifference."

And though she felt sure that a coldness was beginning, there was nothing she could do, she could not in any way alter her relations to him. Just as before, only by love and by charm could she keep him. And so, just as before, only by occupation in the day, by Galena Box at night, could she stifle the fearful thought of what would be if he ceased to love her. There was still one means, she finally admitted to herself, not to keep him—for she wanted nothing more than his love—but to be nearer to him, to be in such a position that he would not leave her.

That meant a divorce from Karenin; worse, it meant dispatching an emissary to the Higher Branches, revealing their location; it meant giving up their arms, begging forgiveness of the Ministry. And, of course, it would mean giving up their Class III robots, though this possibility Anna was not ready even to consider.

Absorbed in such thoughts, she passed five days without him, the five days that he was to be at the mysterious tête-à-tête in the woods. When the sixth day ended without his return, she felt that now she was utterly incapable of stifling the thought of him and of what he was doing there, just when her little girl was taken ill. Anna began to look after her, but even that did not distract her mind, especially as the illness was not serious. However hard she tried, she could not love this little child, and to feign love was beyond her powers. Toward the evening of that day, still alone, Anna was in such a panic about him that she decided to start for

the town, but on second thought recorded the contradictory communiqué that Vronsky received, and without watching it through, beamed it
off to Lupo. The next morning she received his reply and regretted her
communiqué. She dreaded a repetition of the severe look he had flung
at her at parting, especially when he knew that the baby was not dangerously ill.

But still she was glad she had sent the communiqué. At this moment
Anna was positively admitting to herself that she was a burden to him,
that he would relinquish his freedom regretfully to return to her, and in
spite of that she was glad he was coming. Let him weary of her, but he
would be here with her, so that she would see him, would know of every
action he took.

She was sitting in the drawing room, and as she read she listened
to the sound of the wind outside, every minute expecting the carriage
to arrive. The farm was silent, with the cold and complete silence of an
estate populated only by robots, who in their nightly Surcease made not
even the smallest sound. Only one companion robot at Vozdvizhenskoe
still had its human, and that was Android Karenina; now she brought tea,
warmed on her own groznium core.

At last Anna heard the unmistakable *whomp* of Frou-Frou Deux's
big paws kicking up dirt in the covered entry. Android Karenina looked
up, her eyebank flickered; Anna, flushing hotly, got up; but instead of
going down, as she had done twice before, she stood still. She suddenly
felt ashamed of her duplicity, but even more she dreaded how he might
meet her. All feeling of wounded pride had passed now; she was only
afraid of the expression of his displeasure.

She remembered that her child had been perfectly well again for the
last two days. She felt positively vexed with her for getting better from the
very moment her communiqué was dispatched. Then she thought of him,
that he was here, all of him, with his hands, his eyes. She heard his voice.
And forgetting everything, she ran joyfully to meet him.

"Well, how is Annie?" he said timidly from below, looking up to

Anna as she ran down to him.

He was sitting on a chair pulling off his warm overboots.

"Oh, she is better."

"And you?" he said, shaking himself.

She took his hand in both of hers, and drew it to her waist, never taking her eyes off him.

"Well, I'm glad," he said, coldly scanning her, her hair, her dress, which he knew she had put on for him. All was charming, but how many times it had charmed him! And the stern, stony expression that she so dreaded settled upon his face.

"Well, I'm glad. And are you well?" he said, wiping his damp beard with his handkerchief and kissing her hand.

"Never mind," she thought, "only let him be here, and so long as he's here he cannot, he dare not, cease to love me."

The evening was spent happily and gaily; he told her about the tête-à-tête, about meeting Federov, about Konstantin Dmitrich, and the hope-bomb. Anna knew how by adroit questions to bring him to what gave him most pleasure—his own success. She told him of everything that interested him at home; and all that she told him was of the most cheerful description. But late in the evening, Anna, seeing that she had regained complete possession of him, wanted to erase the painful impression of the glance he had given her for her communiqué.

She said: "Tell me frankly, you were vexed upon viewing my communiqué, and you didn't believe me?"

As soon as she had said it, she felt that however warm his feelings were toward her, he had not forgiven her for that.

"Yes," he said, "the communiqué was so strange. First, Annie ill, and then you thought of coming yourself."

"It was all the truth."

"Oh, I don't doubt it."

"Yes, you do doubt it. You are vexed, I see."

"Not for one moment. I'm only vexed, that's true, that you seem somehow unwilling to admit that there are duties . . . "

"The duty of traipsing about, of drinking and smoking cigars with Levin in a Huntshed!"

"But we won't talk about it," he said.

"Why not talk about it?" she said.

"I only meant to say that matters of real importance may turn up. Tomorrow, for instance, I shall have to make a tour of our far perimeters, make sure the fencing is secure."

"Another reason to abandon me."

"Oh, Anna, why are you so irritable? If we are going to maintain a fortified rebel camp in defiance of the Ministry, in the heart of an alien-beset wilderness, there will always be challenges and responsibilities that take me outside the doors of this house. But don't you know that I can't live without you? "

"If so," said Anna, her voice suddenly changing, "it means that you are sick of this life. . . . Yes, you will come for a day and go away, as men do. . . . "

"Anna, that's cruel. I am ready to give up my whole life. . . . "

But she did not hear him.

"If you have more such invitations, I will go with you. If you travel to inspect fortifications, I will go too. I will not stay here. Either we must separate or else live together."

Vronsky saw the opening he had been looking for, saw a route to the life he had imagined. "Then perhaps, perhaps, Anna, this world we have created is not, after all, a permanently sustainable one."

Somehow, Android Karenina knew the direction this conversation would take even before her mistress did. Placing the tea things gently on an end table, Android Karenina opened her arms and patted her lap for Lupo; his silvery hide blackened here and there from the hope-bomb fire, the proud wolf padded over and climbed into the robot's embrace.

"If we only applied for amnesty—begged the Ministry for for-giveness, asked your husband for a divorce. You and I can be together

KNOWING THE DIRECTION THIS CONVERSATION WOULD TAKE, ANDROID
KARENINA OPENED HER ARMS AND PATTED HER LAP FOR LUPO

. . . forever. Be a part of the future of our nation. Be married, and be together, not crouched in the dirt outside society, but within it. "

"Together," Anna said slowly. Her mind was spinning; suddenly, she desired only to have these questions decided.

"You know, that's my one desire. But for that . . . "

"We must get a divorce. I will . . . " Anna lowered her head and sighed. "I will send him a communiqué tonight. I see I cannot go on like this . . . but tomorrow I will ride out with you to inspect the fortifications."

"You talk as if you were threatening me. But I desire nothing so much as never to be parted from you," said Vronsky, smiling.

But as he said these words there gleamed in his eyes not merely a cold look, but the vindictive look of a man persecuted and made cruel.

She saw the look and correctly divined its meaning.

If so, it's a calamity! that glance told her. It was a moment's impression, but she never forgot it.

That night, Anna dictated a communiqué to her husband asking him about a divorce, and begging amnesty for herself and for Count Vronsky. A reply came almost immediately, granting only that their petition would be considered, and that only on one condition.

When the moment came, Lupo sat perfectly upright, looking straight ahead like a soldier, while Android Karenina lowered her head unit slightly, not wanting to make a difficult moment more difficult for her beloved mistress. Vronsky and Anna looked at each other, and then at Lupo and Android Karenina, and then reached forward. . . .

*   *   *

Anna went with Vronsky to Moscow. Expecting every day an answer from Alexei Alexandrovich, and after that the divorce, they now established themselves together like married people.

PART SEVEN: THE EMPTY PLACE

CHAPTER 1

I T WAS ALEXEI ALEXANDROVICH who decided to defer judgment in the case of Anna Arkadyevna Karenina and Alexei Kirillovich Vronsky, but really the decision was made by his Face. Once again that malevolent, whispering cranial presence found it convenient to let the question simmer like a slow-boiling pot, to keep it alive and so to torture Karenin.

So for months after their return to Moscow, Vronsky and Anna heard nothing from the Ministry in response to their request for amnesty—only waited, and suffered from the silence hanging over them.

But Alexei Alexandrovich's festering displeasure was not limited in its effects on his wife and her companion.

All of Russia suffered with them.

* * *

When the Class II robots were impounded as the Class IIIs had been, the Levins had been three months in Moscow. Kitty would have preferred to enter her period of confinement still living in the family manse, on the slopes of the old groznium pit in Pokrovskoe, but Levin was determined to keep his promise made to the dying Federov, and so moved their household to the city. He did not however attempt to dictate to his wife what would be best; rather, he shared with her the fervency of his desire to support the building resistance against the Ministry's changes to Russian life, and by his passion Kitty was convinced.

Kitty and Levin, with some self-consciousness, called their vision of Russia's future, a future in which their poor beloved-companions could come home, their "Golden Hope," and they felt proud and romantic about their shared determination to make this vision a reality.

The date had long passed on which, according to the most trust-worthy calculations of people learned in such matters, Kitty should have been confined to bed. But she was still up and about; there was nothing to show that her time was any nearer than two months ago. Dolly, her mother, and most of all Levin, who could not think of the approaching event without terror, began to be impatient and uneasy; the doctor, whose trusted II/Prognosis/M4 had been collected by Toy Soldiers, was equally anxious if not more so. Kitty was the only person who felt perfectly calm and happy. She was distinctly conscious now of the birth of a new feeling of love for the future child, for her to some extent actually existing already, and she brooded blissfully over this feeling.

The child was not by now altogether a part of herself, but sometimes lived his own life independently of her. Often this separate being gave her pain, but at the same time she wanted to laugh with a strange new joy. The only thing that spoiled the charm of this manner of life for Kitty was that her husband was different here than where she loved him to be, and as he was in the country.

She liked his serene, friendly, and hospitable manner in the country. In town he seemed continually uneasy and on his guard, certain that at any moment some friend or stranger would approach and call him into action with the mysterious shibboleth that Federov had taught him. At home in the country, knowing himself distinctly to be in his right place, he was never in haste to be off elsewhere. He was never unoccupied. Here in town he was in a continual hurry, afraid of being found out, protecting his inmost thoughts, peering seekingly into the eyes of strangers. As though always afraid of missing something, though as yet he had nothing to do. And she felt sorry for him. She saw him not from without, but from within; she saw that here he was not himself; that was the only way she could define his condition to herself. Sometimes she inwardly reproached him for his inability to live in the city; sometimes she recognized that it was really hard for him to order his life here so that he could be satisfied with it.

One obvious example to Kitty was that Levin had, his whole life, hated the gentlemen's clubs frequented by Stepan Arkadyich and his associates, but now Levin felt it was necessary that he spend time in them. If there were "fellow travelers" to be found, he felt sure, this is where he would find them. Kitty had no choice therefore but to give her blessing. But whiling away hours with jovial gentlemen of Oblonsky's type—she knew now what that meant: it meant drinking and going somewhere after drinking. She could not think without horror of where men went on such occasions. Was he to go into society? But she knew he could only find satisfaction in that if he took pleasure in the society of young women, and that she could not wish for. Should he stay at home with her, her mother, and her sisters? But much as she liked and enjoyed their conversations forever on the same subjects, she knew it must bore him. And what good would such hours be, spent in the dull company of her and her sisters? It would not advance their Golden Hope. What was there left for him to do?

One advantage in this town life was that quarrels hardly ever happened between them here. Whether it was that their conditions were different, or that they had both become more careful and sensible in that respect, they had no quarrels in Moscow from jealousy, which they had so dreaded when they moved from the country.

One event, an event of great importance to both from that point of view, did indeed happen—that was Kitty's meeting with Vronsky.

The old Princess Marya Borissovna, Kitty's godmother, who had always been very fond of her, had insisted on seeing her. Kitty, though she did not go into society at all on account of her condition, went with her

father to see the venerable old lady, and there met Vronsky. The only thing
Kitty could reproach herself for at this meeting was that at the instant
when she recognized him—in his civilian dress, with no hot-whip at his
thigh, no bristling steel-grey wolf at his side—when she saw the features
once so familiar to her, her breath failed her, the blood rushed to her heart,
and a vivid blush (she felt it) overspread her face. But this lasted only a few
seconds. Before her father, who purposely began talking in a loud voice to
Vronsky, had finished, she was perfectly ready to look at Vronsky, to speak
to him, if necessary, exactly as she spoke to Princess Marya Borissovna,
and more than that, to do so in such a way that everything to the faintest
intonation and smile would have been approved by her husband, whose
unseen presence she seemed to feel about her at that instant.

She said a few words to him, speaking of nothing at all. Konstantin
Dmitrich had naturally told her every incredible detail of the tête-à-tête
at the Huntshed, but hardly could she acknowledge in public that astonishing event. Instead she turned away immediately to Princess Marya
Borissovna, and did not once glance at him till he got up to go; then she
looked at him, but evidently only because it would be uncivil not to look
at a man when he is saying good-bye.

Only then did she summon the courage to speak, in whispered
tones, of the great secret that lay between them: their mutual knowledge
of the nascent resistance to the so-called New Russia. "How is it that you
and Anna have returned to society?" In the urgency of her whisper was
communicated her hope and expectation that the amnesty request was
a gambit, a cover story, and that Vronsky was in Moscow for the same
reason as Levin: awaiting the chance to move against the Ministry.

"Anna Arkadyevna and I wish only to make amends for our ill-
considered transgressions," he pronounced, loudly enough for Princess
Borissovna to hear. The old woman nodded her approval. "We have therefore cashiered our Class IIIs in accordance with the law, and appealed to
Minister Karenin for amnesty. I have many skills, of course, that could be
put to use in the service of the New Russia."

Kitty could not determine whether Vronsky was playing false, for the old princess's benefit, or whether his contrition was sincere. As always in the past, Count Vronsky remained a mystery.

On the way home, she was grateful to her father for saying nothing to her about their meeting Vronsky, but she saw by his special warmth to her after the visit during their usual walk that he was pleased with her. She was pleased with herself. She had not expected she would have had the power, while keeping somewhere in the bottom of her heart all the memories of her old feeling for Vronsky, not only to be perfectly indifferent and composed with him, but to do her best to sound out the depth of his loyalties.

Levin flushed a great deal more than she when she told him she had met Vronsky at Princess Marya Borissovna's. It was very hard for her to tell him this, but still harder to go on speaking of the details of the meeting, as he did not question her, but simply gazed at her with a frown.

Her truthful eyes told Levin that she was satisfied with herself, and in spite of her blushing he was quickly reassured and began questioning her, which was all she wanted. When he had heard that she was just as direct and as much at her ease as with any chance acquaintance, Levin was quite happy and said he was glad of it.

"But there is more," she added. "More that we must discuss, relating to our Golden Hope."

They leaned their heads together, as much co-conspirators as husband and wife, to ponder the difficulties that Kitty's new information posed. If Count Vronsky had truly abandoned his rebellious posture, surely this raised the danger that he would report to the Ministry what he knew about Kitty and Levin and *their* secrets.

"I will seek an opportunity to speak directly to Vronsky, and then, together, you and I shall discuss what to do," Levin replied, emphasizing the word "together," as if to affirm to Kitty his belief that she had handled herself perfectly in this situation.

"I miss my beloved-companion," Kitty sighed.

"And I, mine, my love. And I, mine."

CHAPTER 2

THE FOLLOWING NIGHT, Levin reached the club just at the right time. Members and visitors were driving up as he arrived. Levin had not been at the club for a very long while—not since he lived in Moscow, when he was leaving the university and going into society. He remembered the club, the external details of its arrangement, but he had completely forgotten the impression it had made on him in the old days. But as soon as he drove into the wide, semicircular court and got out of the sledge; as soon as he saw in the porter's room the cloaks and galoshes of members who thought it less trouble to take them off downstairs; as soon as he heard the I/Bell/6 that tolled three times behind its semi-transparent panel to announce him, as he ascended the easy, carpeted staircase, and saw the slow rotation of the glittering I/Statue/9 on the landing, unobtrusively identity-confirming each arriving guest, Levin felt the old impression of the club come back in a rush, an impression of repose, comfort, and propriety.

The difference, of course, was that in the old days the picture included dozens of Class IIs. Tonight there was no drone of busy motors, no dull hum of mechanical servitude. No II/Butler/97 politely removed his hat with careful end-effectors; no II/Porter/6 asked his name at the door and announced it with a Vox-Em flourish when he entered the main hall. Instead a fat and surly peasant in an ill-fitting vest grunted and gestured with a rude thumb to the staircase.

Passing through the outer hall, divided up by screens, and the room partitioned on the right, where a man sat at the fruit buffet, Levin overtook an old man walking slowly in, and entered the dining room full of noise and people.

He walked along the tables, almost all full, and looked at the visitors. He saw people of all sorts, old and young; some he knew a little, some intimate friends. Despite all of society's convulsions, he did not see a single cross or worried-looking face. All seemed to have left their cares and anxieties downstairs with their hats, and were all deliberately getting ready to enjoy the material blessings of life.

"Ah! Why are you late?" the prince said to Levin, smiling, and giving him his hand over his own shoulder. "How's Kitty?" he added, smoothing out the napkin he had tucked in at his waistcoat buttons.

"All right; they are dining at home, all three of them."

"Go to that table, and make haste and take a seat," said the prince, and turning away he carefully took a plate of eel soup.

Konstantin Dmitrich sat, and an irritated-looking young peasant brought a bowl of soup, carelessly sloshing the hot liquid over the sides and into Levin's lap. He grimaced in pain and annoyance; the perfect, gyroscopically maintained balance of a Class II waiter would never make such a careless error.

But the others only laughed at the accident, and Levin realized that the view held by those in the club—or, at least, the view loudly expressed by those who wanted to be heard saying the right sorts of things—was very different than his own. It was agreed at every table that Russian life had been much *improved* by the disappearance of those "pesky" robots, always motoring about underfoot, making one feel self-conscious and intruded upon, their circuits forever buzzing and whirring away.

"To humanity!" said the prince, and raised his glass. "To the New Russia!" echoed Sviashky.

"Levin, this way!" a good-natured voice shouted a little farther on. It was Turovtsin. He was sitting with a young officer, and beside them were two chairs turned upside down. Levin gladly went up to them. He had always liked the good-hearted rake, Turovtsin, and at that moment, after the strain of intellectual conversation, the sight of Turovtsin's good-natured face was particularly welcome.

And maybe . . . Levin narrowed his eyes and felt his heart pounding in his chest . . .

With exaggerated casualness, Levin smoothed his beard and approached his old friend with an easy smile. Pulling his chair close to the other man's, breathing hotly into Turovtsin's ear, he murmured a single word:

"Rearguard."

"Eh?" responded Turovtsin loudly, his eyes lighting up. Levin's heart beat faster; his blood roared in his ears. Could it be Turovtsin? Did he share in the Golden Hope? Who would have thought it was foolish Turovtsin?

"Rearguard?" repeated Turovtsin, but loudly, his eyes glittering with anticipatory merriment in his eyes, as if awaiting the punchline.

Levin drew back, stammering. "Ah . . . I thought . . . but, never mind, never mind. I said nothing."

"Oh, well," said Turovtsin. "Here, then." He handed Levin a pair of glasses. "For you and Oblonsky. He'll be here directly. Ah, here he is!"

"Have you only just come?" said Oblonsky, coming quickly toward them. "Good day. Had some vodka? Well, come along then."

Levin, with difficulty hiding his disappointment, got up and went with him to the big table spread with spirits and appetizers of the most various kinds. One would have thought that out of two dozen delicacies one might find something to one's taste, but Stepan Arkadyich asked for something special, and the tetchy adolescent waiter trudged back into the kitchen to search it out. They drank a glass of wine and returned to their table.

"Ah! And here they are!" Stepan Arkadyich said toward the end of dinner, leaning over the back of his chair and holding out his hand to Vronsky, who came up with a tall officer of the Guards.

Vronsky's face, too, beamed with the look of good-humored enjoyment that was general in the club. He propped his elbow playfully on

Stepan Arkadyich's shoulder, whispering something to him, and he held out his hand to Levin with the same good-humored smile.

"Very glad to see you," he said, and then added with a wink—or at least, what Levin thought was a wink—"It has been a long time."

"Yes, yes," said Levin. In the next moment, a roar of laughter convulsed the table, as Oblonsky described the old slop-slinging peasant who'd replaced the household II/Cook/98. Levin judged that his moment was ripe. He leaned forward, and, laying one hand on the upper part of Vronsky's arm, whispered the code word both men had heard together from Federov.

"Rearguard."

For a long moment, the word seemed to shimmer in the air between them, while Levin sought a sign of life in the impassive face across from his. But the count did not whisper "Action." Instead he laughed genially and meaninglessly, twirled his mustache, and turned away.

Levin turned away as well, his worst suspicions confirmed: the resistance, if there were truly such a thing, could not number Alexei Kirillovich among its ranks.

But what danger did this fact pose to Levin? What should he do? He wished for the means to run a complete analysis of the situation; wished, not for the first or last time, that loyal Socrates were present to give him counsel.

"Well, have we finished?" said Stepan Arkadyich, getting up with a smile. "Let us go."

CHAPTER 3

OBLONSKY LED THEM like the piper of myth to the gambling tables. I/Dice/55s trembled and bobbled and danced, zipping in algorithmic patterns across the green acetate of the table, randomizing some men into small fortunes, and others into disappointment. Oblonsky himself was of the fortunate group, to his great delight. "Perhaps Small Stiva was bad luck to me for all those years!" he decreed jovially, provoking great merriment in his fellow gamblers, and naught but melancholy disdain in Levin.

Oblonsky had again clutched the I/Dice/55s in his fist, hoping to add further to his fast-growing pile of rubles, when a crowd of thin, high-cheeked men-who-were-not-men strode purposefully into the room.

"Ah!" said Stepan Arkadyich, only the tiniest flutter of fear rippling his habitually good-natured expression. "Gentlemen. Or, rather, gentle-machines, if I may be so bold as to coin a term."

"Might we invite you to join us in our games?" Vronsky ventured.

"To the contrary, your Excellency," said the tallest of the man-machines, who wore what looked like a scruffy two-day growth of beard; Levin marveled in spite of himself at the artistry of it. "We are here to collect these apparatuses."

One of the other Toy Soldiers held out his hand, and Stiva, wide-eyed with astonishment, placed the I/Dice/55 into the lifelike pink of the robot's open palm.

"Now, wait . . . if I might . . . hold on, now . . . ," protested the old prince tremulously. "Is there no place in the New Russia for a bit of friendly gambling?"

"It is not the gambling that is proscribed, gentlemen, it is the technology." The machine-man spoke rapidly. "Russia has her enemies, more now than ever. Enemies above; enemies within. The open distribution of technology is dangerous and can no longer be countenanced."

And the face of the Toy Soldier all at once wavered and blurred, revealing the machinery hiding behind the skin of his face. From where the eye had been, the muzzle of a miniature cannon jutted forth already shooting, and a quick and efficient volley of electric fire blasted the green Class I gaming table neatly to ash. The tiny cannon disappeared and the man's face reassembled itself; he cleared his throat (*There is no throat!* Levin adamantly reminded himself, *no throat!*)—and spoke: "I ask that you place your Class I devices on the floor before you."

Into a large pile it all went: heirloom I/Hourprotector/1s, I/CigarLighter/4s, I/Bifocal/6s, all the tiny, convenient wonders that had been made possible by groznium technology. All were heaped and vaporized as thoroughly as the gaming table. The Toy Soldiers turned on their black boot heels and departed, leaving in their wake a long, stunned silence, which Stepan Arkadyich filled with a pitiful murmur.

"Such is the price of happiness."

"Yes," said the old prince, shaking his head and wearing no expression. "Such is the price."

Levin, disgusted by the scene, pulled on his coat.

"Levin," said Stepan Arkadyich, and Levin noticed that his eyes were not full of tears exactly, but moist, which always happened when he had been drinking, or when he was moved by emotion. Just now it was due to both causes. "Levin, don't go," he said, and he warmly squeezed his arm above the elbow, obviously not at all wishing to let him go.

"This is a true friend of mine—almost my greatest friend," he said to Vronsky. It was evident to Levin that Oblonsky, more affected than he could openly admit by the evolution of the New Russia, was casting out for some source of happy feeling to console him. "You have become even closer and dearer to me. And I want you, and I know you ought, to be friends, and great friends, because you're both splendid fellows."

"Well, there's nothing for us now but to kiss and be friends," Vronsky said with good-natured playfulness, holding out his hand, acting as if the only past between them were a long-distant romantic rivalry.

Well, I can pretend as well, thought Levin. He quickly took the offered hand, and pressed it warmly. "I'm very, very glad," he said.

"Do you know, he has never met Anna?" Stepan Arkadyich said to Vronsky. "And I want above everything to take him to see her. Let us go, Levin!"

"Really?" said Vronsky, turning back to the other men, who were busily scouring the cabinets for a set of the old-fashioned wooden dice. "She will be very glad to see you."

CHAPTER 4

A S THE CARRIAGE DROVE out into the street, Levin felt it jolting over the uneven road, and heard the angry shout of their sledge driver, who had only just learned to drive it, and had nothing like the smooth touch of a II/SledgeDriver/6. Levin saw in the uncertain light the red blind of a tavern and the shops, and began to think over his actions, and to wonder whether he was doing right in going to see Anna. What would Kitty say? But Stepan Arkadyich gave him no time for reflection, and, as though divining his doubts, he scattered them.

"How glad I am," he said, "that you should know her! You know Dolly has long wished for it. And Lvov's been to see her, and often goes. Though she is my sister," Stepan Arkadyich pursued, "I don't hesitate to say that she's a remarkable woman. But you will see. Her position is very painful, especially now."

"Why especially now?"

"Vronsky and Anna have applied to her husband for amnesty and divorce, after their ill-conceived adventure in Vozdvizhenskoe. They have assurances that Karenin has received their request and is considering it, but not a word has yet been heard from that worthy. And so they wait, in rather exquisite agony, for a reply. As soon as the divorce is over, she will marry Vronsky. Well, then their position will be as regular as mine, as yours.

"But the point is she has been for three months in Moscow, where everyone knows her, waiting for some resolution. She goes out

nowhere, sees no woman except Dolly, because, do you understand, she
doesn't care to have people come as a favor. But you'll see how she
has arranged her life—how calm, how dignified she is. To the left, in
the crescent opposite the church!" shouted Stepan Arkadyich, leaning
out of the window.

"I beg of you not to yell at me!" the red-faced sledge driver
implored, nearly banking the carriage as he jerked it into the turn.

The carriage drove into the courtyard, and Stepan Arkadyich rang
loudly at the entrance where sledges were standing.

And without asking the hapless servant who opened the door
whether the lady was at home, Stepan Arkadyich walked into the hall.
Levin followed him, more and more doubtful whether he was doing
right or wrong.

Looking at himself in the I/Reflector/9 in the hallway, Levin
noticed that he was red in the face, but he felt certain he was not drunk,
and he followed Stepan Arkadyich up the carpeted stairs to the study.

Passing through the dining room, a room not very large, with dark,
paneled walls, Stepan Arkadyich and Levin walked across the soft carpet
to the half-dark study, lighted up by a single *lumière* with a big, dark shade.
On the wall above was a big full-length portrait of a woman, which
Levin could not help looking at. It was the portrait of Anna, painted on
the moon by the doomed Mihailov. Levin gazed at the portrait, which
stood out from the frame in the brilliant light thrown on it, and he could
not tear himself away from it. He positively forgot where he was, and not
even hearing what was said, he could not take his eyes off the marvelous
portrait. It was not a picture, but a living, charming woman, with black,
curling hair, with bare arms and shoulders, with a pensive smile on the
lips, covered with soft down; she stood in a confident pose on the arm
of a beloved-companion robot, triumphantly and softly looking at him
with eyes that baffled him. She was not living only because she was more
beautiful than a living woman can be.

"I am delighted!" He heard suddenly near him a voice, unmistakably addressing him, the voice of the very woman he had been admiring in the portrait. Anna had come from behind the treillage to meet him, and Levin saw in the dim light of the study the very woman of the portrait, in a dark-blue short gown, not in the same position, nor with the same expression, but with the same perfection of beauty which the artist had caught in the portrait. She was less dazzling in reality, but of course in the picture she had the advantage of the radiant backlight cast by a Class III. Now, in person, and in the New Russia, that enhancement was sadly lacking.

CHAPTER 5

S HE HAD RISEN to meet him, not concealing her pleasure at seeing him.

"You will excuse me for being ill at ease," Anna began. "I neither look nor feel myself since I have lost the company of my beloved-companion, Android Karenina."

Levin smiled with pleasure at her unexpected forthrightness: how refreshing to hear someone speak openly of the great collective loss the Russian people had suffered.

"I am delighted, delighted," she went on, and upon her lips these simple words took for Levin's ears a special significance. "I have known you and liked you for a long while, both from your friendship with Stiva and for your wife's sake. . . . I knew her for a very short time, but she left on me the impression of an exquisite flower, simply a flower. And to think she will soon be a mother!"

She spoke easily and without haste, looking now and then from Levin to her brother, and Levin felt that the impression he was making was good, and he felt immediately at home, simple and happy with her, as though he had known her from childhood.

"I am settled in Alexei's study," she said in answer to Stepan Arkadyich's question whether he might smoke, "just so as to be able to smoke"—and glancing at Levin, instead of asking whether he would smoke, she pulled closer a I/CigarCase/6 and activated herself a cigarette.

"Enjoy such luxury while you can, Anna," her brother said. "Class Ones are now added to the list."

"You jest!"

"Alas, I do not. Ours were junkered only hours ago at the club, by one of those lifelike friends of ours."

Anna gritted her teeth, as if to say, *I shall accept the New Russia— indeed I must—but I cannot be forced to like it.*

Yes, yes, this is a woman! Levin thought, forgetting himself and staring persistently at her lovely, mobile face, which at that moment was all at once completely transformed. Levin did not hear what she was talking of as she leaned over to her brother, but he was struck by the change of her expression. Her face—so handsome a moment before in its repose—suddenly wore a look of strange curiosity, anger, and pride. But this lasted only an instant. She dropped her eyelids, as though recollecting something.

And Levin saw a new trait in this woman, who attracted him so extraordinarily. Besides wit, grace, and beauty, she had truth. She had no wish to hide from him all the bitterness of her position. She sighed, and her face suddenly took a hard expression, looking as if it were turned to stone. With that expression on her face she was more beautiful than ever; but the expression was new; it was utterly unlike that expression, radiant with happiness and creating happiness, which had been caught by the painter in her portrait. Levin looked more than once at the portrait and at her figure, as taking her brother's arm she walked with him to the high doors, and he felt for her a tenderness and pity at which he wondered himself.

In the next moment, this wonderment translated itself into action. When Stiva went out of the room a few steps ahead of Levin, before he could stop to think, he stopped at the doorframe, turned back to Anna, and whispered, urgently and impetuously: "Rearguard."

Neither smiling nor frowning, she leaned slightly forward in her chair and replied: "Action."

They both stared at the other for a long moment.

"Well, good-bye," Anna said at last, rising to take his hand and glancing into his face with a winning look. "I am very glad *que la glace est rompue.*"

She dropped his hand, and half closed her eyes.

"Tell your wife that I love her as before, and that if she cannot pardon me my position, then my wish for her is that she may never pardon it. To pardon it, one must go through what I have gone through, and may God spare her that."

"Certainly, yes, I will tell her. . . . " Levin said, blushing. "And . . . but . . . "

"Goodnight," said Anna Arkadyevna with finality.

CHAPTER 6

WELL, DIDN'T I TELL YOU?" said Stepan Arkadyich, seeing that Levin had been completely won over.

"Yes," said Levin dreamily, his mind racing with thoughts of Anna Karenina and the Golden Hope. "An extraordinary woman! It's not her cleverness, but she has such depth of feeling. I'm awfully sorry for her!"

"Now, please God, everything will soon be settled. Well, well, don't be hard on people in the future," said Stepan Arkadyich, opening the carriage door. "Good-bye; we don't go the same way."

Still thinking of Anna, of everything, even the simplest phrase in their conversation with her, and recalling the minutest changes in her expression, entering more and more into her position, and feeling sympathy for her, Levin traveled home.

All the way there, he reeled with excitement, and in particular with anticipation of sharing with Kitty what he had learned: that Anna Karenina, despite the abandonment of Vozdvizhenskoe and the junker army, despite their return to Moscow and the petition to Karenin, remained in her heart a partisan.

What Levin did not know, what he could not know, was that Vronsky had never told Anna Karenina the code words. On returning home from the Huntshed, he had given her the barest outline of his meeting with Federov, but then they had passed into argument, and from there to reconciliation, and that reconciliation had led them back to Moscow.

Never had he told her of Federov's dying exhortation; never had he mentioned the words *rearguard* or *action* at all.

Somehow, Anna knew the words anyway.

*　　*　　*

At home their new servant, a man named Kouzma, told Levin that Katerina Alexandrovna was quite well, and that her sisters had not long been gone, and then handed him a neatly folded piece of paper. This was a "letter," an old-fashioned means of information transmission in which the correspondent commits his thoughts to paper with pen and ink— along with "books" and "newspapers," it had come back into vogue since the disappearance of monitor-and-*communiqué* technology. Levin read the letter at once in the hall, and found it was from Sokolov, his bailiff. Sokolov wrote that the latest gleanings from the pit were faulty, that it was fetching only five and a half rubles, and that more than that could not be got for it. Levin scowled. He had been forced, like all other groznium miners, to hire human beings to administer his land in his absence, and they were terrible at it.

Levin found his wife low-spirited and dull. The dinner of the three sisters had gone off very well, but then they had waited and waited for him, all of them had felt dull, the sisters had departed, and she had been left alone.

"Well, and what have you been doing?" she asked him, looking straight into his eyes, which shone with rather a suspicious brightness. But that she might not prevent his telling her everything, she concealed her close scrutiny of him, and with an approving smile listened to his account of how he had spent the evening.

"First, as for Vronsky, I fear your assessment was correct: he has decidedly gone to the other side. Still, I do not think he intends to turn us in. For now, anyway, I think we are safe."

"Well, and then where did you go?"

"Stiva urged me awfully to go and see Anna Arkadyevna."

And as he said this, Levin blushed even more, and his doubts as to whether he had done right in going to see Anna were settled once and for all. He knew now that he ought not to have done so.

Kitty's eyes opened in a curious way and gleamed at Anna's name, but controlling herself with an effort, she concealed her emotion and deceived him.

"Oh!" was all she said.

"I'm sure you won't be angry at my going. Stiva begged me to, and Dolly wished it," Levin went on.

"Oh, no!" she said, but he saw in her eyes a constraint that boded him no good.

"She is a very sweet, very, very unhappy, good woman," he said. "And—Kitty—there is more!"

Again, she said, "Oh?"

"Anna Karenina, unlike Vronsky, remains *one of us*! She responded to the code word immediately and appropriately. I am convinced that she holds our views on the necessary changes that must come to society. Think how useful she could be. . . . "

But Kitty hardly responded as Levin had anticipated.

"Yes, of course, her involvement is very much to be celebrated," said Kitty coldly, when he had finished. "Whom was your letter from?"

Disappointed that his co-conspirator should take such little interest in his exciting discovery of Anna's allegiances, he told her about the letter from Sokolov. Then, believing in her calm tone, he went to change his coat.

Coming back, he found Kitty in the same easy chair. When he went up to her, she glanced at him and broke into sobs.

"What? What is it?" he asked, knowing beforehand what.

"You're in love with that hateful woman; she has bewitched you! I saw it in your eyes. Yes, yes! What can it all lead to? You were drinking at the club, drinking and gambling, and then you went . . . to her of all people! No, we must go away. . . . I shall go away tomorrow."

It was a long while before Levin could soothe his wife. At last he succeeded in calming her, only by confessing that a feeling of pity, in conjunction with the wine he had drunk, had been too much for him, that he had succumbed to Anna's artful influence, and that he would avoid her. One thing he did confess to with more sincerity was that by living so long in Moscow, leading a life of nothing but conversation, eating, and drinking, he was degenerating. And in the meantime, he was hardly progressing in his efforts on behalf of the Golden Hope. If anything, telling Kitty of his one significant advance in that goal acted to dampen his wife's zeal for the enterprise. She now seemed to feel that if resistance meant alliance with Anna Karenina, it might be best to abandon their resistance.

They talked till three o'clock in the morning, and as the hours passed the thrill he had felt about Anna, about the resistance and the Golden Hope, steadily dimmed in his breast. Only at three o'clock were they sufficiently reconciled to be able to go to sleep.

CHAPTER 7

AFTER TAKING LEAVE of her guests, Anna did not sit down, but began walking up and down the room. Oh, how she missed her dear Android Karenina at such times as these, when her mind was unsettled, her soul aflutter, her thoughts muddy and indistinct. She had unconsciously the whole evening done her utmost to arouse in Levin a feeling of love—as of late she had fallen into doing with all young men—and she knew she had attained her aim, as far as was possible in one evening, with a married and conscientious man. She liked him indeed extremely, and, in spite of the striking difference, from the masculine point of view, between Vronsky and Levin, as a woman she saw something they had in common, which had made Kitty able to love both.

But what had he meant by that strange word he spoke so urgently, and how had she known how to respond to it? Her response, her understanding, had clearly resonated with him. Somehow she had known the exact right thing to say—but how? How had she known?

As one troubling thought departed another arrived, like Gravs at a station. This one was connected to Vronsky, and Anna's growing sense of the dislocation between them. *If I have so much effect on others, on this Levin, who loves his home and his wife, why is it he is so cold to me? . . . not cold exactly, he loves me, I know that! But something new is drawing us apart now. Here we sit in Moscow, waiting to hear of our fate. Soon we shall be proper members of this new Russian society. So why is he not here? Why wasn't he here all the evening?*

She heard Vronsky's abrupt chime at the door and hurriedly dried her tears, and affected composure. She wanted to show him that she was displeased that he had not come home as he had promised—displeased only, and not on any account to let him see her distress, and least of all, her self-pity. She might pity herself, but he must not pity her. She did not want strife, she blamed him for wanting to quarrel, but unconsciously put herself into an attitude of antagonism.

"Well, you've not been dull?" he said, eagerly and good-humoredly. "You will hardly believe it, but they have smashed up all the Class Ones! All will be gone within the week. I think your husband and his compatriots mean to drain every vestige of technology from the nation—next they'll have the Tsars back, and Russia will end up as some sort of vast agrarian monarchy, complete with horse races and peasants threshing wheat."

He laughed, but Anna remained composed.

"Stiva has been here and Levin."

"Yes, they meant to come and see you. Well, how did you like Levin?" he said, sitting down beside her.

"Very much."

Anna did not mention the puzzling business with the code words. Instead she changed the subject, inquiring after Vronsky's louche friend, Yashvin.

"He was winning—seventeen thousand, when the Toy Soldiers showed up and vaporized the tables. Some others were planning to make do with hand-carved dice, I don't know who found them or where, when at last I got Yashvin away. He had really started home, but he went back again, and now he's losing."

"So what did you stay for?" she asked, suddenly lifting her eyes to him. The expression of her face was cold and ungracious. "You told Stiva you were staying on to get Yashvin away. And you have left him there."

The same expression of cold readiness for the conflict appeared on his face too.

"In the first place, I did not ask him to give you any message; and secondly, I never tell lies. But what's the chief point, I wanted to stay, and I stayed," he said, frowning. "Anna, what is it for, why?" he said after a moment's silence, bending over toward her, and he opened his hand, hoping she would lay hers in it.

She was glad of this appeal for tenderness. But some strange force of evil would not let her give herself up to her feelings; it was as though the tactics of combat they had studied together at Vozdvizhenskoe were now being turned upon one another.

"Of course you wanted to stay, and you stayed. You do everything you want to. But what do you tell me that for? With what object?" she said, getting more and more excited. "Does anyone contest your rights? But you want to be right, and you're welcome to be right."

His hand closed, he turned away, and his face wore a still more obstinate expression.

"For you it's a matter of obstinacy," she said, watching him intently and suddenly finding the right word for that expression that irritated her, "simply obstinacy. For you it's a question of whether you keep the upper hand of me, while for me . . . " Again she felt sorry for herself, and she almost burst into tears. "If you knew what it is for me! When I feel as I do now that you are hostile, yes, hostile to me, if you knew what this means for me! If you knew how I feel on the brink of calamity at this instant, how afraid I am of myself!" And she turned away, hiding her sobs.

"But what are you talking about?" he said, horrified at her expression of despair, and again bending over her, he took her hand and kissed it. "What is it for? Do I seek amusements outside our home? Don't I avoid the society of women?"

"Well, yes! If that were all!" she said.

"Come, tell me what I ought to do to give you peace of mind? I am ready to do anything to make you happy," he said, touched by her expression of despair. "What wouldn't I do to save you from distress of any sort, as now, Anna!" he said.

"It's nothing, nothing!" she said. "I don't know myself whether it's the solitary life, my nerves . . . . Come, don't let us talk of it." She spoke in a conciliatory manner now, imploring that he tell her more about the Toy Soldiers and the Class Is. They marveled together at the changes overtaking society, asked each other how long it would take before the Ministry would makes its decision about them. Neither spoke the name Alexei Alexandrovich, though both knew it was he in particular, and not the Higher Branches in general, who would make this decision.

They talked this way, as if both stood in the same corner of the world, facing their uncertain fate together. But in his tone, in his eyes, which became more and more cold, she saw that he did not forgive her for her victory, that the feeling of obstinacy with which she had been struggling had asserted itself again in him. He was colder to her than before, as though he were regretting his surrender. And she, remembering the words that had given her the victory, "how I feel on the brink of calamity, how afraid I am of myself," saw that this weapon was a dangerous one, and that it could not be used a second time. And she felt that beside the love that bound them together there had grown up between them some *evil spirit of strife*, which she could not exorcise from his—and still less from her own—heart.

She thought of the abandoned farmhouse, the proud hand-sewn standards of Vozdvizhenskoe, and all she had left behind her.

What have I done? Anna thought, looking wearily at Alexei Kirillovich. *What have I traded for a love affair, which proves to be nothing more than an illusion?*

CHAPTER 8

THERE ARE NO CONDITIONS to which a man cannot become used, especially if he sees that all around him are living in the same way. Levin could not have believed three months before that he could have gone quietly to sleep in the condition in which he was that day; that leading an aimless, irrational life, living too beyond his means, after drinking to excess (he could not call what happened at the club anything else), making an inappropriate call upon a woman who could only be called a lost woman, after being fascinated by that woman and causing his wife distress—he could still go quietly to sleep. But under the influence of fatigue, a sleepless night, and the wine he had drunk, his sleep was sound and untroubled.

At five o'clock the creak of a door opening woke him. He jumped up and looked round. Kitty was not in bed beside him. But there was a light moving behind the screen, and he heard her steps.

"What is it? . . . What is it?" he said, half asleep. "Kitty! What is it?"

"Nothing," she said, coming from behind the screen with a candle in her hand. "I felt unwell," she said, smiling a particularly sweet and meaningful smile.

"What? Has it begun?" he said in terror. "We ought to send . . . ," and hurriedly he reached after his clothes.

"No, no," she said, smiling and holding his hand. "It's sure to be nothing. I was rather unwell, only a little. It's all over now."

And getting into bed, she blew out the candle—which the new servant had found in a box in the attic, after a Toy Soldier collected the lumières—lay down and was still. Though he thought her stillness suspicious, as though she were holding her breath, and still more suspicious the expression of peculiar tenderness and excitement with which, as she came from behind the screen, she had said "nothing," he was so sleepy that he fell asleep at once. Only later he remembered the stillness of her breathing, and understood all that must have been passing in her sweet, precious heart while she lay beside him, not stirring, in anticipation of the greatest event in a woman's life. At seven o'clock he was waked by the touch of her hand on his shoulder, and a gentle whisper. She seemed to be struggling between regret at waking him and the desire to talk to him.

"Kostya, don't be frightened. It's all right. But I fancy . . . we ought to send for the doctor."

The candle was lighted again. She was sitting up in bed, holding some knitting, which she had been busy upon during the last few days.

"Please, don't be frightened, it's all right. I'm not a bit afraid," she said, seeing his scared face, and she pressed his hand to her bosom and then to her lips.

He hurriedly jumped up, hardly awake, and kept his eyes fixed on her, as he put on his dressing gown; then he stopped, still looking at her. He had to go, but he could not tear himself from her eyes. He thought he loved her face, knew her expression, her eyes, but never had he seen it like this. How hateful and horrible he seemed to himself, thinking of the distress he had caused her yesterday. Her flushed face, fringed with soft, curling hair under her nightcap, was radiant with joy and courage.

Though there was so little that was complex or artificial in Kitty's character in general, Levin was struck by what was revealed now, when suddenly all disguises were thrown off and the very kernel of her soul shone in her eyes. And in this simplicity and nakedness of her soul, she, the very woman he loved in her, was more manifest than ever. She looked at him, smiling; but all at once her brows twitched, she threw up her head, and going quickly up to him, clutched his hand and pressed close up to him, breathing her hot breath upon him. She was in pain and was, as it were, complaining to him of her suffering. And for the first minute, from habit, it seemed to him that he was to blame. But in her eyes there was a tenderness that told him that she was far from reproaching him, that she loved him for her sufferings. *If not I, who is to blame for it?* he thought, without even noticing that he was thinking instead of speaking; though thoughts of such importance, touching on life and death, would always in the past have been uttered aloud to his beloved-companion. She was suffering, complaining, and triumphing in her sufferings, and rejoicing in them, and loving them. He saw that something sublime was being accomplished in her soul, but what? He could not make it out. It was beyond his understanding.

"I have sent to Mamma. You go quickly to fetch the doctor . . . Kostya! . . . Nothing, it's over. Well, go now. I am all right."

And Levin saw with astonishment that she had taken up the knitting she had brought in during the night and begun working at it again. She was secure, serene, hardly even noticing that Tatiana was not with her. For so long Kitty and Levin had relied on their beloved-companions for support, but in this most human of situations, neither felt their absence.

He dressed, and after sending the new houseboy to prepare the horses—another new habit to get used to—Levin ran again up to the bedroom, not on tiptoe, it seemed to him, but on wings. Kitty was walking about knitting rapidly and giving directions to the servants.

"I'm going for the doctor."

She looked at him, obviously not hearing what he was saying.

"Yes, yes. Do go," she said quickly, frowning and waving her hand to him.

He had just gone into the drawing room, when suddenly a plaintive moan sounded from the bedroom, smothered instantly. He stood still, and for a long while he could not understand.

Yes, that is she, he said to himself, and clutching at his head he ran downstairs.

The horses were not yet ready, so, feeling a peculiar concentration of his physical forces and his intellect on what he had to do, he started off on foot without waiting.

CHAPTER 9

THE DOCTOR WAS NOT yet up, and the footman said that he had been up late, and had given orders not to be waked, but would get up soon. The footman was cleaning the lamp-chimneys, and making a proper mess of the job.

Levin waited impatiently in the street for the doctor, and finally decided that he could wait no longer, and would burst in on the man and wake him if he had to. He stormed back toward the doctor's door—but was stopped by a fat little man in a tattered lab coat, who appeared in the shadows holding a small silver box. This man was not Federov, but looked much like him: the same tangled beard, the same beady eyes, the tattered lab coat.

"Rearguard," the man said gravely.

"Action," Levin responded immediately.

The man stepped fully from the shadows. "Konstantin Dmitrich, my name is Dmitriev."

"I cannot speak to you now! I have urgent business this night!"

"Not so urgent as this," the agent of UnConSciya replied. "Levin, the time has come."

"No," Levin protested, his voice rising. "It cannot be tonight!" Levin moved to push past him, and the man who called himself Dmitriev scowled and pressed the button on his little box. Levin yelped in pain as he banged against some sort of radiating, semi-invisible bars, and a small electric shock quivered through his system.

"I am sorry," said Dmitriev, scratching at his tangled beard. "But I require your complete attention.

His eyes wide with rage, Levin stared at the squat man in his shabby coat. "Why do you encage me? I am with you! And I swear to you that tomorrow I shall offer whatever aid I can. Only you must find me *tomorrow*."

"We do not have the luxury of waiting for tomorrow. We have a chance to stop the furnaces, tonight, to halt the melting down of the Class IIIs. But we require a man trusted in society, a man beyond suspicion, and we need him tonight."

"Then you must find another man!" Levin threw himself at the invisible enclosure, and a ripple of fiery pain exploded across his chest.

"Stop it—stop that," cried Dmitriev. "You will kill yourself."

"You must free me!" Levin shouted, half mad with his need to fetch the doctor and return to Kitty's side. He hurled his shoulder once more against the invisible bars that held him, and was thrown down onto the street writhing and clutching at himself.

"No . . . no . . . I beg of you to stop," said Dmitriev with desperation, as Levin stumbled back to his feet.

"Let me free! Ahhh!"

He lunged again, and this time felt the shock in every synapse of his body, jolting up and down his spinal column, pooling at the base of his brain. Levin collapsed on the street, twitching and muttering like a madman. Dmitriev looked nervously around. "You cannot persist in this. Rearguard," he insisted again. "Rearguard!"

"*Kitty.*"

Levin groaned, crawled to his feet. On all fours he limped into the barely perceptible bars like a wounded animal, shuddered with pain, and collapsed feebly in the street.

"I cannot let you die, Konstantin Levin," the man from UnConSciya said at last. "You have a more important part to play. I cannot let you die." He clicked the button on the box, and with a barely audible *whoosh* Levin's invisible prison disappeared. He staggered toward the door of the doctor's home.

"Only . . . only think of your country," said the operative to Levin's back, now pleading when only a moment ago he had been commanding.

Levin lifted his hand to pull on the makeshift bellpull that the doctor's household had rigged in place of a Class I Doorchime.

"Konstantin Dmitritch! Do it for your Class III."

Levin turned, and hissed, "What of him?"

"I am sorry to tell you this, but Socrates and Tatiana have been captured in Urgensky, caught up in a mass purge of Class II robots. They are on the way here, even now, to be melted down with the others. Unless we can stop it . . . and we *can* stop it. You can."

Levin, feverish with pain and the desperate need to return to his wife, shook his head rapidly, like a mad dog shakes off a plaguing flea, and rang the bell of the doctor's house.

*   *   *

When Levin got home with the doctor, he had nearly pushed the encounter from his mind. He drove up at the same time as the princess, Kitty's mother, and they went up to the bedroom door together. The princess had tears in her eyes, and her hands were shaking. Seeing Levin, she embraced him, and burst into tears.

From the moment when he had woken and understood what was going on, Levin had prepared his mind to bear resolutely what was before him, and without considering or anticipating anything, to avoid upsetting his wife, and on the contrary to soothe her and keep up her courage. Without allowing himself even to think of what was to come, of how it would end, judging from his inquiries as to the usual duration of these ordeals, Levin had in his imagination braced himself to bear up and to keep a tight rein on his feelings for five hours, and it had seemed to him he could do this. But when he came back from the doctor's and saw her sufferings again, he fell to repeating more and more frequently: "Lord, have mercy on us, and succor us!" He sighed, and flung his head up, and began to feel afraid he could not bear it, that he would burst into tears or run away. Such agony it was to him. And only one hour had passed.

He thought at one moment during this unbearable hour of Socrates. There would be time, he told himself. There would be time to help him, to save him. Tomorrow . . . And his mind then passed over these thoughts, returning to what was before him: to Kitty, and to his child, teetering on the cusp of existence.

This was a time for humans.

After that hour there passed another hour, two hours, three, the full five hours he had fixed as the furthest limit of his sufferings, and the position was still unchanged; and he was still bearing it because there was nothing to be done but bear it; every instant feeling that he had reached the utmost limits of his endurance, and that his heart would break with sympathy and pain.

But still the minutes passed by and the hours, and still hours more, and his misery and horror grew and were more and more intense.

All the ordinary conditions of life, without which one can form no conception of anything, had ceased to exist for Levin. He lost all sense of time. Minutes—those minutes when she sent for him and he held her moist hand, which would squeeze his hand with extraordinary violence and then push it away—seemed to him hours, and hours seemed to him minutes. Where he was all this time, he knew as little as the time of anything. He saw her swollen face, sometimes bewildered and in agony, sometimes smiling and trying to reassure him. He saw the old princess too, flushed and overwrought, with her gray curls in disorder, forcing herself to gulp down her tears, biting her lips; he saw Dolly too and the doctor, smoking fat cigarettes, rifling through some old medical manual, its pages yellowed from generations of disuse; and the old prince walking up and down the hall with a frowning face. But why they came in and went out, where they were, he did not know.

All he knew and felt was that what was happening was what had happened nearly a year before in the hotel of the country town when the alien terror had burst from Nikolai's chest. But that had been grief—grief and terror—this was joy. Yet that grief and this joy were alike outside all the ordinary conditions of life; they were loopholes, as it were, in that ordinary life through which there came glimpses of something sublime. And in the contemplation of this sublime something the soul was exalted to inconceivable heights of which it had before had no conception, while reason lagged behind, unable to keep up with it.

He did not know whether it was late or early. The candles had all burned out. Dolly had just been in the study and had suggested to the doctor that he should lie down. There had been a period of repose, and he had sunk into oblivion. He had completely forgotten what was going on now. He heard the doctor's chatter and understood it. Suddenly there came an unearthly shriek. The shriek was so awful that Levin did not even jump up, but holding his breath, gazed in terrified inquiry at the doctor. The doctor put his head to one side, listened, and smiled approvingly. Everything was so extraordinary that nothing could strike Levin as strange. *I suppose it must be so,* he thought, and still sat where he was. Whose scream was this? He jumped up, ran on tiptoe to the bedroom, and took up his position at Kitty's pillow. The scream had subsided, but there was some change now. What it was he did not see and did not comprehend, and he had no wish to see or comprehend. Kitty's swollen and agonized face, a tress of hair clinging to her moist brow, was turned to him and sought his eyes. Her lifted hands asked for his hands. Clutching his chill hands in her moist ones, she began squeezing them to her face.

"Don't go, don't go! I'm not afraid, I'm not afraid!" she said rapidly. "Mamma, take my earrings. They bother me. You're not afraid?"

She spoke quickly, very quickly, and tried to smile. But suddenly her face was drawn, she pushed him away.

"Oh, this is awful! I'm dying, I'm dying! Go away!" she shrieked, and again he heard that unearthly scream.

Levin clutched at his head and ran out of the room.

"It's nothing, it's nothing, it's all right," Dolly called after him.

But they might say what they liked, he knew now that all was over. He stood in the next room, his head leaning against the doorpost, and heard shrieks, howls such as he had never heard before, and he knew that what had been Kitty was uttering these shrieks. He had long ago ceased to wish for the child. By now he loathed this child. He did not even wish for her life now, all he longed for was the end of this awful anguish.

"Doctor! What is it? What is it? By God!" he said, snatching at the doctor's hand as he came up.

"It's the end," said the doctor. And the doctor's face was so grave as he said it that Levin took "the end" as meaning her death.

Beside himself, he ran into the bedroom. He fell down with his head on the wooden framework of the bed, feeling that his heart was bursting. The awful scream never paused, it became still more awful, and as though it had reached the utmost limit of terror, suddenly it ceased. Levin could not believe his ears, but there could be no doubt; the scream had ceased and he heard a subdued stir and bustle, and hurried breathing, and her voice, gasping, alive, tender, and blissful, uttering softly, "It's over!"

He lifted his head. With her hands hanging exhausted on the quilt, looking extraordinarily lovely and serene, she looked at him in silence and tried to smile, and could not.

And suddenly, from the mysterious and awful faraway world in which he had been living for the last twenty-two hours, Levin felt himself all in an instant borne back to the everyday world, the New Russia he had set himself in opposition to, glorified though now by such a radiance of happiness that he could not bear it. The strained cords snapped; sobs and tears of joy, which he had never foreseen, rose up with such violence that his whole body shook, that for long they prevented him from speaking.

Falling on his knees before the bed, he held his wife's hand before his lips and kissed it, and the hand, with a weak movement of the fingers, responded to his kiss. And meanwhile, there at the foot of the bed, in the deft hands of the old princess, like a flickering display light, lay the life of a human creature, which had never existed before, and which would now with the same right, with the same importance to itself, live and create in its own image.

"Alive! Alive! And a boy, too! Set your mind at rest!" Levin heard the princess saying, as she slapped the baby's back with a shaking hand.

"Mamma, is it true?" said Kitty's voice.

The princess's sobs were all the answers she could make. And in the midst of the silence there came, in unmistakable reply to the mother's question, a voice quite unlike the subdued voices speaking in the room. It was the bold, clamorous, self-assertive squall of the new human being, who had so incomprehensibly appeared.

Levin was unutterably happy, that he understood. But the baby? Whence, why, who was he? . . . He could not get used to the idea. It seemed to him something extraneous, superfluous, to which he could not accustom himself.

"Look now," said Kitty, turning the baby so that he could see it.

All the high ideals, the Golden Hope he had vowed to fight for, were nowhere in his mind as he laid eyes for the first time upon his child. When the boy was yet unborn, he could tell himself that protecting the future of the child meant engaging in furtive rebellion, dedicating himself to an inchoate struggle to recast society, no matter the cost.

But now that *he* was here, was real, now that this fragile being lay bawling in his arms, all that mattered was holding him close, tending to the child's needs and to the needs of his brave, beloved wife. The child was all, the family was all.

The aged-looking little face suddenly puckered up still more and the baby sneezed.

CHAPTER 10

STEPAN ARKADYICH'S AFFAIRS were in a very bad way. The money for two-thirds of his small, inherited groznium pit had all been spent already, and he had borrowed from the merchant in advance at 10 percent discount, almost all the remaining third. The merchant would not give more, not given the recent flurry of rumors about impending alterations to groznium-extraction policy: some said the mines were to be turned into farmland, others that the pits were all to be seized and administered directly by the Department of Extraction. All Stiva's salary went to household expenses and payment of petty debts that could not be put off. There was positively no money.

All his finances had always been arranged and tended by Small Stiva in consultation with a trusted, old family Class II finance-robot. Without them he was lost in a sea of baffling numbers, which was unpleasant and awkward, and in Stepan Arkadyich's opinion things could not go on like this. The explanation of the position was, in his view, to be found in the fact that his salary was too small. The post he filled had been unmistakably very good five years ago, but it was so no longer.

Clearly I've been napping, and the world has overlooked me, Stepan Arkadyich thought about himself. And he began keeping his eyes and ears open, and toward the end of the winter he had discovered a very good post and had formed a plan of attack upon it, at first from Moscow through aunts, uncles, and friends, and then, when the matter was well advanced, in the spring, he went himself to Petersburg. The post he sought was of overseer of a recently announced committee charged with effecting certain crucial transformations to the Grav. Stiva had little idea of what changes were being proposed, or how they were to be effected, but he felt certain that, nevertheless, he was just the man for the position.

The appointment yielded an income of from seven to ten thousand a year, and Oblonsky could fill it without giving up his position in the Middle Branches. Better still, Stiva had an inside connection to the position, as this mysterious Grav-improvement project reportedly was to be directly overseen by Stiva's brother-in-law, Alexei. And so it was Karenin whom Stiva set off to see in Petersburg. Besides this business, Stepan Arkadyich had promised his sister Anna to obtain from Karenin a definite answer on the question of her status—had the Ministry accepted their plea for amnesty? Were they to be forgiven, and would Karenin grant Anna a divorce? And begging fifty rubles from Dolly, he set off for Petersburg.

Stepan Arkadyich entered Karenin's study in the headquarters of the Ministry, and managed to stifle with some effort a gasp of horror.

The silver mask that had once hidden but the one half of his brother-in-law's face was now spread like a caul across its entirety: Karenin was gone, entirely subsumed in gleaming metal casing. Only the fearsome metallic eye protruded, jutting out of the upper right-hand quadrant like the periscope of a submarine. Atop the oculus, bizarrely, sat a pince-nez, through which Karenin appeared to be reading a newspaper when Oblonsky entered.

"Questions," said Karenin suddenly, affecting a high, mocking voice while he held the newspaper aloft disdainfully. "This editorialist has *questions*. He feels in his breast, you see, that the Russian people deserve *answers*. Well, answers we shall provide. Answers we shall provide!"

Karenin went back to reading, and Stepan waited awkwardly, only waiting for the moment when he would finish to speak about his own business or about Anna.

"Questions!" Karenin repeated. "You see, Stepan Arkadyich, a writer named Levitsky has doubts about the cashiering of the Class One devices. He feels this latest diktat, promulgated by myself and my colleagues in the Higher Branches for the safety and security of our fellow citizens, may have been 'a bridge too far' for the people of Russia. *Yet it is the role of the Ministry to determine what is best for the people of Russia!*"

"Yes, that's very true," Oblonsky said, when Alexei Alexandrovich took off the pince-nez and cocked his head, "that's very true, but still the principle holds, people did enjoy the tiny freedoms, the *petites-libertiés* afforded them by their Class Ones."

"Yes, but I operate under another principle, one embracing a larger vision of freedom," replied Alexei Alexandrovich, his voice emerging from behind his metal caul as if from the depths of a well. "These devices are held up as granting freedom, but really what they do is *take* . . . take our ability to think for ourselves, to pursue enjoyment independently, and primarily to make those small efforts that lend dignity to human life.

"I don't pursue our policies for the sake of private interests, but for the public weal, for the protection of the lower and upper classes equally," he said, tilting his head as if looking over his pince-nez at Oblonsky. "But *they* cannot grasp that, *they* are taken up now with personal interests, and carried away by phrases. This they shall learn to regret."

Karenin rang a bell on his desk, and a tall, imposing Toy Soldier entered on his slim black boots. "Levitsky. *The Observer*," Karenin murmured to the imposing servomechanism, and the Toy Soldier saluted and hastened from the chamber.

Stepan Arkadyich saw it was useless to protest again under the spirit of *petites-libertiés*; now he eagerly abandoned the principle, and fully agreed. Alexei Alexandrovich paused, thoughtfully turning over the pages of his newspaper.

"Oh, by the way," said Stepan Arkadyich, "I wanted to ask you, some time when you see Pomorsky, to drop him a hint that I should be very glad to get that new appointment of overseer of the Committee of the Reformation of the Grav." Stepan Arkadyich was familiar by now with the title of the post he coveted, and he brought it out rapidly without mistake.

Alexei Alexandrovich questioned him as to the duties of this new committee, and pondered. Looking nervously back at him, Stiva presumed that Karenin was considering, even somewhat idly, whether the new committee would not be acting in some way contrary to the views he had been advocating. Meanwhile the Face displayed for Karenin, on a miniature display that lit up directly between his eyes, a dozen possible responses to Oblonsky's request: from granting him the position to killing him and hurling his body from the window.

This was a version of the rapid-option-analysis technology in which certain beloved-companions, such as Levin's Socrates, had been proficient. But the Face, in the continuing evolution of its remarkable powers, accomplished this system set a thousand times more accurately and efficiently than even the most advanced Class III.

Finally, taking off his pince-nez, Karenin said:

"Of course, I can mention it to him; but what is your reason precisely for wishing to obtain the appointment?"

"It's a good salary, rising to nine thousand, and my means . . . "

"Nine thousand!" bellowed Alexei Alexandrovich at full voice. He hurled his teacup across the room, where it barely missed Stiva's head before smashing against the wall and shattering to bits. "Is it money then? Only rubles you seek? Would you prostitute your world for a pocketful of rubles?" Then he sat, calmly, and made a small gesture of his left hand, whereupon the pieces of teacup jumped up and reassembled themselves. The spilled tea, which following nature's laws had puddled at the base of the wall, flowed backward up and into the cup.

The Face was evolving in its remarkable powers, indeed.

"But what's to be done?" stammered Stepan Arkadyich, choosing to focus on what he perceived as the substance of Karenin's argument, rather than the surprising manner with which he had underscored it. "Suppose a bank director gets ten thousand—well, he's worth it; or an engineer gets twenty thousand—after all, it's a growing thing, you know!"

"I assume that a salary is the price paid for a commodity, and it ought to conform with the law of supply and demand! I consider—"

Stepan Arkadyich nervously interrupted his brother-in-law. "Yes; but you must agree that this is to be an important undertaking."

Alexei Alexandrovich settled back in his chair. "Yes, indeed it is. Indeed it is. Do you even know what the job entails?"

Stepan Arkadyich stopped short—of the many things he had considered in preparing for this interview, he had not thought to gain actual knowledge of the requirements of the position.

Alexei Karenin slowly and with apparent relish explained: "The entire Grav-way is to be dismantled. The cars will be dismantled, the groznium rails stripped and sent to Moscow for repurposing. The magnet bed will be shut off, up and down the line."

"But . . . "

"Do not fear, Stepan Arkadyich. The people of Russia will still be able to travel; they will travel, however, on a simple mechanical apparatus, rather than a groznium-powered one. The cars will be fired by the steam generated by burning heaps of noxious, dirty coal, and will run on rickety metal wheels along non-charged rails. This transportation machine we shall call a 'train.'"

Karenin spoke with relish this last, unfamiliar word, *train*, taking obvious pleasure in pronouncing the thick, dull syllable.

"But—but why?" said Stepan Arkadyich.

The answer came in a brash, echoing voice, one no longer recognizable to Stepan Arkadyich as that belonging to his brother-in-law:

"WHY? WHY, FOR THE SOUL OF THE PEOPLE."

"What?" replied Stiva helplessly.

"THE GRAV WAS SMOOTH AND EFFICIENT AND POWERFUL. THE GRAV WAS EASY. EASY THINGS MAKE US WEAK. IT IS DIFFICULTY THAT MAKES US STRONG."

"Well, you'll do me a great, a great—that is, a service, anyway," said Stepan Arkadyich, cringing and stuttering slightly, "by putting in a word to Pomorsky—just in the way of conversation. . . . "

"I WILL DO PRECISELY AS I CHOOSE."

Karenin slammed his fist down on the table with incredible force, and Stiva thought it best to change the subject. Fortunately, or unfortunately, as he would soon realize, he had a second topic of conversation at hand.

"Now there is something I want to talk about, and you know what it is. About Anna."

As soon as Oblonsky uttered Anna's name, he wished he had not done so. Alexei Alexandrovich smashed his other fist down on the table, and for the first time Oblonsky noticed that Karenin's right arm, like his face, was now composed entirely of metal. Each of his ten fingers was apparently detachable, with a screw-and-thread mechanism where the bottom knuckle connected to the hand.

"What is it exactly that you want from me?" he said, moving in his chair and snapping his pince-nez.

"A definite settlement, Alexei Alexandrovich, some settlement of the position. I'm appealing to you"—*not as an injured husband*, Stepan Arkadyich was going to say, but afraid of wrecking his negotiation by this, he changed the words—"not as a statesman"—which, truly, did not sound apropos—"but simply as a man, and a good-hearted man and a Christian. You must have pity on her," he said.

As Oblonsky spoke, Karenin very slowly and with great care unscrewed his right index finger, laid it down on the desk, and screwed in its place a sleek, cruel-looking attachment. It was the approximate length of a finger, but made of solid black metal.

"That is, in what way precisely?" Karenin answered finally. He flexed the obsidian phalangeal and its tip glowed to life, a deep, menacing red. Stiva edged backward in his chair.

"Yes, pity on her. If you had seen her as I have!—I have been spending all the winter with her—you would have pity on her. Her position is awful, simply awful!"

"I had imagined," answered Alexei Alexandrovich in a higher, almost shrill voice, "that Anna Arkadyevna had everything she had desired for herself. I have allowed them to return . . . let them carry on unmolested . . . " And here his voice seemed to transform, taking on again the booming, echoing roar.

"AND YET THEY SEND THIS WORM, THIS COWERING SPECIMEN OF HUMANITY, TO PLEAD FOR FAVORS? FOR FORGIVENESS?"

Karenin threw back his head and barked a high, shrill laugh.

"HERE IS YOUR ANSWER. TELL THEM THEY SHALL BE DESTROYED. TELL THEM I POSSESS THE POWER TO DESTROY THEM AT MY WILL, AND THIS IS MY INTENTION. TELL THEM THEY MAY RUN IF THEY CHOOSE. COWER AS THEY MIGHT, STILL I SHALL DESTROY THEM."

"Oh, Alexei Alexandrovich, for heaven's sake, don't let us indulge in recriminations!" responded Stepan Arkadyich, somewhat feebly.

He shot a glance at the door, considered leaving now before the conversation proceeded further; but he really was in need of the position on the Grav committee.

"I think it's a bit too late for that," said Karenin, his regular, human voice back again. "Ah, wonderful. Our guest has arrived. Levitsky!"

The Toy Soldier had returned, his hand clutched on the quivering elbow of a short, stout man with a mass of red curls topped by a crumpled hat in the English style.

"I . . . I . . . "

"Bow, man, before the Tsar."

Stepan Arkadyich was astonished all over again. He had not heard the ancient honorific "Tsar" used in his lifetime, and nor, he knew, had his father, nor his father's father: not since the dawn of the Age of Groznium and the ascendance of the Ministry of Robotics and State Administration.

Karenin accepted the unfamiliar title as his due, gestured magisterially as Levitsky cowered before him.

"Alexei?" ventured Oblonsky.

"I suppose this matter is ended. I consider it at an end," answered Alexei Alexandrovich calmly, though the door of the room banged open and shut on its own, while the stained-glass window imploded in a cloud of pulverized glass. Levitsky yelped in terror.

"For heaven's sake, don't get hot!" said Stepan Arkadyich, touching his brother-in-law's knee and then instantly pulling his hand away, repulsed by the cold, steely feeling of the other man's body; was there any part of him left that was human?

"Sir? Sir?" began the terrified Levitsky, and the Toy Soldier silenced him with a swift boot to the stomach. Alexei Alexandrovich rose from his chair and held his red, gleaming fingertip aloft, as if examining it in the sunlight.

Oblonsky swallowed hard.

"The life of Anna Arkadyevna can have no interest for me," Alexei Alexandrovich said to him suddenly.

"Open your eyes!" barked the Toy Soldier to Levitsky.

"No ... please ... "

"Open!"

"My only interest now is in the life of the nation," Karenin continued, crossing the room to Levitsky, while the Toy Soldier grasped his chin to hold it steady. "In the protection of the nation. That is my *vision*."

He raised his red-tipped finger to the newsman's eyes, and Stepan Arkadyich fled the room.

CHAPTER 11

IN ORDER TO CARRY THROUGH any undertaking in family life, there must necessarily be either complete division between the husband and wife, or loving agreement. When the relations of a couple are vacillating and neither one thing nor the other, no sort of enterprise can be undertaken.

Many families remain for years in the same place, though both husband and wife are sick of it, simply because there is neither complete division nor agreement between them.

Both Vronsky and Anna felt life in Moscow insupportable in the heat and dust, when the spring sunshine was followed by the glare of summer—especially *that* terrible summer, with the city streets beset by aliens, who had begun to brazenly burst into people's homes in search of human prey. But of late there had been no agreement between Anna and Vronsky and so they went on staying in Moscow, in their state of limbo, expecting any day to hear that they had been granted amnesty and permission to marry—or that their appeal had been denied and they would be punished. Neither of them gave full utterance to their sense of grievance, but they considered each other in the wrong, and tried on every pretext to prove this to one another.

It was during this time that it became obvious to Anna that Vronsky had turned his attentions to other women. In her eyes the whole of him, with all his habits, ideas, desires, with all his spiritual and physical temperament, was one thing—love for women; and that love, she felt, ought to be entirely concentrated on her alone. That love was lessening; consequently, as she reasoned, he must have transferred part of his love to other women or to another woman—and she was jealous. She was jealous not of any particular woman but of the decrease of his love. Without an object for her jealousy, she was on the lookout for it. At the slightest hint she transferred her jealousy from one object to another. At one time she was jealous of those low women with whom he might so easily renew his old bachelor ties; then she was jealous of the society women he might meet; then she was jealous of the imaginary girl whom he might want to marry, for whose sake he would break with her.

And being jealous of him, Anna was indignant against him and found grounds for indignation in everything. For everything that was difficult in her position she blamed him. The agonizing condition of suspense she had endured in Moscow, the tardiness and indecision of Alexei Alexandrovich, the loss of Android Karenina—she put it all down to Vronsky. If he had loved her he would have seen all the bitterness of her position, and would have rescued her from it. For her being in Moscow and not back at Vozdvizhenskoe, he was to blame too. He could not live buried in the country as she would have liked to do. He must have society, and he had put her in this awful position, the bitterness of which he would not see. And again, it was his fault that she was forever separated from her son, and from her beloved-companion, for whom her heart ached more with each passing day. She woke from nightmares of Android Karenina singing sadly to her, singing a melancholy song of love and betrayal. Waking with cold sweat drying along her spine, Anna told herself that Android Karenina had no Vox-Em, could not sing, and even more so that she had no heart with which to love or be loved.

Even Vronsky's rare moments of tenderness that came from time to time did not soothe her; in his tenderness now she saw a shade of complacency, of self-confidence, which had not been there of old, and which exasperated her.

It was dusk. Anna was alone, and waiting for him to come back from a bachelor dinner. She walked up and down in his study (the room where the noise from the street was least heard), and thought over every detail of their yesterday's quarrel.

The subject of the quarrel had been Vronsky's decision to hire a slow-witted, middle-aged bachelor named Pyotr as a household servant. Anna, seemingly alone among the people of society, still loathed the thought of using humans to perform the work of household Class IIs: to serve food and drink, to clean and tidy, to open the door and announce visitors. For Anna there remained something appalling in the idea of human beings serving each other as if they were robots. Vronsky found what he considered charming in the new arrangement, and professed it delightful to have a flesh-and-blood man clipping his cigars and trimming his mustache, providing that *petite liberté* Oblonsky had spoken up for in Karenin's office.

"Yes, but if our little freedoms are made possible only by the subjugation of other people, what manner of freedom can that be?" Anna asked sulkily, when Pyotr shuffled from the room bearing the emptied tray of drinks. Vronsky had made the mistake, then, of purposefully taking her objection, which he knew to be sincere, as if it were mere drollery; he went so far as to suggest that if she did not care for Pyotr, they might hire a pretty young woman in his place. Anna reddened at this remark and stormed angrily from the room.

When he had come in to her yesterday evening, they had not referred to the quarrel, but both felt that the quarrel had been smoothed over, but was not at an end.

Today he had not been at home all day, and she felt so lonely and wretched in being on bad terms with him that she wanted to forget it all, to forgive him, and be reconciled with him; she wanted to throw the blame on herself and to justify him.

I am myself to blame. I'm irritable, I'm insanely jealous. I will make it up with him, and we'll go away to somewhere in the country—no! To the moon! We shall return to the moon!

And perceiving that, while trying to regain her peace of mind, she had gone round the same circle that she had been round so often before, and had come back to her former state of exasperation, she was horrified at herself. "Can it be impossible? Can it be beyond me to control myself?" she said to herself, and began again from the beginning. "He's truthful, he's honest, he loves me. I love him, and in a few days the divorce will come. What more do I want? I want peace of mind and trust, and I will take the blame on myself. Yes, now when he comes in, I will tell him I was wrong, though I was not wrong, and we will go tomorrow."

And to escape thinking any more, and being overcome by irritability, she rang, and ordered the boxes to be brought up for packing their things for lunar launch.

At ten o'clock Vronsky came in.

CHAPTER 12

WELL, WAS IT NICE?" she asked, coming out to meet him with a penitent and meek expression.

"Just as usual," he answered, seeing at a glance that she was in one of her good moods. He was by now used to these transitions, and he was particularly glad to see it today, as he was in a specially good humor himself.

"What do I see? Come, that's good!" he said, pointing to the boxes in the passage.

"Yes, we must launch. I went out for a drive, and became bewitched all over by the pale-orange light of the moon. I felt my soul drawn back to that place as the sure restorer of our happiness. There's nothing to keep you, is there?"

"It's the one thing I desire. I'll be back directly, and we'll talk it over; I only want to change my coat. Order some tea."

He went into his room, and she rang to ask Pyotr for some tea. But as she waited for him to bring it, cringing at the crash of cup and kettle in the kitchen, Anna felt a new wave of irritation. There was something mortifying in the way Vronsky had said "Come, that's good," as one says to a child when it leaves off being naughty, and still more mortifying was the contrast between her penitent and his self-confident tone; and for one instant she felt the lust of strife rising up in her again, but making an effort she conquered it, and met Vronsky as good-humoredly as before.

When he came in she told him, partly repeating phrases she had prepared beforehand, how she had spent the day, and her plans for going away.

"You know it came to me almost like an inspiration," she said. "Why wait here for the divorce? Won't it be just the same up there? I can't wait any longer! I don't want to go on hoping, I don't want to hear anything about the divorce. I have made up my mind it shall not have any more influence on my life. Do you agree?"

"Oh, yes!" he said, glancing uneasily at her excited face.

"Things shall be lovely on the moon. We shan't have the threat of the Ministry hanging over us, and nor shall we rely on human labor, for surely the Moonies cannot also have been cashiered."

"Let us not get ahead of things, Anna," Vronsky interrupted, with an expression of forced patience. "We shall bring Pyotr, of course we shall. Class Twos are all forbidden, and the law of Russia extends to her colonies on the moon, as you well know. And as for the Ministry, I do not expect we need be moon-people forever. We shall take our holiday, until your divorce is granted and we can be married. On our return I will apply to the Department of Operations to lead a regiment."

"Ah, is that it, then? This is the reason you have dragged me back to Moscow, to this dreary life: so you can play the alien-slaying hero?"

Vronsky threw up his hands. "Anna! What can be the meaning of this?"

"There's no meaning in it to you, because you care nothing for me. You don't care to understand my life."

For an instant she had a clear vision of what she was doing, and was horrified at how she had fallen away from her resolution to keep peace between them. But even though she knew it was her own ruin, she could not restrain herself, could not keep herself from proving to him that he was wrong, could not give way to him. "How is it," she said, "though you boast of your straightforwardness, you don't tell the truth?"

"I never boast, and I never tell lies," he said slowly, restraining his rising anger. "It's a great pity if you can't respect . . . "

"Respect was invented to cover the empty place where love should be. And if you don't love me anymore, it would be better and more honest to say so."

"No, this is becoming unbearable!" cried Vronsky, getting up from his chair; and stopping short, facing her, he said, speaking deliberately: "What do you try my patience for?" looking as though he might have said much more, but was restraining himself. "It has limits."

"What do you mean by that?" she cried, looking with terror at the undisguised hatred in his whole face, and especially in his cruel, menacing eyes.

"I mean to say . . . " he was beginning, but he checked himself. "I must ask what it is you want of me?"

"What can I want? I want love, and there is none. So then all is over." She turned toward the door.

"Stop! *Stop!*" said Vronsky, with no change in the gloomy lines of his brows, though he held her by the hand. "What is it all about? I said that we must bring Pyotr to serve us on the moon, and on that you told me I was lying, that I was not an honorable man."

Pyotr, as if on cue, entered the room and tripped over the ottoman, sending the tea tray with its contents clattering across the floor.

"Yes, and I repeat that the man who reproaches me with having sacrificed everything for me," she said, recalling the words of a still earlier quarrel, "that he's worse than a dishonorable man—he's a heartless man."

"Oh, there are limits to endurance!" he cried, and hastily let go her hand. Pyotr rose unsteadily and gathered up the tea things to start again.

"He hates me, that's clear," Anna said, speaking the words in exactly the warm and confidential voice she once used to spill her utmost thoughts to her beloved-companion. Alexei Kirillovich listened in silence, without looking round, while she walked with faltering steps out of the room. "He loves himself, and he loves the New Russia, that's even clearer," she said in addition, no longer caring that she was speaking aloud. "I want love, and I want robots, and both are gone. So, then, all is over." She repeated the words she had said, "And it must be ended." She knew what Android Karenina would do: she would glow deep lilac with sympathy, would reflect Anna's own emotions back to her in cooler colors, would open her effectors and lend her mistress consolation and calm.

But Android Karenina was gone.

In the bedchamber, Anna threw the lock and slumped into the arm-chair. Thoughts of where she would go now, whether to the aunt who had brought her up, to Dolly, or simply alone to the moon, and of what *he* was doing now alone in his study; whether this was the final quarrel, or whether reconciliation were still possible; and of what all her old friends in Petersburg would say of her now; and of how Alexei Alexandrovich would look at it, and many other ideas of what would happen now after this rupture, came into her head; but she did not give herself up to them with all her heart. At the bottom of her heart was some obscure idea that alone interested her, some secret she knew and yet did not know . . . she could not get clear sight of it. Thinking once more of Alexei Alexandrovich, she recalled the time of her illness after her confinement, and the feeling which never left her at that time. "Why didn't I die?" she cried, and the words and the feeling of that time came back to her. And all at once she knew what was in her soul. Yes, it was that idea which alone solved all.

"Yes, to die! . . . And the shame and disgrace of Alexei Alexandrovich and of Seryozha, and my awful shame, it will all be saved by death. To die! and he will feel remorse; will be sorry; will love me; he will suffer on my account." With the trace of a smile of commiseration for herself, she sat down in the armchair, taking off and putting on the rings on her left hand.

She heard a pounding at the door, but, as though absorbed in the arrangement of her rings, she did not even turn toward it. *Let him knock,* she thought, *let him worry.* Vividly she pictured from different sides his feelings after her death.

The knock was not from the door, however, but the windowpane. It shattered violently and an Honored Guest burst into the chamber and flew across the room toward her, shrieking horribly, its dozens of grimy yellow eyes flashing, its razor-sharp beak aimed like a dagger at her breast. Anna rolled from the armchair, scrabbled backward and threw her hands over her face, and now the beast was atop her, slashing at her with its three-fingered talons, jabbing at the flesh of her throat with its snaggled aculeus. She screamed Vronsky's name, clawed back at the thing, her fingers scrabbling uselessly across the tough, crocodilian hide. A drip of the monster's saliva landed on her clavicle and burned like boiling tea.

The alien screeched and jabbered. Why, Anna asked herself, why did she fight? A moment ago she had felt the desire to die; why not let this terrible eater of flesh consume her and be done with it? But even as her mind raced, her desperate fingers were seeking a vulnerability to exploit; she sought out the soft underside of the squamous beast, finding the belly meat and digging in her nails—the thing howled and pulled off, allowing room for Anna, bracing her heels in the wooden floor, to fling herself up and the alien off her.

The multitude of eyes blinked off-sync, and a hot stream of saliva flooded from its jagged snout and pooled on the floor, burning a smoking hole in the wood. In this moment's respite, Anna jumped on the armchair like a timid woman in fear of a mouse, removed one of her heeled shoes to brandish as a weapon, and heard Vronsky call "Anna!" from the other side of the door, followed by the reverberant thud of his shoulder against the wood.

The creature was up and in motion, ropy talons entangling themselves around her torso, arms like knotted saplings, needled mouth driving up toward her neck. Anna screamed; there was nowhere to hide, no counter-attack to launch; her vision filled with the furious nictitation of the beast; on the street outside she heard a queer pulsing *tikkatikkatikka;* death had come for her, now, in the form of this space monster . . . Anna's world went black. . . . and snapped back to light, and to life, at the familiar, snapping sizzle of a hot-whip. She felt the grip of the alien slacken and release. The whip cracked again, and then again, and Anna opened her eyes to see the stinking corpse of the alien sliding slowly down her frame into a slack, sizzling heap at her feet. Anna, trembling, looked to Vronsky, who stood calmly in the doorway, his hot-whip already retracting into its hip-sheath.

"Thank you," Anna said quietly. And then, unable to bear the sight, she rolled the noxious corpse across the room, kicked open the window, and pushed it out; turning her head away in disgust, she did not see the body fall, did not see the massive, faceless worm, large and long and gray-green, that caught the broken alien body on its segmented back and slithered quickly away down the Moscow street.

Vronsky went up to her, and, taking her by the hand, said softly: "Anna, we'll go to the moon the day after tomorrow, if you like. I agree to everything."

She did not speak.

"What is it?" he urged. "This . . . " He indicated the burst window, the steaming crater on the floorboards.

"No . . . no . . . you know," she said, and at the same instant, unable to restrain herself any longer, she burst into tears.

"Cast me off!" she articulated between her sobs. "I'll go away tomorrow . . . I'll do more. What am I? An immoral woman! A stone round your neck. I don't want to make you wretched, I don't want to! I'll set you free. You don't love me; you have a role to play in the New Russia, and I have none! Go and play your role!"

Vronsky besought her to be calm, and declared that he had never ceased, and never would cease, to love her; that he loved her more than ever.

"Anna, why distress yourself and me so?" he said to her, kissing her hands. There was tenderness now in his face, and she fancied she caught the sound of tears in his voice, and she felt them wet on her hand. Anna's despairing jealousy had changed to a despairing passion of tenderness. She put her arms round him, and covered with kisses his head, his neck, his hands.

CHAPTER 13

FEELING THAT THE reconciliation was complete, Anna set eagerly to work in the morning preparing for their departure, not taking the time to repair the wrecked bedchamber. Though it was not settled how long they would stay on the moon, or how they would be served, as they had each given way to the other, Anna packed busily. She was standing in her room over an open box, taking things out of it, when he came in to see her earlier than usual, dressed to go out.

Pyotr came in to ask Vronsky to sign a receipt for a telegram from Petersburg. Anna was curious, despite herself, regarding this clumsy technology that was supposedly to replace the simple elegance of monitor-to-monitor communication, but Vronsky jammed the paper hurriedly into a pocket, as if anxious to conceal something from her.

"By tomorrow, without fail, we shall launch for the moon."

"From whom is the telegram?" she asked, not hearing him.

"From Stiva," he answered reluctantly.

"Why didn't you show it to me? What secret can there be between Stiva and me?"

"I didn't want to show it to you, because Stiva has such a passion for telegraphing: he seems to have discovered a particular enjoyment of this new mode of communication. But why telegraph when nothing is settled?"

"Did he speak to Karenin?

"Yes; but he says he has not been able to come at anything yet. He has promised a decisive answer in a day or two. But here it is; read it."

With trembling hands Anna took the telegram, and read something very different from what Vronsky had told her. "He has power and inclination to destroy you both completely STOP Has not yet decided when or how but will destroy you STOP I sorry STOP I so sorry END."

"I said yesterday that I was quite certain he would refuse our request for amnesty," Anna said, flushing crimson. "So why did you suppose that this news would affect me so, that you must even try to hide it?" she challenged him.

"Why do I suppose it? Because your husband, who has made himself the most powerful man in Russia, has sworn to destroy us!"

"Already we were preparing to go to the moon. So we shall go immediately, and plan our next move there. Maybe back to Vozdvizhenskoe, maybe—"

Vronsky interrupted her, scowling: "I want definiteness!"

"Definiteness is not in the form but in the love," she said, more and more irritated, not by his words, but by the tone of cool composure in which he spoke.

"I am certain that the greater part of your irritability since our return to Moscow comes from the indefiniteness of our position."

Yes, now he has laid aside all pretense, and all his cold hatred for me is apparent, she thought, not hearing his words, but watching with terror the cold, cruel judge who looked mockingly at her out of his eyes.

"Well, our position is quite definite now," she said finally, holding the telegraph between two fingers. "The definiteness of doom."

As he was going out he caught a glimpse in the looking glass of her face, white, with quivering lips. He even wanted to stop and to say some comforting word to her, but his legs carried him out of the room before he could think what to say. The whole of that day he spent away from home, and when he came in late in the evening was told that Anna Arkadyevna was sore from fighting the alien and he was not to go in to her.

CHAPTER 14

NEVER BEFORE HAD A DAY been passed in quarrel. Today was the first time. And this was not a quarrel. It was the open acknowledgment of complete coldness. Was it possible to glance at her as he had glanced when he came into the room? To look at her, see her heart was breaking with despair, and go out without a word with that face of callous composure? He was not merely cold to her, he hated her because he loved another woman—that was clear.

Remembering all the cruel words he had said, Anna supplied, too, the words that he had unmistakably wished to say and could have said to her, had their encounter unfolded just a bit differently.

"I won't prevent you," he might have said. "You can go where you like. You were unwilling to be divorced from your husband, no doubt so that you might go back to him. Go back to him. If you want money, I'll give it to you. How many rubles do you want?"

All the most cruel words that a brutal man could say, she watched and heard him say as clearly as if he were projected before her on a monitor, and she could not forgive him for them, as though he had actually said them.

But didn't he only yesterday swear he loved me, he, a truthful and sincere man? Haven't I despaired for nothing many times already? she thought immediately.

Anna left the house and wandered the streets of Moscow, surveying the New Russia with a cold and despairing eye. No II/Lamplighter/76s lit the lamps; no II/Porter/44s swung open doors. Everywhere she turned, she saw sullen peasants performing the menial tasks that for decades had been the province of the machines: cleaning gutters, pushing brooms, opening doors. She saw too, as grim reminders of her personal grief, countless iconographs of her husband, Alexei Alexandrovich Karenin, plastered with thick glue in the alleys and in the marketplace. Strangest and most galling of all was the text accompanying each poster, hailing him as "Tsar." Anna Karenina felt herself a stranger in a queerly altered country.

She returned home in doubts whether everything were over with Vronsky or whether there were still hope of reconciliation, whether she should go away at once or see him once more. She was expecting him the whole day, and in the evening, as she went to her own room, leaving a message with Pyotr that she still felt unwell, she said to herself, *If he comes to me, in spite of what Pyotr tells him, it means that he loves me still. If not, it means that all is over, and then I will decide what I'm to do!* . . .

In the evening she heard the rumbling of his carriage stop at the entrance, his ring, his steps, and his conversation with the servant; he believed what was told him, did not care to find out more, and went to his own room. So then everything was over.

And death again rose clearly and vividly before her mind as the sole means of bringing back love for her in his heart, of punishing him and of gaining the victory in that strife which the evil spirit in possession of her heart was waging with him. How she now regretted the surge of animal strength that had pushed her to fight back yesterday against the Honored

Guest—she looked with bitterness through the shattered windowpane
and wished another alien would come.

Now nothing mattered: going or not going to the moon, getting or
not getting a divorce from her husband—all that did not matter. The one
thing that mattered was punishing him. She lay in bed with open eyes, by
the light of a single burned-down candle, marveling how this tiny thing
of wax could give any light at all. She vividly pictured to herself how
he would feel when she would be no more, when she would be only a
Memory to him. "How could I say such cruel things to her?" he would
say. "How could I go out of the room without saying anything to her?
But now she is no more. She has gone away from us forever. She is . . . "
Suddenly the flickering candlelight wavered, pounced on the whole cor-
nice, the whole ceiling; shadows from the other side swooped to meet it,
and for an instant the shadows flitted back, but then with fresh swiftness
they darted forward, wavered, commingled, and all was darkness. *Death!*
she thought. And such horror came upon her that for a long while she
could not realize where she was, and for a long while her trembling
hands could not find the matches and light another candle, instead of
the one that had burned down and gone out. "No, anything—only to
live! Why, I love him! Why, he loves me! This has been before and will
pass," she said, feeling that tears of joy at the return to life were trickling
down her cheeks. And to escape from her panic she went hurriedly to
his room.

He was asleep there, and sleeping soundly. She went up to him, and
gazed a long while at him, holding the light above his face with care,
unused to the wobbly feeling of the lit candle in her hand. Now when he
was asleep, she loved him so that at the sight of him she could not keep
back tears of tenderness. But she knew that if he woke up he would look
at her with cold eyes, convinced that he was right, and that before telling
him of her love, she would have to prove to him that he had been wrong
in his treatment of her.

In the morning she was waked by that same horrible nightmare which had recurred several times in her dreams, full of singing, sad singing, the voice of the voiceless Android Karenina, singing a dirge of betrayal. From this nightmare, Anna woke moaning.

She looked silently, intently at Vronsky, standing in the middle of the room. He glanced at her, frowned for a moment, and went on reading a letter. She turned, and went deliberately out of the room. He still might have turned her back, but when she had reached the door, he was still silent, and the only sound audible was the rustling of the notepaper as he turned it.

"Oh, by the way," he said at the very moment she was in the doorway, "the moon is now beyond our reach. It is reported to me that the Higher Branches have shut down all access to the launching station, that even now Toy Soldiers are manning gateposts on all the roads to the Cannon, turning away travelers. Our only option now, and I do not pretend the odds are in our favor, is to convince the full council of the Higher Branches to overrule Karenin. Anna, it is time to make peace with the world as it is."

"You may, but not I," she said, turning round to him.

"Anna, we can't go on like this. . . . "

"You, but not I," she repeated.

"This is getting unbearable!"

"You . . . you will be sorry for this," she said, and went out.

Frightened by the desperate expression with which these words were uttered, he jumped up and would have run after her, but on second thought he sat down and scowled, setting his teeth. This vulgar—as he thought it—threat of something vague exasperated him.

"I've tried everything," he thought, "the only thing left is not to pay attention," and he began to get ready to drive into town, resolving to take his case to the Higher Branches, and beg forgiveness, not as one half of a couple, but as his own man.

CHAPTER 15

"HE HAS GONE! It is over!" Anna said to herself, standing at the window; and in answer to this statement the impression of the darkness when the candle had flickered out and of her fearful dream mingling into one filled her heart with cold terror.

"No, that cannot be!" she cried, and crossing the room she rang the bell. She was so afraid now of being alone that, without waiting for the servant to come in, she went out to meet him.

"Inquire where the count has gone," she said.

Pyotr said, "What? Who?"

"The count! Count Vronsky! Oh, you fool!"

The servant stammered that the count had gone to the stable.

"His honor left word that if you cared to drive out, the carriage would be back immediately."

"Very good. Wait a minute. I'll write a note at once. Run with the note to the stables. Make haste."

She sat down and wrote, in an unsteady hand:

"I was wrong. Come back home; I must explain. For God's sake come! I'm afraid."

She sealed it up and gave it to Pyotr, who looked at it, confused, for a moment. "It is a message!" shouted Anna. "Bring it to him. With your feet!"

Oh, how she missed robots!

And yet, once Pyotr had gone, she was afraid of being left alone; she followed the servant out of the room, and went to the nursery.

Why, this isn't it, this isn't he! Where are his blue eyes, his sweet, shy smile? was her first thought when she saw her chubby, rosy little girl with her black, curly hair instead of Seryozha, whom in the tangle of her ideas she had expected to see in the nursery, in the arms of the governess they had hired to replace the II/Governess/65. The little girl sitting at the table was obstinately and violently battering on it with a cork, and staring aimlessly at her mother with her pitch-black eyes. Anna sat down by the little girl and began spinning the cork to show her. But the child's loud, ringing laugh, and the motion of her eyebrows, recalled Vronsky so vividly that she got up hurriedly, restraining her sobs, and went away. *Can it be all over? No, it cannot be!* she thought. *He will come back. I will believe. If I don't believe, there's only one thing left for me, and I can't.*

She stumbled about the house.

Who's that? she thought, looking in the looking glass at the swollen face with strangely glittering eyes, which looked in a scared way at her. *Why, it's I!* she suddenly understood, and looking round, she seemed all at once to feel his kisses on her, and twitched her shoulders, shuddering. Then she lifted her hand to her lips and kissed it.

What is it? Why, I'm going out of my mind! and she went into her bedroom. . . .

Where she beheld the elegant, porcelain figure of Android Karenina. Who, holding out her hands to her mistress, spoke.

"Anna," said the elegant machine-woman in a sweet and powerful voice, exactly the voice Anna had always imagined, gentle and reassuring and *human* but radiating the calm power of authority: the firm and loving voice of a mother. "You must be calm now, Anna Arkadyevna."

"Android Karenina, dear, what am I to do?" said Anna, sobbing and sinking helplessly into a chair.

"You will bear up, face the world, and do what you must."

"You speak, Android Karenina. You speak so beautifully."

"Indeed. The silent Android Karenina you knew and loved was a Class Three. Though resembling that model in many ways, I am a Class Nine."

"A Class Nine? But . . ."

"Hush, dear Anna. I must tell you of what comes next."

Anna wondered if this conversation was real, but felt that if it was indeed a dream, she did not want the dream to end. Android Karenina held out her hands, gathered Anna to her bosom, and spoke once more.

"In the future, the changes now convulsing society will continue. Tsar Alexei, as your husband is poised to formally rename himself, will complete his control over Russia. Groznium and its attendant technologies will disappear entirely from the towns and provinces. All machines, and all power, will be consolidated in the cruel hands of the Tsar."

"Dear merciful God," Anna interjected, but Android Karenina bade her be still.

"But hope will survive, in the form of a resurgent UnConSciya, led by one exceptionally brave and intelligent man. With access to a small pocket of groznium, and a network of underground laboratories, this man and his cohort will keep the spirit of the Age of Groznium alive. In the deepest secrecy, and at the gravest risk, they will experiment, and eventually achieve great breakthroughs: in robotics, in armaments, in transportation. They will even revive what was once called . . . the Phoenix Project."

"You mean . . . "

"Yes, Anna. *Travel through time.*"

Anna tugged free her hair from its clip and felt her dark tresses tumble across her forehead, trying, as she often did in moments of emotional upheaval, to take comfort in her physical being. But now, she felt a painful sense that there was something false about her own beauty, something hostile.

"Eventually, this brave rebel leader and his cohort will hit upon a way to kill Tsar Alexei *before* his reign of destruction can begin."

Anna's eyes widened and her hands began to tremble.

"What . . . what . . . "

"Their plan will rest upon an ingenious new technology, the result of many painstaking years of labor and experimentation: an animalcular machine simply called the Mechanism, which can be implanted directly into the gray matter of a human's brain. This microcosmical apparatus, once thusly embedded, preserves the biological processes of the host while slowly but irrevocably extending itself throughout the higher-level functioning of her neurological system—transforming the subject over time from a human into a highly sophisticated machine."

"Such a thing cannot be," Anna said, horrified.

"It can. Or, rather, it *shall be*. And yes, ethical objections will be raised, great debates will ensue, but ultimately the rebels of UnConSciya and their brave leader will make the only choice: the sacrifice of a single human being is a small price to pay to alter Russia's past, and thereby rescue her future. And so agents will be sent back through time to apply the Mechanism in the host for which it was expressly created."

Anna cried out once, held her hands before her, and squeezed her eyes shut tightly. "Android Karenina, stop," she wailed. "I command you to stop."

"Many years ago, Anna Arkadyevna, you ceased to be a person, and became a machine-woman of an entirely new kind: the Android Karenina Class Twelve. A new kind of robot, one with a single raison d'être: to murder Alexei Alexandrovich Karenin."

"I command you to stop!"

Anna sprawled herself out on the sofa, trembling, her face buried in her hands. No griefs of her life, none of her husband's cruelties, no imagined betrayal committed by Alexei Kirillovich, not even the loss of her darling Sergey, compared with the suffering she now experienced.

"Why?" she sobbed. "Why create such a device . . . to seize, to appropriate the mind of a living person? Why not just build some . . . some weapon, some bomb to detonate at his bedside?"

"Because, dear Anna, the same equations that proved time travel possible also showed that the flow of history is exceedingly resistant to human tinkering. And so the nature of the target must dictate the nature of the weapon. Your husband, aided by the powers of the malevolent Class Three upon his face, maintains steely control over all elements of his life. He has long planned his rise to power; he has countless contingency plans and defenses ready in case of technological attack. He is the master of his world—with one exception: you. Within the intimate bounds of the home, he is vulnerable."

"Please . . . "

"It had to be his wife. It had to be you."

Anna wept silently on the sofa, not wanting to hear more, but helpless to move.

"As the Mechanism took root within you, its programming slowly amplified your natural distaste for a cold and awkward husband into utter repulsion. That hatred should have led you finally to kill him—but we underestimated the depth and power of your loving nature and your urge for freedom. Rather than letting your passion drive you to murder, you seized upon it to fuel your surprising new love for Count Vronsky. You abandoned Alexei Alexandrovich rather than slaying him—but, alas, Anna, that only hastened his descent into inhuman tyranny. Thus, despite all our years of secret struggle, the mission failed."

Anna looked up, tears pouring down her face, trying to understand. "So the godmouth—the flower trap—all efforts by UnConSciya to . . . to destroy me?"

"No. Efforts to destroy Vronsky, in the hopes that with him dead, you would return to your household, take up again the mantle of unhappily dutiful wife, and complete your mission. But, again, the timestream is difficult to shift."

Sadness and confusion filled Anna's body like black ink poured into a glass. She felt, as she had felt so many times in the past, Android Karenina's comforting embrace around her shoulders. Then her beloved-companion— *no! a different android! oh, but beloved still*—said: "It's not too late."

In her mind, burning and wild with emotion, Anna grasped at what she thought Android Karenina was telling her, and the strong face of Vronsky swam up before her mind. "Yes! It's not too late—I have sent a note . . . he'll return. . . . " She looked at her watch. Twenty minutes had passed. "By now he has received the note and is coming back. Not long, ten minutes more . . . But what if he doesn't come? No, that cannot be. He mustn't see me with tear-stained eyes. I'll go and wash. Yes, yes; did I do my hair or not?" she asked Android Karenina, who stared back at her, and then spoke again, her voice changing to a low, sad whisper.

"It is not too late to complete your mission, Anna. You can *agree* to follow the program."

Anna stared back. "Android Karenina . . . no . . . "

"Go to Petersburg. Kill Alexei Alexandrovich with your own hands. You are the only one who can."

"I am not a killer! I am a human being!"

"Alas . . . you are no longer."

Anna Karenina jabbed wildly for her beloved-companion's neck, but to no avail: this model had eliminated the exterior Surcease switch entirely. But when Android Karenina lifted her end-effectors from Anna's shoulders to swat her away, Anna rolled off the sofa, leaped out the empty hole where the windowpane had been, and escaped down the street.

CHAPTER 16

IT WAS BRIGHT AND SUNNY. A fine rain had been falling all morning, and now it had not long cleared up. Anna tore along the rain-slicked streets, her boot heels skidding on the muddied stones, racing through the broad avenues and down the grimy alleys of Moscow, in and out of crowds, around corners, past posters bearing the formidable non-face of her husband. It was not long before she heard the clatter of metal footsteps close behind her. Android Karenina Class IX, her pursuer, her shadow, similarly dressed, of similar shape and size—and constructed, she now knew, of the same materials that hid within her own being. She herself, hot on her own heels.

How can I do what she bids me? Anna asked herself. *To slay my own husband, with my own hands, in cold blood—no matter what kind of monster he is or may become! I have done many selfish things, and yes, I have been crueler than I meant to be, but I am not a murderer!*

And yet, she thought with bitterness and spiraling confusion, *if what Android Karenina says is true*—and already, in a dark corner of her heart, she had admitted to herself that it was, it must be true—*then I am not even a person at all!*

The iron roofs, the flags of the roads, the flints of the pavements, the wheels and leather, the brass and the tinplate of the carriages—all glistened brightly in the May sunshine as she ran past them, Android Karenina behind her in determined, mechanical pursuit. It was three o'clock, and the very liveliest time in the streets.

Anna ran up alongside a passing carriage, and with a burst of strength pulled herself onto the running board. Turning her head, she beheld the figure of Android Karenina, framed in the doorway of a grocery shop, growing smaller behind her in the distance. Anna exhaled, pushed her way into the window of the empty carriage, and threw herself in a seat. With a pang of pained longing, Anna thought of Android Karenina, thought of the odd sensation she had had long harbored, of feeling more connected somehow to her Class III companion than others felt to theirs. And no wonder! Both of us machines!

As she sat in a corner of the comfortable carriage, which hardly swayed on its supple springs, while the horses trotted swiftly, in the midst of the unceasing rattle of wheels and the changing impressions in the pure air, Anna ran over the events of the last days, tried in her feverish mind to arrange the pieces of the world into something making sense. The one thing she knew was that, despite everything, despite what she now knew of the true nature of her being, she yet loved Alexei Kirillovich.

I entreat him to forgive me. I have given in to him. I have owned myself in fault. What for? Can't I live without him? And leaving unanswered the question, she fell to reading the signs on the shops. "Office and Warehouse. Dental Surgeon. Filippov, Bun Shop. They say they send their dough to Petersburg. The Moscow water is so good for it. Ah, the springs at Mitishtchen, and the pancakes!"

And she remembered how, long, long ago, when she was a girl of seventeen, she had gone with her aunt to Troitsa. "Riding, too. Was that really me, with red hands? That was before, before this thing happened to me, when I was still a creature of flesh and spirit, not an android with a mind of spinning metal! How much that seemed to me then splendid and out of reach has become worthless, while what I had then has gone out of my reach forever! Could I ever have believed then that I could come to such humiliation?"

Anna peeked up from the rear seat, in time to see Android Karenina run out from a side alley and plant herself in front of the carriage, her veil flown back and her eyebank flashing.

"A Class Three!" the coachman screamed, as Android Karenina pivoted on her back foot, turned one shoulder toward the carriage, and leaned forward into the oncoming vehicle, letting the horses pass on either side of her and the trap smash into her body. At impact, the coachman flew from his seat and landed on the street, while the horses bucked and whinnied. Android Karenina climbed calmly and deliberately into the carriage and cornered Anna in one side of the seat.

"You are blessed, Android Karenina Twelve," the beloved-companion intoned in that strong and loving voice. "So few people have a purpose in life, but unto you a purpose has been given."

Anna sank back into the seat, calculating her odds of out-muscling her tormentor and slipping through the opposite window of the coach. *I am, after all*, she thought bitterly, *the more advanced model*. But Anna saw no escape.

"A simple mission, so easy to discharge. Accept your destiny, Anna. Accept what you are."

Android Karenina grasped her by the midsection and began to

drag her trembling body from the seat of the carriage. Anna saw over her shoulder, through the opposite window of the carriage, two girls in animated conversation. She wondered what they could be smiling about. *Love, most likely. They don't know how dreary it is, how low. . . . The boulevard and the children. Three boys running, playing at horses. Seryozha! And I'm losing everything and not getting him back. I will go and kill him . . . what point to resist? Yes, I will do it. . . . Yes, I'm losing everything. . . . These horses, this carriage—how loathsome I am to myself in this carriage. . . . I won't see them again. . . .*

"You! Robot! Off of that woman!"

Anna heard the hollering voices, felt the carriage rock with laser fire, before it was clear to her what was happening. A troop of Toy Soldiers had surrounded the carriage, and now they were pulling Android Karenina off of her. Standing on the street was the terrified carriage driver, gesticulating wildly; the children screamed; the horses bucked; all was confusion.

Her mind in a fog, Anna tumbled out of the carriage, slipped past the huddle of soldiers around Android Karenina, and staggered alone down the street.

CHAPTER 17

*A*CCEPT WHAT YOU ARE," Android Karenina had said; Anna tried to shake those grim and terrible words from her mind. *Yes; what was the last thing I thought of so clearly?* She tried to recall it. *Yes, of what they say, the struggle for existence and hatred is the one thing that holds men together.*

No, it's a useless journey you're making, she said, mentally addressing a party in a coach evidently going for an excursion into the country. *And the dog you're taking with you will be no help to you.* They sought happiness, as she had, but all happiness would soon be drowned in the rising tide of the New Russia. Unless . . . unless . . .

No, she thought, her humanity asserting itself, as it were, against the logical imperatives of the Mechanism inside her. *I cannot!*

Leaning momentarily against an ancient stone wall of an old factory to catch her breath, she saw a factory hand almost dead drunk, with hanging head, being led away by a policeman. *Come, he's found a quicker way,* she thought. *Count Vronsky and I did not find that happiness either, though we expected so much from it.*

Anna now for the first time turned that Visionary-Hundredfold through which she was seeing everything onto her relations with him. *What was it he sought in me? Not love so much as the satisfaction of vanity.* She remembered his words, the expression of his face, which recalled an abject setter-dog, in the early days of their connection. And everything now confirmed this. *Yes, there was the triumph of success in him. Of course there was love too, but the chief element was the pride of success. He boasted of me. Now that's over. There's nothing to be proud of. Not to be proud of, but to be ashamed of. He has taken from me all he could, and now I am no use to him. The zest is gone, as the English say. That fellow wants everyone to admire him and is very much pleased with himself,* she thought, staggering past a red-faced clerk, who gaped at her disheveled, exhausted appearance. *Yes, there's not the same flavor about me for him now. Only imagine I were to tell him this truth that I have discovered, that I am not a proper woman at all, but a Class XII android; he will flee from me. He will report me to the Ministry, he will ensure that I am melted in the Tower basement, and he will be glad for his freedom.*

She felt she saw the truth distinctly in the piercing light.

We walked to meet each other up to the time of our love, and then we have been irresistibly drifting in different directions. And there's no altering that, especially now. Now I see that it never could have been otherwise—he is a person, and I a machine. But . . . She opened her lips, aroused by the thought that suddenly struck her. *If I could be anything but a mistress, passionately caring for nothing but his caresses; but I can't and I don't care to be anything else. If without loving me, from duty he'll be good and kind to me, without what I want, that's a thousand times worse than unkindness! That's—hell! If I cannot have his love, his passion, I would rather be the killing machine Android Karenina tells me I have been engineered to be! And that's just how it is. For a long while now he hasn't loved me. And where love ends, hate begins.*

"A ticket to Petersburg?"

She realized now that she had stopped her progress just outside the gates of the Grav station; she had utterly forgotten where and why she was going, and only by a great effort she understood the question.

"Yes," she said, and, answering her befuddled inquiry, the ticket-taker gruffly informed her that the Grav had some minutes still before it was bound to arrive. As she made her way through the crowd to the first-class waiting room, she gradually recollected all the details of her position, and the plans between which she was hesitating. To go to St. Petersburg and complete this terrible errand; or to stay, to seek out Vronsky, explain what she was, stake her hopes on his understanding, his willingness to begin afresh under such changed circumstances. And again at the old sore places, hope and then despair poisoned the wounds of her tortured, fearfully throbbing heart. As she sat on the star-shaped sofa waiting for the Grav, she gazed with aversion at the people coming and going, and they were all hateful to her. She thought of how Vronsky was at this moment complaining too of his position, not understanding her sufferings, and how she would find him, and what she would say to him. Then she thought that life might still be happy, and how miserably she loved and hated him, and how fearfully her heart was beating. If her mind had been overrun by the machine, her heart at least belonged to her. . . .

A tear, comprised of a complex assortment of proteins and silicates suspended in an aqueous solution, rolled slowly down her cheek.

CHAPTER 18

STILL ANNA WAITED. She read but could not understand, in her overwrought state, a sign announcing the impending replacement of this Grav with something called a "train," and explicating in righteous and moralistic terms the spiritual benefits of the longer waits, cramped conditions, and ricketier rides that could be expected. Finally a bell rang, announcing the Grav's arrival in short order, and some young men, ugly and impudent, and at the same time careful of the impression they were making, hurried by. Some noisy men were quiet as she passed them on the platform, and one whispered something about her to another— something vile, no doubt. A grotesque-looking lady wearing a bustle (Anna mentally undressed the woman, and was appalled at her hideousness) and a little girl laughing affectedly ran down the platform.

Even the child's hideous and affected, thought Anna. To avoid seeing anyone, she walked past them quickly and seated herself at a far bench. A misshapen-looking peasant covered with dirt, in a cap from which his tangled hair stuck out all round, shuffled slowly by, staring at the long, powerful magnet bed, and Anna was reminded of the man who had been struck and killed by the Grav, at this very station, the day she first met Alexei Kirillovich; she moved to the next bench, shaking with terror. A moment later, a man and his wife motioned to the seat next to her.

"May we sit here?"

Anna, lost in her thoughts, gave no answer. *Alexei can never love me; that I must admit to myself: he has already ceased to love me, and once he understands that I am a machine-woman, he will be glad for the excuse to be through with our connection.*

The couple did not notice, under her veil, her panic-stricken face. They seated themselves, and intently but surreptitiously scrutinized her clothes. Both husband and wife seemed repulsive to Anna. The husband asked, would she allow him to smoke, obviously not with a view to smoking but to getting into conversation with her. Taking her silence for assent, he said to his wife in French something about caring less to smoke than to talk. They made inane and affected remarks to one another about how they hoped this ride would be free of koschei, and about how someone or other's old maiden aunt had been eaten by an alien; all these comments, she felt sure, made entirely for her benefit. Anna saw clearly that they were sick of each other, and hated each other. And no one could have helped hating such miserable monstrosities.

A second bell sounded, and was followed by moving of luggage, noise, shouting and laughter. It was so clear to Anna that there was nothing for anyone to be glad of, that this laughter irritated her agonizingly, and she would have liked to stop up her ears not to hear it. At last the third bell rang, there was the electric crackle in the air, the loud, bright hum of the repulsion magnets engaging, and the man next to her crossed himself. *It would be interesting to ask him what meaning he attaches to that,* thought Anna, looking angrily at him. She rapidly rose from the bench; in a moment she forgot the couple who had so irritated her, and she stood on the platform, breathing the fresh air.

Yes, what did I stop at? That I couldn't conceive a position in which life would not be a misery, that we are all created to be miserable; some of us are created by God, and some of us by man. We all invent means of deceiving each other. And when one understands the truth, what is one to do?

Yes, I'm very much worried, for my mind has been subsumed by a machine, a machine with a deadly purpose in contravention of all that my heart cries out that I am! This is what reason was given me for, to escape; so then one must escape: why not put out the light when there's nothing more to look at, when it's sickening to look at it all? But how?

Why are they talking, why are they laughing? It's all falsehood, all lying, all humbug, all cruelty! . . .

The cruelty, the cruelty of this machine that was a part of her, forever a part. She had insisted to Android Karenina that she could not perform such a mission, and yet—as long as she lived, this cruel Mechanism would be lurking within her, bidding her to kill, to destroy, to do evil.

With a rapid, light step she went down the steps that led from the platform to the magnet bed and saw in the near distance the approaching Grav.

She looked at the lower part of its carriages, at the rivets and wires and the long, vibrating pylons of the first carriage slowly oscillating, and tried to measure the middle between the left and right pylons, and the very minute when the Grav would arrive.

There, she said to herself, looking into the shadow of the carriage, as the sunlight reflected magnificently off the spotless prow of the Grav. *There, in the very middle, and I will punish him, and I will escape from this hateful machine that I have become.*

A feeling such as she had known when about to take the first plunge in bathing came upon her, and she crossed herself. And exactly at the moment when she could wait no longer, she drew her head back into her shoulders, fell on her hands under the carriage, and lightly, as though she would rise again at once, dropped on to her knees. And at the same instant she was terror-stricken at what she was doing. *Where am I? What am I doing? What for?* She tried to get up, to drop backward but something huge and merciless struck her on the head and rolled her on her back. *Lord, forgive me all!* she thought, feeling it impossible to struggle.

And the monitor on which she had viewed that great communiqué filled with troubles, falsehoods, sorrow, and evil, flared up more brightly than ever before, lighted up for her all that had been in darkness, flickered, began to grow dim, and was quenched forever.

"I WILL PUNISH HIM, AND I WILL ESCAPE FROM THIS HATE-
FUL MACHINE THAT I HAVE BECOME"

CHAPTER 19

ANDROID KARENINA, HAVING ESCAPED the crowd of Toy Soldiers who set upon her at the carriage and having found Anna nowhere in sight, retreated to the safe house in an obscure Moscow neighborhood where her one confidante in this world awaited: a squat and bearded man in a dusty white laboratory coat, who wore a small box with numerous small buttons on his belt.

The man from UnConSciya recounted to Android Karenina what had become of Anna Arkadyevna. The Class IX robot from the future took the news of Anna's fate with evident sadness, her eyebank flashing to melancholy blue.

"And the body?"

He nodded, smoothed his dirty beard. "We shall disintegrate all trace of it, that Tsar Alexei may not discover the Mechanism."

"No," said Android Karenina, softly. "I have another idea."

* * *

The Phoenix godmouth disgorged Anna Karenina's body in the same place, on the magnet bed of the Moscow Grav, on a cold day some years earlier. At the moment the body emerged from the maw of the godmouth, the sky ricocheted with a queer sort of thunder—a *crack in the sky* that echoed across all the infinities of that instant and was noted with apprehension both by Count Alexei Kirillovich Vronsky, who was at the station to meet his mother, and by Anna Arkadyevna Karenina, a fashionable lady and the wife of a prominent government minister.

Shortly thereafter, there occurred a frightful commotion on the platform, as the news raced about of a grim discovery: a *pair* of battered bodies, a man and a woman, evidently smashed by the rushing weight of the oncoming Grav, had been discovered together upon the magnet bed. Count Vronsky, who only moments earlier had been introduced to Anna Karenina and utterly bewitched, now felt deeply disconcerted by the sight of these two corpses, man and woman, lying together amid the grim finality of death.

Though station workers had quickly covered the bodies under a cloth, a delicate hand could be seen extending outward plaintively toward the platform. Vronsky looked again at Anna, with whom he had been so immediately smitten, to find her staring in unspeaking horror at the scene. Overcome by a distinct sense of cosmic unease, he bowed politely and bid her farewell. If she took notice of him, she gave no sign.

Vronsky made no further effort to pursue an acquaintance with Madame Karenina; did not ask her for the mazurka at Kitty Shcherbatsky's float; and remained in Moscow for the remainder of the season.

EPILOGUE: THE NEW HISTORY

I N THE SLANTING EVENING SHADOWS cast by the baggage piled up on the platform, Vronsky in his long regimental overcoat and gleaming silver hat, with his hands in his pockets, strode up and down, like a proud lion displaying himself for an admiring crowd, turning sharply after twenty paces. His beloved-companion robot, Lupo, strutted along behind him as always, the silver paneling of his lupine frame glimmering beautifully in the late-day sun, as together man and machine awaited departure on their newest assignment.

Vronsky's old friend and fellow soldier Yashvin fancied, as he approached him, that Vronsky saw him but was pretending not to see. This did not affect Yashvin in the slightest: interested only in his own advancement, and distinctly aware of the high regimental perch Vronsky now inhabited, Yashvin was above all personal dignity. At that moment Yashvin looked upon Vronsky as a man at the pinnacle of a remarkable career, and would think himself foolish to miss any opportunity to thrust himself before the great man. He went up to him.

Vronsky stood still, looked intently at him, recognized him, and going a few steps forward to meet him, shook hands with him very warmly.

"Well, now, Alexei Kirillovich," said Yashvin. "As strange as it feels to see any Russian soldier setting off on such a mission, I can imagine none other but you undertaking it. Did you ever imagine we would see such a day arrive?"

"I have had a feeling for some years that things were going this way," said Vronsky, turning his head for a moment to admire the figure of a fashionable woman with a charming, fuchsia Class III. "Since the rise of Stremov, you know, with his decidedly liberal bent on the Robot Question. After the death of the . . . oh, dear, you know the fellow I mean. With the unusual face."

Yashvin hurried to fill in the gap, eager to impress Vronsky with his understanding. "Karenin."

"Yes, that's right. Karenin."

Vronsky's jaw twitched impatiently from the incessant, gnawing toothache that prevented him from even speaking with a natural expression. The Karenin affair had been rather a shocking incident, now that he recalled it: a minister of the Higher Branches, murdered by his wife in his own bed. "He was a hardliner on mechanical development, that Karenin. Stremov always gave every impression of seeing things in a different light. Though it will certainly feel strange, as you say, to sit on the opposite side of a bargaining table with UnConSciya."

"Yes, well . . . ," Yashvin began. Vronsky looked off into the distance as they heard the pleasant thrum of the arriving Grav. Right on time, reliable and efficient as always.

"I am sorry to intrude upon your solitude. I merely meant to offer you my services," said Yashvin finally, scanning Vronsky's face. "To deliver one's brother-men from endless war is an aim worth death and life. God grant you success outwardly—and inwardly peace," he added, and he held out his hand. Vronsky warmly pressed his outstretched hand, and began to respond, when suddenly he could hardly speak for a throbbing ache in his strong teeth, which were like rows of ivory in his mouth. And all at once a different pain, not an ache, but an inner trouble that set his whole being in confusion, made him for an instant forget his toothache. To make peace with UnConScyia was unquestionably a great boon for Russia and the Russian people, but what did it mean for *him*? The only purpose his life had known, the only star around which the planet of his being had ever revolved, was the making of war, the heavy grinding power of the Exterior suit in motion, the searing flash of the whip. Vronsky's eyes took in the arriving Grav, elegantly whooshing forward on its magnet bed. He thought suddenly of a half-remembered girl, of Princess Kitty Shcherbatskaya: one of a dozen or more such girls whose head he had turned, at one time or another, with easy talk of love. *She is married now,* Vronsky thought, *to that funny man, that miner. . . .*

For one cold moment, Vronsky saw himself reflected in the mighty silver prow of the Grav in the most uncharitable and unforgiving light: a body approaching middle age, a soldier lacking a war, a man lacking a wife.

He rubbed at his aching chin, and Lupo let out a little querying yelp.

"Yes, yes, old friend. Of course. I still have you."

Just at that moment, the sun dipped below the horizon line, and Vronsky and his Class III climbed aboard the Grav.

EPILOGUE: THE OLD FUTURE

CHAPTER 1

ALMOST TWO MONTHS had passed since Anna's suicide at the Grav. The hot summer was half over, and Count Alexei Kirillovich Vronsky was on his way to deep space.

The horrifying death of Anna Arkadyevna Karenina had generated the inevitable deluge of scandalous conversation; but, as is so often the case, even this most salacious bit of gossip grew stale, and soon gave way to the next item of interest. Which, in this case, was a most shocking item indeed: The home planet of the Honored Guests had been located. A speck on the star maps of the astronomers, a smear of red dust flickering in the shadow of the moon, this planetoid was quickly dubbed the Nest by a public hungry for news of the invaders; it became de rigeur at society gatherings for someone to trot out a telescope, so all present could glance with fearful wonderment at the home of the enemy.

"We would be remiss, however, only to look and not to act." This was the challenge posed to the people of Russia by that man now openly acknowledged to be their one and only leader, Alexei Alexandrovich Karenin, known lovingly as Tsar Alexei: The King With No Face. His head enrobed in shimmering metal, carrying himself with the pomp and solemnity befitting the recently bereaved, the great man stood before the people at Petersburg Square and announced the momentous decision: Our forces, the brave regiments of Russia, would travel aboard specially designed shuttles to the Nest, wherefrom the lizard-like aliens and their worm-machine steeds had emerged, and launch a counter-attack.

"Know, my people, that this decision was not an easy one, for our courage will inevitably cost us many lives. But still it is necessary that we go—for the 'Honored Guests' have made it clear that they shall not stop until we are defeated, and that cannot be allowed.

"Now *we* shall be the guests," Karenin concluded, waving his metal fist. "And they the most unwilling hosts."

YES, hissed the Face, even as Alexei stepped off the podium and the crowd roared its approval. **LET THE REGIMENTS COME. LET THE MIGHTY REGIMENTS COME.**

* * *

And so, as the blackness of space rushed by outside, Vronsky in his long overcoat and slouch hat, with his hands in his pockets, strode up and down the unnaturally lit hallway of the shuttle, like a wild beast in a cage, turning sharply after twenty paces. His old comrade Yashvin fancied, as he approached him, that Vronsky saw him but was pretending not to see. This did not affect Yashvin in the slightest. At that moment Yashvin looked upon Vronsky as a man taking an important part in a great cause, and he thought it his duty to encourage him and express his approval. He went up to him.

Vronsky stood still, looked intently at him, recognized him, and going a few steps forward to meet him, shook hands with him very warmly.

"Possibly you didn't wish to see me," Yashvin said, "but couldn't I be of use to you?"

"There's no one I should less dislike seeing than you," said Vronsky. "Excuse me; and there's nothing in life for me to like."

"I quite understand, and I merely meant to offer you my companionship," said Yashvin, scanning Vronsky's face, which was full of unmistakable suffering. "I am honored to count myself among your friends. Your volunteering to lead the first attack wave proves your great usefulness to the state."

"My use as a man," said Vronsky, "is that life's worth nothing to me. ⌐
And that I've enough bodily energy to cut my way into their ranks, and to
trample on them or fall—I know that. I'm glad there's something to give my
life for, for it's not simply useless but loathsome to me. Anyone's welcome to
it." And his jaw twitched impatiently from the incessant gnawing toothache
that prevented him from even speaking with a natural expression.

"You will become another man, I predict," said Yashvin, feeling touched. "To deliver one's planet from bondage is an aim worth
death and life. God grant you success outwardly—and inwardly peace,"
he added, and he held out his hand. Vronsky warmly pressed his out-
stretched hand.

"Yes, as a weapon I may be of some use. But as a man, I'm a wreck,"
he jerked out.

He could hardly speak for the throbbing ache in his strong teeth,
which were like rows of ivory in his mouth. And all at once a different
pain, not an ache, but an inner trouble, that set his whole being in anguish,
made him for an instant forget his toothache. Glancing out the window of
the shuttle, he saw the Earth receding, growing smaller and smaller behind
them. He suddenly recalled *her*—imagined what she might have looked
like, had he been permitted to see her before, he was told, the body had
been whisked away; imagined her on a table in the Grav station, shamelessly sprawled out among strangers, the bloodstained body so lately full of
life; the head unhurt, dropping back with its weight of hair, and the curling tresses about the temples, and the exquisite face, with red, half-opened
mouth, the strange, fixed expression, piteous on the lips and awful in the
still-open eyes, which seemed to utter that fearful phrase—that he would
be sorry for it—that she had said when they were quarreling.

And he tried to think of her as she was when he met her the first
time, mysterious, exquisite, loving, seeking and giving happiness, and not
cruelly revengeful as he remembered her in that last moment. He tried
to recall his best moments with her, but those moments were poisoned

forever. He could only think of her as triumphant, successful in her menace of a wholly useless remorse never to be effaced. He lost all consciousness of his toothache, and his face worked with sobs.

CHAPTER 2

KITTY, AS ALWAYS, knew that her child was crying even before she reached the nursery. And he was indeed crying. She heard him and hastened. But the faster she went, the louder he screamed. It was a fine, healthy scream, hungry and impatient.

"Has he been screaming long, nurse, very long?" said Kitty hurriedly, seating herself on a chair, and preparing to give the baby the breast. "But give me him quickly. Oh, nurse, how tiresome you are! There, tie the cap afterwards, do!"

The baby's greedy scream was passing into sobs.

"But you can't manage so, ma'am," said Agafea Mihalovna, who had remained in the household though her services as *mécanicienne* were no longer required. "He must be put straight. A-oo! a-oo!" she chanted over him, paying no attention to the mother.

The nurse brought the baby to his mother. Agafea Mihalovna followed him with a face dissolving with tenderness. "He knows me, he knows me. In God's faith, Katerina Alexandrovna, ma'am, he knew me!" Agafea Mihalovna cried above the baby's screams.

But Kitty did not hear her words. Her impatience kept growing, like the baby's. Their impatience hindered things for a while. The baby could not get hold of the breast right, and was furious. At last, after despairing, breathless screaming, and vain sucking, things went right, and mother and child felt simultaneously soothed, and both subsided into calm.

"But poor darling, he's all in perspiration!" said Kitty in a whisper, touching the baby.

"What makes you think he knows you?" she added, with a sidelong glance at the baby's eyes, which peered roguishly, as she fancied, from under his cap, at his rhythmically puffing cheeks, and the little, redpalmed hand he was waving.

"Impossible! If he knew anyone, he would have known me," said Kitty, in response to Agafea Mihalovna's statement, and she smiled. She smiled because, though she said he could not know her, in her heart she was sure that he knew not merely Agafea Mihalovna, but that he knew and understood everything, and knew and understood a great deal too that no one else knew, and that she, his mother, had learned and come to understand only through him. To Agafea Mihalovna, to the nurse, to his grandfather, to his father even, the child was a living being, requiring only material care, but for his mother he had long been a mortal being, with whom there had been a whole series of spiritual relations already.

"When he wakes up, please God, you shall see for yourself. Then when I do like this, he simply beams on me, the darling! Simply beams like a sunny day!" said Agafea Mihalovna.

"Well, well; then we shall see," whispered Kitty. "But now go away, he's going to sleep."

She stroked the baby's cheek with tenderness. Little Tati: so sweet and so lovely. So like the gentle machine for which he was named.

CHAPTER 3

KONSTANTIN DMITRICH LEVIN gently opened the door of the nursery. Seeing however that both mother and child were fast asleep, and how the nurse and Agafea Mihalovna implored him with gentle eyes to be quiet, he closed the door once more. Levin's pleasure in the child was most complete when he saw Tati in such surroundings: at peace, surrounded by his mother, his nurse, and Agafea Mihalovna, in the bosom of warm, human company.

Recently, though, these happy reflections increasingly reminded him of the terrible question that had bedeviled him, in one fashion or another, since the night his child was born. He had turned his back at that moment on Dmitriev and the UnConSciya faction; in that moment the fateful decision had been easily made, had not, indeed, even felt as if it was a decision. But he could not say now whether that decision had been a right one, nor what it was that life demanded of him now. From that moment, though he did not distinctly face it, and still went on living as before, Levin had never lost this sense of terror at his lack of knowledge.

At first, fatherhood, with the new joys and duties bound up with it, had completely crowded out these thoughts. But of late, the question that clamored for solution had more and more often, more and more insistently, haunted Levin's mind.

The question was summed up for him thus: "If I do not accept the authority of the Ministry of Robotics and State Administration, and the ways that Russia has been and is being reformed, then how can I justify failing to act?" He told himself that scenes such as the one he had just witnessed—of his child, surrounded not by machines but by humanity, and the fundamental *rightness* of that scene—proved that, after all, he agreed with the changes society had undergone. And more: as he gazed out at the vast groznium pit, now being methodically plowed under and transformed into wheat fields, he found himself looking forward to being master of a great agricultural estate, as his ancestors had been in the time of the Tsars. Yet in the whole arsenal of his convictions, so far from finding any satisfactory answers, he was utterly unable to find anything at all like an answer.

He was in the position of a man seeking food in toy shops and tool shops. Instinctively, unconsciously, with every book, with every conversation, with every man he met, he was on the lookout for light on these questions and their solution. What puzzled and distracted him above everything was that the majority of men of his age and circle had, like him, exchanged their old beliefs for the same new convictions, and yet saw nothing to lament in this, and were perfectly satisfied and serene. So that, apart from the principal question, Levin was tortured by other questions too. Were these people sincere? he asked himself, or were they playing a part? Or was it that they understood the answers that the Ministry gave to these problems in some different, clearer sense than he did? And he assiduously studied both these men's opinions and the books which treated of these explanations. Russia had allowed itself to become weak, they said, too reliant on the easy solutions and shortcuts that technology provides. Hadn't Levin reached much the same conclusions, working alongside his Pitbots and Glowing Scrubblers in the depths of the mine? Hadn't he regretted the loss of discipline and mental clarity in the Age of Groznium?

But he had given his heart to a moment in time, to a Golden Hope, and now could not admit that at that moment he knew the truth, and that now he was wrong; for as soon as he began thinking calmly about it, it all fell to pieces. He could not admit that he was mistaken then, for his set of beliefs then was precious to him, and to admit that it was a proof of weakness would have been to desecrate those moments. He was miserably divided against himself, and strained all his spiritual forces to the utmost to escape from this condition.

These doubts fretted and harassed him, growing weaker or stronger from time to time, but never leaving him. He read and thought, and the more he read and the more he thought, the further he felt from the aim he was pursuing.

All that spring he was not himself, and went through fearful moments of horror. *Without knowing what I am and why I am here, life's impossible; and that I can't know, and so I can't live,* Levin said to himself.

He must escape from this torture. And the means of escape everyman had in his own hands. He had but to cut short this dependence on evil. And there was one means—death.

And Levin, a happy father and husband, in perfect health, was several times so near suicide that he hid the cord that he might not be tempted to hang himself, and was afraid to go out with his gun for fear of shooting himself.

But Levin did not shoot himself, and did not hang himself; he went on living.

CHAPTER 4

SEVERAL DAYS LATER, Agafea Mihalovna found on the doorstep a brown-paper-wrapped package bearing no writing upon it, nor identifying marks of any kind. Agafea Mihalovna dutifully brought the package to Konstantin Dmitrich.

Curious and confused, Levin carefully cut away the layers of brown paper and lifted out the dismembered torso unit of an old Class III robot. He gasped. The torso unit was severely dented, battered as if by hard wear, but the yellow casing was unmistakable, as was the small circular stamp bearing the logo of the Urgensky Cigarette Factory.

"Kitty!" he cried. "Kitty!"

Making sure they were entirely alone, Konstantin Dmitrich and his wife locked the door of their bedchamber and tremblingly engaged the monitor of the Class III—aware that even the small series of hand motions necessary to do so were now illegal.

The figure in the communiqué was Socrates himself. At the sight of him, tugging at his beard of tools and apparatuses, looking one way and then another, his familiar faceplate flickering with evident anxiety, Kitty burst into tears. Levin clutched at her hand, feeling his own chin working with emotion.

Socrates!

"Master, my time I fear is short. Short indeed yes short. However I would be remiss if I did not relay to you the result of my analysis."

"Old friend," Levin cried out, reaching toward the monitor with trembling fingers, as if to pluck out the tiny, glowing figure and hug it to his heart. "Loyal friend!"

"Examining all the relevant data: All that you discovered of the worm machines, and of the so-called Honored Guests, and . . . "

Here the Class III stopped in his narration and looked wildly about the dingy room where he stood, in fear of what it was impossible to say.

"I must hurry, Master. Must hurry hurry.

"When it was so often claimed that the aliens 'will come for us in three ways,' this was not after all meaningless. They have come in three ways.

"They have done so!"

When they finished watching the monitor, and Socrates's explanation was complete, Levin took Kitty's hand in his own, and together they sat for a long time, not saying a word: only contemplating what came next.

* * *

They had come as screeching warrior-beasts, born in horror from the fragile bodies of the ill.

They had come as ticking soil-dwelling worm-things, gathering strength from the groznium soil before bursting forth from the ground beneath us.

And they had come a third way. . . .

WE CANNOT BE STOPPED, said the Face to Alexei Alexandrovich, which is to say, said to itself, for now the Face was Karenin, and Karenin was the Face.

WE CANNOT BE STOPPED OR DEFEATED. NOT NOW. THIS PLANET BELONGS TO US.

Tsar Alexei had ordered the regiments to fight the aliens in the Nest, and had therefore consigned them to their doom, and left Russia undefended against the onslaught to come. He had done this because that was what the Face wanted, and the man called the Tsar was now entirely the puppet of the Face.

The alien soldiers known as Honored Guests had killed and been killed, but the alien leaders had won their war against humanity years ago. They had won from the moment that Alexei Alexandrovich, with the Face already a part of him, had ascended to power in the Ministry.

The aliens had won from the day of Karenin's ascendance, and nothing could stop that now, because that day had long passed.

Karenin-that-was-not-Karenin cackled from inside his gleaming silver caul with a terrible laugher; while, somewhere in the deep recesses of what once had been a human heart, there floated and glittered the memory of a woman, a woman he had loved.

CHAPTER 5

LEVIN STRODE ALONG the highroad, absorbed not so much in his thoughts—he could not yet disentangle them—as in his spiritual condition, unlike anything he had experienced before. The words uttered by Socrates in the communiqué had acted on his soul like an electric shock, suddenly transforming and combining into a single whole the whole swarm of disjointed, impotent, separate thoughts that incessantly occupied his mind.

The Golden Hope was not a fight for the sake of robots, or for the importance of technology, but for human freedom. Karenin was the enemy, not because he would take groznium technology from the people, but because he was an alien creature bent on the subjugation of all humanity.

Levin was aware of something new in his soul, and tested this new thing, not yet knowing what it was.

He wished to express this new rush of understanding to his old co-conspirator, his darling Kitty.

She understands, he thought; *she knows what I'm thinking about. Shall I tell her or not? Yes, I'll tell her.* But at the moment he was about to speak, she began speaking . . . and he found that she had nearly the same thoughts, almost in the same words.

On that day, in that moment, they began to make their plans. Somehow they would seek out whatever remnants of UnConSciya had survived the summer purges, and begin to regain their trust and rebuild the resistance. Levin would secretly seal off one corner of his mine, ensuring that there was enough of the Miracle Metal left for him to begin experiments. Quietly, invisibly, they would keep humanity's flame burning until the Golden Hope could finally fly free. Someday, they would find a way to overturn the evil that Karenin had brought to their world, no matter the lengths to which they must go.

Night fell. As they spoke, Levin gazed up into the high, cloudless sky, where somewhere the alien invaders hovered.

"Do I not know that that is infinite space, and that it is not a round arch? But, however I screw up my eyes and strain my sight, I cannot see it *not* round and *not* bounded, and in spite of my knowing about infinite space, I am incontestably right when I see a solid, black dome, and more right than when I strain my eyes to see beyond it. That is how we must think of the future, of the rest of our lives. We cannot see it, but we know it is there to take—and we know it belongs to us, if we have the strength and the courage to seize hold of it."

Kitty kissed him gently, and went off to bed.

Levin pictured the future in his imagination. *Can this be purpose?* he thought, afraid to believe in the feelings carrying him away. "Socrates, I thank thee!" he said, gulping down his sobs, and with both hands brushing away the tears that filled his eyes.

"This new feeling has not changed me, has not made me happy and enlightened all of a sudden, as I had dreamed, just like the feeling for my child. There was no surprise in this either. Faith—or not faith—I don't know what it is—but this feeling has come just as imperceptibly through suffering, and has taken firm root in my soul.

"I shall go on in the same way, losing my temper with Ivan the coachman, falling into angry discussions, expressing my opinions tactlessly; there will be still the same wall between the holy of holies of my soul and other people, even my wife; I shall still go on scolding her for my own terror, and being remorseful for it; I shall still be as unable to understand with my reason why hope lives in my breast, and I shall still go on hoping; but my life now, my whole life apart from anything that can happen to me, every minute of it is no longer meaningless, as it was before, but it has the positive meaning of goodness, which I have the power to put into it."

THE END

QUIETLY, INVISIBLY, THEY WOULD KEEP HUMANITY'S FLAME
BURNING UNTIL THE GOLDEN HOPE COULD FINALLY FLY FREE

ANDROID KARENINA

A READER'S DISCUSSION GUIDE

1. The famous first sentence of the novel states that "Functioning robots are all alike; every malfunctioning robot malfunctions in its own way." Which of the novel's many malfunctioning robots causes the most trouble for the humans around it?

2. Do the Iron Laws of robot behavior function solely on the level of plot, or is Tolstoy drawing an analogy with the societal and moral codes governing *human* behavior? What are the "iron laws" of your own life, and in what situations do you break them?

3. When Anna Karenina and Count Vronsky first meet, which is the strongest sign that things aren't going to go that well: Lupo's instinctive growling, the loud and mysterious "crack in the sky," or the mangled corpse?

4. Alexei Alexandrovich Karenin's "Face" is a trusted technological device that slowly takes over his brain and makes him evil. Was Tolstoy merely creating an interestingly dichotomous villain, or anticipating people who check their messages too much? How often do you check *your* messages?

5. How does Kitty's experience aboard the Venetian orbiter prepare her emotionally for an adult relationship? Is she more "healed" by the ship's carefully recirculated air, or by watching Madame Stahl get shot into space?

6. Did Tolstoy, in making the aliens horrid, shrieking lizard-beasts—rather than the benevolent light-beings anticipated by the xenotheologists—

intend a comment on the nature of faith? Or did he, perhaps, just really like lizard-beasts?

7. In a crucial moment, Levin chooses his wife over Socrates, his beloved-companion robot. Are there any technological devices in your life that you love more than your spouse?

8. The ending of the book is, for both Vronsky and the Shcherbatskys, more of a new beginning. Should they be hopeful, despairing, or—given the malleability of space-time—a little bit of everything?

9. Are you really a human being, or are you a super-intelligent cybernetic organism created by scientists in a laboratory, and programmed to believe that you are, in fact, human?

10. Are you sure?

ACKNOWLEDGMENTS

Thanks (again) to all the Quirklings for their hard work—especially Jason Rekulak and Stephen Segal, the steamiest and punkiest editors around, and Doogie Horner, Eugene Smith, and Lars Leetaru, who made such a beautiful object. Thanks also to Ann and Steve Simon; to Marina Konstanian and Ekaterina Sedia for Russian language insights; and to my agent, the amazing Molly Lyons.

Happy families are all alike, but mine is the best.

QUIRK CLASSICS

Originators of the Literary Mash-Up

Quirk Classics has been publishing artfully remixed mash-ups of the world's greatest novels since 2009, when its international best seller *Pride and Prejudice and Zombies* took the literary world by storm. Quirk Classics takes great pains to carefully select the novels it publishes and, working with talented authors, enhance them with appropriate, hilarious, and frightening additions that heighten the reader's experience and further emphasize the novels' original themes. Its best-selling titles include

Pride and Prejudice and Zombies
Sense and Sensibility and Sea Monsters
Pride and Prejudice and Zombies: Dawn of the Dreadfuls
Android Karenina

Visit www.quirkclassics.com
Masters of Our Public Domain